SEEKING TWO ELKS FIGHTING

Also in this series by Joseph Dorris:

Sheepeater: To Cry for a Vision
Katrine: High Valley Home
Sojourner of Warren's Camp
Salmon River Kid

SEEKING TWO ELKS FIGHTING

ERIK LARSON: SHEEPEATER SERIES

JOSEPH DORRIS

SEEKING TWO ELKS FIGHTING
ERIK LARSON: SHEEPEATER SERIES

iUniverse books may be ordered through booksellers or by contacting:

iUniverse
1663 Liberty Drive
Bloomington, IN 47403
www.iuniverse.com
844-349-9409

ISBN: 978-1-6632-1267-2 (sc)
ISBN: 978-1-6632-1266-5 (e)

Library of Congress Control Number: 2021903274

Print information available on the last page.

iUniverse rev. date: 03/05/2021

In Memory of Jack and Doris Chamberlain

and for the

McCall-Donnelly High School Class of 1970

PORTIONS OF 1872 IDAHO AND MONTANA TERRITORIES

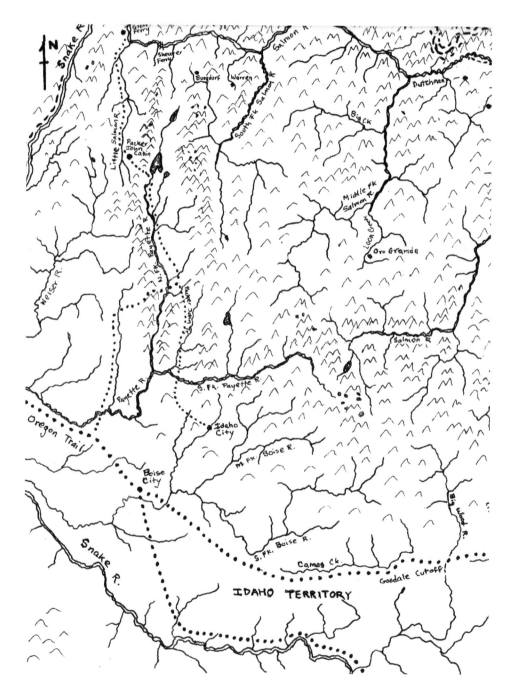

SOUTH SECTION SEEKING TWO ELKS

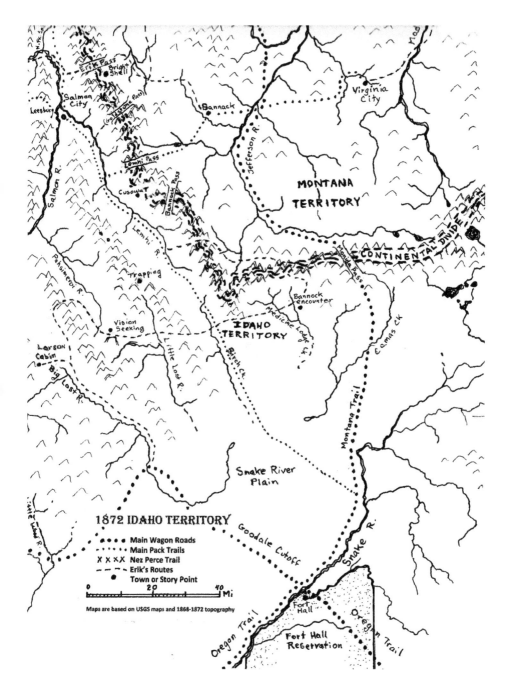

Salmon City
Leesburg
Erik Pass
Bright Shell
Bannack
Virginia City
Lemhi Pass
Cusowat
Bannock Pass
MONTANA TERRITORY
Jefferson R.
CONTINENTAL DIVIDE
Lemhi R.
Monida Pass
Pahsimeroi R.
Trapping
Bannock encounter
Vision Seeking
IDAHO TERRITORY
Medicine Lodge Cr.
Larson Cabin
Big Lost R.
Little Lost R.
Birch Cr.
Camas Ck.
Montana Trail
Snake River Plain

1872 IDAHO TERRITORY

- ●●●● Main Wagon Roads
- ••••• Main Pack Trails
- X X XX Nez Perce Trail
- – – – Erik's Routes
- ● Town or Story Point

0   20   40 Mi

Maps are based on USGS maps and 1868-1872 topography

Goodale Cutoff
Snake R.
Oregon Trail
Fort Hall
Oregon Trail
Fort Hall Reservation

PORTIONS OF 1872 IDAHO AND MONTANA TERRITORIES

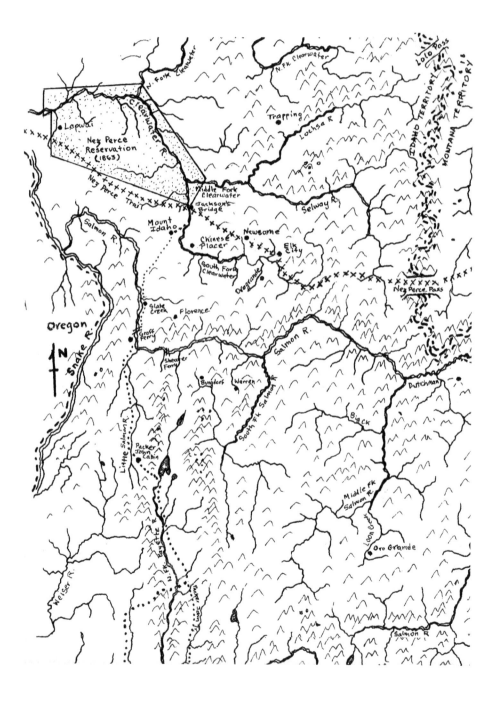

NORTH SECTION SEEKING TWO ELKS

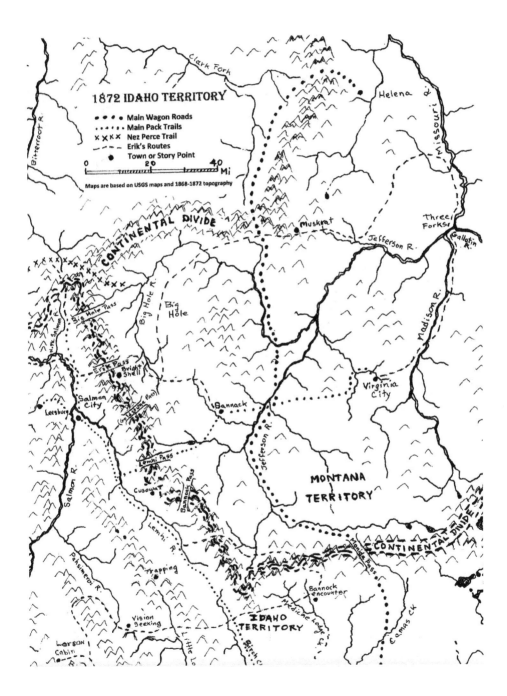

BURNING ROCKS LAND

CHAPTER 1

Erik Larson, now miles east of Fort Boise, told himself the high valley no longer mattered. It was as it was meant to be. His sister, Katrine, now promised in marriage to Björn, would fulfill the dream his parents had intended for Erik when they headed west in 1862, six years ago. He had been twelve. He shook his head, recalling Björn as a young boy then. Even now, he was not much more than a boy, and Katrine was not much more than a girl. Erik would return one day to visit them—to visit his nephew or niece, whose birth had been revealed by his *poh-nymy-pya*, his spirit helper. For now, he followed his own path.

Deftly, he worked his way well off the trail across the broken basalt country north of the Snake River in southern Idaho Territory. Erik traveled alone and avoided others. He was two months shy of nineteen and youthfully small and slight in stature.

The late-August sun beat warm. He pulled off his buckskin shirt and rolled it behind his saddle. He welcomed the slight, cooling breeze on his bare chest and pushed his unkempt blond hair back. With his clothing and the sheep horn bow he carried, he easily could have been mistaken for an Indian unless one looked closer and took note of his light hair and saddles. Erik preferred not to be seen—a trait he shared with his Sheepeater Indian family.

He gazed north toward the mountains that rose in folded brown ripples into black timber. Beyond the vast mountain barrier lay the broken canyon land of the Salmon River—the River of No Return. It was the home of White Eagle, a Sheepeater Indian bound to him not by blood but by spirit.

Erik clucked to Hatchet, his roan Indian pony, as the animal hesitated at some downed aspens. Normally, Leaf, his red-and-white pack pony, would have been the one to shy. Erik let Hatchet have his head, and the horse turned above the barrier.

Erik had had no direction or intended route when he left the Swedish settlers. He had drifted south to Fort Boise and talked with some of the freighters and packers, intending possibly to do some packing. Boise Basin was still booming, and he had heard about the gold camps opening in eastern Idaho Territory.

That was as good as any reason for heading east from Fort Boise and retracing the Goodale Cutoff, the route his sister and the wagon train had traveled. The cutoff took emigrant trains well north of the Snake River and the Oregon Trail to avoid Indian attacks. The train following the Swedes, which had not turned north, had been attacked. Their stock and wagons had been destroyed, and ten settlers had been murdered. Ironically, the Swedes had fared little better. A sickness had swept their party, killed several, and left Erik's mother gravely ill.

Erik sat Hatchet for a moment, taking in the empty but strangely familiar country. Grass and sagebrush stretched upward to a few scattered junipers and piñon pines on the slopes that rose to the north. The sharp sage and tangy pine fragrance stirred by the heat permeated the still air. The grasses had long ago burned to amber and gold in the late-summer heat. The scanty-leafed shrubs bled streaks of russet and orange. Thin clouds masked the pale sky; most were haze from the forest fires or dust raised by stiff winds that scoured the near-desert country. Jackrabbits, a few coyotes, and pronghorn antelope inhabited this otherwise empty land, as well as a few hawks and eagles.

Erik fingered his medicine bundle, which swung free on his bronzed chest. "So, Great Mystery," he whispered, "what is your path for me?"

He watched a hawk glide on outstretched wings perhaps a hundred feet above the sun-drenched landscape. It stuttered and then keeled over, diving toward the short, bleached grasses below, and hit the ground, pinning some small creature beneath its talons, peering in Erik's direction as if challenging him to take its prize.

Caught by the drama unfolding before him, Erik failed to see the man rise from the draw below and raise his rifle.

The bullet's high whine and explosion snapped Erik's reverie. Instantly, he kicked Hatchet's flanks, causing the animal to bound, as Erik swept his eyes toward the sound. There were two figures. One held a rifle. A puff of smoke and a second shrill whine, enveloped in an echoing report, shattered the silence as another bullet zipped between Hatchet's neck and Erik's chest. Hatchet jumped. Erik grabbed but found only air. He hit the ground hard and rolled, gasping and dazed. Hatchet took a couple of hops and then broke off down a slight draw, dragging Leaf by his lead rope.

Erik lay in the grass, smarting from the impact. He sucked in some air. Whoever had fired had intended to kill him. He rolled over and crawled to where he could see the two men below—an older man and a youth. Both were on foot and approached his position. The top of a wagon, which had been masked by junipers before, was now visible beyond the rise in the bottoms. Erik chided himself for having not seen it earlier.

He caught a muffled voice: "Finish 'im off."

The two angled toward where Hatchet had jumped.

With his heart quickening, Erik pulled his skinning knife.

The voices grew nearer. "We'll get his horses. They might fetch us a few dollars."

Erik rolled backward into thick sagebrush. The direction the two headed would take them below him.

With knife in hand, Erik circled away.

"He's over thisaway, I'm certain," the older voice said. "I'll cover ya, Son."

Erik swallowed. The older man had no qualms about possibly sending his boy into harm's way—unless he was confident of his aim. The second round had come within inches—close enough to spook Hatchet, which did not often happen.

Erik considered his choices: jump the son and hope the father wouldn't be fool enough to try to shoot him, or take the father and assume the son was, at best, armed with only a knife.

Fate determined Erik's actions. The boy, hardly in his teens, came to within a few yards of where Erik hid. The boy nervously scanned the sagebrush and waved a trembling knife in front of himself.

Erik waited until the youth turned slightly. Instantly, Erik swept up from the brush, twisted away the boy's knife, and put his own knife to the boy's throat. He spun him toward his father. "Drop the rifle, mister."

The boy cried out, "D-don't kill me, mister! Don't kill me."

Erik felt the skinny youth quiver, struggling, and almost tear loose.

The man swung his rifle toward Erik. His face blanched. "Let 'im go." The man's voice quavered.

"Dammit, I'm not bluffing. Unless this boy doesn't mean anything to you, drop that rifle!"

Hesitantly, the man lowered his rifle. "You ain't an Injun?"

"Dress isn't what makes an Indian," Erik snapped. He saw the tension leave the man's face.

The man slid the rifle into the grass and raised his hands. "Don't hurt my boy. You can have the rifle. Leave us be."

"Step away," Erik demanded. He dragged the youth toward the rifle. Reaching it, he stepped on the weapon and then released the boy, shoving him, stumbling, toward his father. Erik quickly brought the rifle up to bear on the man.

The man's eyes became frantic. "Don't kill us. I mistook ya."

"I don't aim to kill anyone unless I'm not given a choice, and you nearly didn't leave me one," Erik said. "What in blazes are you doing out here—a lone wagon and trying to bushwhack someone?"

The man clutched his son. "Some Injun beggars threatened us. We gave them the last of our flour and some sugar. They wanted more, and I refused. I thought you were them comin' back to finish us off and take everything."

Erik handed the man his rifle. "*Nej*, not me."

"I sure am sorry, mister. Sure sorry." He pulled off his hat, ran an arm across his sweaty brow, and then reset it, covering scraggly dark hair that matched his beard. "Name's Minton. Randolph Minton. My son's name is Drake." He reached out a slender, work-worn hand.

"Erik Larson."

The two men shook. Erik nodded toward Drake. The youth barely acknowledged Erik with a slight nod, his eyes flashing.

"What can I do for ya, Mr. Larson? I owe ya. You want some chow?"

"Help me get my horses. Shouldn't have gone far," Erik said. "Sure, I'll join you for supper. Sun's getting low."

Shortly, the men had retrieved Hatchet and Leaf and led them to the wagon. Another surprise greeted Erik: two towheaded, blue-eyed children, a boy and a girl, tumbled from beneath it. They appeared unlike Drake, who had darker hair and brown eyes like his father's.

"They're twins," Minton said. "Wesley and Alice." The small boy and girl clutched their father.

Erik offered to help with supper.

"No, sir," the man said. "It's the least we can do for ya."

The Mintons had a beat-up wagon and a team of four trail-worn mules. It appeared they had no riding stock. Like many of the emigrants who headed west with high hopes, it appeared they were busted and were now headed east.

"None of my business, but it looks like you could use a hand if you're heading much farther."

Minton shook his head. "I'm headin' back to Kansas. Taking the twins to their aunt."

Drake's eyes darted from Erik to his father. Erik sensed that Minton would be leaving Drake there as well.

Like his father, Drake was lanky. Erik guessed he was twelve or thirteen. Whereas his father showed the wear and tear of sun and wind, Drake had not yet grown out of boyhood.

Erik took the plate of food offered to him by Alice. He guessed she was five or six. Judging by the look of the mostly watery beans, he figured the family had little remaining in the way of food. He would not refuse the meal since Minton intended to make amends. Erik didn't ask about coffee. None was offered.

Randolph Minton ate little. Drake ate hungrily. The twins shared a plate and looked toward their father as if hoping for more.

"Thank you for supper," Erik said.

"No, sir," Minton answered. He fingered his beard. "Thank you. It was me that was in the wrong, and yes, I'd be obliged for your company."

"Just to the junction," Erik said. "I'm figuring on heading north from there."

"North? Nothing's north 'cept the Salmon River, unless you head east up the old Overland."

"*Ja*, and you'd be right, but I have an interest north." Erik felt no need to tell the Mintons that he and his parents had gone that direction six years earlier when he was about Drake's age. He stood. "I'll bed down over yonder." Then his thoughts got the better of him. "It is not my business, but why are you willing to risk heading back east this late in the season? Your provisions seem a bit scanty."

"I reckon it ain't much of a meal, if that's what you're gettin' at, but we're bound to find some game. We're plannin' on resupplyin' at Fort Hall."

Drake shifted on his seat and shot his father a look. Erik guessed they had little or no money for resupply.

Minton returned a cautioning look. "We'll make it. And I reckon once we cross into Wyoming Territory, we'll be on well-traveled roads. We'll make it to Atchison all right."

Erik considered the man's comment. Atchison was on the Missouri River, a good three months' travel. They would arrive in winter.

"What became of their mother, if I may ask?"

Minton's eyes smoldered. He set his jaw. "I have nothing to say about their ma."

Drake's eyes filled with distress.

Erik thought the mother's absence might have something to do with Drake, and he wanted to ask him to explain, but neither the man nor the boy was of his concern. Nevertheless, he had agreed to travel with them to where the Goodale trail branched south toward Fort Hall. He'd leave them there and head north into the Salmon River country, at least for now.

CHAPTER 2

A few days later, Erik took Drake hunting, intending to help the Mintons supplement their remaining food. Erik's own provisions were light, and although he did not mind sharing, particularly because he could feed himself from the land, the Mintons were not that capable.

They had seen pronghorn antelope, but after several attempts to get within range, Erik told Drake he would be wise to save his ammunition and forgo hunting the fleet creatures.

"I learned the hard way," Erik said. "First time in this country, my father and I wasted a lot of shot and powder before we gave up. Antelope see you and take off. They're not like a mule deer. Now I hunt with a bow. I find it better for the rabbits and prairie chickens we're seeing."

"I don't have a bow," Drake replied. "Wouldn't know how to use one anyhow."

"I may be able to show you some tricks where you don't need one."

"Ya think so?" The youth grinned.

The following day, they entered a draw lined with thick orange-red chokecherry shrubs heavily laden with stems of blue-black berries. A trickle of water traced across the trail.

"Good place to water the stock, Mr. Minton," Erik suggested. "It may be the last for a good day or more. The children can pick some chokecherries. They don't have much meat on them, but you can dry them and take them with you. The Indians swear by them."

"We'd be wastin' time pickin' berries," Minton said.

"Berries help against scurvy, and you'll find everything east of South Pass has been stripped bare or trampled into the trail. You'll be fortunate to find much, particularly with winter coming your way before you finish-crossing the plains."

7

Minton worked his jaw. "I can resupply some at Fort Hall."

Erik considered Minton did not appreciate taking advice from him. This late in the season, few wagons would be coming through, and few supplies would remain at Fort Hall.

Erik pointed toward a narrow, spruce-carpeted ridge. "Drake and I might be able to find some grouse. We likely won't be near timber like this again."

Minton glanced toward his son. Drake appeared eager to go. "Maybe you're right. I can give the stock a break. We've been pullin' hard."

Erik rode out with Drake. When within a few yards of the spruce trees, Erik dismounted and studied them. Grouse ate almost anything, including moths that clustered around the spruce. They were more likely to frequent isolated stands such as this one. Shortly, Erik spotted what he'd hoped to see. A spruce grouse, its head bobbing, strutted around in the shadows beneath the limbs. Carefully, he picked up a stout stick about two feet in length.

"Let me see if I can still do this," Erik murmured. Crouching, he moved toward the bird.

When a dozen feet away, Erik spotted two other grouse. He judged his distance to the nearest bird and flung the stick, spinning it. It caught the bird in the neck, and the grouse flopped onto the ground. The other birds exploded upward into the trees. Erik stepped to the flopping grouse and wrung its neck.

Erik handed the stick to Drake. "See if you can knock one off its perch." He pointed to the lowermost grouse.

Drake threw the weapon and missed wildly. He repeatedly tried until the grouse laddered upward out of his throwing range. "Blame it!" he exclaimed. "You made it seem easy enough."

"Try that one." Erik pointed to another grouse that was hiding in the lower branches of a second spruce. The bird had remained frozen, instinctively avoiding movement that would give it away to a predator.

Drake drew back and sent the stick spinning. It awkwardly hit the grouse, which launched itself upward but tangled momentarily in the branches above it. Erik grabbed the bird and killed it.

Drake laughed. "Well, I guess that works."

"I used to do like this as a boy nearly every day. It was important not to waste an arrow if it could be helped, especially before I learned how to make a decent bird point."

Drake stared at Erik. "Were ya really an Injun?"

"I lived three years with them when I was about your age." Erik nodded toward the mountains rising to the north. "They're called the Sheepeaters and live along the Salmon River." He pulled his skinning knife and began dressing one of the birds.

"That's why ya know so much," Drake said. "So how come ya joined up with them? They capture ya when ya was little? My pa says they do that. He was afraid those we ran into were gonna take the twins."

Erik shook his head. "I wasn't a captive, but not far from here, my parents and I got separated from the wagon train. I lived with the Sheepeaters so I could survive."

"Is that why you're goin' north at the junction? You gonna go back to them?"

Erik paused. "I rightly don't know." He handed his knife to Drake and nodded at the second bird.

"You don't think we'll make it to Atchison, do ya, Mr. Larson?"

"If you can hunt some game like you've been doing, you'll make it." In truth, without help, Erik believed the Mintons had little chance. He changed the subject. "So tell me—what about your mother?"

Drake's eyes flashed. "My real ma died when I was born. Afterward, Pa married the tramp. Now she's took off with some of our money and a fancy man. She took our ridin' horse too." Drake tightened his jaw. "That's why Pa's going after her. He's gonna leave the twins with my aunt." He bit his lip. "I think he's plannin' on leavin' me there too."

"I'm guessing that," Erik said with a voice to give Drake the impression it was not his business but to encourage him to continue his story.

"I won't stay. I'm goin' with him." Drake started to cut the bird and then glanced up at Erik. His shoulders trembled.

"And when you find your stepmother?"

"Pa will kill her," Drake said. He slit open the belly of the bird. "I'm gonna help."

A chill washed over Erik. "Does your father guess your intentions?"

9

Drake spun toward Erik, pointing the knife. "Hell no. And if ya so much as say anything, I'll—"

Erik recoiled from the boy's sudden anger. "It is of no concern to me, Drake," Erik said. He held out his hand and received his knife back. He wiped the blood on the grass.

"She deserves it." Drake's tone indicated he sought approval.

"I see," Erik said, nodding. He took Drake's bird and placed both birds in his saddle pouch.

Drake tried to catch Erik's eyes. "Well, hain't ya gonna say something?"

Erik swung up onto Hatchet. "Nej. Looks like you've got things figured out."

"I have," Drake spat. He grabbed ahold of Leaf, started to mount, and then stopped. He trembled. "She shouldn't a done what she did with that man," he choked out. "Pa caught them." Drake shook harder. "Pa loved her. So'd me and the twins. Why'd she do it?" His eyes glistened.

"I have no answer for you, Drake. That is something best to be left between you and God."

Anger flooded Drake's questioning eyes.

"That's something I learned when I lived with the Sheepeaters," Erik said. "You'll learn it someday. Only promise me you'll be listening when he talks to you."

"Talks to me?" Drake scoffed.

Erik nodded. "You'll know."

Still shaking, Drake hoisted himself onto Leaf. Erik led the way back to the camp, not looking back toward the youth.

In camp, Erik did not mention any trouble. Drake had calmed as well. Erik presented the birds to the twins, who were eager to show him the chokecherries they had gathered. Both had red-and-black-stained fingers, as did Minton.

"What do you think of what your brother and I got?" Erik asked. He presented the two grouse.

Their eyes flew wide. Wesley petted one of the birds. "You got one?" He peered questioningly at Drake.

"He sure did," Erik said. "He swatted one with a stick."

Wesley beamed with admiration.

"You two can help me roast them. You think some onions would go well with them?" Wild onions grew everywhere and were easily identified by their odor. "You can help me dig some."

That night, Erik sat with Randolph Minton while Minton smoked his pipe. Drake fought sleep, but the two men won out, and Drake turned in. The twins had rolled up inside the wagon box an hour earlier.

"I spect Drake told you what's up," Minton said evenly. "He hasn't said anything to me, but somethin' happened while you two were out hunting, I have a feeling."

"You'd be correct, Mr. Minton," Erik said.

"Ain't any of your cussed business what I do to that wench. Ya hear me?" he spat.

"I reckon not." Erik checked his own sudden anger.

They sat in silence for a moment. Erik studied Minton's face until he felt certain the man had run the scenario through several more times.

"You know Drake intends to go with you, don't you?"

Minton glared at Erik. "I spect he'll try. He won't get far."

"Well, sir, I'm going to disagree. I've been hunting with Drake a few days. I can tell you that he'll be with you."

Minton's shoulders sagged. Then his eyes narrowed. "Go to hell. I have to do what's right."

"I reckon you will." Erik stood and walked a few yards to a gnarled juniper above their camp. In a couple of days, three at most, they would part company. He gazed at the stars. He had taken a man's life when he was sixteen. There were times when killing was necessary. Taking the life of a woman who had committed adultery did not seem to him to be such a case.

The following morning, they pushed on toward the junction, making good miles. In a gully among some jagged basalt, they discovered a destroyed wagon.

Drake turned to Erik. "Was it Injuns?"

"Nej. Just the heat and rock in these parts. It's what we call lava rock. Some of the ancient Sheepeaters claimed to have seen the earth torn apart with molten lava pouring out."

Drake studied the landscape. "It looks like it coulda been flowin' at one time. I noticed that in a few places. Other pieces of broken wagons too, not just this one."

11

"Something works at it long enough, it can wear even the best-built wagon down."

"I reckon. We busted a wheel before."

"How old are you?"

"Prit near thirteen."

"You are young, Drake, but know this: humans wear out as well. It doesn't matter what we're made of. You said you loved your stepmother—what's her name?"

"The tramp?" Drake hesitated as if wrestling with whether or not to answer. "Wilhelmina."

"Wilhelmina," Erik said quietly. "You all loved her. You said so. Maybe those are the memories you should keep of her. At the very least, she has given you a brother and sister."

"It hain't none of your blamed business," Drake spat. "My pa even said so. I heard him."

"You wanted to make it my business, Drake. Otherwise, you wouldn't have told me."

"Damn you," Drake whispered.

Erik stepped away. He had said all he could. He touched his medicine bundle. This truly was between the Great Mystery and Drake.

Late the following day, they reached the junction.

Memories washed over Erik. This was where the wagon train had split up and left him and his parents behind. They had left Minnesota much too late. He understood that now. The Swedes had been overconfident that they could reach the valley and still have time to prepare for winter. They were accustomed to snow country. They hadn't made it. His sister had told him about the brutal winter they had spent at the site of Fort Boise.

Randolph Minton thanked Erik for accompanying them. "We'll get some supplies at Fort Hall before headin' east. I still have a little money. Maybe we'll find some others we can travel with."

"Just give warning to whoever you plan to shoot."

Minton grinned for just a moment. Then his lips tightened. "You and I just don't see eye to eye on this."

Erik shook his head. "Though you may not have a wife at present, nor do the children have a mother, Mr. Minton, you still have a family. They'll grow up no matter what happens."

Minton cursed under his breath.

"Good luck to you, Mr. Minton."

Erik turned away toward the trail as Drake watched from a distance. He motioned for the boy to come over.

"Take this." Erik pulled an arrow. "I paint my arrows with this red marking. That lets all who would inspect a kill know whose arrow took the animal."

"Yes, sir," Drake mumbled.

"Take care of your father and your brother and sister, will you? And promise me you'll be listening when the time comes."

Drake nodded. "Yes, sir." His eyes glistened.

Erik shook Drake's hand. It was all he could do.

WOLF-BEAR VISION

CHAPTER 3

Erik swung north. Sharp memories of heading in that direction with his parents enfolded him. His father had stayed at the junction for a few days to give Erik's mother a chance to strengthen.

Erik had ridden past there two seasons ago when he left the Sheepeaters to seek his sister. He had always presumed he would remain with the Swedes when he finally reunited with them. Oddly, he had been surprised at how easy it was to leave again. In some ways, Katrine had seemed more real when they were apart than when he finally found her. While apart, she had been in his thoughts each day, but when he had finally rejoined her, he had accepted that each day she would be there—she would always be there. Now they were apart again. He disliked the feeling.

"Come on, Hatchet. Nothing but memories here for me." He clucked to the horse, hurrying his pace. Leaf followed.

The country faded from prairie covered by bunch grasses and sage to a gently rising slope barren except for an occasional solitary juniper or stubborn piñon pine. The slopes above him became spotted with scattered fir trees and mountain ash ablaze with orange leaves and berries. Smaller shrubs had withered in the heat and donned reddish-brown leaves. Sharp memories returned as he followed the invisible tracks of their wagon from years ago.

Katrine had told him some soldiers had tried to find their parents. Erik smiled inwardly; anyone could have picked the route his father had driven. There was only one direction to go to get off the barren prairie. Had his father been familiar with the Goodale trail and the likelihood of finding shelter along it, he might have continued west; however, the broken basalt in that direction would have been less inviting than this, and had they continued west, they could have just as likely destroyed their wagon, like the one he and Drake had come upon. If so, they would have been stranded in a more hostile place.

Three days after leaving the junction, Erik topped a rise that divided the Salmon River and Snake River drainages. Spreading below him was the small valley his father had chosen—the first place where they had found trees. Wrinkled and heavily forested mountain ridges unfolded in shadows to the north. Behind and toward the east, fractured mountains jutted upward, stark and barren, except where occasional streaks of autumn foliage spotted them.

The long rays of the late-day sun caught the remains of his parents' cabin in the small basin below. Nearby, the skeleton of their wagon rested where it had stopped. He remembered how his father had pointed toward the spot beneath the hill and declared that was where they would build their cabin. Erik had made tea for his mother from rosehips he collected. He'd swum in the yet warm water of the beaver pond. His father had confided that the basin was like the valley where the Swedes were heading, and they could survive the winter in it just as well. They'd had hope.

But only Erik had survived.

He dismounted and wandered toward the grove of aspens, with their trembling leaves, many now yellowing. Although leaning at angles, the two crosses he had cut and carved remained, displaying the names Ruth Larson and Jon Larson. They stood within a thicket of rosebushes now speckled with bright red-orange rosehips—the very bushes from which he had picked rosehips for his mother's tea.

Erik's eyes flicked between the graves. He accepted the knowledge that under the earth, his parents were but skeletons. He had not been able to fashion coffins. He had hardly been able to dig to a safe depth where their bones were protected from the animals.

"Mamma, Pappa, det är jag—Erik" (Mama, Papa, it's me—Erik). Erik spoke his native Swedish. "As I promised, I found Katrine. I told you I would. She is well. She and Björn are to marry in a season. You will remember Björn. He pestered us on the trip west. He was the one who put the grass snake in Katrine's bed. You never knew." He smiled, shaking his head. "He's grown up. Of course, so has Katrine." He pushed at the dirt with his moccasined toes. "In two seasons, Katrine will have a child, I'm certain. You will be grandparents. *Mor Mor* and *Mor Far.*"

Erik glanced around. Would any ears hear his words? Perhaps the spirit of the woods had returned—*Sohobinehwe Tso`ape*. Gray Owl, the wizened chief, had named the spirit. Sohobinehwe Tso`ape had whistled to Erik and guided him back to the cabin when he became lost.

"You never approved of the Sheepeaters, Mama, but they became my family. God's plans for me are hidden, but Katrine is home. It is my turn to find my way. I asked Katrine if she wanted to come here, but she said her life was in the valley with Björn. I do not think you would have wished for her to come here, but for me, this is where my life becomes a circle."

Erik leaned down and straightened the cross on his mother's grave. "Mama, Papa, you rest easy. Your children are well."

Erik straightened and removed his medicine bundle from around his neck. The contents were blessed items that represented the spirits of creatures connected to his boyhood vision-seeking. He frequently touched the bag during the day and asked for intervention, strength, or direction. Through those totems, the Great Mystery provided him assistance or protection.

Gray Owl had interpreted Erik's vision and prepared his bundle, as he did for all boys when they completed their vision-seeking. Erik last had opened it before his stay among the Swedes. During those months, whenever he'd touched the bag, the Swedes had frowned, especially Sven Olafson. Sven would have nothing to do with suggestions of spirits being carried about with Erik through the totems in his pouch. Erik laughed. Of all the Swedes, it was Sven who recited tales of Swedish trolls and elves—all supposedly with magical powers.

He pulled out the blunt and polished elk tooth, fingered it, and recalled his vision of the fighting elk. He examined the sharp, curved mountain lion tooth—his most powerful helper. The night cat had reminded him of his promise to find Katrine. Lastly, he rubbed the blue-green stone. Gray Owl had said it was for the pika, the bringer of song and joy—his mother's song. He returned each item to the pouch and retied it. More significant than the items themselves was what they suggested about his future, and much of that remained clouded.

Erik did not enter the cabin. Nothing remained there any longer for him. It was right that the earth and brush reclaim it. In time, Earth would reclaim all things that had risen from her.

He moved away from the graves and found a sheltered spot for an evening fire and supper. Hatchet and Leaf busied themselves with the long grasses.

He gazed toward the shadows of the Salmon River canyon. The river lay hidden several thousand feet below him, running swift and clean. He had first met the Sheepeaters there, and they called the Salmon River the River That Cries. The river swung north and then westward in a huge arc. The land encompassed within was cut into lacy canyons and crisscrossed by turbulent streams. Alpine-glaciated basins, pockmarked with granite amphitheaters and sapphire lakes, spread high above the canyons. The Sheepeaters adapted to the land by living in the lower regions along the canyons during the harsh winters and then migrating back to the higher elevations following the game cycles and seasons. As a boy, Erik had crossed this region during four seasons and then back.

Erik reflected on White Eagle. He and other hunters would be in the high country, seeking elk. Quickly Smiles would be waiting to prepare meat and hides from the animals he was sure to kill. Erik longed to see them. "It's no use," he whispered. "My life belongs elsewhere."

His life did belong elsewhere, but for what reason, and where? For a moment, Erik believed he might make a difference with Randolph and Drake, but in the end, he could not alter the path they had chosen. At least the twins might have a better life with their aunt in Kansas. Although the Mintons should have been at Fort Hall and soon to head east, they still might not make it. If they did, next season, Randolph and Drake would be back somewhere in the gold country, seeking a wayward woman.

CHAPTER 4

Erik retraced his steps to the valley floor and then continued for several miles northward along a grassy trough to a barren, windswept saddle where he crossed into the Salmon River drainage. This was the route he and White Eagle had followed two seasons ago. He studied the eastern peaks, which were seemingly unbroken and impassable. This was dry land—near-desert scantily clad with short grasses pestered by the wind. There were no trees or brush. Giant rock and sand fans spread outward from the gulches and canyons that spilled from the pinnacles. Midway toward their summits, the slopes became spotted with pockets of juniper and then, higher up, stands of stunted pine and fir until the trees gave way to barren alpine slopes above timberline. Dark shadows marked a cleft north of one of the peaks.

Erik clucked to Hatchet. "Come on, boy. If we're going to cross them without backtracking for a few days, that shadow might mark a route."

Surprisingly, when Erik reached the foot of the cleft, he found a game trail marked with pony tracks. He followed the dry gulch upward until he found trickling water. This was where the stream tumbling from above sank into the ground. He continued until he found thick grass and stopped for the night. He hobbled his horses, made a small fire from dry conifer branches, and cooked some supper. He watched the stars for a moment before rolling out his bedding.

At morning light, Erik woke to frigid air. Continuing upward, he reached an open basin fringed with bright yellow aspens, dusty beige willows, and dense, dark timber. A cow elk and her calf rose from where they were bedded and trotted into the timber.

When he reached timberline, the small stream again became a dry gully. Scant, bleached grasses carpeted the areas between slabs of gray rock, and scattered blazing orange and red shrubs clung to the edges.

The trail veered to the north and climbed steeply upward to the ridgeline where Erik crossed to the eastern slope. Another barren desert valley lay dizzily below, similar to where he had come from, except some patches of yellowing cottonwoods and willows lined the ravines and gullies where they emerged onto the valley floor. A narrow fringe of yellowing brush stretched toward the north, marking a streambed. He dropped into a narrow gorge that plummeted steeply toward the valley floor. When he left the rocky tundra, water bubbled up in the gorge, and a creek soon flowed strongly, sparkling and clear through the fringe of fir and pine. Erik followed it downward across a gently descending talus slope to where the stream again sank into the dry earth.

Erik turned south and, in a few miles, ascended and crossed a low, grassy saddle back into the Snake River drainage. He did not intend to continue much toward the south but angled eastward toward a series of isolated hills that rose like blunted fingers emerging from the broader dry plain. Another line of peaks crowned the hazy distance in the east. He guessed it was similar to the range he had crossed. There was little wonder why the wagon route lay farther to the south along the Snake River, where it could bypass these narrow, steep ranges.

Erik found what he sought. Several huge blocks of black basalt had been thrown upward as if thrust onto the earth's surface by a demon below. A solitary pinnacle stood apart from the others, silhouetted against the evening sky. He made camp.

The morning brought a bright sky streaked with a few high clouds. A breeze had kicked up, bringing on it the scent of pine and sage. Erik cached his belongings and released his ponies near a trickle of water. If he continued much farther, this water would disappear into the ground as well. Here the water and grass would be enough to keep his horses from wandering.

"Just hope no Indians discover you," he whispered. "I'll be back in a couple of days."

If Erik lost his horses, it would be as it was meant to be. He would consider that he had returned his earthly goods to the Great Mystery from whom they had come. It was part of the Great Circle.

Erik reached the base of the rocky outcrop and climbed, pulling himself up the scaly basalt cliffs, until he reached the summit. Barren, scoured rock, except for a few grass clumps, stretched a stone's throw across. Scuff marks and charcoal spoke of previous use, probably by Bannocks or Shoshones signaling or scanning the surrounding countryside for game.

Erik faced around and gazed outward toward the horizon. Open, barren vistas spread toward the south and disappeared into purple shadows. Behind him and on either side rose fractured peaks.

Erik stripped out of his buckskins and spread his arms to the sky. "I'm asking you to hear me, Great Mystery, as you once did when I was still a boy known as Sky Eyes. This day, hear me as Two Elks Fighting. Show me what you have in your great plan for me."

He stood above the countryside that spread below him—the piñon pine, juniper, sagebrush, and fractured black rock.

He began walking a small circle, praying, reflecting on his life and on what had passed—his sister, the Swedish settlers. The basalt grated his feet.

"What have you in your great plan for me, Great Mystery? Is Erik Larson gone? Am I truly Two Elks Fighting? If so, to what is my purpose?"

The day grew warm, and the heat radiated upward from the dark rock. Erik's thirst grew, and beads of sweat rolled from his forehead and across his chest. At length, he rested, took a deep drink, and then returned to walking a slow, torturous circle while he prayed.

A few thunderheads built and sent cooling shadows across the pinnacle. There was no rain, although a dark curtain appeared in the distance. Occasionally, a thread of lightning snaked through the darkness, and long moments later, thunder rumbled outward.

The sun sank. Its long orange rays cast across the landscape and sent lengthening purple shadows outward. Blue and then violet velvet crept into the sky. Stars blinked and then blazed brilliantly. A waxing crescent moon ascended in the east. Painfully slowly, the hours passed as the moon crossed the sky and began descending behind Erik.

The night turned cold, and the sunbaked basalt cooled. Erik walked his circle. His being filled with sharpening memories—so much so that he expected to see White Eagle.

A night breeze kicked up. He walked rapidly, seeking warmth. His breath hung on the cold air.

Imperceptibly and then faintly, the eastern sky lightened and dimmed the stars. A glowing light spread above the returning sun, and at last, a golden sliver broke the horizon and jumped across the landscape, bathing the pinnacle in brilliant light, painting the tips of the tallest trees, and lighting the scattered basalt blocks. Birds twittered, announcing their joy that life had returned.

The warmth touched Erik, and his ordeal continued. He walked the circle and prayed.

The sun climbed to directly overhead. Clouds began building and soon darkened the sky. Bright mushroom white lit their edges, and inky black painted their bottoms. Lightning split their bellies, snaking downward. Thunder grumbled and boomed more loudly.

Erik paused and watched the approaching thunderstorm. "Perhaps you might spare me this time, Great Mystery. Was it not enough when I was a boy?"

Wind buffeted him. Juniper on the hills below shuddered and swayed, bent by the approaching wind. Birds burst upward, scattering. Dust kicked up, pushed out by unseen forces.

Lightning flickered from sky to ground, and a loud, booming crackle split the air. Instantaneous thunder boomed and chased after, exploding about Erik's being, deafening him. Electricity hung on the air. A curtain of gray and purple-black steadily advanced. The first spatter of rain hit, blasting against Erik's bare flesh.

"If this is to be the way it is, so be it," Erik murmured. He spread his arms at the advancing storm, feeling the rain slam against him, sending a shudder of cold throughout his being. Water flowed freely from his head across his shoulders, down his legs, and onto the basalt outcrop.

Erik leaned into the cold rain and wind, gasping for breath against the stinging drops. The vision of his youth enfolded him as he stood gazing into the midnight blue of roiling clouds. A blast of wind and icy water knocked him back a step and then two steps. His feet slipped against the rock, and he fell to a knee as his foot slid from under him and cut against the rock. He squatted with his arms about himself, shivering against the cold, and braced himself against the downpour.

Flashes sang above his head while earsplitting thunder exploded about him. Erik grabbed his ears, and a numbing sensation danced through his body. Slivers of blue arched across the rock, flowing, skittering, and then disappearing off the edge.

Erik shook his head, now deadened of sound. He blinked his eyes, trying to see. The numbing cold penetrated him. He shivered uncontrollably, bit his quivering lip, and staggered back to his feet.

Erik held his hands up again and turned into the wind. "Great Mystery, I lack the strength. It is only through you that I have strength." With faltering steps, he resumed his circle.

Abruptly, the torrent slackened to a spattering of rain. The wind continued whistling about him, drying his skin, and further chilling him. Erik continued to walk.

A faint glow from behind the black curtain grew stronger, and the wind began dying.

The storm raced past, fading toward the north. The sun broke through, and the air burst into a myriad of sparkling rainbow droplets. Light blazed from the rushing water that drained the rock and from the pools that filled the crevices.

Erik faced the dying sun. He was still shivering but felt a slow warmth returning to his body.

The world was at peace. Erik had been tested, and he had been accepted.

The sun sank below the horizon. He continued his walk and prayed. He had relived much since climbing to this spot early yesterday. He'd had little water, no food, and had not allowed himself any sleep. The storm had further sapped his strength.

Erik sat and crossed his legs. The first star hung above the horizon. Heavy velvet crept down from the heavens overhead and slowly masked the lingering light until it was no longer discernible. Soon a myriad of stars blazed cold and frozen in the indigo sky above.

Erik shakily stood. "Maybe I truly do not have the strength, Great Mystery," he whispered. "Am I Erik Larson, or am I Two Elks Fighting?" He spoke to the empty sky.

A faint light began edging the eastern sky, and the moon began ascending. Erik watched until the silvery lemon crescent broke free and rose silently into the night. Its cold light cast Erik's shadow against the rock.

He shook his head, now dizzy, and began his walk again. The cool air tugged at his body; the rough rock bit his feet. Hazy thoughts blossomed vividly and swamped his being. He paused each time, trying to fathom them. Flickering visions of Quickly Smiles and White Eagle came and went. Images from his youth flooded his being. He found himself swimming after Badger and fighting the great bear.

Then he woke, realizing he was sitting on the rock.

Erik stumbled up. With renewed determination, he began walking again. "Great Mystery, what have you in your plan for Erik Larson? What have you in your plan for Two Elks Fighting?"

He didn't remember sitting again, but now he found the cold rock underneath. His body was bathed in brilliant moonlight, and he turned and faced the moon.

A whistle caught his attention. He smiled to himself. "Sohobinehwe Tso`ape? I have missed you."

Silence greeted Erik. He called out again and strained to hear something in the empty night. He felt himself fading away, when a second whistle met his ears.

Erik's senses sharpened. "Ah, you are here." He spoke the people's language.

He found himself in a meadow surrounded by willows and tall timber. A mountain lion emerged with its glowing green eyes fixed unwaveringly on Erik.

"You have come back, little white boy," the night cat said.

"Yes, I had to," Erik replied. "I have lost my vision."

"Ah, you have not lost your vision, *Wahahte' Paadiha Nikkumpah*, Two Elks Fighting. You have forgotten your vision. And have you forgotten the people and your true brother as well?"

Erik felt stunned. "My vision is lost. I do not seek the people or my brother."

"Ah, but to have a vision, Two Elks Fighting, you must seek the people. Do you not wish to seek the people?"

"No," Erik said. "I do." The clammy night turned to steam. A vision would show him the direction he should go. Why could he not have one? "I seek a vision so I know if I should seek the people."

"Ah, Two Elks Fighting, then you have your answer."

24

Erik trembled. "What answer? This is no vision."

A light began glowing around the mountain lion. Two creatures, like wolves but with bear-like tails and long claws and fangs, rose from the thick grass. The wolf-bear creatures quickly circled and then struck at the mountain lion.

"Leave, Two Elks Fighting," the night cat said. "This is not for you."

With great effort, the lion viciously struck back until the creatures faded.

The night cat addressed Erik. "Why is it you stay? Only you can say when it is time to seek the people."

Again, the misty light billowed up and engulfed the mountain lion. More wolf-bear beasts emerged, seemingly more powerful and more vicious. One leaped on the mountain lion and sank its fangs into the lion's back. Another bit at a hind leg, ripping it and spraying blood. The lion screamed and smashed back at the creatures, sending one and then another spinning into the darkness. A third slinked away. The lion bled and limped. It turned around, and its steady green eyes again found Erik.

"Why are you here, Two Elks Fighting? You should not be here."

Erik felt fastened to where he stood. His legs were stone. He could not move—either to intercede or to escape.

A third time, the glowing mist spread outward, and the wolf-bear creatures emerged, snarling and slashing. One closed its jaws about the mountain lion's neck, tugging at it. A second latched on and brought the lion to its knees. The lion's glowing eyes began to dim.

Erik turned away, unable to watch. A single light caught his attention and advanced his direction, bobbing and shimmering, emerging from the line of trees. A voice like the mountain lion's sounded from the light, and the sounds of the fight behind him began to fade.

"Your brother will be there when you decide."

The light faded.

The rays of the morning sun softly walked across the black basalt that yet glittered with yesterday's rain.

Erik shook his head. This vision had been unlike the one he received as a boy. It had been a great fight between his spirit helper and creatures he had never seen before. The night cat had said it was not his fight. But why had it been revealed to him if it was not his fight? His stomach tightened. The night cat had said he could not have a vision unless he returned to the people. His brother would be there when he did. Had the image been a reflection of Erik's own subconscious decision that he was not ready to go back? What had he seen? He recalled the demon creatures attacking his spirit helper and his overwhelming feeling of helplessness. Gray Owl might find more meaning in the vision than Erik could find. Had he been foolish to attempt a vision-seeking?

"What world did I enter?" Erik asked aloud. He pushed his hand across the rough rock.

Erik dressed and climbed from the pinnacle. He found his two ponies, and as he'd guessed, they had not strayed far. They nickered, seemingly telling him they had wondered about his disappearance.

Erik rubbed down both animals. "We will be on our way in a short while," he whispered. He would not travel northwestward, which would have returned him to Sheepeater country. That direction was for his future.

He opened one of his packs and took from it some dried venison. He chewed it and swallowed a few gulps of water. After abstaining from food for two days, he knew that having too much too fast could make him ill.

He stretched and turned toward the sun. He raised his face and arms. He bathed in the beauty of the world about him, which was shimmering and clean after the rain, with the scent of sage and juniper wafting around him.

"I am here this morning before you, Great Mystery. I have no answers, and so I turn to you. I ask you to watch over those I've left behind. Watch over my journeys. Keep me safe in the future I face. Allow me to be worthy of this day you have loaned me."

When he had left the Swedes, Katrine had asked if he would get lonely. He had never thought of being lonely. The world about him, God's creation, was comfort enough—the visible world as well as the spirit world.

What were the spirits? They were of the First Creator's spirit— the same spirit the Sheepeaters sensed in all things—which this day, Erik again sensed more deeply.

Junipers glowed with the morning's full light. The scrub jays argued more loudly with each other. A lark climbed upward into the sun and dove again to settle on the tips of bright sage, where it broke into song, disrespecting the jays. All things had a spirit within them. No, it was not like mankind's spirit, for the living world did as it was created to do. Only man could choose which direction in life he followed.

CHAPTER 5

Little had been answered from Erik's vision. He felt more than he knew. He would return to the Swedes. He would return to his Sheepeater brother. But the time was obscured. For now, he had no path. The wolf-bear creatures bothered him, but the night cat had said they were not for him. Was this a test from the Great Mystery? Each man was tested, Gray Owl had said, not only during his boyhood vision-seeking but also throughout periods of his life.

Erik continued eastward through dry, barren country to the west slope of the Lemhi Range, where he turned south, eyeing the mountains for a possible pass to the east. He checked each gully that emptied into the intermittent stream he followed. Each gully he encountered was dry. Streams simply vanished into the ground. Erik gazed south through the hazy autumn heat. To go south was worse. He was familiar with that country. There, they had covered their mouths to protect themselves from the alkali dust. They had delayed a full day to fill the water barrels at a barely trickling seep. They had buried his friend.

At length, a fringe of willows came into sight, and Erik found water. A tributary descended from the east. Erik followed a game trail for a distance along its banks until he found a suitable camp. Both ponies drank heavily and grazed the deep grasses along the creek.

The following morning, Erik continued upward, into mostly barren and rocky ground. As he crossed the summit, the air bit cold. Another empty desert valley opened on the eastern side. He worked his way downward and out onto a barren valley that was again traced by an intermittent stream that worked its way through mostly sand and clay. Adjacent to it, he found faint wagon tracks, the first evidence of gold prospectors heading into the gold camps scattered along the Salmon River drainage far to the north.

After watering his horses, Erik continued across the valley and headed upward through some sage-spotted hills. Late day, he topped the small range.

"This looks much better, Hatchet," Erik muttered. Folded ridges descended from a low line of mountains that extended toward the east, which he presumed was the Continental Divide. Conifers spotted the summits and the west-facing slopes. Aspens and willows stretched downward into the valley below him. "Got to be water down there," Erik said.

He rode down into the first basin. A cottontail jumped from the rocks in front of Erik and bounded, zigzagging, into the sagebrush, where it froze in the shadows.

Erik slipped from Hatchet and pulled his bow from its buckskin sleeve. The rabbit's bright black eyes revealed where it hid.

Erik fit an arrow to his bow and pulled back, steadying his aim, knowing and feeling the arrow's flight before he released. Silently, the arrow found its mark, and the cottontail quivered, now pinned to the earth.

"Thank you, Great Mystery, for keeping my arrow straight and merciful. Thank you, brother rabbit, for giving your life to me," Erik whispered.

Erik gathered shredded sagebrush bark and tufts of dry bunchgrass into a small bundle. He pulled a small piece of charred cloth from his tinderbox and tucked it into the nest. He struck the back of his knife sharply against the flint and sent a shower of brilliant sparks into the cloth. The sparks instantly caught, winking and glowing red. He pulled the nest to near his lips and blew the ember into a wisp and then a bright flame. He added twigs to the tiny blaze until he had a small cooking fire. After gutting and skinning the rabbit, he skewered it on a slender juniper twig and slanted it across the fire. This was meal enough for the day and tomorrow, but he intended to soon camp where he could lay in some winter meat.

He filled his canteen at a small seep. Sagebrush and grasses carpeted the hills. A few junipers and piñons grew from crevices in basalt outcrops. He had reentered the burning-rocks land. Somewhere in this country, the Indians quarried the black glass rock—obsidian—for tipping their hunting arrows. The Sheepeaters had also spoken of a nearby land where scalding water shot into the air. The Swedes had shared similar stories about Colter's Hell. Perhaps they were the one and same. Someday he might like to see such a place, he thought.

He searched for an area where Indians had worked on points, in hope of finding a few large obsidian chunks he could take and work later. He needed more arrows, especially since he no longer had a rifle. He had traded his to some Shoshones for Torsten's release.

In some respects, Erik wished he could have anticipated how Torsten would idolize him. Katrine had understood why Erik left, but Torsten, at age five, had not. Erik had been a year older than Torsten when he came to America, and he had seen the world through a child's eyes—an exciting adventure. He'd had no idea of the life-and-death trials in going west. Torsten saw the world the same. Erik sensed he would not become a farmer, as his father wished, but would strike out on his own.

Erik followed the seep to where it emptied into a quiet pool near the base of a basalt flow. Juniper grew from pockets in the rock. Grasses whispered tall in the evening breezes and wafted their dusty scent. Erik slid off Hatchet and turned his ponies loose to water. Tracks at the water's edge showed mule deer and a coyote. This would be a good camp for the evening, but he would sleep up in the rocks, where he would be protected from the cool wind, and not down by the pool.

The sun settled beyond the clouds and sent its last rays outward above the horizon and across the pond where Erik stood. A fragment of obsidian lay in the damp soil, and Erik picked it up. It had been worked.

He flipped the broken point across the pool's quiet surface and watched each strike blossom into ringlets.

Was he willing to follow an unknown path? Did he have faith that meaning would someday come?

The morning light caught a band of mule deer browsing near Erik's camp. He killed a young doe, packed the meat in its hide, and strapped it onto Leaf. He would seek a short-term camp and cure the meat in addition to other game he would kill. He angled downward toward a medium-sized stream known as Medicine Lodge Creek. The Montana Trail, the main supply road from Salt Lake City to Bannack and Virginia City, was but a day's ride east. Erik figured Bannack was four days north, and Virginia City was another two days east. *Why not go there?* A bath and a hot meal appealed to him. He had been on the trail long enough.

The creek ran deep and cool, and its crystal waters bubbled across a scrubbed gravel bottom. Thick, autumn-clad willows and russet foliage lined its banks. A spring bubbled up through bright-green yellow cress near one bank, and a game trail meandered along its length. Erik turned downstream and scattered some trout from under the shadows of the long, nodding grasses.

Erik noticed a brush wickiup in the tree shadows near a clay cutbank. He caught sight of another. These were Sheepeater structures, but this camp was days south of where Erik had first met the people. At least Gray Owl had never spoken of this area.

Rocks outlined the circular edge of one of the wickiups. A few skeletal poles rose from its perimeter. The remainder of the dwelling had been lost to wind and weather. A soapstone bowl rested inside the shallow pit, presumably left behind until the family returned.

Erik clucked to Hatchet and eased his pony into the fast-flowing stream. He waded across and climbed the far bank. Just as abruptly as he had come upon the lush grasses and bubbling creek, he returned to dry, hard-baked earth, scattered sagebrush, and prickly pear.

Some birds erupted from the brush near a basalt outcrop. Maybe a pronghorn antelope or mule deer was coming down to water. Erik braced for the chance for more meat.

The red roan pricked his ears forward. "Easy, boy," Erik murmured to Hatchet. Leaf had alerted as well.

Erik stared past the spot where the birds had risen and tried to catch movement at the edge of his eyes. This was not a pronghorn or a deer.

He turned Hatchet's head. "We'd best get out of sight," he whispered. "I don't need to get shot at again by another stranded pilgrim."

A scrub jay burst from the piñon in front of Hatchet, squawking. Cautiously, Erik pulled his bow to within reach. He caught a form against the sky to his right and slight movement to his left. He had company.

CHAPTER 6

Erik steadied himself as a Bannock brave brought his pony quietly into view from under a dense juniper. The man's forelock was cropped and bound so it stood up. Two other braves emerged on the man's flanks with their bows strung. Erik left his own bow in its sheath and drew a breath. They knew he had no firearms, or they would not have approached.

Erik had no trust in the Bannock. Numerous depredations against the emigrant trains and prospectors were rightfully attributed to them. He considered spurring Hatchet past the nearest man with the hope he would not catch an arrow, but there was too great a likelihood they would grab Leaf.

The men were dressed in loincloths and moccasins; their bronze bodies glinted in the late light. They wore no paint. Possibly they were a hunting party from Fort Hall reservation a few days to the southwest. It was just as likely they had intended to jump and plunder a freighter or lone traveler such as himself.

Erik sat quietly. Had they wanted to kill him, he would already have been dead, but there would have been little honor in killing an enemy without a fair challenge.

The man who approached Erik paused his pony and spoke rapidly, gesturing. Wiry and lean, he appeared to be the oldest of the three and had most likely organized the party. Erik understood what he signed but understood only a few of his spoken words. Although the Bannock were known to hunt with the Shoshone, both peoples had retained their different languages. Erik's people, the Sheepeaters, spoke a dialect of Shoshone.

Erik raised his hand. "I am who Gray Owl of the Tukudeka names Two Elks Fighting." He spoke and signed his words.

The older man scowled more deeply. The two braves drew to within a few feet on either side of Erik, loosely holding their bows ready. The youngest of the three, the man to his right, had a scar across his shoulder. He abruptly laughed, spoke, and gestured.

Erik recognized his meaning: *Tukudeka live in bushes, not lodges.* His sign was dismissive and the same sign as for a worm.

Erik shook his head and signed and spoke in return. "Not brush dwellers. Meat eaters." Meat eaters were honored among the Shoshone. Those of the lowest order were the root eaters or diggers.

"But walkers, not horse riders." The second brave to his left spoke. His deep-set eyes appeared to be set in a permanent scowl, although he grinned while he signed his message.

Erik recognized the mild challenge. They at least would give him a chance and most likely were curious as to who he was—a white man who spoke Shoshone and used hand talk.

"But as you can see, I have two horses," Erik said and signed. "I do not walk."

"Yes," the older man said, "and how does a white man come to call himself Tukudeka and own two horses?"

"Ah, we should talk," Erik said. "We will make camp. I have meat." He nodded toward the doe lashed to his pack pony. Erik hoped the offer would work. At the least, they would first see who he was and what good things he carried before they killed him. Already they eyed his bow. The Bannock hunters' bows were not horn but were sinew-reinforced wood. All their possessions—their ponies, bows, and knives—would not equal the value of Erik's sheep horn bow. Besides, Erik had white men's goods, which were coveted among the Indians. Erik felt like a mouse that three foxes were about to bat back and forth before ripping it apart and devouring it. He was about to become their entertainment before they took what they wanted, including his scalp.

A bead of sweat trickled down Erik's back. He swung himself off Hatchet and began preparing a cooking fire. The three men sat, forming a semicircle about him. Their eyes keenly followed his movements. Erik could have killed one of the Bannocks but not all three. He might win favor, he thought, especially if one or more of them saw strength to be gained from befriending him.

Erik went to Leaf and started opening a pack. Instantly, the youngest Bannock jumped to his feet and flashed a knife.

Erik stood his ground. "I retrieve my things to make our meal," he signed.

Erik set his coffeepot on with water to boil and laid venison chunks in his skillet. The coffeepot and skillet were two utensils he had grown fond of since life with the Swedes.

"I have told you my name." Erik gestured toward the older man with the cropped forelock. "You have not told me yours."

"I am Lame Coyote." The man signed the words *injured* and *coyote* and touched his chest.

Erik guessed they knew what coffee was, but he figured to also spare some of his sugar. The sugar might be sufficient to bring favor.

He seared the venison and offered the skillet to each man to take a piece. They ate noisily, smacking their lips and licking their fingers, and then sat back and nodded their approval.

Erik threw some coffee into the boiling water. In a minute, he pulled the pot off the coals and settled the grounds with a splash of cold water. He poured a cup and made a big show of adding some sugar. He passed his cup around. Lame Coyote tasted it and grinned. He drank more.

"Go easy," Erik whispered in Swedish. "Others want some."

Instead, Lame Coyote drained the cup. Erik poured more and added more sugar until the pot was emptied.

Despite his efforts, Erik had learned little of the three men and nothing of their intentions. The sun settled below the distant ridge, and the cool air gathered.

Erik addressed Lame Coyote. "I know a man of your people. He is called Broken Blade. He and I traded when I was with the Tukudeka."

Lame Coyote spat. "Broken Blade is no longer of the Bannock. He is his own man."

A sudden rush washed over Erik at the connection. Lame Coyote knew of the man, although not favorably.

"His son, Black Legs, is now of the Tukudeka," Erik said and signed.

Lame Coyote's eyes flashed. "It is good Black Legs is of the Tukudeka. He has no stomach for the people's ways."

Black Legs had departed from the Bannock with some disfavor. Each tribe called itself "the people." All other tribes were inferior others and frequently mortal enemies. Given the Indians' predominant feelings concerning this belief, it mystified Erik that the Bannock and Shoshone often hunted together.

Taking a chance, Erik asked, "Do you know of my brother, White Eagle?"

Erik thought he saw a quick flash in the youngest man's eyes; however, none of the men ventured any additional conversation. Instead, their eyes settled on his packs. For what reason would they not now take everything—his bow, his horses, and his life?

Erik began weighing his options. His skinning knife was at his waist. His ponies were packed but not hobbled.

"You call yourself Lame Coyote, but who are your companions with whom I've shared meat?" Erik reminded Lame Coyote of his generosity.

Lame Coyote nodded to the one with the scowl. "Bent Nose is son of Pi-ze." He jutted his chin toward the younger man. "Cut Tongue is son of Horse Runner."

Erik breathed a little more easily. Lame Coyote was willing to converse. It was likely, however, that he wished for Erik to lower his guard.

Erik nodded. "I lived with the Twisted River band of Gray Owl, but I am now seeking a new path. I do not intend to remain here near Lame Coyote's people."

"We go to hunt," Lame Coyote said.

Erik gestured and asked, "Do you travel to hunt buffalo?" He was not convinced they were not intent on striking some traveler along the Montana Trail.

"We hunt big-ears deer." Lame Coyote gestured his meaning of a mule deer by mimicking the animal's mule-like ears.

Erik repeated in Shoshone, "Deheya`."

Lame Coyote nodded. "I see you have a Tukudeka bow. It is fitting to have one for hunting the big ears. We would be able to feed our families."

Erik knew what Lame Coyote suggested. "I have nothing to trade," he said abruptly, signing with a cutting motion. He caught the glimmer in Lame Coyote's and the others' eyes. "Surely Bent Nose and Cut Tongue are great hunters, as is Lame Coyote." Erik stretched, indicating he was tired. "Perhaps, if you agree, we should see in the morning whether Two Elks Fighting is a better hunter. If he can bring down a big ears before you, he will continue on his trail. If not, this shall be yours." Erik touched his bow.

Lame Coyote glanced at Bent Nose and Cut Tongue.

Erik suspected they had considered jumping him, but they had assessed his abilities and had figured that one of them would be dead if they tried. Erik had eyed Lame Coyote with the most intensity, trying to make it clear to Lame Coyote that he would be the one Erik favored to kill. Now he had made an offer that seemed too easy: if they brought down a mule deer before he did, his bow would be theirs.

"We shall have your bow then, Two Elks Fighting," Lame Coyote said, laughing.

"It is good that you accept," Erik said. "Too many already walk the sky trails."

Lame Coyote's eyes flashed, and his hand made a move toward his knife.

Erik smiled and then laughed. "You shall have a good hunt tomorrow." He stood and walked toward his ponies. Cut Tongue again scrambled to his feet and followed, but Erik ignored him. He retrieved some dried fruit from one of Leaf's packs. The ponies had strayed only a few yards and busily cropped the short-grass tufts, seeking them out in the gathering darkness.

"Here. For my brothers." Erik handed out pieces of dried fruit to the three men. They studied the pieces momentarily until he began eating one himself. "Peaches," he said.

The three men settled back, eating heartily. Erik regretted seeing his supply of dried fruit quickly disappear and wondered how the Bannocks would feel when it began swelling in their guts.

He gathered up the coffeepot and skillet and stowed them. He checked to see that Leaf's lead was still tied to Hatchet and then leaped onto Hatchet and slapped his heels against his flanks. "Get up," he hissed. From the corner of his eyes, he saw the three Bannocks hesitate before they realized what he was doing. Quick disbelief flashed into anger. Screaming, they scrambled for their ponies. Bent Nose loosed an arrow in Erik's direction. It hissed past.

Erik did not look back. Leaf would keep up. He had run his horses at night before. He clung low to Hatchet's neck to avoid possible piñon branches.

The Bannocks' cries and ponies' hoofbeats soon echoed behind Erik.

"Go, boy!" Erik hammered Hatchet's flanks. The pony entered an opening and crossed it, reentering scattered piñon and juniper on the opposite side. Leaf thundered behind. The animals raced on, twisting and turning among the scattered trees. The yelling dimmed, and darkness enfolded them.

Erik prayed Hatchet wouldn't hit a hole. He angled uphill. The divide rose about ten miles to the north and ran easterly to where the Montana Trail crossed. He turned north and hoped he could find a pass west of the trail and possibly mislead the Bannocks.

He picked a long upward traverse across the flanks of gentle swells. The cries behind him had ceased. Hatchet's and Leaf's hooves drummed the earth. Both animals breathed hard, and lather coated their shoulders.

Finally, Erik decided he had used up his luck and slowed. The Bannocks would not run their animals hard in the dark; they would depend on their tracking skills at first light. If they set their minds to it, they would pursue mercilessly until they caught him. "Which they very well might do since I made them the fools," Erik muttered.

Erik kept Hatchet at a trot until he entered a broad opening in a dry wash. Erik searched for stars between the gaps in the surrounding trees. He slowed Hatchet to a walk so the animal could pick its way around the rocks. The waxing moon, now nearing its full phase, ascended and spread its light across the countryside.

"Thank you, Lord."

Had he not run, Erik was certain he would have awakened to his throat being slit. He had been a prize too tempting to overlook.

"Come on, Hatchet. Just find us a way now. You have better sense at night than a coyote."

Erik located the North Star, the one point in the night sky that would not shift. The Great Dipper spread toward the east. That constellation would pivot about the North Star as the night passed, giving him a sense of time as well as direction.

Erik followed the dry streambed toward the north. He had no way of knowing if he would reach an insurmountable ridge or if the ascending valley would come out onto a gentle saddle where he could cross the divide.

The wash turned to mud and then flowing water. He found a small pool and watered his horses.

The slopes above glowed pale in the moonlight. They appeared relatively barren. Deep shadows marked where ravines reached upward toward a gentle notch.

Erik breathed easier, now certain he could cross. He encouraged Hatchet onward and began traversing back and forth across the clay slopes while steadily climbing toward the saddle. The mountain shadow spread below and behind him. Above, the stars stretched, frozen in milky clusters.

He crossed a broad, grassy saddle into Montana Territory. Bathed in moonlight, scattered conifer stands spread across the slopes in gentle swales toward the east. Erik cut a long downward traverse until he reached water in the bottom of a gulch. He followed the stream, which drained toward the northwest, where it entered a steep, tree-shrouded chasm.

With the stars still ablaze, Erik found a sheltered cove beneath a pine-blanketed bluff. He picketed Hatchet and Leaf to where they could reach water and good grass. He rolled out his blankets on a hillside above, from which he could watch his horses.

CHAPTER 7

At early light, Erik resumed traveling. He no longer concerned himself with the Bannocks. They were far to the south, and if they followed, they would likely continue eastward toward the Montana Trail.

The stream descended more rapidly. Timber-cloaked mountains lined the northern horizon, but an open prairie extended to the eastern horizon.

Erik swung west and began crossing the folds of the mountains. The land was barren and consisted of mostly clay and wind-scoured short-grass hills. A narrow valley ran to the northwest. Ghostly crags marked its western edge. He considered recrossing the divide and heading west again, but the unbroken pinnacles appeared impassable.

For the next two days, Erik continued roughly northwest, watching for a break in the western range. Presently, he followed a gently rising open and grassy valley that angled due west. A few clumps of aspen were ablaze in yellow and filled the draws. A few ponderosa pine and scattered fir lined the upper edges. Late day, he came out of the valley and topped the saddle, a broad, windswept mountain that straddled the Idaho and Montana territories.

Erik paused to view the country. To the north, the divide became a line of fractured, foreboding peaks. Another rugged line jutted up in the south, but as it swung eastward, the direction from which he had come, the rocky edge dampened into rounded ridges. Erik realized there were numerous passes along the divide. Likely, they were known to the Indians but not necessarily to the whites.

Due east, the land rippled downward in folds and merged with the broken prairie. The silvery headwaters of the Jefferson River sparkled in the late sun. That was bison country. Westward, timbered mountains descended into the shadows of a deep, rugged gorge, which was certainly a tributary of the Salmon River.

Erik sucked in the cool air and tasted moisture, a pleasant surprise. Wispy, high clouds filled the sky. The last weeks had been dry. The breeze carried a slightly smoky odor, and Erik caught the scent of elk mingled within. The grasses had shriveled, and the scanty shrubs had shed their leaves.

"We'd better get off of here," Erik whispered. He nudged Hatchet across the ridge and downward into Idaho Territory toward a grassy draw where he hoped he would soon encounter water. He had ridden much of the day without.

The scattered timber grew more thickly, and shortly, Erik picked up a flowing stream. Almost like magic, it bubbled up from the rocks and flowed toward the northwest. He stopped for his horses to water and scooped water for himself to drink. He refilled his canteen.

He resumed, following the crystal stream in the lengthening shadows. The country steepened, and the surrounding narrow ridges became densely carpeted in timber.

Erik found himself in thought. Life had been good in the small valley near the Swedes, where he had spent the winter trapping. This was similar country. He could trap and, when necessary, strike out for one of the mining camps for supplies. He could build a cabin and raise horses. He would not be far from the Sheepeaters and his brother, White Eagle—and Quickly Smiles. He chastised himself for allowing the thought that accompanied his images of Quickly Smiles, and his face warmed.

He needed a rifle. He could get one after a good winter of trapping. If he'd had one a few days past, there would have been no contest between him and the Bannocks.

Erik angled Hatchet up and across the shoulder of a thickly forested ridge. A snowshoe bounded out of the thickets in front of him and froze. It showed spots of white on its brown coat, a reminder that it would be snow white within a few weeks.

Erik slipped his bow from its sheath and killed the rabbit.

"Thanks for holding steady, Hatchet."

He retrieved the animal.

"Do you want to bet there's water down this gully? This fellow wouldn't be far from it."

Erik nudged Hatchet downward with Leaf following. He reached another small stream that wound its way north through thick underbrush and timber. He was done traveling for the day. He found a somewhat level beargrass-covered bench among the trees, picketed his ponies, and roasted the rabbit. The wind bit cold.

"Winter's on the wing," Erik whispered.

A mountain lion's scream woke Erik. Hatchet and Leaf stamped and snorted nervously. Erik touched his medicine bundle, which held the mountain lion's tooth. "It won't bother you," he whispered.

The lion screamed again, closer and to his left. Erik stepped out and peered beyond his uneasy horses. The moon shone full, lighting up the withered grasses. A memory flashed back. Six winters ago, in the high basin where his father had tried to winter, a mountain lion had killed their ox and stranded them. Erik fingered his skinning knife, the one his father had given him at the time.

The mountain lion flashed between the trees. His horses snorted. It was gone.

Another memory washed over Erik. *Quickly Smiles*. The night cat had visited their wedding lodge.

"You do not let me forget," Erik whispered. Then, loudly, he demanded, "Are you here to remind me? Do you taunt me? Or is this how you tell me I should embrace this life?"

Erik clasped his arms about himself and then opened them to the surrounding country. "Maybe it's your way of telling me this is a good place to winter. What do you think, Sohobinehwe Tso`ape?"

Erik listened for a whistle. Only the wind through the tall timber answered.

CHAPTER 8

The following morning, frost carpeted the beargrass and Erik's bedroll. As he shook it off, his breath hung on the autumn air. At length, the sun broke through the timber and warmed the small clearing, curling steam wisps upward and glinting, sparkling, off the melting frost.

Erik continued downstream, studying the country for sign of fur-bearing animals. The small stream he followed soon entered a wide, grassy valley and dumped into a medium-sized, meandering river. Here the valley spanned a mile, but north, in the direction the river flowed, the walls abruptly pinched. A steep range towered toward the east, the direction from which he had come. To the west, the distant mountains were less rugged but more heavily timbered. Their flanks were barren and covered with short grasses and sagebrush, except for along the drainages, which were choked with willows and aspens. This was good fur country, Erik mused.

Game trails crisscrossed the valley floor. His heart caught when he spotted pony tracks.

"This might change things a bit," Erik muttered. "I don't mind having Indians to trade with, but I need room for trapping."

The valley continued to broaden for several miles and then abruptly narrowed. Erik caught the smell of woodsmoke. Two riders approached. *Indians.* One wore a single braid over his bronze chest, with long hair draping his other shoulder. The second wore no braids, but his brushed hair reached over his shoulders. Erik recognized them as Shoshones.

Erik signed the word *peace.* "I am Two Elks Fighting. I seek to visit with your chief."

"Are you a trader?" the man with the braid asked. He gestured toward Erik, displaying a bronze cuff about his upper left arm. Both men wore traditional multiple strands of white beads. Both appeared surprised that he spoke their language.

"I am, but today I come to visit."

"How is it that a *taipo,* white man, speaks our language?" the other asked.

"I once was of the Tukudeka. This day, I seek to speak with your head man. To whom do you warriors turn?"

"We are Lemhi of the Sacred River band. Tendoy is our chief. He is not here. Cusowat is to whom we turn," the first man answered.

Erik felt a quickening. So these were the Lemhi. While with the Sheepeaters, he had often heard of them. One man whom Erik hoped never to meet again—Runs Fast, who had tried to kill him—had left the Sheepeaters and joined the Lemhi. Possibly, he still lived among them.

"I would speak to Cusowat," Erik said, gesturing. Of all the Shoshone tribes, the Lemhi were the most closely related to the Sheepeaters. Erik recalled that the Big Sheep band often hunted with them.

The men turned toward the eastern peaks, and Erik followed.

Shortly, they reached a cluster of tepees spread loosely through a sheltered basin a short distance up a small tributary. Erik saw few horses. The tepees stood frayed, with thin bison hides stretched sparsely over slender poles. Brush had been thrown over some. The ground had been trampled to hardpan. Scraggly, snapping dogs rushed toward them until an older boy took a stick to them, yelling and swinging until the dogs slinked away.

Eleven tepees. They appeared not much better than the brush lodges Erik had grown accustomed to while with the Sheepeaters. Only a couple of the lodges had good hide covers. Perhaps there were forty to fifty people in the camp, including, at best, a dozen warriors.

Several women clasping ragged hides or tattered blankets and their near-naked children came out and gathered about as Erik was led into the camp.

Although it was October, the moon of the fattening animals, Erik noticed no racks of drying meat, nor did he catch the smell of cooking meals. Instead, the odor of dead and decaying things hung over the camp. The aspens and cottonwoods surrounding the basin had shed their leaves and now appeared as gray skeletons scraping the sky. A few crows hopped about on their naked limbs, intently watching for any unattended scraps.

The two men who escorted Erik stopped in front of one of the finer tepees. Its sides were marked with faded figures of bison and horses. A young woman with a toddler papoose tended a nearby cooking fire.

"Cusowat's lodge," the single-braid man said. He called out.

An elderly man with long graying hair, draped in a yellow-and-black blanket about his shoulders, emerged. An older woman with a young girl and boy also appeared. Erik figured the woman was Cusowat's first wife. The much younger woman with the toddler was likely his second wife.

As was customary, Erik remained astride Hatchet until Cusowat indicated for him to dismount.

Erik did so but retained his bow. A young boy led Hatchet and Leaf away but tended to them within sight of the lodge. Other men gathered around.

Cusowat motioned for Erik to sit and join him. He laid aside his blanket and revealed a handsomely beaded vest with a bone breastplate. He also wore multiple rows of white neck beads. The two women immediately brought bowls of meat soup and a skin of water.

It seemed the entire camp had gathered to observe Erik as he ate. Indians were hard to read, but there seemed a spirit of joy about them. Cusowat grinned and ate with him, his sharp eyes glinting.

Erik scooped the meager pieces of meat into his mouth. He recognized it as elk, probably with other small animals, possibly a ground squirrel. As was customary, he turned his bowl down when finished. In truth, he would have enjoyed a second bowl.

His host gestured to himself. "I am Cusowat. My chief is Tendoy. He is with others in Virginia City." He pronounced it *Jin-ah-sit-ee*. "We are the Sacred River band and care for this, our home." He spread his hands toward the valley. The gesture for *Lemhi* was the same as for *the people*.

Erik nodded and pointed to himself. "I am Two Elks Fighting of the Twisted River band of the Tukudeka."

Cusowat nodded. "I know of the Tukudeka. Some hunt with us and lodge with us. They make fine bows." His eyes flicked toward Erik's sheep horn bow. "How is it a young taipo is of the Tukudeka?"

44

Before Erik could respond, he caught sight of a man about three years older than he was. A chill washed over him. *Runs Fast.* Erik recognized his same long black hair, angular face, and deep-set eyes. Intense hostility shone in the man's eyes. Runs Fast's lips curled. He had not changed.

Erik avoided glancing toward the man but focused on Cusowat. "I lived with Gray Owl's people when my father and mother walk the sky trails. With the Twisted River band, I became a man. I now follow my vision for five seasons."

"The man who killed a Blackfeet warrior was Tukudeka," Cusowat said. "His son is now of us." His eyes swept to Runs Fast.

Erik recognized that Cusowat spoke of Runs Fast's father, Fighting Bear, as being dead. He wondered whether Fighting Bear's wife and daughter were yet here.

"Yes, the man who killed a Blackfeet warrior brought my horse to your people," Erik replied. In truth, Fighting Bear had stolen Erik's horse when Erik was but thirteen and had stranded him with the Sheepeaters. "It is good Runs Fast has come to live with you. But those seasons have passed."

Abruptly, Runs Fast leaned into the circle. "This is little white boy who brought bad medicine to our Tukudeka brothers and disgraced my family. Do not listen to him. Do not accept him among us. He will poison Cusowat's people," he spat. "He brings only death."

Others voiced displeasure at Runs Fast's rudeness.

Cusowat stiffened and raised a cautioning hand. "I can see myself who brings bad things, Runs Fast. Until Tendoy returns, Two Elks Fighting is welcome among our lodges."

Runs Fast pulled back. Erik sensed the buried hatred resurfacing. The man abruptly turned away with two others in his company.

Cusowat sat quietly for a moment. "It is good Two Elks Fighting has come to visit with his brothers. Is he not sent by our Great Father in Washington?"

Erik did not understand. "I wish only to visit. I shall build a white man's lodge in the mountains and hunt. In the spring, I will trade for good things and bring them to Cusowat's people."

Erik caught a flash in the man's eyes. Others who listened appeared puzzled. An unease had risen.

Erik restated his intent. "I visit. Soon I come to trade."

Cusowat lifted his eyes toward the river, spread his fingers, and stretched out his arms. "Tendoy says this is our land now. The Great Father has given us this land." He returned his gaze to Erik. "Have you not been sent to be with us and to teach us?"

"Is this to be a reservation?" Erik asked. He was beginning to understand.

"Yes." Cusowat nodded sharply. "The Great Father has returned our land to us here along Sacred River. Soon we will no longer go to the buffalo-hunting grounds and be attacked by the Crow or the Blackfeet. Soon the redfish will come back up the river. Soon we will have white man's cattle. We will receive many presents. We put our marks on the paper that says this. Tendoy is gone to receive the gifts." Cusowat stood and, clutching his blanket about his shoulders, gestured to Erik. "Come."

Erik followed. This was nothing he had expected. The elderly man stopped at the camp's edge, where they could see the river below.

"Soon we grow wheat and potatoes. Once, we did this when our Mormon brothers were here."

They continued back through the camp. The people watched as they passed.

Cusowat called out to two men, the same two who had escorted Erik into the camp. "Strong Wolf and Crooked Leg," he said, introducing them. "They are hunters and make meat for the people. You should stay with us and hunt with them with your Tukudeka bow."

It was not lost on Erik that the two men had earlier noticed his bow, especially Strong Wolf, the taller of the two men, the one who wore the single braid and the arm cuff.

"Perhaps Two Elks Fighting only carries a Tukudeka bow and does not know how to hunt," Crooked Leg said. Like the other Shoshone men, his middle hair was cropped and brushed back from his forehead and eyes. He wore a simple buckskin shirt braided with tufts of hair, most of which was covered by his bushy, chest-length hair.

Strong Wolf grinned. He patted his chest. "I agree. We should hunt tomorrow and see whose bow shall bring down a big-ears deer."

Erik felt somewhat trapped. "It shall be Cusowat's decision. He and I have much to discuss." He had intended not to stay but to move on and search for a valley where he could trap.

When they returned to Cusowat's lodge, Cusowat invited Erik inside, and it became clear to Erik that he was expected to stay. Cusowat's first wife and the older girl rose and left. His second wife and other children were not present, and Erik presumed they were at a relative's lodge.

The chief again explained Tendoy's absence—his lodges had gone east to hunt bison near their ancestral lands in the Three Forks area, but it was now dangerous since their enemies had driven them out. Tendoy also sought the gifts promised them. Cusowat again wondered if Erik had been sent to assist the Lemhi. Erik repeated his intentions.

Cusowat's first wife and daughter returned. Erik requested her name and learned she was called Black Feather. She did not acknowledge Erik, nor did Erik learn the name of Cusowat's daughter, but that would have been improper. The two prepared their sleeping place on one side of the lodge. Cusowat slept in the customary position at the back of the lodge, opposite the door. Erik was given a pallet of robes near the door.

Years had passed since Erik had slept inside an Indian lodge, and then it had been his own lodge before he left the Sheepeaters. This was not unpleasant. Even so, Erik planned to depart in the morning.

CHAPTER 9

Surprisingly, Erik slept well. He woke only when he became aware of the younger wife working outside the tepee. Her gentle talking told him that Black Feather's children were with her. Woodsmoke and the fire's crackle drifted into the lodge.

Erik slipped outside and greeted the woman simply. "It is a good day."

She averted her eyes. Her toddler son was at her side. It would not have been customary for her to return his greeting.

Erik considered her attractive. Like all the younger Shoshone women, she wore vermilion along the part in her long black hair and on the upper line of her cheeks. He dared not catch her eyes, for it was improper, but Erik could not avoid noticing her arching dark eyebrows. She reminded him of Quickly Smiles, and he pulled his eyes away.

She spoke gently to the two children, treating them as if they were her own; the children treated her as their mother, responding to her directions and showing their affection.

Other voices and sounds of a waking camp interrupted his reverie. Other women were at work. Children and camp dogs darted about. A few men emerged. Some walked in his direction. He recognized Crooked Leg, the man who had chided him about hunting.

Another man joined Crooked Leg and abruptly introduced himself as Black Buffalo. He wore a loose-fitting buckskin shirt decorated heavily with rows of yellow beads. He demanded to trade. Erik had not intended to do any trading; however, he now wondered at the possibility. In doing so, he might gain favor with these people.

"Perhaps I will do some trading," Erik answered. He had a butcher knife and hand ax. He also had some cooking utensils. It might be possible to trade a few items and still resupply before winter, he thought. "I should first like to trade with Cusowat."

Black Buffalo nodded and rose to leave, probably deciding he could now have his morning meal since Erik had assured him there would be no early trading. Crooked Leg followed him.

A couple of children wandered over and squatted near Erik. Their dark eyes were wide, following his movements. Erik could not help but notice Cusowat's second wife as she and the oldest child, a girl of about six, added heated stones to the skin that contained meat and pieces of root.

About the time Erik dared to ask her name, Black Feather emerged. She glanced at Erik and then harshly scolded the younger wife. "You should have risen earlier, woman. Our guest waits for something to eat."

"No," Erik said. "I do not wait to eat; I wait for Cusowat." He gestured toward the sky. "Presently, I am enjoying this morning." It was not proper for him to address Black Feather, but Erik had long followed his own ways.

Black Feather glared and expressed her displeasure in unintelligible mumbling. She huffed about. Erik smiled inwardly. Her manner was not unlike the Sheepeaters'. Black Feather would do little to assist the second wife; rather, she attended more closely to Cusowat's immediate needs.

Shortly, another woman joined the two wives. Erik caught his breath. The resemblance between the two younger women was apparent, and he immediately figured them for sisters. Both had the same thin, arching eyebrows and golden-brown eyes. Erik was captivated by the younger sister. He guessed she might be a couple of years younger than he was, possibly seventeen.

The younger sister took the toddler onto her hip for a moment, smiling and singing to him. Erik was further taken by the woman's smile and soft voice. He caught the baby's bright eyes and smiling face as his aunt entertained him. Of course, the woman ignored Erik, as she should have, but Erik snuck glances while she was occupied with her nephew. She had a graceful, well-defined figure. Yes, she was more beautiful than her sister, and Erik's heart quickened.

It had been months since last he had been in the presence of a woman, and he was surprised at how her beauty quickly warmed him. He shifted uneasily, unable to escape his thoughts. Erik flashed a smile and started to greet her. He caught himself. What was he thinking?

Fortunately, before Erik could make a further fool of himself, Cusowat emerged. Erik stood and greeted him, hoping Cusowat had not noticed his preoccupation.

The man grinned and nodded toward the youngest woman. "You notice Bright Shell," he said. Of course Cusowat had noticed.

"Yes." Erik had to be truthful. "Is she also yours?"

Cusowat shook his head. "Bright Shell is sister of Jumping Deer." He gestured toward his second wife. "They are daughters of Strong Wolf."

Erik recognized Strong Wolf as one of his escorts. He was the taller man who wore the single braid and the arm cuff. Erik suddenly wondered if he should not agree to his challenge to hunt.

"Come. We should eat." Cusowat gestured toward Jumping Deer.

Quickly, Jumping Deer set bowls of meat in front of Erik and Cusowat. The women and children would have their meal later.

"Perhaps Two Elks Fighting has some things to trade?" Cusowat asked. "Black Buffalo says this."

"I have fine things for your wives. I would trade with you for good furs."

"Perhaps I will trade for things for my wives, but I would trade for your bow," Cusowat said. "Today we visit. Tomorrow we will trade."

Erik's chest tightened. He had intended to leave that day. He would never trade his bow and now felt trapped.

After eating, Erik dismissed himself and walked about the village. Cusowat allowed him to do so. Even so, he was aware of several men who followed him. He walked through the camp, realizing he now hoped to catch sight of Bright Shell and to visit her father, Strong Wolf. If he traded with anyone, it should be with Strong Wolf. Perhaps he could offer a gift to him.

Runs Fast stood near one of the tepees, along with Black Buffalo. His lips curled. Erik believed that given the chance, Runs Fast would attempt to poison Black Buffalo against him for long-ago misfortunes he blamed Erik for.

Erik caught and boldly held both men's eyes. Then he spotted Bright Shell. She was outside the adjacent tepee with an older woman, likely her mother, and a younger girl, perhaps a younger sister. It was as if Bright Shell sensed he was near. She glanced in his direction for a fleeting moment before quickly averting her eyes. In that fleeting moment, it was as if the heavens had opened. It was good, but Erik was certain Runs Fast and Black Buffalo had noticed.

Erik considered visiting Strong Wolf. Likely he was not home. He saw only a small boy and a couple of camp dogs. Bright Shell and her mother were busy fleshing a hide. From the corner of his eye, he saw Runs Fast and Black Buffalo approach.

Heat tightened inside Erik's chest. He had done Runs Fast no wrong. Although he was but three years older than Erik was, Runs Fast now appeared much older. He held the same scowl from his youth, but his face was rough, and he now wore a scar across his cheek.

"Ah, little white boy, I see what you see. Should I tell Strong Wolf that little white boy has eyes for his daughter? He would cut them from your head and feed them to the dogs." Runs Fast spat. "Should Cusowat know this? He is to marry Bright Shell so she might join Jumping Deer."

A chill washed over Erik as he fought to keep his face expressionless. He did not want to accept it, but what Runs Fast said was likely true. Frequently, when a man married a woman who had a sister, the younger sister became his second wife.

Runs Fast's fingers hovered near his knife, and his scowl deepened. Erik thought of his own knife and hoped it would not bind in his clothing if he suddenly had to grab it.

He noticed that Strong Wolf had appeared. The tall man folded his solid arms and eyed Erik and Runs Fast. Bright Shell and her mother straightened up from their work.

Erik spoke. "Ah, Runs Fast, you should know Gray Owl has named me Two Elks Fighting. Or should I share with the Sacred River band that Runs Fast was sent away from the Tukudeka?"

Runs Fast's face darkened, and his jaw tightened.

Erik braced himself but continued. "Runs Fast, I hold no anger toward you. We have both left behind what happened before, have we not?"

Runs Fast spat into the dirt. "What happened before I do not forget. The boy who is like the medicine bird dies, and the great fire destroys the people's food. These things came from the evil you brought. It comes with me to these people. Why else would my

51

father walk the sky trails and my mother and sister be taken by the Blackfeet? Do you deny that you bring bad medicine?"

Strong Wolf's eyes moved from Runs Fast to Erik, but neither he nor Black Buffalo moved to intervene.

Erik fought for composure. He regretted that no mention had been made of Runs Fast's mother and sister, who were apparently captives. "Your father did right to kill the Blackfeet warrior. He has honor." Erik presumed as much since Cusowat had addressed Fighting Bear with respect.

"Bah," Runs Fast spat. "You know nothing, little white boy. You pretend to be of the people. You will never be of the people. Evil spirits deceived Gray Owl to make him believe you were a gift to the people. I am not fooled. A bad spirit comes with you. I will speak of this to Tendoy, and others will listen. They will cut your tongue from your head and puncture your ears. Then you may remain with the people. An old grandmother will spit up food for you to eat. All the people will see this."

Runs Fast's hand touched his knife threateningly, inviting Erik to challenge him and fight. Black Buffalo stiffened, and Strong Wolf's hand dropped to his knife as well.

Erik remained calm. He did not fear that Runs Fast would do anything more than threaten. Cusowat had demanded that Erik be welcomed. However, if Erik engaged, Runs Fast could exact revenge.

"I only intend to bring good things to the Sacred River band," Erik said. "It is for Cusowat to decide if I should return or not, not you, Runs Fast." He hoped Cusowat would speak to Tendoy on his behalf. "To show this, I have some gifts." Erik turned toward Black Buffalo and Strong Wolf. "I see you and your wives and daughters work hard." He nodded in Bright Shell's direction. "Tomorrow you should come to Cusowat's lodge so I may give you gifts for them." Erik was uncertain what he could gift; however, even something small would show his goodwill.

Erik noticed that Cusowat now approached, and he realized much of the day had passed. He felt embarrassed for neglecting his host.

The man had heard some of the exchange. He abruptly dismissed Runs Fast, but he did not seem disconcerted. "I will be pleased to trade with Two Elks Fighting tomorrow." He nodded toward Black Buffalo and Strong Wolf. "You should come." He then nodded toward

Erik. "Come. I wish for you to visit Tissidimit. He is keeper for the people."

They reached an isolated tepee, where Cusowat called out. An elderly man emerged on unsteady legs, his watery eyes blinking.

"I have heard of the white stranger who speaks our language," Tissidimit said. Deep lines etched his face. His long hair shone gray, nearly white, and reached to his waist over a tattered buckskin shirt. "I am pleased Cusowat has brought him to me." Tissidimit pushed bony fingers across Erik's face. His eyes appeared blue white, and Erik presumed the man to be nearly blind. "You will stay tonight in my lodge. We will talk."

Erik did not believe that had been the original plan, but when Cusowat turned and departed, Erik knew he was pleased.

"Come," Tissidimit said. A youth standing nearby caught up the old man's arm and helped him reenter his tepee along with Erik.

Inside, an elderly woman tended a small fire. Her scraggly hair was white gray as well, and her face was even more heavily lined. She appraised Erik with a toothless grin.

Dried plants, animal skulls, and stuffed bird skins, including a large raven, hung from the poles. Erik became aware of a sweetish odor, something like anise and sage. He guessed Tissidimit was also a healer.

With the youth's assistance, Tissidimit settled to the ground and leaned against a willow backrest. The youth helped him find and pull up a bison robe.

Tissidimit said, "My time is becoming used up. My eyes are faint, and I no longer hear soft rain on my lodge cover. Soon I will walk the sky trails. Soon Stone Boy will become Tissidimit."

The youth, whom Erik guessed to be in his midteens, was Tissidimit's chosen replacement and would become the next oral historian for the Sacred River band. Erik presumed the woman prepared their food and kept the lodge. Her eyes keenly followed Erik, suggesting she was not a wife but her own person.

Tissidimit patted a rolled robe for Erik to sit and motioned for Stone Boy to bring him a tied bundle. Carefully, Tissidimit unwrapped the bundle and produced a pipe. He filled the bowl and lit it. As was customary, he inhaled twice and then offered the pipe in the four directions before passing it to Erik. Erik followed Tissidimit's actions. He understood that everything now spoken would be truthful or could warrant death.

Erik gestured toward the old woman. "Who keeps your fire? I wish to know her name."

Tissidimit gave Erik a questioning look and then spoke, as if deciding to forgive his visitor for his lack of etiquette. "Raven Woman. She is a healer."

Erik had guessed Tissidimit wrong. The plants, stuffed skins, and skulls belonged to Raven Woman, and as a healer, she had a status similar to that of Tissidimit.

The old woman fixed her eyes on Erik, grinned, and cackled like a raven, momentarily startling him, until he recalled that these people, like the Sheepeaters, were experts at mimicking animal sounds.

Tissidimit instructed Stone Boy to bring forth some skins. When unrolled, they displayed primitive paintings of people and animals. While peering closely, Tissidimit traced a thin finger over the pictures. He gazed at Erik as if to confirm his thoughts and nodded.

"I see you, Two Elks Fighting, and I know you are a true man. You are like the first white men who came to the Lemhi. Then we were a strong people. We had many lodges." He opened his hands six times. "We had many warriors." He gestured the same number again. "We had horses without count. We did not fear the Blackfeeet. We did not fear the Crow. We feared no enemy. We went to the burning-rocks land and dug the camas. We caught many redfish from Sacred River. We hunted beyond the mountains where the sun rises and brought back much meat and robes."

Tissidimit pointed to two faded figures standing as if talking to each other. Based on their dress and long rifles, Erik presumed they were white men.

"I was eight winters when the first white men came. A sister who is gone for many seasons leads them to us. They talk with our chief, my uncle. They desire to travel Great River to the lake with salty water, where the sun goes when it sleeps. My uncle says that in two days' journey, Great River becomes white with dashing water, and its sides cannot be climbed. People who go down the river never return." Tissidimit worked his creased lips and smiled faintly. "The white men listen and go north to the Nez Percé. They do not return."

Tissidimit rubbed his bony hands one over the other and held them out to the fire. His blue-gray eyes focused on Erik. "Some white men come and hunt in other seasons, but only a few. They trap beaver and trade with the people. These white men bring good things. Our people trade for many things. Some of our women marry the white trappers. We have some of their children. But soon they also go away."

He traced his fingers over a sketch of a fortlike structure. "Soon other white men come from the bitter lake to be with us. They show us to grow food and raise white man cattle. Some also marry our women and give us more children. Most are friends to these Mormon brothers, but some are not, and there is bad blood. They return to the bitter lake. We no longer grow crops or white man's cattle. We do not live like before. The Crow and Blackfeet and Sioux are too many and have white man rifles. We do not have white man rifles. We go to hunt buffalo, but we cannot. Our enemies kill our warriors and take our horses. They come also to Sacred River and kill our warriors and take our horses. Soon we live only here on Sacred River."

Tissidimit hunched forward, clasping the robe more tightly before resuming. "In more winters, perhaps this many"—he opened his hands once—"many white men return to where the sun rises, where the buffalo are, and to where the sun sets. They dig in the dirt. They make a city where Sacred River joins Great River. The deer and elk go away. Sacred River is stopped up, and the redfish do not return. We are not welcome to dig for camas in the burning-rocks land. We go to hunt the buffalo, but now our enemies are very strong. Some of us stay here. We have no food. Our children go hungry."

Tissidimit's pale eyes burrowed into Erik's. "Now you come, Two Elks Fighting. You are sent by the Great Father in Washington. You know our language and our ways. You are like the brothers from the bitter lake and can grow things. You can make the white men let the redfish come back to us. We can have white man's cattle. We can become strong again."

Erik's blood raced. He fought his thoughts. Cusowat and Tissidimit expected him to stay to bring back farming, reopen the river to the salmon, and help them against their enemies. "I am Two Elks Fighting. The Great Father did not send me to the Sacred River band. I came because I wish to be a friend of the Lemhi. When I come again, I wish to trade and bring good things."

"Yes," Tissidimit said, nodding. "I know this. Even before this day, I know this. My heart is glad that you are here with us." He opened his arms and reclasped them, rocking slightly.

He had finished talking. Stone Boy took away and rolled the picture hides.

Tissidimit nodded toward Erik. "Two Elks should share my lodge tonight. Tomorrow we will talk some more." The old man retired his pipe, knocking the ash from the bowl, wrapping it, and handing it to Stone Boy for stowing.

Erik had no intention of staying or of teaching the Lemhi to farm, and tomorrow Cusowat expected to trade for his bow. He had no answer to prevent it.

CHAPTER 10

Erik was awakened by Stone Boy and Raven Woman as they began preparing a meal. Erik took his leave while Tissidimit slept. Perhaps he would talk to the man later, but he reasoned he should return to Cusowat.

Frost coated the grass, and steam drifted above the small creek beside the camp. Here the valley spanned about a half mile before it ended abruptly on either side against the mountains. The Continental Divide towered on the east, and heavily timbered mountains rose from the grassy valley in gentle swales toward the west.

Erik tried to imagine sixty lodges scattered throughout the valley, sixty warriors, another three hundred people, and hundreds of horses scattered across the hillsides. The eleven tepees stood wretched and forlorn in this mental comparison. Chief Tendoy was somewhere east with most of the Lemhi, maybe another thirty lodges. Tendoy had gone to Virginia City, the capital of Montana Territory, where he believed he would be provided gifts resulting from an apparent treaty.

Erik reached Cusowat's lodge. His wives and children tended a cooking fire. Jumping Deer shielded her young son as she stirred the fire, explaining how the fire bit. Erik thought again of her younger sister, Bright Shell.

Black Feather muttered under her breath. She seemed to take a keen interest in Jumping Deer and often scolded her. Black Feather reminded Erik of Raven Woman, except Black Feather still retained a few of her teeth.

She soon disappeared into the tepee, muttering all the louder. Shortly, Cusowat appeared, and they were served a meal. While Erik ate, the sun broke over the canyon rim and flooded the camp. The

Lemhi had located the camp well, especially for the winter, when the sun would be at a much lower angle.

"You should stay. We shall make you a lodge. You can help when Tendoy returns," Cusowat said.

"And when does he return?"

Cusowat spread his hands. "Soon."

Erik did not respond. He finished his meal and waited for Cusowat.

An eagle flashed its wings in the morning sunlight as it swooped down and skimmed along the river. Erik wondered about the salmon it hunted. After the fish spawned, their carcasses washed ashore and fed the great birds. Although he had followed the river for several miles, he had not particularly seen any salmon. Tissidimit had said something about the salmon not coming.

"We shall trade now," Cusowat said, and he gestured toward his wives, who quickly hurried away.

Erik gathered the items he had in mind to trade, and shortly, the two women reappeared with two bundles of furs. Their return was like a signal to the others, who began gathering nearby, intent on watching the trading or participating. Trading had long been a favorite pastime.

Erik settled across from Cusowat with his pack.

"All this for your bow," Cusowat said. He pulled the furs toward Erik.

Erik chilled. He shook his head. "I cannot trade my bow. I must have my bow to make meat during the cold snows. I can trade only some things." He opened his pack and removed his hand ax and some utensils. "If you trade furs with me now, I can go to the white man's city and get nice things to trade. In the new season, I will bring many things to trade for your furs."

Cusowat gestured to Black Feather. "Bring my bow."

When she returned, Erik recognized it as a fine wood bow reinforced with sinew, but it did not compare to his horn bow.

"I kill my enemies and provide for my family with this bow," Cusowat said. He demonstrated it to Erik. "I trade my bow for your bow and give you these furs."

"I cannot," Erik said, but he desired to complete some sort of trade to secure Cusowat's trust for next season. He also desired to present gifts to Strong Wolf and Crooked Leg and perhaps Black

Buffalo, men he had determined were important. Most of the men had now gathered as well, including Strong Wolf and Crooked Leg. Runs Fast was noticeably absent.

Erik spread out the items he believed he could part with. "I would give Cusowat this hand ax as a gift for his wives. And since Jumping Deer is wife to Cusowat and Bright Shell is sister to Jumping Deer, I would give Strong Wolf this knife as a gift for his wife and daughter." He pushed the hand ax toward Cusowat and the butcher knife toward Strong Wolf, wondering for just a moment if they might reject the gifts. He need not have worried. The women immediately reached for the items.

Cusowat did not object to the trade.

"If Cusowat wishes to leave me some furs, I can bring more things to trade next season. I do not have many things to trade this day," Erik said again. "However, I would present these things to Black Buffalo and Crooked Leg." He handed out a tin cup and plate. With those last items, he had gifted all the men he believed most important. "That is all." Erik brushed his hands and pushed them outward.

Cusowat shook his head. He had his wives put his bow in front of Erik and pushed the furs toward him. He addressed a young boy, who disappeared and then quickly reappeared, leading a black horse.

"This for your bow," Cusowat said more firmly. "At white man city, you can get rifle and will not need your bow."

Erik shook his head. "I cannot. Runs Fast speaks truth of one thing. I have a spirit, which is not my spirit helper"—he touched his pouch—"but of which Gray Owl knows. This spirit is known by the Tukudeka as Sohobinehwe Tso`ape, the spirit of the trees. Gray Owl says this spirit can bring good, or it can be a trickster. Gray Owl says it lives within my bow. That is why Runs Fast says Two Elks Fighting brings evil."

Cusowat drew back. The others who watched began murmuring, and some shook their heads.

"If I trade my bow, Sohobinehwe Tso`ape would be displeased and would bring bad things to the Sacred River band, as Runs Fast has claimed."

Cusowat hesitated. "How can this be? I know of no such spirit."

"Gray Owl says it is so. Porcupine Woman says it is so. She is a healer," Erik said. "Does the Sacred River band not have spirits that are sometimes good and sometimes tricksters?" Erik glanced around the circle of those who had gathered. The Lemhi's spirits would not necessarily be the same as the Sheepeaters'. "Raven Woman knows of this as well. She will say that she cannot take away the spirit, only that Two Elks Fighting must take it away." He gambled that if asked, Raven Woman would agree. She did not know anything about what he had just said.

"You should bring Raven Woman. Bring Tissidimit," Crooked Leg said.

Cusowat nodded. He sent a young boy in the direction of Tissidimit's tepee. Erik drew a slow breath. He doubted Tissidimit would come. But in minutes, they both arrived. Stone Boy led Tissidimit as someone might have led a blind person and then helped the frail man sit. He covered his thin shoulders with his bison robe. Tissidimit appeared more asleep than awake.

Cusowat explained what Erik had shared. He also said he wished to trade for the bow. When he said it, Erik's hopes sank. He figured both Raven Woman and Tissidimit would wish to please Cusowat and agree with the trade.

Raven Woman peered into Erik's eyes. "You are young to have such a bow." Her voice was dry and crackled.

"It is a gift to me from my uncle upon my man naming," Erik said. His heart hammered.

Tissidimit peered silently in Erik's direction. Erik hoped the old man would guess what he needed.

Raven Woman stretched her hand over Erik's bow. She rolled her eyes upward, muttering a song of sorts. She touched the bow and then, screeching, withdrew her hand and held it as if burned. She pointed at Erik. "It is true. The spirit within answers to Two Elks Fighting. Another may not be strong and keep the evil one away." She waved around toward the others. "Two Elks Fighting must take this bow from the people." She cackled like a raven, turned, and shuffled back toward her lodge. Others nodded and murmured agreement.

Cusowat raised a hand. "It is so." He frowned. "Two Elks Fighting should have first said this."

"I did not know Cusowat only had eyes for my bow," Erik said. "That is why I give away these things." He gestured toward the others who had received some gifts. "I show Cusowat and all the Sacred

River band that I have a good heart, and I will return with more good things when the long nights' snow returns to the north."

"It is as Two Elks Fighting says," Tissidimit said. "He shall keep his bow." He lifted his eyes toward Erik. "I see that like the seasons, sometimes Two Elks will be with us. Sometimes he will not be with us." He reached a hand to Stone Boy, indicating he wished to return to his lodge. Stone Boy helped the old man to his feet and then helped guide him away.

Cusowat nodded. "Yes, Two Elks Fighting will return. He will not forget Sacred River band." He clasped Erik's arms.

A welcome relief washed over Erik. It was finished. He began bundling his things.

Erik had pushed his luck. Cusowat would remember his promise and expect him next season. His gift to Strong Wolf suggested his interest in his daughter, Bright Shell. Likely, Erik had hoped for too much. Tendoy might have other ideas for the goods he would bring. But Erik had considered that. Cusowat's Sacred River band did not leave this valley. If Tendoy did return for this winter, he would likely go east again next summer to hunt bison. Erik would visit when Tendoy was absent.

Erik found that two young boys had brought up Hatchet and Leaf. The people who had gathered around now paid little attention as he swung onto his pony. Erik was pleasantly surprised when Strong Wolf and Crooked Leg came forth and lashed some furs onto Leaf. Cusowat indeed wanted him to return to trade, and he would not accept the gifts Erik had given his wives and the others without returning something to him.

CHAPTER 11

When Erik left the Sacred River band, he traveled southeast up the Lemhi River. He followed the trail awhile and then waded into the river for a distance. Although Cusowat and Tissidimit wished for Erik to return, Indians were fickle. They might get the notion that it would be safer if his bow were destroyed since they now believed it was inhabited by a malevolent spirit. Runs Fast harbored ill will toward him and could justify following and killing him.

Erik did not strike a fire when he stopped for the evening, although a fire would have been welcome comfort against the late-autumn chill. He picketed his ponies, rubbed them down a bit, and then rolled out his bedding. He couldn't help but reflect on the day's events and on Tissidimit, the keeper of the people, and Cusowat, who believed Erik had been sent to assist the Sacred River band. But mostly, his thoughts were on Bright Shell and how her beauty had warmed him. He had heard her voice but once, when she had sung to the child. He scarcely had caught her eyes, but such eyes—deep brown with gold—and her beautiful face with slight, arching eyebrows and rosy, high cheeks. And her breast to which she had held the child.

For a long while, Erik had blocked thoughts of another woman who similarly stirred him: Quickly Smiles. Those memories had flooded forth when he met Bright Shell. Quickly Smiles was equally as beautiful. On the night they had been to marry, the night cat had come to their wedding lodge and revealed to him that he could not marry into the Twisted River band. To do so would have meant he would never leave, and he had promised to find his sister. Thus, Quickly Smiles had become the wife of his brother friend, White Eagle.

Then, for a single night, Quickly Smiles had been made a gift to him, and their coupling was Erik's most intimate memory. He often found himself reaching for that memory, trying to bring it back, trying to relive the memory of their entwined bodies. Afterward, he had known if Quickly Smiles were gifted to him again, he would not be able to refuse. He realized then what the seasons with the Sheepeaters had done. It was not his way of life—it was theirs. He was not Sheepeater, nor was he white. Erik grasped at things from both worlds, but many fit neither. Soon afterward, he'd left the Sheepeaters and White Eagle and Quickly Smiles.

This night, he thought of Bright Shell. Bright Shell was beside him in his thoughts; he saw her golden-brown eyes and the line of her lips breaking into a smile, especially within his imagined embrace. The thoughts stirred him.

He broke from his reverie when Hatchet nickered.

Instantly, Erik found his knife. His other hand found his bow. He rolled from his bedding into the underbrush, listening. He could see nothing—only stars above the timberline. His heart hammered, and sweat gathered on his brow, but it was not for fear. He laughed to himself. If it had been Runs Fast, both ponies would have alerted. They had not, and the night was empty.

Erik returned to his bedroll and tried to squeeze Bright Shell from his senses. He breathed deeply and caught the scent of snow. He listened to the night sounds—an owl answered by a second more distant one, the flutter of wings, and the wind sighing in the firs.

No, this was right. It was what the Great Mystery had intended.

During the following days, Erik explored the Lemhi Range to the southwest of the Sacred River band's winter camp. He sought fur country but with some nearby winter range for big game.

This day, he entered a drainage near the headwaters of the Little Lost River and immediately liked its look. A couple of mule deer browsed near some aspens; neither was alarmed at his presence. Heavily timbered ridges spread westward—indicative of prime fur country.

The sun settled low, and Erik swung off Hatchet. He removed the horse's saddle and his bedroll and released his packs from Leaf. He rubbed the animals before hobbling them.

He kindled a small fire and produced his coffeepot, one of the utensils he was happy he had not traded. The Swedes had been responsible for his acquired love of coffee. Before, he had hardly touched the drink.

He watched the shadows chasing toward the east. Wispy clouds, possibly snow clouds, lined the eastern horizon and caught the fading light, turning pink and lavender. The western sky, which was mostly hidden by the forested mountains, shone a streak of light yellow and gold. He rolled into his blankets to sleep. He had to decide on a location before the heavy snows came, and he yet needed time to obtain supplies.

The morning sun found Erik riding farther up the tree-lined stream. The country soon opened onto a south-facing grassy bowl surrounded by rimrock. A small tributary of crystal water emerged from the basin. Erik found where it bubbled up from the ground below a rock ledge.

He visually traced the main creek to where it repeatedly split and followed ascending fingers into dense timber along the north side of the slopes. "Fur country," Erik mused. Below him, cottonwood trees lined the creek and traced the draws on the open slopes. "And that's mule deer country." Farther below spread the barren scant-grass valley from which he had come. "And if need be, we can go down there to get out of the worst of it."

Erik spoke aloud. He needed a human voice. His ponies did as well.

"Just do not wander too distant, you two. Could be a mountain lion about." He would know shortly after putting in his trapline.

Erik immediately began work on a lodge. He cut and hauled slender poles to his campsite. When he had several dozen, he trimmed the longest and stood three up in a tripod spread about twelve feet apart. He set additional poles between the three until he had a well-formed conical shape. He had no hides or canvas for a covering. Instead, he continued piling on smaller poles and then weaved in some brush to form a waterproof shell. He dug down in the center of the tepee and piled the dirt around the base. The coming snows would insulate and seal out the cold.

Erik built a small platform at the side opposite the doorway. He laid some spruce boughs on the platform and covered them with one of the hides he had. On top of this, he unrolled his blankets. He tied another small hide to the door opening and to a slender pole by which he could pull the hide across the opening.

"I guessed that just about right," Erik mused. He adjusted the opening.

It was a simple dwelling but effective. The depression would collect the cold air and allow for a small fire.

A storm brought a few inches of snow about the time Erik finished his camp. Hazy, high clouds drifted in from the northwest. Erik had sensed the gathering change. He packed the furs that Cusowat had given him onto Leaf and swung up onto Hatchet.

"Come on, boy. Time to go to town."

Erik's lodge was below the summit on the east side of the mountain range, but he desired to explore the country to the west. He would drop down into the Pahsimeroi River drainage, follow that river to its confluence with the Salmon, and then continue to Salmon City, the new city Cusowat had described.

Erik headed uphill, following one of the small tributaries he intended to trap. When he broke out above timberline, he angled toward a saddle between two rocky peaks. He did not like the look.

"Don't know if we can get over that, Hatchet. I probably wasted our time." He nudged his pony upward, leading Leaf, picking his way between rocks, and aiming toward the notch between the two peaks. There was no trail, not even a game trail. If animals were not crossing this direction, it was likely the other side was blocked by cliffs.

"Only one way of knowing," Erik muttered. "When we get up there, at least we'll have a good view of the country. Just don't be mad at me if we're coming back down."

Then he found deer tracks and a thin trail. Hatchet took to it immediately. Horses were normally not hesitant if they could follow even a small trail.

He reached the saddle. Thin-crusted snow carpeted the tundra, and an icy wind buffeted him. The opposite slope fell gently away and disappeared into timber and a narrow valley below.

Erik took in the country. Another jagged mountain range, the Lost River Range, unfolded on the valley's western edge. The Continental Divide lay over his shoulder toward the southeast. This was the middle chain of three narrow mountain ranges. The valleys separating the ranges were barren, dusty deserts nearest the Snake River, but northward and nearer the Salmon River drainage, thick grass and willows traced the rivers and creeks in their bottoms.

"Well, Hatchet, see if you can find us a way down." Erik turned Hatchet down another narrow game trail, traversing across the saddle covered with sparse grass. Game customarily crossed at the lowest points, and when funneled into such a narrow area, they created a zigzag of trails that topped out over the saddles.

He reached a hanging gorge, which he followed due west for about half a mile until it emptied into a lower valley that turned southward. Timber carpeted its steep walls and filled areas with deadfall. Game trails wandered in and about the timber, but unlike deer, Erik's ponies could not slip under most of the downed timber.

Erik steadied himself. "We've got all day, Hatchet." He picked his way around the timber, often climbing the sides of the gulch to get above the deadfall and then dropping back down to the narrow floor.

Water finally seeped up in the bottom of the gulch—not a heavy stream but pools here and there that eventually formed into a flowing trickle. The floor broadened, and the stream spilled outward and downward into the open country below. Then abruptly, the stream sank into a dry apron of rock and gravel that descended from the gorge toward a small fringe of willow.

He emerged onto a wide expanse of alluvial outwash covered only by scattered sagebrush and short grasses. The tops of a few white-and-gray cottonwoods grew farther below.

Erik followed the dry bed, which served as a good trail. After several miles, he began picking up wet areas and some small pools and, finally, flowing water. Erik stopped to water his horses.

Thick grass spread out in a narrow edge along the stream, gradually growing wider downstream. Willows clumped themselves into thickets near the water. Erik pulled away and hugged the drier edge. Other streams merged with the one he followed, meandering, splitting, and reuniting as several narrow waterways flowed toward the northwest. They merged into a larger stream that flowed crystal clear across a scrubbed gravel bottom. Trout raced away.

"The Pahsimeroi River," Erik murmured.

The day became late, the sun set, and the November cold clamped down tightly. Erik found an area off the small river and camped. He figured he had made twenty miles. Considering the rugged peaks he had crossed, his day had been good. He doubted he would retrace this route. Good fur sign abounded along the narrow valley he had descended, but it was not as rich as the drainages on the eastern slope near his lodge.

The following morning, Erik traveled a good trail along the Pahsimeroi toward the northwest. The river continued meandering and braiding itself with other small streams that emptied from the bordering mountain ranges. It grew to several yards wide. Grassy meadows and naked willows spread farther from the river's banks.

Old beaver sign appeared. Chiseled gray cottonwood and willow stumps that had been felled and denuded seasons ago spread on both sides of the river. Fresh sign appeared in only a few isolated places.

"Good that we aren't trapping beavers," Erik whispered.

A couple dozen pronghorn antelope—burnt orange with white throat patches, bellies, and rumps—flowed away across a sagebrush-covered rise. The pungent silver-gray brush reached to near his ponies' height. Deer and pronghorn, except for their brighter color, were invisible in the thickets. Erik watched several prairie chickens scatter away from the trail.

The rugged mountains of the Lost River Range and the Lemhi Range unfolded on either side. The mountains toward the north rippled barren upward into scattered ponderosa pine. The ridges reminded Erik of ribbons of wax that had dripped from a taper and flowed in layers across a table.

He reached the Salmon River—black and solemn and muted in autumn colors. A well-traveled trail followed its south bank. There was no ice. Erik had dropped a mile in elevation, and the cold had not reached the canyon. Shrubs cloaked in a few remaining amber and rust leaves lined the gullies and riverbanks. Dark velvet-green ponderosa pine and blue-black Douglas fir, many of which were four feet in diameter, towered to 150 feet from the grassy slopes on the river's north banks.

When Erik had left the Sheepeaters, he and White Eagle had not followed the Salmon River to this point but had cut across the mountains to the west and returned more directly to his father's cabin. The winter camp where he had first met the Sheepeaters was but a few miles upstream from where he now stood. The hairs on Erik's neck whispered. In some respects, he felt as if he had returned home. *Are you here, Sohobinehwe Tso'ape?*

For the remainder of the day, Erik followed the twisting, sharp bends of the trail as it led downstream until the canyon walls again pulled back and the valley broadened. The river had cut its way through the mountain range he had earlier crossed. He was again on the east side of the Lemhi Range.

Some cattle grazed a nearby slope. A few log cabins and some tents crept into view. He had reached the confluence of the Lemhi with the Salmon River and Salmon City.

CHAPTER 12

Several men gave Erik a good look when he entered Salmon City, likely because he resembled a mountain man in his buckskins and with a pack load of furs.

A mule train stood in the street, as did a couple of wagons. The few buildings were log or rough-sawed lumber. Several canvas tents with smoke pouring from stoves within them were scattered about.

Erik passed a livery and blacksmith. What he took as the main street held several saloons, a hotel and boardinghouse, and at least three mercantiles. Disjointed music filtered from Martinelli Saloon. He saw a sign on one of the more prosperous-appearing stores: Geo. L. Shoup and Co. A smaller sign in one of its tall windows touted "Wide variety of dry goods and canned goods, furniture, clothing, and hardware." Another building—Samstrung and Harpster General Store and Freight, according to its sign—appeared less prosperous.

He swung off Hatchet, unlashed his meager furs, and decided to try Samstrung and Harpster.

A man in his midthirties with dark brown hair and muttonchops met Erik. He raised his eyes questioningly and shook his head but smiled. "Not much in the fur trade these days," he said. He waved at a table where Erik could put down his bundle. "I know there's still plenty in this country. Since the days of Sublette and Bonneville thirty-five years ago. Always has been. Today people want canvas pants and wool shirts instead." He eyed Erik's buckskins and waved at some heavily stocked shelves.

"Seems I know trapping," Erik said. "So I trap." He stood uneasily, trying to guess the man's thoughts.

"Ain't seen you in these parts." The man squinted. His right eye drooped a little under thick eyebrows. He held out his hand.

69

"Name's Chet Harpster. My partner in Bannack is Pete Samstrung. We run this outfit." Harpster wore a striped collared shirt, string tie, and multicolored waistcoat. Erik considered it the perfect look for a successful merchant.

"I'm Erik Larson."

Harpster's handshake was solid. "I spect you're in for supplies. Intending on wintering, I spect."

Erik nodded.

Harpster inspected the furs. "Not much better than for leather, Mr. Larson. Should've left these in the mountains."

"Nothing?"

Harpster shrugged.

"Maybe Mr. Shoup can offer me something then," Erik said. "I don't need much, just a few supplies." He moved to pick up his furs.

Harpster narrowed his eyes. His right eye was barely a slit. "How well you know the country around here, Mr. Larson?"

"I spent a few years west of here. I've traveled it some." Then, to answer Harpster's concerns, Erik said, "I have some coin."

Harpster raised his eyes. "Pick out what you need, Mr. Larson, and I'll also consider something for your furs."

Erik ordered up some coffee, tea, salt, sugar, bacon, beans, and cornmeal. "I reckon with some game, this can see me through to spring." He located a large kettle, replacement utensils, and a bundle of candles. Finally, he piled up a few looking glasses, several butcher knives, and half a dozen awls.

Harpster studied Erik and shook his head. Except for the muttonchops, he was clean-shaven. "Don't understand why you're not chasing gold instead of fur, Mr. Larson. Leesburg is jumping. It's a day the other side of the mountain. Other camps are still opening up." He squinted—compensating for his eye, Erik guessed.

"I have little interest in gold, Mr. Harpster. Suppose I'd dig some if I ever stumbled on it." But Erik would not. White Eagle had found gold. It had brought death to the one man Erik had believed could get him out of the wilderness.

Harpster began wrapping the tea. "There is a big hole of nothing west of here that still needs prospected, not until you reach Florence." He pushed the packaged tea toward Erik. "You run into any Indians?"

Erik nodded.

"Yes, seems by your hand talk, you've been around them."

"I have spent time with them," Erik admitted. The gestures Harpster had noticed were unconscious.

"I had a notion so. Ever do any packing? Might be my partner and I could use you come spring. Have you been around the Shoshone by chance?" He began packing the coffee.

"Close enough," Erik said. "I intend to do some trading with them."

"I was guessing you might be thinking that," Harpster said. He nodded at the butcher knives and mirrors. "You'd make better money just packing supplies into the gold camps. That's why this place exists. Oh, people are raising beef, fishin' for salmon, and growin' crops and such, but none of that would be happening without the gold."

Harpster added the packaged coffee to the pile. "Just two years from ground to this. It's always been a crossroads for trappers and Indians, but now it's gold. I spect it'll just keep growing. There's been a few wagons up the trail over Birch Creek, bringing supplies from Salt Lake City and taking some over to Bannack. Wagons don't do you any good west of here, though. Everyone has to switch to horses and mules. Take Leesburg, for instance." He pointed southwest. "The strike was two years ago. Everyone up there near starved the first winter until we got a mule train in. Fared better last season. I'm guessing about four thousand souls are up there right now. Still, the only way to get grub in is for us to pack it in on mules."

For some reason, Harpster was set on talking. Erik didn't mind. He appreciated learning about the country. Harpster began loading Erik's goods into a canvas bag.

"If you get tired of living in the high lonesome this winter, come spring, head over to Bannack. New freight will arrive soon as the wagons can get over the Montana Trail. Mr. Samstrung will be wanting to get the jump on the freighters. He'll pay good." Harpster squinted and smiled.

"I'll keep it in mind," Erik said. "Thanks, Mr. Harpster." He dumped his coins, and Harpster pulled out three dollars. Erik was surprised. "Sure that's a fair trade to you, especially seeing the furs aren't much?"

"Sure is." Harpster reached into a canvas bag, pulled out a handful of dried fruit, and wrapped it. "And take this with you, Mr.

Larson. Some peaches. I have a feeling you might be ready for a change before spring thaw."

Erik hefted the bag of peaches. "I'm obliged," he said. He almost told Harpster about watching his peaches disappear down Lame Coyote's gullet.

As he packed Leaf, Erik considered that his luck had turned. For some reason, Chet Harpster favored him. He just might head over to Bannack to meet up with Pete Samstrung. For now, he had supplies enough and a winter's work ahead of him.

He headed out along the street, taking in the buildings again. The honky-tonk music from Martinelli's saloon seemed even louder. The Salmon City hotel sign tempted him: "Baths. Meals."

"Maybe that as well, come spring," Erik said as he patted Hatchet. "You won't be minding me that much, will you? You and Leaf and I aren't expecting visitors this winter, are we?"

WINTER TRAPLINE

CHAPTER 13

Erik did not return to his camp by way of the Pahsimeroi River; instead, he headed southeastward from Salmon City, following the wide trail up the Lemhi Valley. At half a mile, he reached Thomas McGarvey's salmon weirs, which spanned the river. He immediately realized why the Sacred River band had no salmon. Although it was not the season for the salmon to be running, had they been, few fish could have swum past the weirs. Erik shook his head. McGarvey might have fished himself out of a livelihood. Like a bear destroying an apple tree for a single meal, McGarvey was destroying the future salmon runs. The bear could be forgiven for his ignorance, but McGarvey?

Erik reached the cutoff toward Cusowat's camp. He teased with the idea of visiting but then decided against it. Likely as not, he would have foolishly ended up trading away his new supplies. The temptation would have been too great.

Three days later, he reached the small basin that held his lodge. Another skiff of snow had been added to the previous one. At this elevation, about four inches covered the ground. The wind had swept some areas free, and the south-facing slopes above his lodge were barren. It had been one of his reasons for picking this location. The wind would keep it mostly clear of snow and, by so doing, provide forage for his ponies. If the basin got too buried, the cottonwoods not far below would get them through the winter.

That night, Erik heard a wolf howl. Hatchet and Leaf stamped and snorted, and Erik's scalp prickled. Likely, the animal was passing through. This was not their favored country. They preferred the broken plains and open hillsides like those he had just traveled through rather than this thick timber. Nevertheless, a wolf pelt was highly prized, and he might get lucky.

This country was more favorable to mountain lions and coyotes. Neither would likely bother him, unless a coyote stole from his snares. A lion might if it became stressed by the winter and turned to trying to get one of his ponies. The worst danger to his trapline was the devil bear, *pah vi-chah*. A wolverine would systematically pick clean every snare and foul the area with its musk.

Erik shoved another piece of willow into the fire and pulled the coffeepot to a corner, where the handle would cool. Neither his small stock of coffee nor his tea would last the winter. He would make it last by steeping kinnikinnick berries and spruce needles and, if any could be found, rosehips.

He poured a cup of coffee and leaned back against the boulder behind the fire. In the morning, he would return to the lower elevations and begin hunting and laying in a store of meat.

The wind sighed in the pine boughs overhead. Their silhouette branches spider-webbed the indigo-velvet sky. A few stars glittered intermittently as the limbs swept the canopy above. *An evening breeze. The morning should be fair weather.*

"But maybe you are trying to tell me something, you trees are," Erik said aloud. Yes, he had been lucky to get past the Bannocks and fortunate to make contact with the Lemhi. Although Cusowat had honored him, Runs Fast would have all winter to poison the others against him. Erik needed to remain alert. A lone man, member to no tribe, was easy prey to others.

Weeks later, Erik snowshoed into a small reentrant where he had placed a baited deadfall. For bait, he had to make do with a mixture of salt pork, blood, and musk. Fortunately, most of the small fur animals were vicious predators eternally on the hunt for smaller prey, such as mice, squirrels, or rabbits. They had a habit of dashing into tight areas to investigate unusual smells, especially odors that mimicked stressed or injured prey.

Erik reached the reentrant, from which a tiny trickle of partially frozen water had worked its way into a faint gurgle downhill toward the larger creek. The log had fallen. The several inches of new snow that had blanketed the limbs above had shaken loose.

Erik found the tail of an ermine in its white winter coat trapped under the log. "Perfect," he whispered. The ermine, investigating the bait, had nudged the trigger, and eighty pounds of wood had crashed down onto it before it had taken another step, despite its normally lightning-quick speed.

Erik examined the animal—slender and beautiful white, with a black-tipped tail. A prize to the Indians.

He took some new bait and scraped a small portion onto the trigger. He respected the delicate task of setting a deadfall. It took a tricky balancing act, and more than once, he'd had a log or rock come down while his hand was underneath. He hoisted the log back into position, wedged it against his chest, and carefully set the trigger into the slot of the supporting stick. He fit a second stick at an angle to hold the two, forming something like a triangle. Gently, he released the log. It held. As long as pressure pressed the two trigger sticks into place, the supporting stick held the weight. The moment something brushed against the baited point, the trigger would disintegrate like a house of cards, and the log would crash down.

He slipped the ermine into his pack and said a quick prayer of thanksgiving that the animal had given its life to him. The woods surrounding were a silent witness. Nothing. But what was there to hear? Erik smiled to himself, remembering Gray Owl's words: *No man truly knows silence unless he has walked the winter woods.* He refixed his snowshoes and turned up the creek, heading for his next trap.

Six feet of snow now filled the drainages and blanketed the surrounding peaks. Erik had proven correct in picking the lower open basin for his lodge. There the sun and wind had kept the snow to only a couple of feet. Certain areas nearby had been scoured to the grass, where often he found his ponies. When the wind picked up, they moved into the cottonwoods farther below, where they browsed on the trees as well as the willows that poked above the snow.

Erik had now worked most of the upper drainages. After working one, he had moved his trapline to another and then to a third. Each had produced a good number of animals, but now, with the approaching spring, he caught fewer. The furbearers were leaving the confines of the creek beds and expanding their hunting grounds. The females would seek new country for raising their young, and the numbers born would rapidly expand to fill the voids left by those Erik or other predators had taken. Come next winter, any surplus would again be whittled down to the same number by spring. Winter, not the hunter, was the primary limiting force.

This day, Erik busied himself with the velvety black coat of a mink. He worked rapidly, peeling away the soft fur and deftly cutting the white tissue that held the hide to the animal's flesh, careful not to cut or damage the pelt. He rolled the skin down the animal as if peeling off a sock. Once the skin was off, he scraped the bits of flesh and tissue from the pelt. The Indians would not split open the mink pelt but turn it back to expose the velvety fur. They might cut it into strips for bow decoration, but more than likely, they would use it as a soft lining for a papoose's cradleboard.

Erik did nothing else to the mink and left its carcass inside out to dry. For other furbearers such as a fox, after rough skinning, Erik carefully worked the hide over a smoothed log to scrape away the remaining flesh and fat. When it was thoroughly cleaned, he stretched the hide on a willow frame, scraped away any additional bits of tissue, and then allowed the pelt to thoroughly dry. After a couple of weeks, depending on the weather, it cured stiff like thick, oiled paper. He removed it from the frame and bundled it with the other pelts, which he stored from the reach of other animals.

Erik preferred to work under a pole canopy he had erected a few yards from his tepee, partly to keep the odor from his lodge and partly to enjoy the open sunshine. He could watch his two horses on the hillside above or sometimes down in the cottonwoods below the camp, along the creek. He never worked long before the crows and whiskey jays discovered him and came quickly cawing and squawking. Erik flicked the small pieces of flesh and fat into the snow, where the birds flashed down and grabbed them. The jays flew away with the bits to a nearby fir, where they ate in leisure. The crows wolfed down their pieces where they sat.

The large pieces often invited a battle. In that case, the crows won out. The gray jays kept their distance, but the instant one of the larger ebony birds flapped away, one or more jays slipped in and snatched up any remaining bits.

When not working on pelts, Erik worked on his equipment, particularly mending his snowshoes. He also worked on arrows for the upcoming season. Even then, the birds kept him company, but they soon left once they discovered he wasn't fleshing a pelt, except the chickadees. The tiny black-capped gray birds scurried up and down the lodgepole pine trunks in search of tiny insects that were revived each sunny day.

When the geese started flying, and the robins showed up, bobbing and chirping in the cottonwoods, Erik knew the season had turned.

He pulled his snares and finished drying the final pelts. He had a good number of fine furs—fox, marten, and fisher, along with some mink and ermine. He also had one lynx and two bobcat pelts.

In a strange manner, the winter solitude had offered companionship, but Erik now looked forward to returning to the outside world. At nineteen, Erik had his entire future ahead of him, yet with this life, he figured some bear or wolf or maybe some Indian, such as Runs Fast, would take his life before he reached old age. He touched his medicine pouch and silently asked for protection. "And where have you been all this long winter, Sohobinehwe Tso`ape? You have not once visited."

Erik had enjoyed a sense of family with the Swedes. He longed for a family of his own. Katrine and Björn would soon be a family. But their dreams would be confined to the valley and to raising their children. Erik did not concern himself with the future; his life was in God's hands. His plan would be revealed at some point. In this respect, he understood why the Sheepeaters held such faith in their visions. It was no wonder a boy would continue seeking a vision until he had succeeded, and it was no wonder a man would seek more than one during his lifetime. He had come to that change in paths when he left the Swedes, but his second vision had revealed little—only that his time had not come. Yet the fight between the lion and the wolf-bear beasts disturbed Erik. Though the night cat had said it was not his vision, it meant something. *But what?* Erik wondered.

It was time. He loaded his pelts onto Leaf, bundled his other gear onto Hatchet, and headed northeast down the narrow valley. All winter, he had wrestled with himself about returning to the Sacred River band and offering his bow, and perhaps even his pack pony, to Strong Wolf to win Bright Shell, but it was likely a moot point. Had not Runs Fast indicated that Bright Shell would soon join her sister, Jumping Deer, as a wife to Cusowat?

For that reason, Erik had tried to push Bright Shell from his thoughts, at least until he had done some trading for better goods in Bannack. Although he doubted that Bright Shell would be available, better goods might increase his chance if she were.

From his visit with Chet Harpster, he understood that a trail cut over the Continental Divide almost opposite the mouth of the creek on whose headwaters he had camped. The trail was one the Indians and, recently, packers, used to cross to the head of the Jefferson River country. There it intersected one of the main trails into Bannack, and except for crossing the divide, the distance to Bannack was nearly the same as the distance to Salmon City. The divide might add half a day more, depending on the weather.

He took a final look at his winter lodge. "Shall I be returning, Sohobinehwe Tso`ape? You kept me little company last winter; perhaps you wish to stay, and I will not."

Erik was not one for staying long in one place. He turned Hatchet toward the valley.

CHAPTER 14

When Erik reached the valley floor, he took one look at the swollen river and turned upstream in search of a better crossing. Similar to the Pahsimeroi, the Lemhi picked up numerous meandering streams that emptied from the steep, rocky peaks on either side of the valley. All high with snowmelt, the streams spilled out into the meadows and pooled into a myriad of ponds and marshes.

Ducks and geese swarmed the waterways. Red-winged blackbirds and their equally noisy blackbird cousins cackled from the willows and cattails. A pair of mountain bluebirds flitted across the open hillside, and a hawk hung suspended high above. It appeared all the wildlife were emerging and joyful to be released from winter's grip.

Fresh horse tracks marked the muddy trail, and Erik found where they crossed the swollen river. Hatchet hesitated. Though not deep, the river was wide and swift. Erik nudged Hatchet into the water, and Leaf followed.

Erik turned downstream until he intersected the creek that spilled down to Lemhi River from the eastern divide. He turned upward and followed a faint trace toward a cleft from which the creek emptied. He found a well-traveled trail and noted some recent tracks. Erik breathed a little easier. Recent tracks meant that others had crossed over the snowfields.

Wind buffeted him. High clouds with some lower gray clouds sifted over from the peaks near where his trapline had been. He glanced upward in the direction the trail climbed and was thankful to see mostly blue sky. Likely, the summit was a good ten miles distant. He had hoped to cross today, but his delay in finding a good ford on the Lemhi had likely changed the plan.

The creek had washed a broad cut over time, and except for some strewn boulders, the travel was easy. Late day, Erik reached the headwall of the basin, where a trail cut a traverse through snow patches above. He judged the sky and weather again.

"This will have to do," he said. "No water much farther above, Hatchet, except the frozen kind."

Erik made camp and hobbled his horses. He could hear the wind whistling above him and decided he had made the correct choice. No stars showed, and Erik felt the moisture.

Morning found the sky overcast. Erik felt the wet cold. If the weather had come in, it would be snowing on the pass. He rubbed down Hatchet and then threw on his tack. He rubbed Leaf similarly and repacked the furs.

Erik turned up trail and almost immediately reached a section of deep snow. Fortunately, tracks before him had cut across it.

He climbed out onto the shoulders of the divide, which was windswept, cold, and barren except for scattered snowfields. The trail split into several smaller trails that descended into different draws. Most, he figured, were game trails. Erik followed the trail that was most heavily marked by horse hooves. Snow lined the hollows and crossed the trail in places. The wind tore at him, flicking bits of snow against his cheek.

This was no country to be caught in. There were no trees or rock outcrops, and the unobstructed wind raced across the land, biting and cold and now spitting wet snow. At the summit, Erik hit unbroken snow and followed the tracks before him that cut across. The summit proved broad but shortly began bending downward. At length, the trail descended out of the snow, and he was again following a muddy trail.

"Guess we're in Montana Territory, Hatchet," Erik murmured.

Undulating, barren beige hills fell away before him until they merged into a broken blue-gray plain in the distance. A few conifers spotted the north- and west-facing slopes. Otherwise, the country was starkly barren, covered only with a sparse mat of withered brown bunch grasses.

When he entered a dry streambed, Erik finally dropped out of the wind, but the snow had turned to intermittent rain. Eventually, water seeped into the streambed, and when Erik reached the first pool, he paused to water his horses and stretch his legs. From the appearances of old campfires, he knew others had also stopped there.

He moved on and encountered increasing rain mixed with snow. It was a good twenty miles yet to Bannack, which meant he would spend another night on the trail. It didn't bother him, but generally, he would hole up in this kind of weather and avoid traveling.

"Sorry about the wet," Erik said. His horses were accustomed to it, however, having lived their lives on open range.

By late afternoon, he intersected a heavily traveled east–west trail and noticed wagon tracks. He figured it was the main road to Bannack and intersected toward the east with the Montana Trail. He had come from the south.

Near dark, Erik pulled well off the trail to again camp. Although he had seen no one, the Montana Trail had a bad reputation. If others discovered him alone, they might decide he was easy prey.

The rain had pestered him throughout the day, and Erik was thankful to build a small fire for a hot meal and to dry out. Greening grasslands spread a considerable distance on either side of the creek and carpeted the rising hills. He could see why this was bison country. He could also see it as future grazing land for horses and cattle.

The following morning, Erik woke to pelting rain. He considered waiting it out but then decided he would be just as wet in waiting as in riding on. He headed down the track, which was now marked with water-filled hoofprints and wagon ruts.

About midday, the trail ascended and crossed between two barren hills and then dropped down into an open grassy basin and a spattering of log structures. Bannack was strung out for a mile on the shoulders of the hills along the course of a rapidly flowing, muddy stream. Widely scattered ponderosa pine carpeted the sage-covered hills high above the town, and a few cottonwoods that had escaped the ax grew scattered above the creek. The entire creek had been turned into a barren landscape of rock piles, pits, and gullies.

Erik rode into the town with a steady rain drumming about his head and shoulders, making him wish for a hat. Water trickled down his neck and down inside his coat and shirt, sticking his shirt to his back. His horses' steps slapped in the mud.

The town seemed quiet, probably because of the rain. A few horses and mules were hitched outside Percy and Hacker's Saloon, from which loud talking drifted into the otherwise mostly empty and soggy street. A flash of lightning illuminated the ridgeline and highlighted the thick stands of sagebrush and lonely pines. Another bolt flickered across the sky and illuminated some gallows set behind a drab building. Muffled thunder rumbled from the hills and echoed repeatedly like talus clattering downslope in a rockslide.

Grasshopper Creek had somehow cut through a rocky ridge, the source of its gold, and twisted eastward toward the Beaverhead River. Bannack stood on one side of the creek. Based on the torrent chasing down its bed, Erik figured that had Bannack been built any nearer the creek, it would have been swept away.

Erik had had enough of the rain, although in one respect, it suited him: he could conduct his business largely unnoticed. Sometimes appearing like an Indian was not helpful. He needed a few staples, but he also wanted some goods to trade to Cusowat or other Indians.

In addition to being a gold camp, Bannack was situated at the end of a supply line. Initially a booming placer camp, Bannack had been thrown together almost overnight after the discovery of gold in 1862. A trail leading 350 miles to the south, to Salt Lake City, had soon become a well-traveled wagon route. Freighters brought in supplies, and as men moved into the territory, so came the cattlemen and farmers. Bannack had become a freight center for pack trains to take goods into the less accessible surrounding gold camps. The town also offered protection from Indian attacks like the ones that had recently closed the Bozeman trail, a previous supply route from the North Platte River.

Beyond Percy and Hacker's Saloon, several empty buildings greeted Erik and hinted of more prosperous past days. He noticed a blacksmith, Potter's Hotel, two mercantiles, and a jail. He searched until he found Samstrung and Harpster General Store and Freight.

Erik stepped inside the building, thankful to get out of the rain, and wiped the water from his clothing and hair.

"Mighty wet out there," greeted a man in his early forties with sandy hair and sideburns. "Welcome. I'm Pete Samstrung. If you're just wanting to dry out, I can understand."

Erik took Samstrung to mean that he figured him to be a drifter just needing a place to get in out of the weather for a bit. His buckskins were wet through.

"I'm Erik Larson."

"In tarnation, you say." Samstrung grinned. "My partner in Salmon City mentioned you. Said you brought in some ratty-looking furs and wanted to do some trading."

"The ones I got this past winter ought to be better." Erik gestured toward the street.

"Bring them in. I'll have a look. And while you're doing that, why don't you stable your horses? Get them out of the rain, and then come on back. Louis Thompson's livery is at the end of the street."

Erik hesitated. He was not certain he would be able to absorb the cost.

"I'll cover you, son," Samstrung said. "That and a room as well. I'm wagering you'll be wanting to get some civilizing."

"You haven't seen my furs yet," Erik said.

Samstrung ran his hand through his hair and reset his rimless glasses. His watery gray eyes crinkled as he peered at Erik. "Judging how you're dressed, you likely know your business."

Surprised, Erik brought in his furs. He piled them where Samstrung had indicated.

The man began a cursory examination and then handed Erik two silver dollars. "Here's for the stables and a room. John and Grace Potter have a respectable hotel. You can catch a bath and supper. We can finish things up in the morning."

Erik wasn't entirely sure how to take things. He stared at the silver. Samstrung seemed to be treating him more than fairly. He wondered what Harpster had told him.

Shortly, Erik had stabled his horses and taken his few personal items with him to Potter's Hotel. The building was typical clapboard, which was thrown up in haste as miners and packers came into the country, giving the proprietors a jump on the competition. Like other merchants' houses, Erik figured the Potters were some of the few making more than grub. He had noted that a meal and lodging cost $1.50 a day. He was immediately thankful to Samstrung.

Shortly, he checked in with Grace Potter. As with most hotels and boardinghouses, Erik knew she, the wife, ran the business. Her husband, John, supported her. Possibly, he even had another job.

She was a seemingly nice lady, older, perhaps in her late forties. She fussed over him a bit as if he were her child. At nineteen, he could have been.

Erik didn't catch sight of Mr. Potter except when he brought in wood for the stove and helped carry hot water to where the bath was.

When Erik lay back in the tub, he realized how much he missed the hot springs in the Swedes' valley. Even with the Sheepeaters, he had been accustomed to washing or bathing nearly daily. In winter, they often chopped a hole in the ice. During warmer months, he made it a point to camp near a river or pond.

As he ran the bar of soap over himself, he thought about others' derogatory comments about Indians' characteristic smell. It was not from lack of bathing. It arose from the animal hides and grease they liberally applied to themselves. It was no different from the distinctive odor of sweat and dirt of hardworking miners or ranchers.

Erik wondered if the odor of animal hides had accompanied him and if that was one of the reasons Samstrung had quickly offered to put him up at the Potters'. Likely it was.

Lightning flashed outside the small window above the wood tub in which Erik relaxed. The low rumble of thunder reverberated down the hills. He reveled in the hot water.

Was this what he was looking for? Had life with the Swedes rubbed off on him more than he had thought? He could see himself building a cabin and having a few cattle and maybe some chickens. No, he'd draw the line at chickens. Beefsteak would do. He could trade for eggs.

A wife? His thoughts flashed to Bright Shell, and his heart caught. He would soon be heading in her direction with new trade goods. He hoped she was not already Cusowat's wife.

A knock on the door brought him alert. "Need anything else, Mr. Larson?" It was Mr. Potter's voice.

"No, thank you." Erik splashed water over his head.

"Others await," Mr. Potter replied.

Erik took the hint.

He took a late supper. Two men were the only customers. After listening for a short while, he took them to be hardrock miners.

He thanked Mrs. Potter for the meal. She seemed appreciative that her meal had been noticed. He stumbled to his room, where he fell onto the bed.

Strangely, he found himself awake an hour later.

"This isn't right," Erik mumbled. He tossed around for a bit, got up, and made his bed on the floor instead.

CHAPTER 15

After a breakfast of ham and eggs and biscuits washed down with hot coffee, Erik found himself thinking about taking up a job in the city and staying awhile.

His musing was interrupted by the talk from a nearby table. Two rough-shod men had begun tossing derogatory remarks his way—something about Indians smelling up the place. He ignored them and stepped back out into the street. He knew why he wouldn't soon take up city life.

Pete Samstrung and another man greeted him when he reentered their store.

The second man was built solidly and had dark hair graying at the temples and a dark stubble beard. Samstrung introduced him as his lead packer, Virgil Williams. He appeared to be in his early forties.

Virgil gave Erik a looking over, grinned, and then chuckled. "Pete said you were hardly growed up and part Injun to boot. Guessing he wasn't telling me a tall one like his normal self." He stuck out his hand.

Virgil's handshake was solid, but Erik was not sure how to reply. He had just about had his fill at breakfast; besides, he was Swedish and only Indian by association.

"Might say so in some respects," Erik said.

Virgil wore a well-worn, sweat-stained dark gray shirt and brown leather vest. "Wal, you can't be all that wet behind your ears if you can survive the high lonesome by yourself, though it's not somethin' I'd choose in life."

Samstrung returned to the pile of furs. "To be honest, when you said you had furs yesterday, I was about to say we couldn't do business. Maybe because you looked like a drowned rat, I figured I could at least spot you two dollars."

Erik swallowed. He saw his winter's work suddenly vanishing. "I can work it off, Mr. Samstrung."

Samstrung laughed. "No, sir, I've had a better look. The lynx and bobcat are good. So is pretty much everything else. What supplies do you have in mind?"

Erik felt a rush of relief. He ran off his list. Shortly, he had things collected, among which were a couple of kettles, knives, and ax-heads.

"I'd say it looks like you intend to do some trading with the Indians," Samstrung said, and he laughed. "I'd say you're about twenty years too late."

Erik nodded. "I'm hoping I'm not completely too late. And otherwise, just say I want to build a cabin."

Virgil gave him a quick look.

Samstrung opened a ledger and made some notes. He asked if Erik had come over Lemhi Pass. "How's the snow? I need to be sending Virgil that direction soon. Folks in Leesburg, west of Salmon City, are needing supplies."

Erik shook his head. "I came from the south. I crossed over a pass upstream of the Lemhi's winter camp."

"That's Bannock Pass," Samstrung said. "You were lucky, son. This time of the season, it's usually under deep snow."

"Some parties had already been through and broke the trail," Erik said. "It was snowing there when I came through, so you may be right, and it's buried again. I didn't find bare ground until near the main trail. That's good range, by my inspection. I half thought about laying claim to it."

"You'd have been beat. That's Horse Prairie Creek. Martin Barrett and Joe Shineberger are already running horses and some cattle down there for the mining camps."

"My luck," Erik said. "Looked mighty good."

Samstrung finished bundling up Erik's goods. Erik had come out close to even, for which he was pleased.

"Are you in a hurry, or can you sit a minute?" Samstrung asked as he settled his glasses. "Have some coffee? Virgil and I have a proposition."

Harpster had hinted about Erik packing for them last fall. He didn't refuse the coffee. The three of them sat back next to the woodstove.

Samstrung did not get to the point for a minute. It seemed he just wished to talk. Virgil seemed a little put off, but Erik figured he had heard the stories before.

Samstrung apologized for the state of the town. "Bannack used to be the territorial capital of Montana Territory. Now it's been moved to Virginia City. The rush in this area only lasted about a year before they hit gold in Alder Gulch, east of here. Some miners jumped from here to there and back again. Virginia's still doing well. Here at Bannack, the placer gold, richer than all tarnation, just played out, but we have some quartz mines booming and a bit of a mill, and freight gets positioned here."

Samstrung rocked back on his chair. "Bannack got discovered by prospectors wanting to get to Florence in Idaho Territory. When news got out in '61 about the strike, some fellas saw a map with a wagon road up from Salt Lake all the way down the Salmon to Florence. There sure as tarnation wasn't a wagon road. Not even a decent trail, except some old Indian trails and a game trail here and there. Those that tried it got a rude awakening."

Erik was familiar with the country. He and White Eagle had come up the Salmon River seasons past. Virgil seemed uninterested and busily pressed his thumbs together as he rocked back.

"Some of them went up to old Fort Lemhi and then up the North Fork and crossed into the Big Hole area, where they found some gold. When others came up over Medicine Lodge Pass, intending on getting to the Big Hole, they stumbled onto gold here.

"Lewis and Clark walked right over the top of this place. They called it Willard's Creek. So many grasshoppers here that the first prospectors changed the name. Know much about grasshoppers?" Samstrung asked. He pushed at his glasses and peered at Erik.

Erik knew he wasn't waiting for an answer, and with hardly a pause, Samstrung raced on. Erik chalked it up to a long winter or the fact that business was slow.

Virgil shot Samstrung a look and deliberately stared out the small window as if he had someplace he would rather be.

"Farmers' bane, grasshoppers are. Those pests will wipe out an entire wheat field in an afternoon. Strip the pastures bare. I've seen it. They did it over on the Lemhi River when the Mormons were there and nearly sent them packing." Samstrung emptied his cup. "More?" he asked Erik.

Virgil offered his. He had not joined in with Samstrung's rambling in the least.

"Down near Salt Lake once, I saw it. A sight you do not want to see. The hoppers made the sky turn black. You try burning them or running logs over them, and they just keep on coming. All you can do is stand by and watch." Samstrung shook his head. "The seagulls out of Salt Lake saved those Mormons' hides more than once by gobbling them up. At least something likes hoppers."

Erik wondered at the image. Indians feasted on them, and he had eaten them occasionally.

Finally, Virgil appeared to have had enough. "So, Mr. Larson, now that you're reoutfitted, what're your plans?"

"I reckon I'll do some trading, build a cabin, and go back to trapping," Erik replied.

Both men frowned.

Samstrung said, "You met my partner, Mr. Harpster—did he ask you if you'd be interested in some packing? Not packing so much as scouting?"

Erik straightened. "For what reason would you be needing a scout? I do not believe the Indians present much of a problem."

"Injuns?" Virgil spat. "Road agents. Injuns ain't much a problem at all. Maybe some Blackfeet wantin' to test their manhood. Otherwise just putting up with drunk ones." He leaned forward. "But road agents? Nigh on every packer has had a run-in or two with 'em."

Erik had not considered road agents a serious threat.

"Virgil is correct," Samstrung said. He waved toward the western mountains. "Between Salmon City and Leesburg in particular. It's only about twelve miles, but there's more than a fair sprinkling of highwaymen, particularly if you're running a small outfit like I do."

"I'm afraid I'm not much familiar with the country around the gold camps," Erik confessed. He didn't see himself warding off road agents, particularly with a horn bow.

Samstrung set his jaw. "I know you can read the country. I've already figured that much about you. Not many trappers these days, but if you can manage on your own in the high country and find your way in and out and about with horses, you can find a route if need be for a pack train." He tapped the table. "Besides, if you can read Indians, you can read highwaymen. I figure with you out in front or watching things, you would be extra insurance for getting my pack train through."

Erik nodded. "It's mighty fine of you to ask, and I appreciate doing business with you. If I get a hankering, I'll be back."

"It would pay better than furs," Samstrung said, somewhat insistent. "You can trap in the winter and pack in the summer." He set his cup down. "Folks may believe Bannack is done as a freight center, but my partner and I have a good sense of the gold camps. Some are better served from here, and others are better served from Salmon City. We can put supplies just about anywhere they're needed. The other packers can't do that—or won't do that. Presently, I could use an extra set of eyes, particularly when we're packing out gold."

Gold made the offer even less enticing to Erik. He shook his head. "I'll keep it in mind, Mr. Samstrung. Thanks for the coffee."

Erik returned with his horses to pack up his purchases. Virgil helped him load up and expertly looped a hitch over the supplies.

"The road agents—are they that bad?" Erik asked. He tightened the strap on his personal belongings, which were lashed behind his saddle.

"It ain't like when Henry Plummer and his gang was about. They were the worst of it. Things settled a mite after the vigilance committee stretched their necks. The gallows are still up to remind others." He pointed toward where Erik remembered seeing them in the lightning. "Still happens, though." He finished pulling the rope tight. "Also, you might say Mr. Samstrung's put a burr under a few folks' saddles."

That made a little more sense to Erik. He thanked Virgil and headed south from the city by following the wagon road. The main route to Salmon City was by way of Lemhi Pass. Erik considered it, but if he had raised any attention, those wishing him harm would figure he would go that direction. He did not wish to lose what he had just purchased, and he preferred less company. He left the trail and headed back toward Bannock Pass.

CHAPTER 16

Days later, Erik had recrossed Bannock Pass and reached the Lemhi River. The swollen stream sucked at its banks where it tore through the willows.

Erik chided himself, suddenly unsure of his intentions. The winter had been too long. He had had too many idle nights and too much time to think. He doubted Cusowat would have delayed in making Bright Shell his wife, but Erik had to know. He flicked Hatchet's reins and turned him downriver. Fortunately, Cusowat's camp was on this side of the swollen Lemhi River.

He rode until near dark and made camp. Figuring he was about five miles south of Cusowat's village, he cached some of his goods. Against all odds, he prayed he would be trading nearly all he had, including Leaf. Caching his goods was the only way he could be sure of hanging on to some supplies for his cabin and trapline and for providing for Bright Shell.

Early morning, he reached Cusowat's camp. Five tepees and near silence greeted him. A single dog came out to investigate. The tepees appeared even more tattered. Four women and an equal number of children were about. The women clutched ragged robes and busied themselves around their fires.

Hollow numbness filled Erik's stomach as he rode into the camp's center. A man he recognized as Red Robe emerged from his lodge and solemnly greeted him.

Erik reached Cusowat's lodge, where Jumping Deer tended the fire. The older girl played with Jumping Deer's young son on a nearby robe. A few others began gathering around. Erik did not see Crooked Leg, Runs Fast, or Strong Wolf. The hollow numbness spread deeper into his being.

Erik greeted Cusowat. The man appeared pleased that Erik had returned. They sat, and as was customary, Jumping Deer brought a bowl of soup. It was thin and held little flavor.

Cusowat answered his unspoken questions. "They go to hunt. Strong Wolf and the others go to Virginia City. Maybe find Chief Tendoy. Perhaps they get the gifts the Great Father promised."

Erik learned the wives and children had accompanied the six lodges and hunters who had gone east. They took Lemhi Pass, the ancient route to the bison-hunting grounds. Cusowat and a few others had remained behind at their ancestral home.

"Perhaps they soon return with seeds for planting now that this land on the Sacred River has been returned to us."

A cold, crawling numbness enveloped Erik. He had missed the others by a week. Bright Shell was gone. He had told himself it would not matter, but he had deceived himself. Once before, he had lost a woman. The pain stabbed deeply.

Among those who were still there and able-bodied were Red Robe, Cow Belly, and Deer Horn, men he cursorily recognized. Possibly these three were the only warriors. Two dozen people remained, of which most were the elderly or young. He wondered about Tissidimit and his lodge.

"You say you will be back, Two Elks Fighting, and you are," Cusowat said, grinning. "For sure you bring things to trade."

"I have brought some fine things," Erik said. "I do not desire to trade this day." How could he explain he no longer saw what he wanted to trade for? He wanted to ask Cusowat if he still intended to marry Bright Shell or if she had become the wife of another man, possibly Runs Fast. An urge to immediately leave and follow after Strong Wolf nearly overwhelmed him.

Cusowat nodded. "Yes. You should stay. We can trade another day."

That was not what Erik had intended. He was compelled to visit, however.

It was much as it had been during his first visit. They talked. Red Robe, Cow Belly, and Deer Horn joined them. Erik was unaware that another woman had joined Jumping Deer at the cooking fire, until the woman placed a bowl of meat in front of him. She did not look up but moved quickly back to the fire, covering herself with a robe.

The woman puzzled Erik until Cusowat explained, "This woman is without a husband. He who strikes the stone is lost two seasons with the man who kills the Blackfeet warrior."

Erik nodded. That meant the woman's husband had been with Fighting Bear and had also been killed. "And what do the people name her?" Erik risked communicating other wishes by asking her name, but it was his nature to know.

Cusowat's eyes lit up. "She is Spotted Bird." He beckoned to the woman.

Erik swallowed. Her eyes were crinkled; her long black hair lacked its blue shine. Perhaps she was thirty, but she appeared much older. She wore a stained and ripped sheepskin dress and no beads. But knowing the people, because of her loss, she would not keep herself pretty. After two seasons, the timing was now proper that she might become available to marry again—if a warrior wished for her. Often, none did. Erik's belly tightened.

"Aishenda`qa," Erik said, and he nodded to her, gesturing his thanks for the meal. He should not have, and he immediately knew it. His gesture could be taken for more than a thank-you.

Indeed, Spotted Bird glanced his way, briefly showing her sharp eyes before averting them.

Cusowat beamed, and the other men grunted softly. Erik wondered if he had been set up.

"It is good that Two Elks Fighting is here," Cusowat said loudly. "You shall stay with Sacred River band. Spotted Bird shall keep your lodge."

Erik shivered. The fleeting thought of what could be momentarily warmed him, and then he buried the idea. He had no intention of staying even a night. Bright Shell was not there. He wished to leave; however, it would have been folly to refuse Cusowat's gift.

"Yes, I would be honored to have a lodge tonight. Thank you that Spotted Bird will keep my lodge," Erik said. The woman would keep his lodge but nothing more. It was Erik's decision as to whether he would share his robes with her. Clearly, some hoped that he would, that things would be right between Spotted Bird and Erik, and that he would marry and stay.

"I wish to see my friend Tissidimit." Erik spoke hesitantly. He had no way of knowing whether the old man had survived the winter.

If not, Raven Woman would yet be in his lodge, probably cared for by Stone Boy, who would have replaced Tissidimit as the next keeper.

"Yes, he would wish to visit," Cusowat said.

When Erik entered the old man's lodge, Tissidimit lifted his head and smiled faintly. Erik could see that Tissidimit's eyes had further paled.

"I have expected you, Two Elks Fighting." The old man beckoned him inside and waved to a place near himself. He did not rise. When Erik sat, he ran his fingers over his face. "It is good you are here. I would be glad if you have come to live with Sacred River band. Is this not why you have returned?"

Erik decided to share his thoughts. It was forbidden for Raven Woman or Stone Boy to repeat his conversation to the others, so he was not concerned. "I share a lodge tonight with Spotted Bird, but I do not wish to remain with the Sacred River band. Someone else calls my heart."

"Ah," Tissidimit said. He laughed gently. "This I know. She is gone with Strong Wolf. You will return for her when they are back, and then you shall stay."

He said it as if it were fact, and a strange shiver raced through Erik.

Tissidimit then shared his concern that something was wrong with the white man's paper that was to give the Lemhi their own reservation. "That is why Tendoy does not return."

Erik remained silent.

"Chief Washakie has his own place. Chief Tahgee has his place. Only the Lemhi do not. We have been friends always with the white man. It is not right that the Lemhi do not have their own land."

"Tendoy will get you your land," Erik said. He had no basis for saying it other than understanding the Lemhi's resolve.

When Erik left Tissidimit, he gifted him two blankets and a knife. Tissidimit would consider the gift generous, but two other persons shared his lodge.

Erik found the lodge he had been given for the night. Already his belongings were inside. Spotted Bird tended a fire outside the lodge and added another stone to the paunch of bubbling stew when he approached. He greeted her. It was proper to do so for a white man but not for a Shoshone. She did not acknowledge his greeting but continued adding bits of rabbit to the pouch.

"I know, Grandmother, that you are here to keep my lodge. Thank you." With the term *grandmother*, Erik believed Spotted Bird would understand.

Inside, Erik found his blankets spread on top of some worn hides in the customary place across from the door. Spotted Bird's robes were midway toward the door. This was not unlike many of the Shoshone lodges in which a family took in an elderly person who helped where possible in exchange for meals and a place to sleep.

Spotted Bird entered and offered him the stew.

He ate and thanked her. "It is good," he said. "You should eat as well."

She did. Erik watched. Likely, she was a dozen or more years older than he was. She wore no vermilion, which was a sign she had been married. He wondered about her children. She would have likely had two or three, with the youngest about nine or ten. The older children might well be on their own, a boy in particular. A Shoshone boy left his mother's lodge when twelve or thirteen and often took up residence with other young men until he proved a worthy hunter, and he would then marry. Erik did not ask.

Erik felt moved by the woman. She sat as close as possible within proper bounds and gave hopeful glances. She was not unattractive. She was his for the asking, and he sensed her desire for him as well. Despite Erik's feelings, he would not do this. He stood and turned away while he undressed and then pulled his blankets up around himself and slept.

In the morning, Erik woke to find that Spotted Bird had already risen. He heard her outside the lodge, busy with the fire and making him a meal.

While he ate, Erik addressed her. "My people would consider you a good woman. You will make some man a fine wife someday. The Great Mystery has shown me a different path."

Spotted Bird's eyes flashed. "It is the Great Mystery's path for me to be an old grandmother."

Erik shook his head. The people would have frowned on her for speaking, and by speaking in the manner she had, she reminded Erik of how he had turned her away. "No, you shall see. The one you shared robes with walks the sky trails, and only now you seek someone. Now that person will know."

Spotted Bird did not reply for a moment, but then she nodded. "The people would have you stay, Two Elks Fighting."

"I know some of the Sacred River band who would not see me stay," Erik said.

"That man says evil of Two Elks Fighting, but he is a foolish man," Spotted Bird said. "He takes his wife and goes to hunt, but he should stay here with us and hunt here. We would not be hungry."

They both talked of Runs Fast. Erik stood. "I will go now. I have some gifts for Cusowat. This I give you." Erik took the blanket he had used and presented it to Spotted Bird.

She shook her head. "I cannot take this. I was given to keep your lodge. I do this because I should." She meant she had fulfilled her obligation to an important visitor.

"I understand, but I decide this. You will keep this blanket."

Spotted Bird's eyes shone as she took the blanket and held it to her face.

When Erik joined Cusowat, he answered the man's question before he could ask it.

"Spotted Bird is a good woman and will someday make some man a fine wife."

Cusowat nodded. "Perhaps Two Elks Fighting will stay. He should hunt with us."

"Will not Strong Wolf and the others bring back meat?" Erik asked. "Is that not why they go?"

Cusowat's eyes hardened, and Erik guessed the truth: they might never return. Erik was a week away from them and would be two weeks away unless they had quit traveling, which they would not have. He wondered about their safety. Their greatest danger would be encountering one of their enemies on the open plains. All tribes who hunted in the Big Hole country warred against the Shoshone, the Blackfeet in particular.

"You should stay," Cusowat said again.

Erik said, "I leave you gifts because I cannot." He opened his pack and presented Cusowat with a butcher knife and blanket, along with other small trinkets. He explained that he had given Spotted Bird a blanket.

Cusowat's eyes widened.

"It is mine to give. You understand I decide to whom I give it."

Cusowat nodded. "Perhaps my friend will return someday to live with Sacred River band."

Cusowat's phrasing indicated that Erik's gifts had been accepted and that Cusowat was releasing him.

Erik shook his head. "I have my own path that the Great Mystery has shown me. I will return with good things for Cusowat and his people, but I do not know when." He pressed his hand to his heart.

Cusowat pressed his hand to his chest as well and said, "It is good Two Elks Fighting will remember his brothers of Sacred River band."

Once again, Erik's ponies were brought to him. He packed his remaining goods and headed upstream along the swollen Lemhi River to where he had cached the other items. He turned up the trail toward Bannock Pass, intending to trade the remaining items to Strong Wolf when he caught up to the small party of hunters and their families. He would trade everything, possibly even Leaf, if he could have Bright Shell. Was it possible?

THE NIGHT PACK TRAIN

CHAPTER 17

By the time Erik approached Bannack, his nagging thoughts had bested him.

"I'm not going after Bright Shell, Hatchet."

Strong Wolf and the small party of families had gone for meat, and Erik knew that trying to find them would be nearly impossible. Of some concern, Runs Fast accompanied Strong Wolf and had had ample time to poison Strong Wolf against him. Erik figured he had already poisoned Black Buffalo and Crooked Leg. Even if Strong Wolf saw some benefit in giving up Bright Shell, Erik's life would be endangered. If they had caught up to Tendoy—if they even sought to join him—Tendoy might take an interest in Erik's intentions and would likely have the final say. Erik had lost his best opportunity to win Bright Shell last fall.

"Maybe this winter, when Bright Shell is back on the Lemhi River," Erik said. "Perhaps I will see about joining them." He smiled to himself at the happier prospect and squeezed his eyes, believing it was Bright Shell, not Spotted Bird, with whom he shared a lodge.

He located Pete Samstrung. The man tried to hide his surprise, but Erik read his eyes, even hidden behind his spectacles.

"Your timing could not be better, son," Samstrung said. "Virgil's heading out in a couple of days. Tell Mrs. Potter I've got you covered at the hotel. Sit a bit, and I'll share what's shaping up."

"You're pretty sure I'm not coming in to trade some more furs?" Erik asked, grinning.

"You'd have tried some new fool," Samstrung said. "So what made you decide against trading with the Indians?"

Erik shrugged. "You treated me more than fair. Both you and your partner."

"No, sir," Samstrung said. "I'm a businessman. I call things pretty square."

"Well, I'm thankful I timed it right," Erik said. "And thank you for the room and board."

Samstrung shrugged. "Mr. and Mrs. Potter and I go way back. You might say we're the little guys trying to make it, especially since Bannack isn't in its prime anymore, and now it's likely to take another step down." He eyed Erik and waved at a chair for him to sit.

Samstrung took a chair across from Erik, peering at him with his watery gray eyes. "The railroad is about to be finished. Some men have platted a new city they're calling Corinne at its northern end, about sixty miles north of Salt Lake City. It's going to be a freight terminus for gentiles and give wagons out of there a jump on those coming out of Salt Lake City. It will be about three hundred miles on a straight line to Salmon City, right through the Lemhi Indian reserve and right to my partner's front door in Salmon."

"Are you thinking about procuring wagons?"

Samstrung shook his head and laughed. "Don't need them. I just need to get connections with some of the freighters out of Corinne. We'll keep supplying the small camps with the mules. Two or three men working a gold strike don't have the luxury of leaving their diggins to come in, and most don't want to. They send out word of what they need. I deliver it. The big companies won't bother with them. They want to stick to wagons, and wagons can't get into those places. With Corinne, they'll get into Salmon City a lot easier and faster, but everything's still going to need to be packed out of there on the backs of mules."

Samstrung stood up. "How about some coffee?" He pulled the pot off the woodstove and poured Erik a cup.

"I'm obliged." Erik took the cup.

"What concerns me, Erik, is this. My pack train may become even more at risk. It can become easy prey to a few hands who are down on their luck or someone who just wants to make trouble. More people have been jumped in this country than anywhere in the West."

Erik had not considered how a pack train might become a tempting target.

"You can hit what you're shooting at, I'm assuming?" Samstrung asked. "You do have a rifle, do you not?"

Erik felt his new job slipping away. He shook his head. "I can shoot, but presently, I have no rifle. I was counting on trading furs for a new one. I'm learning there's not much interest in furs."

Samstrung immediately rose. "I can loan you a firearm." He retrieved a rifle from the rack behind him and put a box of cartridges on the counter. "Spencer repeater."

Erik picked it up and sighted down the barrel. He pulled the hammer back, opened the action, recocked it, and squeezed the trigger, hearing a nice click. "It's good." He knew the rifle's reputation. He did not like that he could not hold on the target while putting another round in the chamber, as a man could when using a Henry, but it was a repeater.

"Take care of it, Erik. I'll see how the summer goes. You may come out ahead enough to own it."

"I didn't know packing was so lucrative."

Samstrung shook his head. "Used to be better, and you're not packing. You're escorting."

Erik raised his eyes.

"I expect you to be out in front, behind, alongside, or anywhere but with Virgil. Your job will be out watching for trouble."

Erik slid the rifle back onto the counter, his eyes questioning.

"Put it this way, son. There's a few folks out there that would just as soon not see my freight getting through, either going in or coming out, especially when it's gold that's coming out. When you've been doing this as long as Chet and I have, not everyone is all that friendly to you."

Samstrung had riled someone—possibly outfoxed someone—and the person hadn't liked it. But to send an armed scout out? Erik wondered what other reasons there might be. He did not believe it to be just a precaution.

Shortly, Erik checked in with Mrs. Potter. She welcomed him back and immediately arranged for a bath. Erik wondered if his buckskins were again the reason for her hurry or if he had unknowingly brought something dead in with him.

Soon he lay back, relaxing. Two hot baths within a year seemed a luxury.

The following day, Erik was on another mission. Samstrung had insisted he ditch his buckskins and also acquire some boots in lieu of his moccasins, saying, "It will make it less likely for you to catch a bullet."

Erik doubted Indians were much of a random target these days, but then he remembered Randolph Minton. Erik had a set of "civilized" clothes from the Swedes, but he took Samstrung up on his offer of a new shirt and pants and some boots.

Erik also found a barber and got his hair trimmed. Other than hacking at it himself, he'd last had a real haircut when visiting Lewiston.

Mrs. Potter noticed. "I declare, Erik, now look at you. You are the most handsome man in these parts. Just you remain close until Sunday. The Nillsons will be here for supper. Their daughter Leah is about your age."

Two men at another table laughed. One said, "Better watch out now, stranger. If Mrs. Potter's got you in her mind, you don't cotton a lick."

"Have a seat." The other beckoned for Erik to join them. Both men were in their early thirties.

Mrs. Potter set a loaf of bread on the table with butter and dished up some stew. "Now, Levi, you and Stu don't go scaring Mr. Larson away."

Erik learned the men were awaiting some of the first freight coming up from Corinne. They would transfer it to mules and take it into Crooked Tree, a small mine somewhere to the north.

Erik shared that he was packing for Samstrung and Harpster.

"Samstrung and Harpster?" Levi turned to Stu. "Aren't they the outfit who took over John Welch's store in Leesburg after he got held up and killed?"

"Held up and killed?" Erik asked.

"Yep," Stu answered. "Welch got himself murdered the second year of the strike, December of '67. He was packing out of Walla Walla and brought freight to the Boise Basin for a couple of years. He brought a train in here and sold out and was headed back to resupply, when four men jumped him. John Welch was my friend. Folks called him Packer John."

Erik leaned forward. "What happened?" Everyone spoke of road agents, but Stu had a firsthand account.

"He was heading out with his gold, along with John Ramey—he's the sheriff now. They got over Birch Creek and got held up," Stu said.

"Ramey was taking tax receipts back to Florence—then we were part of Idaho County. He had about twenty-three hundred dollars. Welch had about thirteen hundred dollars."

"They killed Welch but not Ramey?"

Stu nodded.

"I got an idea on that," Levi said. He leaned toward Erik. "After the strike, road agents were thick as flies on a ripe carcass. Leesburg miners formed a vigilance committee and started stringing 'em up. I say Welch was part of the committee. He recognized the men, so they blew his head off. Ramey didn't know any of 'em, or so he claimed, so he lived."

"Probably Levi's right," Stu said. "They did away with my friend so he wouldn't talk."

Erik ran things over in his mind. Samstrung now supplied Welch's old store. Maybe Welch had indeed made enemies by being on the vigilance committee.

"But there's much worse than road agents, Mr. Larson," Levi said. "It's this country. If you don't respect it, it will eat you alive."

With that comment, Erik knew his new clothes and haircut had made him look too young and wet behind the ears.

Mrs. Potter came over again. "Now, don't give a never mind to those two, Mr. Larson. It's right good to see someone around like you. Gives us hopes of getting some civilization." She ladled out some more stew, offering some to Stu and Levi as well, but Erik noticed their second portions were somewhat less than his. The same was true for the slice of apple pie he received later.

CHAPTER 18

With the morning sky brightening, Erik pulled his tattered brown frock coat over his new brown shirt—he'd chosen the dark color so he would be less noticeable. He glanced down at his new beige pants and clean bright boots. Recalling yesterday, the moment Erik hit the street, he scuffed some dirt onto the boots.

He met Pete Samstrung at his store. Virgil was just bringing the mules to a stop in front.

Virgil rolled his eyes when he saw Erik. "Now you're gonna get kilt 'cause you look like some eastern dude."

Erik flushed. "I spect a little dirt and sweat will change things." He picked up some gravel and ran it down his pants, demonstrating.

Virgil laughed and cuffed him on his shoulder. "Ready to go to work?"

"Yes, sir, Mr. Williams," Erik said.

Virgil thumped him again. "*Virgil's* good by me, seein's we're workin' together. You okay with that?"

"Yes, sir."

Virgil squinted at him and almost thumped him a third time. He pulled out some leather chaps. "Here. You might want these in the timber. Unless you have some."

"I do my best to go places where I don't need them."

Virgil laughed. "I figured you did, but you'll find out real quick that mules make it their business to take you places where you will need 'em." He shoved the chaps into Erik's hands.

"Much obliged, Virgil." Erik tried out the man's name.

Samstrung allowed a crooked grin.

Another man, dressed in a stained blue shirt and dark rust vest, rode up. He was a few years older than Erik was. Virgil waved him off his horse and introduced him. "Lemuel, meet Erik Larson. Erik, this is Lemuel Dunlap."

Lemuel stiffly stepped up to Erik as if he had been in the saddle awhile. His sweat-stained hat sat askew, and he wore an equally stained red bandanna. Lemuel had an appearance the exact opposite of Erik's.

The man gave Erik a visual going-over, sniffed, laughed, and rolled his eyes. He appeared to be in his midtwenties and was thin and wiry, with a stubble beard and unkempt blond hair.

It's the clothes again, Erik thought. The only words Erik got out of Lemuel were that he preferred to be called Lem.

Virgil and Lem began strapping on the sawbuck packsaddles, two wooden X's mounted on a leather pad. The pad conformed to the mule's back and was anchored in place with two cinches running under the animal's chest and belly. A breech strap and breast collar kept the saddle from sliding backward or forward.

Pete Samstrung brought packs out of the store, where he and Virgil had previously bundled the goods into roughly rectangular canvas manty packs.

Virgil gave one of the sawbucks a tug. "With these packsaddles, Erik, these critters can carry nigh on four hundred pounds." He hefted one of the packs and, holding it against his chest and against the mule's back, threw a loop of rope around it and tightened it. He stepped back. "We don't carry anything near that kind of load—about two hundred pounds. Problem's not so much the mule. I don't cotton to lifting more than a hundred pounds to strap it on."

Erik laughed. He knew all too well what Virgil meant. He had lifted plenty of elk hindquarters onto Leaf.

Virgil took the free end of the rope, brought it up from the bottom of the hanging pack, brought a bight of its end over the loop he had anchored the pack with, and then half-hitched the bight. The entire pack could be quickly released by jerking the end of the rope. He daisy-chained the ends of the excess rope and tucked it where it would not get snagged.

He moved to the mule's onside and hitched a second pack of equivalent weight into place.

"Going in, we don't have much to pack in terms of weight; it's mostly bulk," Virgil said, "but comin' out, we could be packin' ore to a mill, and that's heavier than hell. Thankfully, I don't think we have any ore this go."

They had twenty-four mules, plus Erik's pack pony, Leaf. Virgil threw an aparejo onto Leaf. It was most like Erik's packsaddle and a modification of what the Indians used, which was not much more than padded hides. It curved over Leaf's back and was cinched once underneath. For the loads Leaf often carried, it sufficed. When needed, Erik added a breast collar.

As Virgil and Lem hitched on the packs, Erik helped Samstrung line up and match packs for weight. After loading, they pigtailed each mule into the string, tying their leads with breakaway knots in the event a mule went off the trail.

The mules shuffled impatiently. A couple of them gave to grating bellowing, with one getting started and another soon answering.

Erik shook his head. Mules made one of the most awful sounds on earth.

Much of the freight going out on this trip would remain at Salmon City with Harpster. From there, they would head into the mining camps to the west and north.

"Daylight's a-burnin'," Virgil said. The mules were ready. He swung up onto his horse, took the lead rope on his bell mare, and led out the first string of thirteen animals, including Leaf. "How I understand it is that you ride with us, Erik, except when you think you should be out looking for trouble, especially when we're coming home with someone's gold. Is that right, Mr. Samstrung?"

Samstrung nodded. "Exactly right. I would just as soon no one knows Erik is with you."

Virgil headed south with the thirteen animals stringing out behind him.

Lem rode up next to Erik. He eyed Erik's bow, which was sheathed next to the Spencer rifle. He then eyed Erik. "Never seen an Injun scout," he said. "How many white men you killed with that bow of yerun?"

"None. Just meat, but there's likely to be a first time." Erik put an edge to his voice.

Lem hesitated. "Well, you best not be thinkin' all you'll be doing is bird-doggin'. I don't care what Virgil and Samstrung said about you being out and about. You'll be needin' to untangle mules and packs as well. I don't appreciate having to wet-nurse someone. Can't believe they dug you up to be a scout. I've seen your type."

Erik bit his lip. Lem had just admitted he had never seen an Injun scout. How had he ever seen his type? Somehow, Erik was not surprised by Lem's comments. He hadn't had two words with the man until just now.

"I know what I'm hired for," Erik said. "You won't need to ask me for a hand when you need it."

Lem straightened. "Yeah, well, I'll be expecting it." He swung his horse back and took up the lead rope on the remaining mules. Effectively, Lem was midway in the string.

Erik felt a little unsure of exactly where he should be. The country was broad and open and offered no reason for Erik to be shadowing the train, certainly not there. He headed off to the side and tried unsuccessfully to lose himself in the grassy bluffs.

Late afternoon, they hit the trail that turned west toward Lemhi Pass. As they climbed in elevation, they finally entered some scattered timber. Erik moved farther to the side and in front, keeping from sight and more or less parallel to the trail. His worst problem was cutting through the lingering snowfields without a trail.

Virgil stopped for the night just across the divide into Idaho Territory. Erik came in when he saw them stop and helped with the string. Each man took a mule, unpacked its load, pulled off the packsaddle, and then brushed the animal and inspected it for sores or bumps.

Erik wondered if this would be a good opportunity for horse thieves, especially if someone needed only a single animal. In answer, Virgil hobbled the horses and the bell mare. The remaining mules were loose, but he quickly explained that they rarely strayed far from the bell mare.

They had some supper, and afterward, Erik grabbed his bedroll.

Virgil gave him a questioning look. "I can't speak on Lem's account, but I don't have hydrophobia."

"Well, *he* might." Lem jutted his chin at Erik and laughed.

Erik glared. "My understanding is this is what your boss wants so I can meet trouble out there if it happens."

Lem rolled his eyes.

"I don't expect anything," Virgil said. "But it is what Pete said. Wouldn't be the first time he's been right."

The comment made Erik hesitate.

He found a sheltered place under some pines and pulled his blankets about himself, listening to the night. They had seen no one that day.

Morning found frost on the grass. The mules, as Virgil had predicted, were within a few yards of their camp. They struck camp and loaded the animals as the sun's rays snaked through the stunted timber. This day, Erik rode even farther out from the pack train. He picked his way while studying the country and tried to imagine who would want to jump the train and where they would pick a spot to do so. It made little sense they would do it on the way in. It seemed more likely on the trip out, particularly if they carried gold. With that in mind, Erik studied the country for the return trip.

In the distance, Erik noticed what appeared to be a second trail. A barren track stretched in a nearly straight line down toward the valley. It also ascended the slope behind him, closer to the pass. It took him a moment to realize the track had been cut by travois. He briefly wondered why the Indians hadn't bothered to follow the contours.

"Well, of course, Hatchet," Erik muttered. "They gotta go straight up and down. You can't pull a travois across a sidehill."

Erik returned to intercept Virgil, who had nearly brought the mules to the valley floor. They nodded to each other, and Erik rode ahead to where the trail opened onto a gentle apron and crossed to the Lemhi River. This spot was a few miles downstream from Cusowat's camp.

They passed McGarvey's fish weirs. Smoke curled from the cabin's chimney. It was early for salmon, but men were about. Erik figured the salmon trout or steelhead—what the Sheepeaters called the spring trout—were coming upstream. They were often equal in size to the salmon.

Virgil commented. "About the easiest way I know of to make a living. Those fish just come to him. All he has to do is catch them and take them over the pass and freight them out."

Erik briefly considered that salmon also ascended the Pahsimeroi, the next river toward the west. The Shoshone could have moved to that valley, except the Lemhi River was their traditional winter camp. Just as logically, McGarvey could have built weirs on the Pahsimeroi. Of course, the weirs would not have been as close to the trails east or to the new Corinne wagon road.

If Cusowat was correct, it might no longer matter. Tendoy would soon return with gifts. They could farm and raise cattle on the new reservation. They would no longer need the salmon. No longer would the Sacred River band be called the Agaidika, the Salmon Eaters. Erik wondered, *Is there an equivalent name for farmers? Taipo? White man?* It did not seem to fit.

They entered Salmon City. Chet Harpster squinted and then grinned when he recognized Erik.

"Glad you took us up on the offer, Mr. Larson," Harpster said. "I know you're wondering why, because I'm sure you recognized there is certainly nothing difficult about coming over from Bannack. I assure you you'll soon get a better understanding west of here."

After unloading and turning the mules out into the corral behind the store, Virgil suggested Erik and Lem join him at Martinelli's saloon. Erik thought of Samstrung's request that he make himself scarce. That was what he understood his job to be. Awkwardly, he said he preferred to check on his horses before turning in.

"No need. George Wentz does a fine job," Virgil said.

Erik shrugged. "It's my way."

Virgil scratched his head. Lem thumped Virgil and said, "Hell, Virg, I'll have his drink. Come on."

Erik found Hatchet in the corner of the corral with Leaf and the other horses, keeping their distance from the mules. He began rubbing down Hatchet.

George Wentz noticed. "I can see you have a way with your stock, young man," he said. "A normal body having just got here would be having a whiskey or other entertainment by now."

Erik nodded and continued stroking Hatchet's muzzle. "Seems these two have me in their debt. I owe it to them to keep them around best I can." He started brushing Leaf.

George pitched some hay from a stack outside the corral to the nearest of the animals. "More folks could do like you. I get some sorry-looking animals coming in. Their owners spect me to patch 'em up and get them back totally new and ready to go again."

"May I?" Erik asked. He took the pitchfork and pitched some hay to Hatchet and Leaf. He watched them eagerly start munching.

"How about some oats?" George offered. He dragged over a bag and dumped some into a nearby feedbox. Hatchet and Leaf immediately dipped their heads in and ate, blowing and snuffing into the box with tails sweeping.

Erik talked to Wentz for a bit and tried fishing for more information on Samstrung and Harpster.

"I mostly work with Chet. Some say their prices tend high, but then, they come through for you."

"Any reason for someone to want to jump one of their pack trains?" Erik asked.

Wentz frowned. "Not that I would know. Of course, every man has rubbed someone the wrong way a time or two, or he just ain't living life."

CHAPTER 19

At daylight, they repacked the mules and headed west to a bridge that spanned the Salmon River. A man shouted a greeting to Virgil and began counting animals. Virgil counted out the toll.

"Just don't get greedy, George, or I'll have these critters swimming." Virgil spat into the dirt.

"I'd like to see that during this runoff, Virgil," George said, chuckling. The Salmon River ran high and spread out of its banks, roiling with flecks of foam.

Virgil explained, "After Girton and Mulkey tried a ferry here, Barber and Jones put in this pack bridge. Toll's set by the legislature, thankfully, or for sure we'd be swimming. George has the best deal in these parts with this bridge."

"I thought McGarvey had the best deal in these parts," Erik said.

"Come to think on it, I've changed my mind. All Barber has to do is sit here and rake in the money. McGarvey still has to gut and clean fish."

Erik glanced back and caught sight of another pack train heading in their direction.

Virgil spat. "See what I mean? He'll be raking in another dozen dollars in just a moment. If it weren't for some deep holes, I'd be fording the river. I can do it later in the season. Barber grumbles about it, but he still has plenty of business. Trouble is this time of year, the current would knock down one of the mules for sure. Mules don't swim good with a full pack, especially one that's waterlogged. If you could get these critters into the river in the first place," he muttered as if he'd had a new thought. "Hard enough to get them onto a rickety bridge. Folks say they're stubborn, but really, they're smart. If they think there's some danger, even just a leaf blowin' in the road, they stop cold." He laughed. "Horses, on the other hand—they're the dumb ones. They see a leaf blowin' and jump at it."

Virgil rode out onto the decking, clucking to Betsy to follow.

Once crossed, he glanced back at the approaching string. "That's likely Fred Phillips and David McNutt behind us. They'll be pushing to get over the trail into Leesburg in front of us. I don't cotton to standin' here waitin' on them." Virgil led the way up the trail and encouraged his mules to pick it up.

The trail followed along a ridge crest that snaked down from the high country. Short grasses and occasional sagebrush carpeted the barren slope until it ascended first into scattered ponderosa pine and then into thick stands of mixed conifers.

The trail was well used. It had been located high along the sidehills to keep out of the narrow gulches and rocky streambeds. Most of the route had been cleared by ax or cut and dug with pick and shovel.

Two miles up, Erik spotted a rider coming down trail with a pack train on his heels.

"Dad blame it," Virgil muttered. "They have the right to pass, and coming downhill, they'll be moving fast. Help me get these mules to the side."

Erik did not favor being caught three or four animals abreast on the narrow trail. Once he and Virgil had pulled Betsy to the outside, however, the oncoming animals slid to the inside and pushed past the remainder of the train. The men hollered greetings as they passed.

"This spot's not bad," Virgil said. "You get in some of the places, and you have no choice but to wait. That is, if you see them in time. I been pushed dang near off a mountain in more'n one place."

Shortly, the pack train topped out on the saddle. Salmon City was cut from view. Beyond, towered the Continental Divide. The Lemhi Valley appeared as a purple shadow toward the southeast. Northwest, hazy timber-covered mountains shrouded the Salmon River drainage. The mule train began descending, following a torturous sidehill trail across narrow timbered fingers. A whitewater creek pounded through a narrow gorge farther below.

Erik wondered about his real assignment. Virgil admitted the horses and mules moving in both directions were so thick that he doubted any danger. Nevertheless, when Erik encountered a ridge rising above him or another snaking off below, he left the trail and scouted the country. With the timber as thick as it was, there was little chance anyone could leave the trail. On the other hand, the timber gave plenty of cover if anyone wanted to ambush a pack train.

Erik urged Hatchet up a ridge just north of the trail. As was typical of timber growing on a ridgeline, he found it more open, and the going became easier. In places, he found and followed faint game trails. Occasionally, the mules were visible on the main trail below. Shortly, the ridge pitched downward to where it converged at a narrow valley that came in from the northeast. Grayish wraiths snaked above the timber, and the odor of woodsmoke wafted from the gulch.

Erik dropped down onto the trail ahead of Virgil. In another half mile, they broke out into scattered openings among the timber. Smoke clung along the edges of a narrow bowl through which a muddy creek flowed—Napias Creek. Erik recalled the Shoshone word *napiasi*, which meant "money." The creek banks pitched steeply upward into impenetrable timber. Erik figured prospectors who had first reached this spot must have fought every foot of the way coming up the drainages from the Salmon River. Unless a man knew this valley lay as it did, he would never have climbed up from Salmon City, from the direction they had just come.

Men, as thick as bees on honey, stood along the creek, swinging picks and shoveling earth into sluice boxes. They had completely dug the creek into mounds of washed cobbles.

A whining buzz interrupted Erik's thoughts, followed by another and then another. In seconds, he felt the stab on his cheek. He slapped it. It quickly was replaced by another mosquito and then others from a swarm that encircled his head.

"Dad blame it. Pesky little devils. One of the problems in this country. You just don't stop where they can catch up to you," Virgil said as he also swatted at the tiny insects. "Thick as hailstones in a July cloudburst."

Erik followed the pack train through the narrow, muddy street that carved its way between two rows of canvas tents and log buildings. Shouting, laughing, and boisterous music enveloped him. In many respects, except for the lack of wagons and more people, Leesburg resembled Bannack. It spread along both sides of a road for about a mile. Men, horses, and mules, including some being packed or unloaded, filled the street.

They reached a low-slung log building that had been John Welch's former store.

Edward Shunk, a slender, gangly man in his late twenties, stepped out to meet them. "Yo boys are a sight for sore eyes!" He pulled a gray coat over his vest and high-collared tan shirt. He had light blond hair, a narrow face, and wispy muttonchops. "'Bout time yo boys got your sorry asses in here. Losin' business."

The men slid from their horses amid greetings and immediately began dropping packs.

Shunk reached down and, defying his light build, hefted a manty. "Until yo boys got here, the only stock I got was what the Aster boys packed in on snowshoes. And that twern't much. Only way in and out of here when the snow settles in."

"Quit chur bellyachin'," Virgil said. "Nothin' like the first winter. When I got here, they were down to their last can a beans and selling it to the highest bidder—ten dollars, it was. Price plummeted when I arrived, but Samstrung made a killing deal on what I packed in. He was so blamed happy he even gave me an entire day off."

"An entire day, Virgil?" Shunk laughed and then eyed Erik, his jaw working, his muttonchops billowing out. "You ridin' new for Samstrung?"

Erik nodded. "First trip."

"Then you ain't been to the Old Man's town before."

Erik frowned.

Shunk laughed. "Leesburg. A lot of Southern sympathizers come here when gold was discovered. They made this their home by namin' it in honor of Robert E. Lee. It became home because most of those boys had no home to go back to." He grabbed another pack. "Of course, the Unionists right smartly named a place downstream Grantsville. Only now, Leesburg's overrun it, so yo can figure a victory for the South." He grinned. "Some of 'em are leaving now—not just Southern sympathizers but everyone—'cause the Chinamen are comin' in."

Virgil removed the rope and canvas from a bundle of goods. "Then you best be on your way, Edward. Once the Celestials start taking over a camp, it's a certainty the easy pickin's are gone. Time to sell and move on."

Shunk laughed. "This country ain't done, Virgil. Not by a long shot. Maybe right here but not the country as a whole." He waved a hand in the direction of the mountains. "Strikes are being made just about every time I turn around. A couple a rich ones are south of here in the thickest gawdawfullest country there is. A place they're calling Oro Grande, over on Loon Creek. If anything, I might be pulling up stakes and heading over there."

Virgil smiled. "Sounds like one of the places that simply delights Samstrung. If it's as godawful as you say, I might as well start packin' my long johns."

"It's a good bet that you should. Samstrung'll give 'em a week so they'll be desperate for supplies and won't be minding his high prices and then send you on in."

"High prices is a matter of perspective, Edward. Especially when all you got left is a can a beans."

Shunk grinned. "Like spring of '67? By the way, last time yo told that story, it was five dollars for that can a beans." He found a ledger and began making notes. "And if Oro Grande don't work out, Virgil, a couple a Dutchmen hit good closer to the Salmon River north of us here. At least a dozen boys headed out of here yesterday, heading there. The strike is supposed to be up a canyon in some gawdawful gulch between Moose Creek and Panther Creek. They went over the peaks west of here, but yo boys'd have to take your mules down Panther Creek and double back. Ain't any way of getting them mules over the peaks. Might as well be packing straight to hell going into that country." Shunk's muttonchops vibrated as he clenched his mouth.

Virgil laughed and eyed Erik. "What's your wager, Erik? Oro Grande or the gulch?" He rolled a canvas and loosely wound a rope around it. "How are you at cutting trail?"

Erik shrugged. "I've done a bit but avoid it best I can." He had been past Panther and Loon Creeks, only he did not know the tributaries by those names at the time. From the description, Loon Creek was near where he'd spent his first winter with the Sheepeaters.

Lem seemed a bit disgusted. Erik guessed it was not the first time he had cut trail either.

Shunk laughed. "Or I might stay here a spell."

"Even with the Celestials coming in?" Virgil asked.

"They need supplies too. At least until they get their own pack strings coming and going. My guess is those they got going into Boise Basin will start coming this direction."

"The Chinese have pack trains going into Boise Basin?" Erik questioned. Some of the Swedes' crops had gone to Garden Valley and then been transferred to pack trains going into Boise Basin.

"The Chinamen follow the booms," Shunk said. "We Americans keep jumping around from strike to strike, hoping to get lucky rich. The Chinaman sees an area and figures he can work out a dollar a day, day in and day out, and he's happy."

"That's because he has nothing in China to go back to," Virgil said. "Least that's how I understand it."

They had finished opening Shunk's packs and put the others to the side.

Outside, Erik caught sight of the pack train that had followed them now strung out at the opposite end of the street. Despite the number of men and the activity, Erik realized that Leesburg, Oro Grande, and the Dutchmen's strike, all totaled, would never amount to more than a flyspeck of mankind's presence within this country. Something told him the gold seekers would last, at best, five years, and then they would be forever gone. The land would feel their impact like a pesky mosquito being brushed from its cheek. This country was not suitable for farming or ranching, and no road would ever cross it. He thought of the Sheepeaters somewhere toward the west, living secluded, as they always had, and it pleased him.

Despite Erik's sobering thoughts, Leesburg had an exciting air. People milled about. Claims were still being discovered, bought, and sold. Gold was still being found and spent. Hopes still ran high. Even with the Chinese coming in—a sure sign the placer camp was heading toward decay, as Virgil had shared—hopes ran high.

Erik noticed two somewhat revealingly dressed women in the noisy company of several men spill out into the street and then back into a building. It stood near Mulkey's saloon. He couldn't help but catch Lem's crooked grin and his eyes that followed them.

"You gonna gawk at them gals, Lem, or you gonna help me get these mules corralled?" Virgil asked. He swung onto his horse and took up Betsy's lead rope.

Lem glowered but took up the lead on the other mules. As they strung out along the street, a couple of the animals let out a bellow, seemingly aware they were about to get some feed and water.

The corral was a mud pit that water trickled across with flies and dung piled about. As with the corral in Salmon City, the caretaker had some stables located nearby. Virgil handled the details with the man. They were given the choice to stable their horses, but Virgil declined, explaining that Samstrung did not feel it necessary for the short time the animals were there. The stableman tossed out enough hay to get the stock through the night but not much more.

Erik noted about three dozen mules were in an adjacent corral. Still another area was fenced off for when a third string might come in. Erik did not like the meager care offered for his horses. He especially did not like their being corralled in such tight quarters. Suddenly, the entire town seemed to be pressing in on him. He hadn't minded Salmon City, but here, things felt different.

Erik caught up with Virgil. "I'm thinking I just might take a journey up there," he said, pointing toward the timber. "Take my horses and wander a bit."

Virgil arched his eyebrows. "Tonight you get a bed at Moss's."

Erik shook his head. "Might be the job Samstrung has in mind for me is out there."

Lem scoffed. "Ya kin learn a lot more by listenin' in a saloon."

"Maybe," Erik said. "Might be I just learn different." He nodded toward the ridge to the north. "Besides, Mr. Samstrung said I should keep scarce."

Virgil scratched his head. "He did at that, but it couldn't hurt, beings as you're here now, and you've been seen."

"Leave him be, Virgil. Let him go play Injun if he wants." Lem rolled his eyes.

"That's what I want," Erik said.

"Then be here tomorrow at daylight," Virgil said. "We're taking freight upstream to another camp and picking up a shipment as well. I'll need a full day."

"I'll be here." Erik turned back toward the corral.

Lem hissed under his breath, "He's loony. Gone Injun, I say, Virgil. What was Samstrung thinking hiring him? If he's watching us, who's gonna be watchin' him?"

Erik took Hatchet and Leaf and headed toward a notch in the timber. "Don't know about this anymore, Hatchet. Don't think I'm cut out to guide mule wranglers."

He worked his way up a small drainage until he found a somewhat grassy glen next to the stream. He wondered briefly if underneath the sod there might be gold. He shook the idea. None of Erik's history with gold had yet been good.

Erik moved off into the timber and waited patiently until he spotted some spruce grouse. He picked up a stout stick but then thought better of it. Drake wasn't with him. He retrieved his bow and put an arrow into each grouse. Soon he had the birds cleaned and roasting over a small fire. Hatchet and Leaf grazed nearby. Their tails swished the mosquitoes away, just as the smudge from Erik's fire did.

"This is more like it," Erik whispered as he bit into the roasted grouse. Woodsmoke and an occasional gunshot drifted to him through the timber.

CHAPTER 20

The following morning, Erik reached the corral before Virgil and Lem did, and he began preparing the mules.

When Virgil arrived, he asked if Erik had learned anything useful.

"A bit," Erik said. He leaned over a mule and began plastering a recent bite with salve. "Learned it was a good thing my horses weren't in with this stock."

"It happens," Virgil said. "I'm talking about out there."

"Nothing that I noticed." Erik finished patching the wound.

Lem, standing by, scoffed. "Loony, I say."

Erik did not rise for the bait but started hauling out packs destined for the next camp.

When packed, Virgil led the string out and headed up Napias Creek. They soon turned up a small tributary toward a snow-shrouded peak.

"Killion's Diggins is near timberline," Virgil explained. "They said we should be able to get in across the snow now."

Erik moved off the trail, disappeared into the timber, and moved up a small ridge.

After several hours of steady climbing, the timber thinned to scattered clumps of whitebark and limber pine. Nearly unbroken snow filled an open basin that held several flimsy log cabins and canvas tents. Smoke curled from the tin smoke pipes. Erik watched from a twisted clump of limber pine. A party of men came forward and greeted Virgil. Some supplies were offloaded and hauled into one of the log buildings. Men brought out several panniers and hung them on four of the mules. They covered them with top packs, which Virgil tied down. A few other mules were loaded with manty packs.

The remaining mules carried only the canvas and ropes that had made up their former packs.

Within a couple of hours, Virgil began leading out again, following the trail he had cut back across the snow. Erik had circled above the camp to another cluster of limber pine and now worked his way back above the trail on the opposite ridge.

Virgil was about two miles down trail out of the snow and back in timber, when Erik caught a flash of movement on the opposite side of the narrow valley. It was too brightly colored for an elk or mule deer. He turned his head slightly to catch the movement at the edge of his eye. Two horsemen stood in the shadows of some thick timber. He doubted they had sighted him. Erik eased Hatchet back down the ridge and turned downstream.

He crossed the trail well below the pack train and began a cautious loop back up to intercept the men. When he next spotted them, they had moved closer to the trail. Virgil was on a line that would soon put him within a few yards of the men. Oddly, Lem and the empty mules had fallen far to the rear. Perhaps he had stopped to untangle something. The two men began moving.

Erik knew that one man could easily stop Virgil, and the second could search the packs, especially if he had any idea where the bullion had been packed. It was on one of the first four mules, in one or two of the panniers. From how the fourth mule had been packed, Erik figured it was the one. If the men had watched, they likely knew as well. Lem was nowhere in sight.

"What the blazes, Hatchet?" Erik urged his horse forward and closed the distance to within a hundred yards of the two men. He pulled up his rifle and made himself visible. One of the men turned in his direction and then caught the attention of the other. They studied him briefly and quickly turned their horses back into the protection of the timber. Erik caught flashes of them moving back in the direction of the mining camp. He knew it would be no trouble to slip over the ridge and into the Salmon River drainage, or if they intended, they could double back and try to intercept the pack train at another point. If that was their intent. But what other intent could they possibly have had?

Samstrung had guessed correctly. The men had not counted on his having an outrider. However, they now might be on the search for Erik. "Let them try, Hatchet," Erik said.

About the time Lem brought his mules up to Virgil's, they had reached Leesburg. They picked up a few more packs and quickly resumed travel up the main trail back toward Salmon City. Erik remained out of sight, shadowing the pack train, working along the ridgeline above them.

He continued shadowing them until Virgil topped the summit, broke out of the timber, and headed down toward Salmon City. Erik rejoined the trail behind Lem's mules, catching his look as he passed, and rode ahead to intercept Virgil.

"You should know that Lem would do you no good where he likes to hang back like he did coming out of that mining camp," Erik said. "You had company back there. They had their eyes on that fourth mule."

Virgil squinted. "Coming out of Killion's Diggins? I'll be dad blamed." He rubbed his jaw. "Guess we won't be stoppin' on the way home. Better get your butt set for goin' straight through to Bannack."

Erik understood Virgil's meaning. They rode together for a short distance before he again split out and shadowed the string. He met them again south of Salmon City before they hit the trail over Lemhi Pass. Erik figured to show himself occasionally so Virgil knew he was still with them and alive.

When Virgil stopped the string for the night, Erik chose not to come into the camp but bedded down nearby. He declined to light a fire and hobbled Hatchet. He tried to figure out the men he had seen. Maybe someone had hired some road agents to take care of the competition, namely Samstrung. Or maybe, as Wentz had suggested, Samstrung and Harpster had simply rubbed hide the wrong direction with someone who now was bent on leveling some old score. Erik knew he'd better get some answers before he had to kill someone to save his hide or Virgil's or Lem's.

Erik rose once and checked on the pack train. He walked a wide circle about the camp. Seeing and hearing nothing, he returned to Hatchet. Then, on impulse, he took Hatchet and moved to a small ridge opposite the one where he had been. It occurred to him that someone wishing to strike the mules would more likely come from this direction.

Erik woke to Hatchet's whicker. He rolled from his bedding with knife in hand. The slight click he had heard had not been an animal sound. He grabbed his rifle, quickly backed into the timber, and crept toward the sound. Moonlight cut patterns through the timber. A rock clattered, and Erik caught an irritated but hushed voice. He scrambled to put himself between the voice and where Virgil was camped.

Erik paused against a tree and peered ahead into dense black timber, his body tense. Moonlight filtered through in several places. Sweat beaded on Erik's temples.

Brush snapped, and Erik caught a quick movement. Two men stepped into the moonlight.

Erik shouldered the Spencer. "You mind telling me what you two are intending?" he demanded.

Both men spun in his direction.

"What the hell?" One raised his rifle.

"You fire that, and it's the last thing you'll do," Erik said. "I'm looking at you down the barrel of a Spencer." He cocked the rifle. The sound carried.

The man froze.

"You're tailing Samstrung's train, and I want to know why." He sighted on the man with the half-raised rifle.

"Let's git," a voice croaked.

The two men bolted back into the timber, cracking branches as they moved.

Erik held his fire. He could no longer clearly see them, but he knew he could still likely hit one of them. He stepped quickly away from where he had been and tried to catch sight of the men if they crossed into another shaft of moonlight.

A spurt of flashing fire lit the night with an explosion as a round shrieked through the timber high and wide toward Erik's previous position. A second explosion followed the first.

Erik led the shot's origin and pulled the trigger of the Spencer. It slammed back into his shoulder as the night lit up. A man cursed. Erik ran forward toward the voice, cranked another round into the chamber, brought the rifle back up, and cocked it, anticipating where to shoot.

The brush continued cracking and snapping. Too many trees were in the way, but Erik fired another round to speed the men on their way. Shortly, he heard drumming hoofbeats crashing through the timber.

Erik lowered his rifle. "Guess they didn't want to answer my questions."

His racing heart slowed. The hoofbeats receded in the direction of the trail.

Erik returned to where Hatchet was. The horse whickered at his approach. "Let's go visit Virgil."

Erik found Virgil with Lem near the coals of their campfire. Both were holding their rifles and peering in his direction.

"Sounds like our visitors were back," Virgil said.

"Couldn't see much, but I have no doubt it was them." Erik slid off Hatchet. "I asked them what they were up to, but they weren't too neighborly about it and threw some lead my way."

"Dad blame it, they know we're packing gold," Virgil said. "Reckon it's time to sharpen our peepers and play mix-'em-up with the packs."

Lem hadn't said anything and appeared to be somewhat in disbelief.

"As long as they don't know where I'm at, I doubt they'll try it again," Erik said. "So I guess that means I should go back out there."

"Help us load up first," Virgil said. "We're awake. We have moonlight. It's a good trail, so we might as well head out."

Erik helped them get the mules packed. When they were ready, he said, "I'll do what I've been doing and show myself on occasion, but otherwise, I'll see you back in Bannack."

"Good enough," Virgil said. He led out.

Erik turned into the timber. It would not be light for a few hours. Erik wondered how he would stay awake for the remaining miles.

In Bannack, Samstrung came out to greet them and help them unload. He alone took the gold bullion to a safe in the back of the store. Erik helped turn the mules out. Afterward, Lem headed toward one of the saloons.

Erik told Samstrung what he knew of the two men who had tailed them.

"The first time was up near Killion's Diggins. I let them know where I was and then disappeared to keep them guessing," Erik said.

"Good. I hired you because I was betting you could appear and disappear when necessary."

"The second time, I asked what they were up to. They hightailed it and let loose a couple of rounds in my direction. I sent a couple back."

"Just make sure you don't get dry-gulched."

Erik said, "I need to know at what point you don't want me to ask questions and want me to make men like them permanently disappear."

Samstrung pushed at his spectacles. "When you are convinced someone's life is in danger."

Erik would need a lot of convincing. He might take someone's life if the threat of death was imminent, and he would certainly shoot back, as he had done, but this was only a job. It was unlike going after Torsten.

Samstrung seemingly sensed Erik's unease. "Likely you won't be called to. Like what just happened. They won't risk it once the word gets out that you're escorting."

"Any ideas on who it could have been?" Erik asked. "I heard about John Welch being held up and killed. Edward Shunk is running his old place for you. Could there be a connection?"

Samstrung shook his head. "None that would make any sense. Might be someone had a grudge against Welch but not against any of us that I know of. I think it's more likely because Leesburg is declining."

Erik lifted his eyes.

"When a camp first opens, a lot of ne'er-do-wells show up, hoping to get rich quick. If they don't, they take it from others who do. Same thing happens when a camp is in decline. Those that didn't get rich decide to grab what they can on their way out."

Samstrung shrugged. "Maybe in my case, it could be as simple as someone thinking I charge too much. Always the way it is when you don't have enough of everything that someone wants. Costs me more, but no one believes that. Instead, I'm raking in money, so I'm the greedy son of a bitch." He smiled at Erik. "It's what they say anyhow. No one considers the cost of getting supplies into this country. It isn't like going to the neighbor's farm for milk."

Samstrung shook his head. "And if I lose one shipment of gold for someone, Erik, I'm done. If I never lose any, well then, yes, it's a good living—while it lasts."

Virgil leaned against the open door and spat. "You might be getting another opportunity, Pete. Edward says a couple of Dutchmen have a good strike somewhere between Moose Creek and Panther Creek. Men are headed there as we speak."

"That surprises me not," Samstrung said, brightening. "You can't get any more rugged country than that, so it figures on being some of the last to be prospected." He laughed. "So the Janssen brothers finally hit. You remember them. Let's hope this strike holds up."

"Johnny and Lars." Virgil shook his head and stepped back inside. "I thought they were in Boise Basin. But now you mention them, it has to be them. They'd be the only fools enough to go there."

"Only fools if it doesn't pay, and this time, it just might."

Virgil chuckled. "You've said that before, Pete."

"Best start getting ready, Virgil. By the time we reach them, they'll require supplies as well as have gold to take out. They and any others who make it in," Samstrung said. He turned to Erik. "That's another thing. I'm about to put my pack train in there, and if it's a bust, I lose everything. Now, who's going to pay for that?"

Virgil laughed. "I haven't seen you go bust yet, Pete. You have a knack for getting to places at the right time. This one might be tougher'n hell getting there, though."

Samstrung eyed Virgil. "You'll figure a way. You always do."

"Main trouble I can think of is Craig Weston. If he's heard about it, you can wager he's thinking the same thing," Virgil said. "Knowing him, he'll wait until we get to Salmon City and then follow us while we cut trail. Then he'll try to outflank us or set up a store with lower prices."

"Which is why he's a henpecking snake," Samstrung said. "Unwritten law says the one who cuts the trail sets up shop. After that, it's the next man's turn."

"There's that much difference?" Erik asked.

Both Samstrung and Virgil eyed Erik.

"About half our profit," Samstrung said. "Beating competition to a new strike is the only way I've stayed in business. I can't afford Weston making a run around us at night and beating us."

"We might get lucky and get out of Salmon City without him seeing us," Virgil said.

"Doubtful. We'll just have to keep him behind us." Samstrung set his jaw.

"Can you avoid Salmon City?" Erik asked.

"Chet has stock there," Samstrung said. "And no, there's no other trail to get into Leesburg, which is where you have to be to head down Panther Creek."

"Maybe there *is* another trail, Pete," Virgil said. "Get your map." He began clearing a table. "You probably don't need what's in Salmon for a first trip. You have plenty of freight here in Bannack. What about taking it up the east side and over the Big Hole? I wager it's about the same distance and probably just as fast."

Erik peered between the two men as they examined the map. Gold camps were indicated in numerous spots. He noted where Bannack City, Lemhi Pass, and Salmon City were. Samstrung had the days to each place recorded, as well as approximate miles. It made sense. A mule train might make five miles a day in extreme country or thirty miles on a good road in open country.

Virgil ran his finger across the map. "Here's the mouth of Moose Creek, and here's Panther Creek. The only sizable drainage between them is this one—with no name on it. Likely the strike's up it."

"Or the strike could be up a tributary of Panther Creek." Samstrung harrumphed.

"Nope," Virgil said, setting his jaw. "Johnny and Lars would be up this gulch." He made a mark and wrote "Dutchmen's Strike." Then he ran his fingers back up Panther Creek, up Napias Creek, and over to Salmon City. "Five days if everything goes well and the mules don't get tangled up somewhere in some bottom."

Virgil next traced up from Bannack City to the area marked "Big Hole," across the divide, back down to the Salmon, and then up the main Salmon to the unnamed gulch. "See what I'm thinking, Pete?" he exclaimed. "Probably shorter by ten miles, and we aren't going through Salmon City. Weston won't even know we've left until we get there."

"If you can get up the Salmon canyon there." Samstrung pointed downstream of Moose Creek. He turned to Erik. "You know any of that country?"

Erik nodded. "There are trails, but it's rugged. I've made it with my packhorse but not with twenty mules."

Samstrung nodded at Virgil. "You and I both know the country down Panther Creek. It's rougher than a snake's belly. Let Weston go that route. Even if his spies tip him off, you'll beat him by going over Big Hole." He began rolling up the map.

"How soon?"

"Two days. Take everything you can." Samstrung chuckled. "Finally. I'll get that henpecker."

Erik wondered if they had been too quick in guessing the camp's location. Why would it be up that drainage and not somewhere else? This was huge country. He could also now see why some of the folks spoke guardedly about Pete Samstrung and Chet Harpster.

CHAPTER 21

Two days later, they headed out. They had twenty-four mules in the string, plus Leaf. Virgil had been instructed to work with the Janssen brothers to set up a store if possible, at least until the merchandise was sold. If it looked to be a good strike, they would turn around and bring in more supplies from Harpster's stock in Salmon City.

They traveled rapidly out of Bannack toward the north. The country was open and dry, with windswept short-grass parks surrounded by low-rising hills. Bluffs toward the east had been cut into mud cliffs capped with rusty red rimrock. Stunted juniper spotted the uppermost reaches of the hills. Pronghorn scattered as the pack train passed through their country.

It was not until they crossed a low divide to the west and began dropping into the Big Hole River drainage that the land began to green up. A myriad of streams, thickly carpeted with grass and willows, drained eastward. Small ponds and marshy meadows filled the broadening valley.

They cut to the east to find dry ground. Erik ranged well away from the pack train. Occasionally, he returned to view its progress. Near midday, he spotted a scattering of black-brown shapes near the eastern horizon. It took him a moment to realize they were bison, the first he had ever seen. He watched the slowly moving shapes. Three smaller shapes broke away and rushed about. *Calves.* The bison were moving across a low rise and dropping from his sight toward the northeast.

"Well, Hatchet," he mused, "where there are buffalo, there are Indians." This was Big Hole country, prime hunting grounds for several tribes at any given time: Flathead, Blackfeet, Sioux, Crow, or Shoshone.

He drifted in the direction of the bison and searched for tracks of any hunting parties. Shortly, he found some—Blackfeet. The small trailers on their moccasins that swept the soil identified them.

On the eastern rise, Erik found he had closed on the bison. Their shaggy dark shapes were more distinct. He could make out the horns and the glints from their small eyes. They seemed unaware of his presence. He found more Blackfeet sign. They were possibly scouts for a hunting party. They could also have been the rear guard for the main village, which he knew could easily be days to the northeast.

The Blackfeet would welcome a fight to prove their mettle and personal honor, but they would not likely make a move against the pack train if it was on alert or if they were outnumbered. Like other Indians, they avoided situations in which they lacked a clear upper hand or were uncertain of the outcome. The pack train was likely safe from a couple of scouts, but that didn't answer concerns about himself. Well, if it should happen, he wouldn't let it be easy, Erik told himself.

Erik pulled back from the rise and picketed Hatchet. He crept back and watched. He wasn't familiar with the specific country, but the nature of the country was clear. The rise of the timber, the jagged openings, and the mix of aspens indicated the finger ridge to the north was rocky. Toward the southwest, the aspens of similar height among naked and scattered snags marked where a fire had moved through a few years past.

He surveyed the country behind him toward the pack train. Its different appearance reminded him of a time when he was a boy. Whistling Elk intentionally had lost him and Badger. "You see," he had cautioned, "it is good to keep your eyes on where you go but also from where you come. See how different the way appears."

Erik recalled how foolish he had felt. He and Badger had found their way back but not easily.

"It is much like life," Whistling Elk had said. "See the man you wish to become, but do not become blind to the lessons of the boy."

Erik circled farther to the east in search of additional sign before he began drifting back toward the pack train. The sun settled to the western peaks. He reached some open hills adjacent to the trail. Virgil was not in sight. Erik angled downward toward the trail, intending to meet up for the evening. Unexpectedly, he found more moccasin tracks. These were fresher and were not from a couple of

Blackfeet scouts. Several Blackfeet had gathered there and likely had watched the trail.

Erik quickly scanned the country. It was open, bordered on the west by the Big Hole River and on the east by steep bluffs that had been cut into deep coulees. The trail disappeared where it dropped into each ravine and then climbed back out. He knew a pack train could easily become boxed in. Mules would try to turn down the coulee rather than climb the opposite side.

Erik pushed up the eastern hillside, climbing rapidly, cutting a long traverse across it, which brought him uphill to where he could cross from above and peer down into the eroded ravines. The sun had set, but there was still an hour or more of light. Virgil might have already stopped.

The tracks bothered Erik. These weren't scouts. Possibly the Blackfeet were pursuing an enemy. Erik thought of Strong Wolf, but he could only hope the man had taken his lodges toward Virginia City and had not come this direction to hunt. Strong Wolf and a few warriors stood no chance against Blackfeet warriors who might be bent on revenge. He had not seen any travois drag marks, but that mattered little. This was immense country.

Erik crossed into the next ravine and angled down into the gathering dusk until he could see that the ravine was empty. A finger ridge projected downward in front of him. An unease overcame him. He caught woodsmoke and bits of muted chanting. Hatchet's ears swiveled. An unsettled whisper raced across Erik's neck. He dismounted and crept to the ridgeline. Two hundred yards below, six Blackfeet shuffled about a fire. Horses flicked their tails under some nearby aspens. The men's voices became more intense and agitated. The Blackfeet warriors were working on each other to heat their blood. This was a raiding party.

Erik retreated and headed back toward Virgil, again watching Hatchet's ears for any sign that he was near other ponies, listening, and straining to see into the gathering darkness.

An hour back, Erik found Virgil and Lem camped along the river, enjoying a cup of coffee. The mules were scattered along the river.

"Thought you lost your hair," Virgil said with a slight grin when Erik rode into the camp.

"Not that far off," Erik said as he dismounted. "I followed some Blackfeet sign and found a war party of at least six. If you add two scouts, there are likely eight and not far ahead."

Virgil's eyes flashed as he handed Erik a cup of coffee.

"They had a good number of horses," Erik added. "I didn't come across any shod hoofprints that indicate any were stolen, so I'm figuring they brought extra mounts."

"Should we douse the fire?" Lem asked.

"If a scout sees the fire go out, they'll get suspicious," Erik said. "It's a good chance they watched me return and are watching us as I'm speaking."

Lem glanced nervously past Erik and stepped back from the fire.

"You think it's a raiding party and not a hunting party?" Virgil asked.

"With that number of ponies, it's likely a raiding party to cross the divide," Erik said.

"They likely won't bother us then," Lem said.

"When Indians are on a raid, they won't overlook an opportunity," Erik countered. "They'll try to separate us from our horses—either come in at night or unseat one of us on the trail and add our horses to their herd. Any mules they run off with packs will be welcome plunder."

"I guessed you'd say that," Virgil said. He spat toward the fire. "Dad blame it, I'm not in the mind to post guards all night, and I sure don't cotton to riding past them tomorrow, tempting them with the goods we're carryin'. There's been plenty of trains hit just so some Indians could ride off with a couple of packs."

Erik nodded toward the mountains to the west, where the light had nearly faded. "We might be wise to attempt a nearer crossing. Don't go over Big Hole."

Virgil shook his head. "There's no route I know of, and that doesn't answer tomorrow." He spat again.

"I've cut through these mountains before," Erik said. "I can get us through short of the Big Hole. As far as tomorrow goes, I suggest we go tonight."

"You're crazy," Lem said. "We'd for sure lose mules. Maybe all of 'em."

"We'll have a waxing moon," Erik said.

"Even with a moon, there's plenty a trouble we can't see," Lem argued. "Mules don't like things they can't see."

Virgil tightened his mouth. "You're right, Lem, but Erik has something. If there's a party of Blackfeet working themselves into a frenzy, it doesn't matter the reason; they'll be delighted to take us on."

"I say let 'em. I ain't afeerd of no Injuns. Just go past 'em tomorrow." Lem raised his rifle as if to make the point.

"It has nothing to do with being afraid," Virgil muttered. "If they have six rifles to our three, even if none of us gets winged, I'd likely lose a mule or two as well as what we're packing. I can't afford that." He threw the remainder of his coffee into the grass. "We're going. Once the moon starts to break the horizon, we'll muffle Betsy's bell and head out. Besides, it'll get us to the Dutchmen even quicker."

Lem muttered something, but it was settled. They let the fire die, and Erik withdrew into the brush to watch and listen.

The glow on the eastern horizon brightened into a sliver of bright light. It was time. Erik made his way back down the bluff and intercepted Virgil.

"Well?" Virgil cocked an eye.

"No scouts out there watching us that I could tell," Erik said.

"Thanks," Virgil murmured. He roused Lem.

Within the hour, they had repacked the mules. They walked each animal a short distance and checked packs for noise and then recinched the ropes and straps as needed. Lem wrapped Betsy's bell.

Virgil and Lem chambered a round in their rifles, intending to cradle them at the ready while they rode. Erik left his rifle in its boot to remain unencumbered. He glanced toward the bluffs that hid the Blackfeet position seen now outlined only by thick stars.

Lem eyed him. "What makes you so cocky?" he hissed.

Erik didn't answer. He knew it might not be wise to let Lem know he had been raised by the Sheepeaters, considering Lem intended to kill Indians.

"We're ready," Virgil said.

"Then I'll see you about five miles down the trail," Erik replied. He swung up onto Hatchet, coaxed him off the trail, and headed back toward the Blackfeet camp.

After a short climb, Erik stopped. He could hear the pack train below him. He counted on the Blackfeet being out of earshot, but if they did hear them, he figured they would not attack at night but shadow them until terrain and opportunity were on their side.

Erik moved quickly but frequently paused to scan the country. He studied the shadows cast by the moonlight. Details were lost, but movement in the moonlight would not be. He drew near where the Blackfeet were. He was not concerned. They would have no guards.

Hatchet's ears pricked forward. Erik swept his eyes and caught something flutter. He swept his eyes back and caught another flicker. *Their ponies.* None of the animals whickered. Like Hatchet, they were trained not to.

"We don't want this way, Hatchet," Erik whispered.

He caught movement farther down the hill. A man had risen. Erik froze as the man stepped into the moonlight to relieve himself. He made out three other forms. He knew they would have liked nothing better than to take his blond hair as a trophy and leave his mutilated body behind.

Erik steadied himself. He could take one or two but not six or eight. A sliver of sweat rolled down his neck.

Gently, he turned Hatchet and moved farther uphill before cutting a long track north around the camp. At two miles, he stopped above the trail and waited for the pack train. A half hour passed before he caught movement. Ghost mules and a rider came into view.

Erik dropped down onto the trail.

Lem jumped. "What the hell?" he hissed.

"You passed the Blackfeet a mile back," Erik said.

Lem glared but then shot a nervous look over his shoulder.

Virgil came up, holding his rifle half raised. "Don't you know it's not healthy to materialize like that?" He spat.

"I skirted their camp. No sign they heard me, so I doubt they will be following."

"Good. Let's keep moving a few miles and then cut for the divide if you think we can cross the valley," Virgil said.

"I say we cut across here," Lem said. "Lose those red devils now."

"I think not," Virgil said. He peered west. "Here's marsh and a bunch of unorganized creeks that haven't decided which way to go yet. We're going on a bit."

Lem muttered something. Erik made his way off the trail and headed back up into the bluffs. Moonlight sparkled off dozens of specks of water toward the west. Several small silver threads winked where water flowed. Virgil was correct. They had to reach a place where the river had come together enough to give stable ground.

Erik judged the time by the climbing moon and receding shadows. The pass appeared ghostly white above black timber across the open meadows toward the west. Erik returned to the trail and caught up to Virgil.

"That's our pass." Erik pointed toward the moonlit gap.

Virgil nodded. "I figured so. See if you can find us a crossing."

Erik led down toward the river and soon intersected it. Virgil brought the pack train behind him. Willows choked the riverbank. Erik turned upstream and rode the bank until he could discern light filtering from a shallow bottom. "Come on, Hatchet. We've done worse."

He rode the horse a few yards out and waited for the mules. Virgil led, and for once, Betsy didn't hesitate but splashed into the river. Maybe she was ready to get finished for the night. The other mules obediently followed, until the rear few mules entered the water.

A mule slipped while coming up the bank and kicked another, which began braying and bucking. It dragged at the others.

"Son-of-a-bitch flea-bit coyote bait," Virgil snapped, heading for the clambering mules. "Grab that critter."

Lem jerked up in his saddle, apparently having been nearly asleep.

Another mule went down into the water. It rolled and stood up, shaking. A pack came loose.

Erik headed for the pack, which was now sweeping into a river bend and willow thicket. He jumped from Hatchet and snagged it. Its weight nearly dragged him into the river.

Cursing erupted a short distance upstream and filled the night.

Erik put the pack in front of himself and headed back to the ruckus.

By the time he reached the mules, they were strung out, some with splayed legs and shaking. Virgil was examining one's hoof the best he could in the moonlight. It was the one who had rolled and lost a pack.

"Told you we'd lose 'em," Lem said. He was busy refixing a pack.

Virgil shot Lem a look. "I sure as hell noticed how quick you were to grab her."

Erik pulled the pack off and dropped the soggy mass onto the ground.

"Hope it wasn't flour or somethin' like that," Virgil muttered.

They spent another thirty minutes sorting out the animals, refixing the breakaway knots in their leads, and tightening packs before heading out again.

"It could have been worse," Virgil said.

Erik rode straight for the rising mountains until he intersected another stream. He located a faint trail that traced its banks. Hoofprints told him what he needed to know. His stomach tightened. It was possible the Blackfeet intended to take this route.

He continued upward, tracing the trail through the narrowing valley, until he figured he had better not further press his luck.

Virgil and Lem brought up the mules, and Erik helped unpack them. By the time they had laid out their bedrolls, the night had nearly passed. Erik took his blanket and found a location a short distance away. He picketed Hatchet nearby. The horse would tell him of any danger.

CHAPTER 22

After hardly catching two hours of sleep and after the sky had grown light, Erik scouted out the trail toward the summit. A strong trail led up a broad valley and skirted a couple of small, timber-fringed lakes. Above the lakes, it cut through some high open meadows, where it then angled south through heavy timber and climbed steeply toward the pass. Erik returned to find Virgil on the trail behind him, making good time.

Erik turned to lead the way again and traversed upward in the steepening terrain until he abruptly pushed through stunted timber and emerged onto wind-scoured tundra. Snowbanks remained in long strips and were gathered in the draws.

Erik eyed the summit. Although he had encountered pony tracks, that did not mean a mule train could get across. He angled for what seemed to be the most open country.

Wind buffeted him, swaying the limber pines and alpine firs. Most of the stunted trees had been scarred by either lightning or avalanches. This was fur country and possibly better than where he had wintered last season. Numerous thickly forested draws branched downward on either side of the divide.

He watched Virgil, far below, steadily winding his way upward with the mules moving briskly as black dots, traversing up and out of the drainage.

Erik crossed to the opposite side to check the downside route. Directly below him, a cirque opened into a wide amphitheater toward the north. A small turquoise lake with snowbanks surrounding much of it shimmered below the bordering cliffs.

"Not going that way, Hatchet." Erik turned south and followed the ridge a short distance.

Although not visible, the Salmon River lay far below, a good half a day distant yet. Erik angled down into the timber and found another substantial game trail with a few pony tracks. Satisfied this was the best trail down, he returned to intercept the mules and waited until they began topping the ridge. He waved at Virgil and then dropped back into the timber, where he followed the trail down into a U-shaped valley.

Abruptly, he reached a massive blowdown. Twisted spruce and fir lay like jackstraws across the head of the descending valley. He skirted the area by climbing back up. The mule train might not be able to follow, he realized. Beyond the blowdown, the valley broadened slightly and opened up again. If they could get this far, they would have a clear trail to the river. If not, he would need to find another route.

Erik returned to intercept Virgil and explained what lay ahead.

Virgil laughed. "You don't know mules," he said. "If you got past the blowdown, these critters can get past it. Lead the way, Erik."

Erik retraced his route up the steep valley wall. Deftly, the mules followed closely on his heels, plodding doggedly along. They descended back into the small valley beyond the blowdown and intersected a distinct trail that pitched steeply down through the timber. Had Erik ever doubted the mules' ability, his doubt had now been assuaged.

"Those critters were made for this country," Erik mused.

By late day, they reached the Salmon River.

Virgil shook his head. "I'll be dad blamed, Erik. Except for that blowdown back up there, you just might have got us a new route." He stood in his stirrups and gazed around. "You couldn't have come down at a better place either. This is about the last ford before the Salmon goes berserk with whitewater."

Virgil stepped his horse out into the river. The mules followed, splashing in to over their knees.

Here the Salmon River braided between several channels. Like a natural dam, the silt and gravel from the upper Salmon had filled the valley and created shallows before the river abruptly swung west to where it cut deeply through the mountains.

Late the following day, Erik led the pack train into Dutchmen's Flat amid cheering from Johnny and Lars Janssen and Levi Van Dijk.

"Ja, I was telling my brother, Johnny, that you'd be here, by gar. We were betting, we were." Lars slapped Virgil on the back. "Ja, if anyone could find us in this hole, you'd be the one."

Erik watched, somewhat bemused, as it appeared old friends had reunited. Even if they had not made it in first, Erik doubted they would have lost the Janssens' business.

White canvas tents were spread everywhere up the narrow gulch. Picks were singing against rocks. Trees were being felled and ripped into lumber for sluice boxes.

The Janssens quickly unfolded and erected a large tent that Virgil had packed in. They moved in some stumps for shelving and counters and started hauling in the freight amid a gaggle of miners already gathering.

From the dozen or so miners dishing out their gold dust, it appeared to Erik that perhaps the Janssens had found a better way to mine gold than by digging in the ravine. By evening, the crude shelves were nearly bare, especially of food stocks. The Janssens and Levi scribbled out a second order.

Virgil weighed out the gold dust and bundled it in leather bags. Erik had never seen so much gold—pounds of it.

Erik spent another near-sleepless night doing sentry duty in the timber near the Janssens' cabin, where Virgil and the Dutchmen slept, and kept watch in the event any hapless miners or camp followers decided they were hungry enough to try for the gold.

The following morning, they were packing to leave, when a shout went up. Miners came running. A second pack train came into view, winding its way up the narrow ravine.

"You need to see this," Virgil said, grinning. He approached the man leading the string and waved. "How you doing, Weston? Seems like Johnny and Lars have themselves a healthy little strike."

A somewhat stocky middle-aged man in a dusty dark coat swung off his horse. Two men brought the mule train into camp. Craig Weston's eyes snapped, and his jaw tightened. He eyed Erik as if he recognized him or at least had heard about him.

"How the hell, Virgil? You were just in Leesburg," Weston said. "You sure didn't come through Salmon City."

Virgil allowed a slight smile. "Nope. I came straight from Bannack, north over the divide." He turned and spat into the dirt. "Got me a half-Injun Swede that can make a trail outta thin air."

Weston gave Erik a harder look and then shook his head. "You cussed son of a bitch," he said. He tried to laugh, but Erik sensed the man's displeasure.

CHAPTER 23

The race to Dutchmen's Flat might have taken the wind out of Weston's sails. After taking in another load from their stocks in Salmon City and not encountering Weston, Chet Harpster confirmed their thoughts. Weston had pulled up stakes and relocated to where he could support the new strike at Oro Grande, on Loon Creek.

After he had heard about the strike, Erik had become more certain Loon Creek was the stream draining the country where he had met the Sheepeaters. The Sheepeaters called it Bird Calls Creek, possibly because of the loons.

A bit of regret washed over Erik. He wondered if the miners had encountered any of the Sheepeaters. Likely the Sheepeaters had made themselves scarce and retreated farther into the mountains and canyons to avoid the white miners.

The summer heat gave way to the first cold snap of September. Erik found himself reflecting on Tendoy's people. Certainly, by now, they would have new bison hides and quantities of dried meat. Cusowat would have caught and smoked what salmon had escaped McGarvey's weirs. The Lemhi would soon prepare for their winter camp.

Erik met with Pete Samstrung. "The seasons are turning," Erik said.

"Yes, I reckon snow is peeking over our shoulders," Samstrung agreed. "News of you must have spread, since we had no additional trouble after Killion's Diggins, and Weston is out of the country. You can sure carry on as a packer, despite you cost me a half eagle."

Erik cocked his head.

"I bet Virgil those mules would have you cursing to high heaven by summer's end. I have to admit you're the first man I ever met who could handle a mule team using a civil tongue."

Erik smiled. "Then I'm blessed that Virgil couldn't hear my thoughts."

Samstrung chuckled. "You'd be welcome to stay on while we resupply camps for winter, Erik. Lem can find another job."

Erik had hardly tolerated Lem, but he did not wish to take the man's job. "Thank you, Mr. Samstrung. It's been a pleasure packing for you, but I intend to do some trapping, and it's time I checked out some of the high country. We'll see about next season if that suits you."

Samstrung shook his head. "I can't figure you, Erik. You're damn good at this. Maybe you did get bit by too much Indian when you were a lad." He pushed at his glasses. "Keep in mind that the winters have a way of cultivating more desperadoes. I reckon I'll have a job for you next spring if you still hanker for one." He shook Erik's hand.

Erik also said goodbye to Virgil. Toward the end, Erik had become more of a hand with the pack train than an outrider. Virgil had respected his help, and Erik respected Virgil. Nothing stopped the man, and they'd had their bellies full a few times, especially when fording rivers and threading the string through timber to some of the more remote camps. Virgil rarely asked for a hand at doing something and never asked his men to do something he wasn't willing to do himself. Erik recognized that, and even when his job was outrider, Erik simply took a hand at whatever Virgil was engaged in doing. Rarely had they talked about it, but Erik knew the man's sentiments when he insisted that Samstrung give him the Spencer without taking it out of his pay.

Erik rode out of Bannack, not heading south toward Bannock Pass and Cusowat but heading north. A week later, he found what he sought: another high basin rich with fur sign and close to the pass he had blazed earlier in the summer. Not far below the basin, he discovered a small elk herd near some hot springs. The springs trickled from a hillside before gathering and dumping into a rapidly flowing stream. The land reminded him of the area he had trapped when near the Swedes' high valley. The warm water had helped him get his ponies through the winter. He guessed the elk would remain nearby as well and only drop lower in elevation if the snow drifted too deep.

At length, he selected a site for a cabin at the edge of the timber where the creek cut through a meadow. Above the site, similar to last season's camp, the stream drained a half dozen thickly forested basins, each prime fur country.

Over the next several days, Erik constructed a rude cabin—not a brush tepee like the one he had built last year. He wanted a sturdy roof that was high enough for him to stand up and would hold up through the winter with five feet of snow on it.

Days later, he relocated the small elk herd and killed two cows. He skinned them, fleshed their hides, and then smoked and cured the meat. He began preparing the hides for a future use.

He cached some of his supplies, crossed the divide into Idaho Territory, and descended to the Salmon River. A few days later, he skirted Salmon City and continued south up the Lemhi River toward the Sacred River band.

WOLVERINE

CHAPTER 24

Erik found the Sacred River band near last season's winter camp but on the opposite side of the river. He had prepared himself for seeing a hundred lodges and several hundred ponies. He expected to finally meet Chief Tendoy and all the Lemhi people. However, a disheartening sight again met him. *How could it be?* No more than a dozen lodges and a dozen ponies came into view. However, the sight meant that Strong Wolf and the others who had gone hunting over the summer had returned, including Bright Shell. He caught his breath. Although she was certainly another man's wife, he could not bury his desire to see her.

Cusowat received Erik with gladness and immediately sent out a young boy to announce a meal. Erik learned that Chief Tendoy was still attempting to get the promised gifts and assurance that the land now belonged to the Lemhi people. Although the area was now treated by Salmon City residents as the Indian camp, the treaty had not been ratified to officially make it a reservation.

Tendoy and the others had camped somewhere outside Virginia City but had not received permission to hunt on what were now considered Crow lands. Tendoy's people had resorted to begging and hunting prairie dogs, and Tendoy remained near Virginia City and Governor Smith, hoping for a reprieve. Strong Wolf had returned with some meager meat and hides and rejoined Cusowat. In some respects, Cusowat and his remnant Sacred River band fared better than Tendoy. Even though almost no salmon had escaped McGarvey's weirs, some game remained in Lemhi Valley despite the increasing wagon traffic coming north from Corinne.

Cusowat expressed hope that Erik had come to be with them. He was anxious to trade, but the man could not offer much, nor could the others.

While talking with Cusowat, Erik caught sight of Black Feather and her children but not Jumping Deer or Bright Shell. He immediately became concerned. Where was Jumping Deer? Was it possible Bright Shell had not married?

"We should hunt," Erik said. "Before you asked that I hunt. I had only my bow. I now have this." He produced his Spencer rifle.

Cusowat grinned and caressed the rifle. "Yes, you should stay with Sacred River band and hunt with us."

Erik was given a lodge, and as he stowed his possessions, he was strangely pleased to again see Spotted Bird. She would know Bright Shell's whereabouts, but to ask was not proper.

That evening, Cusowat gathered the people. Erik was relieved to now see Jumping Deer. She had joined Black Feather to prepare the meal. He still did not see Bright Shell. He tried to seek her out but did not wish to be noticed. She often cared for Jumping Deer's young son, but the boy was near his mother, helping. He noticed another thing: Jumping Deer appeared pregnant. Was it possible Cusowat had not taken a third wife because his second wife was pregnant? He returned his attention to Cusowat and the others. The men prepared to dance.

Then Erik caught sight of Strong Wolf and his wife. *Yes!* There was Bright Shell. He thrilled at her sight. She was even more beautiful than he remembered. She still wore vermillion that highlighted her cheeks and lined her hair. Erik's heart raced. Did he dare?

This time, Erik did not avert his eyes from Bright Shell. She had grown in her beauty. He allowed her to briefly catch his eyes and his smile. He also allowed his eyes to be caught by Cusowat as well as by Strong Wolf, Bright Shell's father. Erik knew the two men would recognize his wishes.

Runs Fast noticed as well and spat. He curled his lips.

At dawn, the men left the camp to hunt mule deer. Whenever the Lemhi failed to get bison meat, they fell back on deer and elk, especially during a difficult winter. Erik reasoned this would be another difficult winter.

Erik chose to follow Strong Wolf as he turned up a narrow cut that emptied into the valley. Cusowat's band possessed three or four firearms at best, and Erik had noticed that Strong Wolf carried only a bow. Both men scanned the stunted aspen groves, which were now stripped of their autumn leaves. Shortly, they spotted a small herd of mule deer grazing above them.

Erik motioned to Strong Wolf and slipped off Hatchet. He pulled his rifle and displayed it for Strong Wolf to see. The man grinned and ran his hands over the weapon. He nodded.

The small herd browsed slowly as it moved across the brush-covered slope and through a grove of naked aspens.

"I will take the lead doe," Erik said. He cocked the Spencer, aligned his sights behind the doe's shoulder, and squeezed the trigger. The explosion ripped the autumn day, and the doe crumpled and lay still.

The other mule deer jumped but did not run. They stared in Erik's direction, swiveling their mule-like ears toward the sound, trying to fathom what they had heard. One at a time, they returned to browsing, seemingly ignoring their dead relative.

"There, my brother," Erik said. "This one will give us meat." He put the rifle in its boot and pulled his bow, strung it, and nocked an arrow. "Now you and I shall hunt."

Strong Wolf grunted and strung his bow as well.

The two men moved off, heading to where the mule deer continued moving slowly across the grassy slope.

Erik dropped into a slight depression and, crouching, moved to where he would be in bow range of one of the animals. Strong Wolf moved in the opposite direction. As Erik had done numerous times, he moved upward, keeping out of sight and keeping downwind. He had guessed correctly. When he emerged from the slight hollow, two mule deer were within a few yards. He sighted on the lead animal, which was oblivious to his presence, and drew back an arrow. He anchored it at his cheek, took a slow breath, and held it. Then, breathing out slowly, he released the arrow and watched its flight as it struck home.

Erik pulled another arrow. The animal bounded, turned downhill, and stopped. Erik's arrow had been true. The doe dropped to its knees. Erik let the arrow do its damage as the doe rolled onto its side with blood draining from its mouth as it died.

Erik said a prayer of thanks as he slit the animal's throat and began gutting the deer. He hoped Strong Wolf had had a similar fortune.

Erik had two animals down. He moved back to where the first doe lay dead and prepared to dress the animal. Well above him and to his left, Erik spotted Strong Wolf. The man was bent over a buck.

Within another hour, they had the animals dressed and slung over their ponies, and they headed back to the village.

There was a genuine celebration as the other hunters brought in several more mule deer. The women butchered the animals and began roasting slices of venison near Cusowat's lodge. The chief had called an honoring for Erik, but there were other intentions as well.

Erik gifted his two mule deer skins to Cusowat's wives. According to custom, the hunter's wife was entitled to the hide. The meat was also customarily first given to the hunter's family before being freely shared. Because Erik had no family, he announced his meat would be for all the Sacred River band.

Erik then brought forth one of the two elk skins from the elk he had killed near his new cabin. He gifted it to Cusowat. While doing so, he nodded to Bright Shell so that Cusowat understood. The man jutted his chin toward Erik; he had released his interest in Bright Shell. Erik had guessed Cusowat would agree in part because it would create a stronger tie between Erik and his people.

The following morning, Erik approached Strong Wolf. His wife, Dancing Swallow, and Bright Shell brought them a meal, after which they departed the tepee. Strong Wolf offered Erik a pipe. They smoked it and emptied the bowl between themselves.

"I wish to give this elk skin to Dancing Swallow," Erik said. "She should have a warm robe for the winter." Of course, Strong Wolf was a good provider. The robe was a gift.

Strong Wolf examined it. He knew Erik had done the work. "Yes, Dancing Swallow may use this to make a robe."

With his heart hammering in his throat, Erik said, "I would have Bright Shell."

Strong Wolf nodded. "It is as the others say. Cusowat releases her. Yet I am saddened that Bright Shell will not be with her sister as wife to Cusowat." He smoothed the elk hide. "If Two Elks Fighting takes Bright Shell, how can my heart be eased?"

"I will care for your daughter. Strong Wolf will be like a father to Two Elks Fighting."

"If I say it is good that you have my daughter, my heart says you will go away with her. Will you not live with Sacred River band?"

Erik's chest tightened. He could not stay and for reasons he could not make Strong Wolf or the others understand. One of those reasons remained Runs Fast and the men who sided with him. Other reasons only he understood.

"The people will be in my heart. It is as Tissidimit says. I will be like the seasons. Sometimes I will be with you. Sometimes I will not. In the seasons that I am here, I will come and trade and bring Bright Shell to see her family. And when she has children, they will come to see their family. I will stay near."

Strong Wolf straightened himself and peered intently at Erik. "I understand the white man ways are strange. Tissidimit tells of the white men who married our women. They promised to stay near as well. They did not. They went away."

Erik could not argue. Most white men who married Indian women chose to take their wives with them. They lived solitary lives, as he planned to live. They brought their wives to their villages only when trading.

"I am also of the people," Erik said. "I received my man's name while I was with the Tukudeka. I share much with the people. Though I will not lodge with the Sacred River band, you shall see me often." He pulled the Spencer from its sheath. "I give Strong Wolf my rifle so that he knows I will not forget the Sacred River band and so that he sees it is my promise that he will see his son and daughter and his grandchildren."

Strong Wolf took the rifle. "It is as you tell us, Two Elks Fighting. Tissidimit says you are like the seasons. You will come like the seasons. For me, that is good. You shall have Bright Shell if she wishes to have you."

A numbness crawled over Erik's skin. He wanted to shout joyously, but this was unusual. How could Bright Shell know if she wished to have him? They had hardly glanced at each other, and he had infrequently heard her voice. Of course, she had seen him and knew of him but not anything more. How could she know?

CHAPTER 25

Erik returned to his lodge in troubled thought. He hardly acknowledged Spotted Bird's presence or the meal she had prepared for him. She sat to the side, watching.

He had gifted his rifle. Two mule deer and two elk hides meant nothing, but his rifle? He fingered his bow as if to reassure himself that he still possessed it. What right did he have to presume he, a white man, would be able to take a Shoshone woman as his wife?

Only after Erik had removed his buckskins and pulled his robes about himself did he notice that Spotted Bird had been watching. Erik smiled and caught her eyes. He should not have. His smile was because of Bright Shell, not because of Spotted Bird.

Spotted Bird did not know this. She rose, bringing her robes with her, and settled beside Erik. She offered herself, and Erik's heart began pounding. He allowed the thought. Both would give to the other. Would it be wrong? But was it because of the thoughts he had for Bright Shell?

He was moved and pushed his fingers through Spotted Bird's hair, which had fallen before her eyes and kindly face. "You are a good woman," Erik whispered. Her robes fell, and he saw her nakedness. He pulled away his eyes and tried to focus his thoughts. "No, my woman, I will not have you." Gently, he took Spotted Bird's hand and pushed away.

A cry escaped Spotted Bird's lips as she again gathered her robes and returned to her place away from Erik.

"You bring me desire, Spotted Bird. You will bring another man desire. You will not be an old grandmother who others keep in their lodges to tend the fire. There is one among the Sacred River band who will have you."

Spotted Bird sat with the robes around her, shaking. "But why does Two Elks Fighting not want me if he says these things?"

"I have spoken for another woman," Erik said.

Spotted Bird's eyes widened and then settled. She understood.

"I know of another who would make his wishes known," Erik said. In truth, the man Erik considered had said nothing as far as he knew.

Spotted Bird raised her eyes. They sparkled. "I wish to know his name."

"You know that is not possible, because only he must make his wishes known."

"Yes, I know this, Two Elks Fighting." Spotted Bird lay down with her eyes still fixed on Erik, but her face held joy.

Erik stretched out in his robes, wishing for what he could not have with Spotted Bird but imagining Bright Shell instead.

But had he made himself a fool? He had made his intentions known, but Strong Wolf had not given an answer—he'd said only that if Bright Shell wished it, she could be his. How could that be if they could never meet? He turned in his robes and spent the night in miserable doubt.

Early morning light and the smell of a cooking fire and fragrant meat penetrated Erik's lodge. Spotted Bird was gone from her robes. Erik was not surprised and was a bit relieved. He had turned her away, and it was not unusual for her to have simply left during the night.

The man Erik had considered for Spotted Bird was Deer Horn. He had remained with Cusowat and cared for those who stayed behind when Strong Wolf and the others left to hunt. He was not much younger than Spotted Bird, and as Erik understood, he had little standing because he was a bit odd and not an able hunter. He had not married because of it. A true man did not take a wife until he had proven himself in battle or as a hunter, and if a man took a wife and failed to provide for her and his family, he was rebuked.

Erik grew angry with himself. *And now what am I doing— playing matchmaker?*

His heart froze when the lodge flap opened, and Bright Shell came inside, carrying a bowl of soup. She wore a white elk-skin dress adorned with elk teeth. He sat up, collecting his sleeping robe about his waist. Without lifting her eyes to his, Bright Shell set the bowl in front of him. Erik saw that she trembled. His blood began pounding. *Could it be possible?*

"Do you bring me this meal as a sister or as a woman who wishes to be my wife? If it is as my wife, I should like to see her."

Bright Shell raised her eyes. Erik fought the rush of feelings that flooded him, and somehow, he held his emotions. He sampled the soup and meat, and as he ate, he tried to keep his heart from racing, certain that Bright Shell could hear it.

"Bright Shell honors her father," Erik said. "She makes a fine meal that would please a husband." Hope stirred within him. "But is this her wish?"

Bright Shell's eyes did not leave Erik's but searched his face. Erik could only wonder the feelings she had for him and whether they matched his. Here she was, the woman who had captured his heart, beautiful young Bright Shell, with high, rosy cheeks highlighted with vermilion, a shapely nose, full lips, and eyes of ebony with flashes of golden light that sparkled with joy but also trepidation as they sought his own eyes.

Erik wished only for her to smile and let him see into her heart and know her true feelings. He wished for her trepidation to pass and for his own to settle. He would never have wished to harm Bright Shell. His desire for her strengthened, and he prayed she felt the same. Did she? The people had ways different from his. She would be his wife because her father said so, because the people wished it to be so, and because Erik desired it. But was that what she wished, or would she do it only because it was demanded of her?

Erik hesitated. "I will share this. My heart is strong for Bright Shell. I would be hunter and warrior for Bright Shell. I would have her accept my seed and grow my child. I know the people's ways are not the same as my ways. I ask Bright Shell if her heart is strong for Two Elks Fighting, or is she here because her father wishes it?"

Erik felt his heart go still. He could not undo what he had said. He recalled what Strong Wolf had said: Bright Shell would be his if she desired it. But a new rifle and a father's request could obscure what Bright Shell desired. She was there and, through her actions, professed her wishes, but Erik's doubts raced. He did not want to take her if she was but a gift, as Spotted Bird had been intended to be.

"I would have Two Elks Fighting as my hunter and warrior and as my husband," Bright Shell said. "I would have his child. My heart is strong for Two Elks Fighting."

Erik's blood rushed, pounding in his chest and head. He was numb with feelings. "I would have Bright Shell then." He motioned for her to come closer and sit beside him. He tugged at her dress. Knowing his desires, she pulled her dress over her head, revealing her nakedness and offering herself to him.

Erik caught himself trying to fathom the beauty before him—her bronze skin glowing softly in the pale morning light, the curves of her waist, her silky smoothness, and her rising breasts.

He wanted to touch, caress, and not show the intensity of his desire. He wanted to cherish this moment, but he could not. He opened the robes he had gathered around himself and gently pulled her down beside him and to himself. He explored her until he could no longer hold back. They lay together, and she received him. He was humbled by Bright Shell's desire for him and shuddered as the intensity of their coupling washed over him. He had never felt such completeness before, and it humbled him to realize that by coming together, they had fulfilled marriage in the ways of the people. Bright Shell was not a gift, as another had been, but was his for as long as they desired each other—for as long as either lived.

Erik marveled in the mystery. He lay with her, touching, tracing his fingers across her beauty, across her rising and falling breasts. He could not tear his eyes away. This was his wife, Bright Shell. They would start a family together; perhaps it had already begun. He shivered. He wished to come together again and linger in the bliss of their entwined bodies, but the people awaited the news.

He rose, gently pulled Bright Shell to her feet, and embraced and kissed her. Confusion came to her eyes. Erik kissed her again. "It is our custom," he said. The confusion in her eyes melted, and she smiled as they held each other tightly, and their lips met deeply a third time.

Erik gathered up Bright Shell's dress and pulled it over her, regretful that he had to cover her beauty so soon but excited by the knowledge that they would soon be together again. He pulled on his buckskins. They walked toward Cusowat's lodge to announce they had joined with one another, but of course, this was already known by the others, who now joyously gathered.

There were congratulations and small gifts. In turn, Erik gave away the remaining trade goods he had brought in guarded hope of this event. The people shared in a community meal. Much of what Erik had expressed privately to Strong Wolf and later to Bright Shell he now expressed to the people. He would go away with Bright Shell, but they would be near, and they would visit often. Cusowat reaffirmed that Erik would always have a lodge when he came to visit and that he should do so frequently. He was of the Sacred River band and always would be.

Erik located Deer Horn. The man was somewhat gangly and not as well kempt as others, but perhaps it was because he lacked the decoration that usually marked a man's important deeds. The man straightened with questioning eyes.

"You and Red Robe and Cow Belly did not leave with Strong Wolf to hunt during this past season. Instead, you remained behind and provided for Cusowat and the others who stayed here. You brought in a fine deer, yet there was no ceremony, or they would have danced an honor for you."

Deer Horn appeared perplexed. "With only a few of us, we did not find reason for a ceremony."

"The women would have wished to see one. I shall tell Cusowat to have one when you again bring meat. It is a good thing what you did."

Deer Horn seemed to stand a little taller but remained confused.

"Certainly you know who kept my lodge when I have been a guest. She fears she is an old grandmother. She is not."

Deer Horn could not hide a smile. "Spotted Bird."

"I am married now, Deer Horn, and I had asked for Bright Shell before Spotted Bird kept my lodge. She honored that, but she shares that she would have a certain hunter to share his robes."

Of course, Erik did not know if Spotted Bird had ever given a single thought to Deer Horn. It was not customary for a Shoshone woman to do so, and what Erik had just done would have never been considered.

"Unless he is not a good hunter and so does not wish to share robes with a woman," Erik added.

Deer Horn's eyes flashed but then settled. Erik knew the man would approach Spotted Bird. Erik had only to suggest it was time.

Only Runs Fast did not share in the joy and celebration. Black Buffalo and Crooked Leg stood with him but cursorily joined in with the celebration, possibly only to receive gifts. Erik recognized their expressions, but there was no wisdom in challenging them or jeopardizing his new relationship with the Sacred River band.

Late day, Erik indicated he had to go. Of course, the others understood it as a desire to be with his new wife and get to know her. It was customary. Strong Wolf wanted to send a riding horse with Bright Shell; however, Erik showed that Leaf could accommodate her and their few remaining possessions. It was right for him to do so. After all, a husband provided for his wife.

Erik led the way with Bright Shell following on Leaf, heading north toward the divide he had crossed with Samstrung's pack train and the small basin where he intended to trap and while away the winter with Bright Shell. The women trilled.

CHAPTER 26

There was little to do on a day such as this. Outside their rough cabin, snow fell steadily. Erik had his trapline to run, but there was little sense in doing so until the snow quit and had settled for a day. Bright Shell sat near the fire, pulling at some fox skins.

Erik glanced around his cabin, the structure he had built before he brought Bright Shell into his life. The cooking fire was not elaborate, not like the settlers' fireplaces, but a pit like those Bright Shell was accustomed to. He had dug a deep hole against a wall and lined it with rocks. From it, he had dug a small trench where Bright Shell could pull coals upon which to cook. He had built a crude chimney of sticks and mud to direct the smoke out. Opposite the door was their bedding, and on the other wall, he had cut a window. The window was unlike anything Bright Shell had experienced, and it had taken her a bit to get used to it. It was a simple opening with a hide covering drawn down at night. Erik desired the window for watching the dawning day or the gathering night and, this day, the falling snow.

The season of the cold moons was upon them. More than three feet of snow blanketed the basin. Erik let the skin flap fall back in front of the window. He momentarily thought about having Bright Shell join him in his robes again; however, she had reminded him she must be about doing her work.

The past weeks had been the best part of life, Erik decided. He had dug a deep pool for the springs' warm water to trickle into and fill, and they had frequently walked there to bathe. At first, Bright Shell had not been comfortable in doing so. Her people did not share a common bathing place among men and women. Erik had made it special, however, and it had become part of their lovemaking. He enjoyed caressing and washing Bright Shell, although she did not often reciprocate. Afterward, at the cabin, however, she joyously accepted him.

Of late, however, their activity had lessened, perhaps because Bright Shell had kidded Erik about always wanting to share the robes and said perhaps he was becoming lazy. It had hurt when she had implied that. It was the opposite. Erik ran his traplines tirelessly, cared for the two ponies, hunted, and brought in game.

This day, Bright Shell sat quietly, sewing a fox pelt. Occasionally, she looked in Erik's direction. Erik decided it was not a good idea for his wife to see him doing nothing and took down one of the skins he had stretched. He sat with it and began scraping carefully. Bright Shell gave him a curious look.

"I realize Shoshone women do this work." Erik spoke in English to help her learn, although she knew few words. "I helped Moccasin Woman do skins when I was with the Tukudeka. The other boys laughed at me for doing women's work."

Bright Shell did not completely understand, Erik knew, but she looked up from her sewing and smiled.

"But I had the last laugh, Bright Shell. The skins I helped Moccasin Woman with became a rabbit skin robe that she gave to me. It was finer than any of the other boys' robes. We wore them in the evenings when it was cool."

Bright Shell smiled again.

"Perhaps this is a fox robe you are making for me?" He spoke Shoshone.

She pulled her eyes away, which told Erik he had guessed correctly.

A warmth washed over Erik. He wondered again how it was possible that this woman who now shared his life had become his life and was the most intimate part of him.

His desire grew, and Erik motioned for Bright Shell to join him. She lifted her eyes and, smiling, shook her head.

Erik felt stunned. "How can this be?"

Bright Shell rose and came and sat beside him. "See for yourself," she whispered. She took his hand to her belly.

Immediately, Erik knew. He shook. He pulled Bright Shell to himself, and they kissed deeply. This custom she had accepted.

"You grow my seed, Bright Shell," he whispered. "Come the summer season, we will have a child." His being raced with joy.

"We shall take our child to the people so that they may share in our happiness."

He kissed her again and then stood and, pulling his coat about himself, stepped out into the falling snow. He wanted to dance and shout, to call out to the woods.

"Do you hear my heart singing, Sohobinehwe Tso`ape?" Erik said. "I will be a father, and Bright Shell shall be a mother." He kicked at the snow, musing to himself. He enjoyed Bright Shell's company in his robes, but now he would have to do without. He knew that among the people, they would not come together again until sometime after the child was born. "I can understand why men have two wives," he murmured. But he could not see himself with two wives. Bright Shell was all he would ever wish for and all he would ever love.

CHAPTER 27

The winter darkness gave way to lengthening sunshine. Erik had decided that after their child was born, he would take Bright Shell and the baby to visit Katrine. She and Björn would have been married for going on two seasons and might also have a child. Of course, he would first take Bright Shell and their child to visit the Sacred River band.

Presently, he had work to finish in curing his pelts. The trapping had been good. He and Bright Shell had prepared several fine fox and bobcat pelts and two lynx pelts. Those would bring good money in Bannack. The other furs—the ermine, mink, and fisher—would be desired more by the Lemhi people for baby cradles and decoration.

The snow had begun receding. In the early morning, the snow remained crusted from the nightly freeze, but by midmorning, it had softened. Erik had kept a good trail down to the meadows and the hot springs. Hatchet and Leaf remained near the open hillsides where they could browse. Today they had strayed farther down the slope, pulling at the greening grasses. It was time.

Erik prepared a travois for the furs and fitted it to Leaf. It was customary that Bright Shell would manage the travois and follow a short distance behind Erik. The practice allowed Erik to quickly meet danger with an unburdened horse if necessary.

He headed east toward the Big Hole country. The season was early, and he didn't need to be concerned with the Blackfeet or other enemies since the Indians would yet be near their winter camps. Road agents, on the other hand, were always a threat, especially after a lean winter.

Heavy runoff and overflowing streams, not people, were their greatest challenges and slowed their travel. A day out of Bannack, they picked up fresh horse tracks. Possibly they were from mining parties headed north, following the receding snow.

When they entered Bannack, Erik discerned Bright Shell's unease, but she said nothing. Erik went directly to Samstrung's mercantile, where Pete Samstrung and Virgil Williams heartily greeted him. Virgil thumped Erik. Samstrung shook hands. Both shifted their eyes to the street and Bright Shell and then back to Erik.

"Lord be!" Samstrung exclaimed. "Now I understand why you were in an all-fired rush to leave last autumn."

Virgil grinned. "I'll be dad blamed. I never could figure you when we were in the mining camps. Couldn't get you to a saloon. You didn't cotton for any—you know. Hell, you probably had your eye on her all that time, keepin' her a secret." He took in Bright Shell. "If she don't beat all. I'd a kept her a secret too."

"Near as I can translate, her name is Bright Shell," Erik replied, grinning. "I first laid eyes on her two years ago, when I first visited the Lemhi. In truth, I never presumed at that time this would be."

Samstrung shook his head. "This calls for a celebration." He eyed Erik, looked at Bright Shell, and then, adjusting his spectacles, looked back at Erik. "I don't suppose you would want to scout again? If it's possible?"

"No, sir," Erik said. "We're expecting a baby, though not until August as I can best figure it, but still—"

"In all tarnation, Erik!" Samstrung boomed. "Now, this does call for celebration. You didn't waste your time, did you, son?"

Virgil thumped him. "You had it in you after all. And here when I met you, Samstrung and I was a-wondering if you was even growed up enough to know what was what for."

Erik flushed. "Not much to do in the winter, I suppose, when all you have is snow and a trapline."

"That's why winters were invented," Virgil said.

"Not just winter." Samstrung's eyes wandered back to Bright Shell. "I'd say she's good for every day of the week."

Erik attempted to derail the conversation's drift. "Good to see the mules haven't beaten you yet."

"Forget the mules, son. Congratulations are in order. We need a drink!" Samstrung shouted. Erik had rarely seen him this excited. He pulled the door to the mercantile shut behind himself, and the three of them crossed the street to Chester Willis's saloon.

Erik felt a bit awkward with Bright Shell in tow, but she remained sitting patiently astride Leaf, watching. The three men downed a whiskey. Others joined in as the news spread. Some Erik recognized. Others were newcomers. It seemed Bannack still had some life to it, at least when there was an excuse to celebrate.

When Erik returned to Bright Shell, she appeared distressed. She and Leaf had not moved.

"Men watch me," she said.

Erik noticed two rough-dressed men outside Madam Holloway's. They might have been wondering if Bright Shell were available. It was not unheard of. Erik shook his head in disgust.

They unloaded the travois and hauled the furs into Samstrung's. Bright Shell pointed out things that delighted her. Erik had to hold back a bit but settled on some beads, vermilion, and a mirror. The sensible items included wool cloth and a large cooking pot. Shortly, Erik had finished trading and pocketed a few dollars. He was thankful Samstrung had not asked if he needed more ammunition for his Spencer, but Erik figured he already had noticed the rifle's absence and, seeing Bright Shell, likely had figured out what had become of it.

Leading out of town, Erik passed the Potters' boardinghouse. "Funny," he mused, "how my life's changed." With the hot springs, he did not miss a hot bath, and with Bright Shell preparing his meals, he did not need a hot meal. Certainly, bread and vegetables would have been good. *And pie. Apple pie.* He'd plant some apple trees. If the Swedes could grow apples in their high valley, he could grow them in his basin.

He headed southwest for Lemhi Pass and Bright Shell's people. The trail was now well marked with wagon ruts and horse tracks. He caught a few stares from travelers and understood why. The days of a mountain man with his Indian wife had pretty much passed.

The Sacred River band remained encamped where they had been last autumn, but Erik's heart fell when he realized there were but seven lodges. Dread seeped through him until he spotted Strong Wolf's lodge. That was what mattered most. He guessed that several families had risked going east to again go hunting and possibly to join Tendoy. He had not expected the chief to return, since he had not done so last winter, but he had not expected the others to leave. Times were not good.

Erik's arrival had been well announced preceding his entry into the village. Despite the few lodges, there would be a great celebration that evening. Already word spread that Strong Wolf would have a welcoming meal for his daughter and Erik. As husband to Strong Wolf's daughter, Erik would be the family's guest. Jumping Deer would join them as well.

A separate lodge was made available for Erik and Bright Shell. Spotted Bird attended it and assisted Erik and Bright Shell. Erik addressed her as grandmother, again signaling the proper relationship, but no sooner had he done so than Spotted Bird shook her head.

"I am wife to Deer Horn. You were right that a certain hunter desired me."

Erik fought his smile. He had held little hope but then recalled his conversation with Deer Horn. Sometimes a man just needed a hint, and that was what Erik had given him.

He was mildly surprised when Deer Horn later approached him and said, "Spotted Bird says I am a good hunter, and we share the robes." It was a reminder of when Erik had asked if he was not a good hunter and so did not share robes with a woman.

Erik grinned. "I am pleased for you, Deer Horn. Spotted Bird is a good woman, and you will have a good family."

"Soon, I hope," Deer Horn said. He laughed. "My brother will visit us then, and perhaps he will have a family as well." He smiled.

Erik was tempted to share the news but did not. Men did not share something of that nature, although the women would do so.

The following day, as custom dictated, Erik held council with Cusowat and the remaining men. The Sacred River band harbored great concern. Too few lodges remained in Lemhi Valley to properly protect the homeland. Tendoy remained to the east. No word had been received regarding the promised gifts. Cusowat believed there would be none. The papers for the reservation remained unsigned. Tendoy and some Bannocks would join with the Crow for a bison hunt this season. It surprised Erik that they would join with their sworn enemy, the Crow. The Bannock and Shoshone often hunted and wintered together for mutual protection, but the Crow? Perhaps hunting with the Crow would help increase their success; however, Erik was certain they would return to raiding each other for horses and demonstrating deeds of bravery as soon as the hunt was finished. Erik was not disappointed that among the hunters who had gone east were Runs Fast, who harbored hate toward him, and Crooked Leg and Black Buffalo, with whom Runs Fast held sway.

That Strong Wolf remained in the valley was fortunate. Perhaps Strong Wolf had anticipated that Erik would return after the winter since Erik had promised to visit often.

"After the hunt, it shall be good," Cusowat said. "Tendoy will bring much meat and hides to make new robes and to cover our lodges before the cold moons return. All the Lemhi will return to Sacred River."

Erik sensed the optimism, even though Tendoy and the people with him had endured a season of starvation last winter. Cusowat's people had fared somewhat better since some game remained in the mountains that surrounded Lemhi Valley, but now, without hunters to provide for them, they faced a lean summer.

The following day, Erik visited with Tissidimit. The man appeared frailer, and his vision had further dimmed, yet he was pleased to see Erik. They smoked a pipe.

"It is good I visit with Two Elks Fighting. It is a glad time for me. I soon travel the sky trails. My time is nearly used up." He placed his hand on Erik's. "Soon I shall have Stone Boy paint a memory of Two Elks Fighting and Bright Shell on the memory hide, but this shall not be until I see his child."

A shiver ran through Erik's scalp. How did the old man know? Although Bright Shell had likely shared the news with her sister, it was not something to share with the men.

Tissidimit leaned toward Erik and carefully traced his fingers over Erik's face. "Yes, I see a child like the father. This child has a good spirit." He pulled his hands into his lap and studied Erik with his dim eyes. "When the cold moons were upon us and a little one was lost, I knew that Bright Shell was with a new life. I announced this to the people, for it was good news.

"Beware, Two Elks Fighting, for Runs Fast tells the others that it is a sign of evil since the little one perishes and an unborn takes on life inside Bright Shell. Runs Fast says Two Elks Fighting and

Bright Shell must never bring the child to the people, for it now has the unborn's spirit and will bring evil."

Erik went cold. It was not surprising for Tissidimit to predict that Bright Shell was pregnant, but why would he have chosen to do so at the time of another baby's death? The chill strengthened as a dim thought rushed forth.

"Who was the little one's mother?" he asked. Jumping Deer had visited with Erik and Bright Shell when they arrived. Erik recalled her toddler son of two winters had been with her, but there had been no papoose. Icy water slammed into him, and a chill penetrated to his center.

"Jumping Deer's child lived a single day."

Erik tried to steady himself. How could this be? The sisters had visited as if all were well. He then remembered: the people did not consider a newborn's sudden death as a death. The child had died because it had been unfinished. But surely Erik would have noticed something.

"The little one's spirit returned to the Great Mystery. And then the Great Mystery sends the spirit to Bright Shell, and it enters her. This is how I know that Bright Shell carries a new life." Tissidimit's waxy eyes brightened.

Erik fought to understand. He did not believe it, or was it possible? Did his unborn child now possess the spirit that had been intended for Jumping Deer's child?

"I call to Jumping Deer and share with her that her unborn's spirit now goes to Bright Shell's child. Jumping Deer is joyful. The people understand this is by the Great Mystery and are joyous. It is Runs Fast who is wrong." Tissidimit spat. "Runs Fast has a troubled spirit. It is fed by something evil. He will not listen. Neither Raven Woman nor I can release him from his troubled spirit. He poisons those who would listen. He poisons Crooked Leg and Black Buffalo. You must not forget Runs Fast's sickness is strong against you."

Raven Woman cackled, which reminded Erik that she and Stone Boy had overheard the discourse. She shuffled over to sit near Erik. Her eyes flashed. She cawed again and then allowed her voice to trail off in short staccato croaks while jerking her head like a raven.

She addressed Erik. "Your child shall be a shaman for the people, Two Elks Fighting. The evil one that Runs Fast shelters will fight the shaman. I will train up your child. I teach Bright Shell the plants to give to your child so that it will grow wise and learn the ways of the shaman."

A shiver coursed through Erik. "Then is my child a boy child, or is it a girl child?"

Tissidimit drew a slow breath. "This is not revealed, but what Raven Woman says is revealed. Your child will be a great healer and one to whom the people will turn."

Erik wrestled with himself. *No, my child will live in the white world. My child will be like the Swedes and grow crops or ranch cattle.* He surprised himself. Until this moment, he had given no thought to his child's future.

Something pressed in on Erik, troubling him. Bright Shell had not shared her meeting with Raven Woman. Why had she hidden it from him? But then he considered that Bright Shell might be fearful that he would not understand or fearful of how he would react.

His child had the spirit that had been intended for Jumping Deer's child. It had returned to the Great Mystery, but why had Tissidimit decided this spirit would meld with his unborn child? Had Tissidimit had a vision? It mattered little. Erik's son or daughter would have a good home. After a child's birth, spirit and body were inseparable. Before and after life, the spirit existed in a different world. The body came from dust and returned to dust. His child's spirit belonged only to his child for as long as his child should live.

CHAPTER 28

Erik and Bright Shell remained another day with the Sacred River band. Erik was troubled by what he saw—an impoverished people. This was no life for Bright Shell and certainly no life for his child. He wondered if he should return to the valley. Sven and the others would have to accept them. *After all, they're now apparently accepting Irish Catholics*, Erik mused. The O'Donnells had arrived in the valley shortly before he left.

He would build a cabin where he had run his first trapline. It would be far enough from the others but not too far. He would raise some horses and cattle.

He thought of the Lemhi. *I cannot. When I asked for Bright Shell, I promised I would remain near.*

And what about his intentions now? He had managed alone while trapping, but what right did he have to take Bright Shell into that kind of isolation? He raised his eyes. *Have I made a mistake, Great Mystery?*

Erik glanced back at Bright Shell, who rode Leaf with their possessions on a travois. She noticed his glance and smiled.

Erik turned back to her and reached her side. "My heart is glad that Bright Shell is my wife. I could not live alone any longer. I will bring her often to visit her family."

She smiled. "I am happy to be where my husband is."

They returned to their cabin, and life was good, except that shortly, Erik caught a sadness in Bright Shell. He wondered if it was because she already missed her family. He did not ask.

This day, Bright Shell sewed some moccasins. Her swelling belly had become much more noticeable. Erik wondered if he should take her to Salmon City and find a midwife for when her time came. It was a full day's ride—that was, unless he cut over a saddle to the south of the cabin. From there, it was nearly a straight line down the west side back to the Salmon River.

Erik decided against such ridiculous thoughts. Bright Shell was of the people; she would know what to do.

Bright Shell seemed preoccupied. They had not spoken much of their visit with her people or of her sister, Jumping Deer. He asked if she wished to go visit soon. Bright Shell nodded but said, "You have much work here."

Something else bothered her. She would not have known what Tissidimit or Raven Woman had shared with him regarding their unborn child. Perhaps Bright Shell knew only what Jumping Deer had shared. Men did not delve into women's affairs, and women's business was kept from husbands.

"You should know, Bright Shell, that I talked with Tissidimit about our child."

"I know this," Bright Shell said. She paused in her work, and her eyes fell.

"He says the spirit that was in Jumping Deer's child left because the little one was unfinished. The Great Mystery gave its spirit to our child."

Bright Shell looked up. "Yes, this is what he says." She seemed anxious and caressed her belly. "But Two Elks Fighting knows it is his seed that grows inside me," she said. "The child has the spirit that once was in Jumping Deer's child, but it is Two Elks Fighting's seed. I was afraid to say, because I do not know my husband's ways, and he might be displeased."

"No, Bright Shell." Erik now understood. He had thought about Tissidimit's claims as well and had tried to reconcile his own beliefs. "Our child comes from you and me. Though the spirit inside our child was once inside Jumping Deer's child, it does not matter. The body and spirit become one when the child is finished. Its spirit comes from the Great Mystery. All spirits are of the Great Mystery, not of the parents. It is so with all the people."

Bright Shell trembled. She looked in his direction, and her eyes brightened. "I was afraid you would think it is not our child. I did not know. You make my heart glad again, Two Elks Fighting."

"You should have said why you were sad, Bright Shell," Erik said. "It is not good for our child to listen to its mother's sad heart before its time to come into the world."

Bright Shell averted her eyes. "This I know. But I sing to our child and think of things happy. And now I am more happy."

"And did you speak with Raven Woman about our child?"

"She came to me and said our child will be a shaman. She told me of plants I should prepare and use." A quick shadow crossed her eyes. "I do not know if this is what I wish. I think my husband would wish for a great hunter. But I do not talk of this at this time."

Erik smiled. "Yes, let us decide these things later. I think our child shall decide this." *Particularly if he is anything like me.* Inwardly, he was pleased Bright Shell showed skepticism about their child becoming a shaman.

He pulled Bright Shell to himself and kissed her deeply, allowing his fingers to gently rub her bulging belly. A small flutter met his hand. *A mystery of life! Simply because Bright Shell and I came together.* The joy he felt burst forth like a spreading fire in his heart.

"See? Your child knows you," Bright Shell said. "It is happy." She held her hand over his.

Erik had his work—a stock shed, a corral, and hunting—all before the summer passed. He primarily worked on a stock shed, which was an open three-sided pole structure with a roof where the two horses could gather during a blizzard. In addition, despite some reluctance, he put in a small garden near the creek. Bright Shell learned to run water to the growing vegetables—potatoes, onions, and turnips. He would show Bright Shell how to use them in their meals, although she was adept at using wild roots, including bitterroot, wild onion, and camas. The Shoshone, more so than the Crow or Blackfeet, used a variety of wild plants and berries.

Erik also continued his unending work on new arrows. He used steel points he had acquired from Samstrung. Many Indians now did so because they were easy to acquire and were often reusable. Even if he had a rifle, he would never give up his bow. It was silent and efficient, especially for small game.

He watched Bright Shell. Her round belly held a special beauty.

"We should go to bathe," Erik said.

She glanced at him; her brow furrowed.

"Not where the water is too hot," he added.

Bright Shell frowned more deeply. Erik wondered if she did not like being seen in her present condition.

"You are beautiful," he said. "Baths are good for unborn babies. Sometimes it helps them arrive earlier. Then we can travel to see my sister."

"*My* sister is at Sacred River."

"Of course. We go to my sister after we visit the people."

Bright Shell asked where Erik's sister lived. Erik attempted to describe where the valley was. By a bird's flight, he estimated it to be 150 miles southwest, but following the canyons and mountain divides, it was likely 200 miles—across the most cut-up and nearly impassible land in America. Erik guessed it would take at least two weeks with the horses.

Bright Shell appeared skeptical. "My husband would go there?"

"I would to show off my wife and our child." *And to let a few stubborn Swedes know I've found love.* Deep down, Erik knew they would embrace her. Despite Sven's rock-hard attitude toward him, the man respected his lifestyle. After all, had he not been half Indian, as some liked to claim, Sven would have never again seen Torsten.

Erik led the way for Bright Shell in the growing dusk. A mountain breeze picked up, cooling the hot day. Hatchet and Leaf grazed above them on the open slope. Soon he would acquire some more horses and perhaps some cattle. He would have two places: one near the valley, where he could grow crops and better care for livestock, and this one from where he could run his trapline.

Erik settled with Bright Shell into the warm water, sitting back against the smooth boulders near where the water trickled down from the hotter upper springs.

Erik spoke. "Does Two Elks Fighting make Bright Shell happy?"

She turned toward him, smiling, and kissed him—something she now did freely.

Erik's heart raced. "My wife makes me happy," he whispered. "And soon we will have our child."

Erik could not stem his desire for her. Bright Shell recognized his need and grasped his hardness, soon bringing him comforting pleasure.

CHAPTER 29

Erik spotted the black-and-gold flash of the wolverine near a silvery alpine lake. "Blazes," he muttered. The animal's foul scent lingered. A trapline would provide the animal with easy prey throughout the winter. Worst of all, the animal had a nasty habit of fouling its meal to ward off other scavengers. Given a chance, it would foul every snare and catch that Erik made during the entire winter.

"Not a good sign, Hatchet," Erik said. "Gray Owl would say to leave the devil bear this place, but I have a cabin and a pregnant wife. I cannot just move on to another valley." He watched among the timber, trying to sight the animal. Most likely, it was a male visiting one of his females in her territory. Wolverines might roam an area of two hundred square miles. "No choice but to set a trap for him. Bait it with something he'd like, like a rotting weasel. Catch him before the season."

Erik set his jaw. Gray Owl would have said that killing it would invite its spirit to taunt him and chase away the furbearers. An unease rankled the hairs on Erik's neck.

He turned Hatchet away from the basin and descended the lake's outlet to a small meadow below, where a couple of mule deer grazed. He slipped from Hatchet and began stalking the larger of the two animals. When within a few yards, he placed an arrow behind the buck's shoulder. He nocked a second arrow and pulled, but the animal went down. He waited for it to bleed and then approached it and gutted it.

He threw the buck over Leaf and hitched it to the packsaddle. He thought about Bright Shell. He decided this would be his last trip away for any length of time, at least until their baby was born. He had been gone two nights. His heart raced at the thought of soon arriving at his cabin and feeling Bright Shell's embrace.

He worked his way through the timber, and an inexplicable unease surfaced. The wolverine provoked images from his vision two seasons ago. An image of the wolf-bear creatures striking and slashing at the night cat, gripping the struggling mountain lion about its throat, and bringing it down suddenly flashed in Erik's mind.

A mile from the cabin, he caught sight of white signal smoke billowing up from the trees. "My kid's coming!" shouted Erik. The disturbing images vanished. "Come on, Hatchet." He nudged the horse into a trot. Leaf protested slightly but, shouldering the weight of the deer, followed.

When Erik caught sight of the cabin, he knew something was wrong. His throat tightened. Smoke billowed from the cabin door— not only from the stick-and-mud chimney. It roiled black, no longer white. Erik jumped from Hatchet and raced the last few steps and into his cabin.

"Bright Shell!"

She lay bloody and naked, weakly coughing. Her hands held a small form to her breasts. Her chest heaved, and she gasped as she choked.

They'd had visitors. Hoof and boot prints marked the cabin's dirt floor and yard.

A wave of nausea swept over Erik. He gasped, choking, understanding what had happened but refusing to believe it. He felt as if his being were being ripped apart. A fleeting image of the two men watching from Madam Holloway's welled up.

He reached under Bright Shell and, cradling her, brought her and their baby girl outside.

The act had likely caused Bright Shell to go into labor. She had delivered their baby, a tiny, trembling form naked against Bright Shell's breast. His daughter made feeble attempts to nurse.

Erik dragged a blanket from the cabin and covered Bright Shell and their baby. "I'm here. I'm here!" he cried, trying to soothe Bright Shell. Her frantic eyes swept aimlessly, and he read her desperation and pain. She mouthed words that Erik did not understand.

He put his fingers to her lips. A great, crushing weight began pressing down. He gasped for breath—breath that was being squeezed from him as his world filled with darkness.

Erik broke away, reentered the cabin, pulled the burning and smoking branches from the fire, and scattered them outside. He found water and put a pot on the remaining fire. He pulled free another robe and returned to Bright Shell.

He had seen foal and calves being born. Sometimes one damaged its mother. Erik didn't know what had damaged Bright Shell—the men or her attempts to pull the child free. It mattered not.

He tried to stem the flow of blood and clean Bright Shell the best he could.

He had faced terror before but nothing like this. *This* had no equal. He coughed, choking, battling to keep his head. Only one of God's miracles could save Bright Shell now.

The smoke cleared. Erik fixed a new bed and carried Bright Shell with their baby girl inside and made her comfortable the best he could.

At length, Bright Shell woke. Her eyes became frantic, and her fists fought some unseen evil.

"Sh. I'm here, Bright Shell." Erik caught her hands and stared into her eyes. "We have a girl child," he whispered.

"Men," Bright Shell gasped.

"I know," Erik said. "They are not men. They live on borrowed breath. This I vow to you, Bright Shell."

She squeezed her eyes and opened them. "One man. He has two fingers gone. I cut the other man's face."

Erik found the knife wet with blood. She had fought the men.

He brought Bright Shell water. She took a few sips. He allowed some hope to fill him.

"Our daughter. What do you wish to call her?"

"Spirit. Glad Spirit."

"Yes," Erik whispered. "That is a good name. Glad Spirit." He pulled his daughter back to Bright Shell's breast, hopeful for the moment.

Erik stayed at their side through the long night, trying to give Bright Shell water. The gray morning told Erik the truth: Bright Shell did not wake; she had bled too much. His daughter was trying to nurse a dying breast.

"God, how can this be?" Erik cried. "How can this be?"

He bent and kissed Bright Shell. Her eyes had stilled.

The crushing weight thrust Erik into blackness. He fought back.

Gently, he pulled the robes over Bright Shell and wondered how long it would be until Glad Spirit joined her mother in death. A few hours? A day? He bundled Glad Spirit with Bright Shell so he would not see his baby girl breathe her last. He was powerless to keep her alive. *God, I cannot bear it. End it soon.* His thoughts choked him.

Other thoughts pressed in. Wrapping Glad Spirit with her mother was the right thing to do. Did Glad Spirit know she suffered? Certainly she felt the pain.

He opened the robe.

A soft whistle reached his ears. It wavered and whistled again. *Sohobinehwe Tso`ape!*

The baby pushed herself against him, bringing him out of his fog.

Is it possible? Glad Spirit is to be a shaman. You have reminded me, Sohobinehwe Tso`ape! "Dear God, do not let me be too late."

He swaddled Glad Spirit under his coat against his chest and swung up onto Hatchet. He pulled Leaf after him for when Hatchet tired. "Go, boy. My daughter does not have much time."

The men's tracks had come from the east, but Bannack was too far to go for help. He nudged Hatchet up the trail and forked to the west, toward the divide that led into Idaho Territory—the divide he had considered crossing but had never attempted. Only deer and elk tracks came from that direction. Could a horse even cross?

Then the soft, wavering whistle came from that direction. Did he imagine it? Did he want it so badly that he created it?

"No! Sohobinehwe Tso`ape tells us there is a way, Hatchet. Come on, boy!"

Erik guided Hatchet toward the notch above them. He judged the distance to Salmon City to be short of twenty miles, but across the divide, he would drop into a deep gorge—one that, once entered, would be nearly impossible to get out of. Erik's chest ached, and each step seemed to take minutes. *Too long.* Hatchet picked his way painfully slowly upward. *Does Glad Spirit still breathe?* Erik brought his ear to her quiet face. She breathed shallow breaths. He tried to squeeze water into her tiny mouth.

They topped the divide, and Erik switched to Leaf. Leaf protested because Erik did not often ride him, but the pony soon settled and obediently descended through the gorge, picking his way around downed timber and fractured boulders. Maybe Leaf settled because he sensed Erik's distress.

The gorge broadened, and the trail flattened. Erik reached the Salmon River and turned upstream. He switched back to Hatchet and urged the animal into a gallop. Salmon City was at best five miles away, but the ground was level, or as near level as ground could be in that country, and Erik rode as quickly as the animal would move.

CHAPTER 30

Erik rode directly to Samstrung and Harpster's mercantile in Salmon City. Chet Harpster greeted Erik, but his smile immediately faded. Erik slid to the ground and pulled Glad Spirit from inside his coat. Harpster asked no questions. Maybe Samstrung had told Harpster that Erik had married a Shoshone woman. Erik mentioned only that Bright Shell had encountered problems in delivery and that he had lost her.

Harpster choked out how sorry he was. "I'm sending for help. Your baby will be all right."

Erik sat in a daze. He held Glad Spirit tightly. Miraculously, the baby yet breathed.

He became aware of two women. One, he learned, was Mrs. Magdalena Shoup.

"Call me Lena," she told Erik. "Now we have Mrs. Baker. She can care for your child. She's nursing one of her own."

Erik would not release Glad Spirit until, gently, Mrs. Shoup pulled away his fingers. He dared not dwell on what had happened. Nothing in his life compared to the feelings he now had. He could not grasp how he could endure the pain another day. But he had Glad Spirit, a tiny spark of light, he told himself. She was now in Mrs. Baker's care; she had a chance.

Mrs. Reverend Cuthbert visited Erik early the following morning.

"With God's grace, the baby is doing well, Mr. Larson. We cannot help you with this tragedy, but we can arrange to take the baby to Virginia City. They have an orphanage where she will be cared for."

Something inside Erik twisted violently. Glad Spirit was of the people. She was not white. Raven Woman had claimed she would become a shaman for the people.

"I cannot assure you that others will overlook her heathen blood. You men who bed Indian women should consider those consequences," Mrs. Cuthbert said with unmasked disdain as she wagged her head. "Be pleased, Mr. Larson, that she will have a chance to be saved. She will certainly have a godlier upbringing than that allowed by your lifestyle."

Mrs. Shoup rested her hand on Erik's shoulder. "This news must be pleasing for you, Mr. Larson. Your baby will be well cared for."

Erik found himself in Martinelli's saloon. He downed a whiskey and asked for another. Chet Harpster found him and tried to talk. Erik wanted nothing to do with him, and Harpster walked out. After four whiskeys, Erik's head swam.

"Ought to be enough," he muttered.

He left the saloon and found Mrs. Baker's home. Mr. Baker frowned but allowed him to enter. Mrs. Baker nursed Glad Spirit. Two other small children ran about.

"I'm much obliged for what you have done, Mr. and Mrs. Baker," Erik said, partly slurring his words. "I can never repay you. You've given her a chance."

"Yes, and I hear Mrs. Cuthbert is making arrangements for the orphanage," Mrs. Baker said. "It must ease you some."

"Yes, ma'am. May I hold her?" Erik took his daughter. Her dark eyes sparkled, and her tiny fingers curled about his small finger. He swaddled her; walked out the door; and, holding her tightly, swung up onto Hatchet. He tucked Glad Spirit under his coat against his chest and turned up the Lemhi River, leading Leaf.

Erik reached Cusowat's camp late in the day. He did not know how he could face the Sacred River band, especially Strong Wolf, but he had no choice. Erik had given Strong Wolf his word that he would care for his daughter and protect her.

When he met the people, there were few words. He explained he would go after the two men. He would return only when he had taken their breath.

Strong Wolf wanted to ride with him, as did others, but Erik refused their offer.

174

"It is my task," Erik said. "I gave my sacred word when I took Bright Shell. I said I would care for her. I failed. Only I can undo my failure. This I owe the people."

As the news spread, women began the mourning sounds. Dancing Swallow and Jumping Deer reached the gathering. Upon seeing Erik holding Glad Spirit, both women began fiercely wailing and pulling at their hair.

Erik motioned to Jumping Deer. "I will go now. I would ask only that Jumping Deer take her sister's child."

Jumping Deer paused her wailing. Her eyes met Erik's as she received the small bundle. Other women gathered around Jumping Deer, and the wailing ceased. Erik wondered if the cessation had something to do with not bringing anything bad to the child. The wailing would resume later but not within Glad Spirit's hearing.

Runs Fast broke through the group with hatred etched on his face. "We must not allow this child to be among us!"

Erik forced himself to sit fast. Blossoming red clouded his vision. He'd intended only to leave Glad Spirit with the Sacred River band and then depart, but Runs Fast had other ideas.

Runs Fast shoved at him. "Little white boy is evil, and he brings evil. Take his child away. It is of evil seed. It has an evil spirit and will bring only evil to us."

"The spirit within my child is not evil," Erik snapped. "Her spirit comes from the Great Mystery, as do all spirits. It is not from me. Her spirit is not evil."

Runs Fast lunged for Jumping Deer and grabbed for Glad Sprit.

"Stop!" Erik shouted. "Tissidimit and Raven Woman know of this child. They say she will become a medicine woman."

Runs Fast spun back toward Erik and shouted toward the others, "You must not listen! Little white boy speaks only evil."

Cusowat straightened. "This is not for you to decide, Runs Fast. Bring Tissidimit and Raven Woman. You forget whose wife now holds this child."

Runs Fast's face darkened. "Tissidimit and Raven Woman will see the evil. They will agree we must destroy it."

A chill gripped Erik. The possibility of this happening sent a numbness through him. He glanced to where Jumping Deer held Glad Spirit and nursed the hungry baby. Although they would not kill Glad Spirit outright, they might abandon the baby to die. His throat tightened.

Erik caught sight of Tissidimit as Stone Boy assisted him, bringing him forward to where Erik remained astride Hatchet. Raven Woman followed. Both Tissidimit and Raven Woman quickly examined the child.

Raven Woman drew back sharply, muttering, nearly shrieking.

Icy cold washed over Erik. Glee crossed Runs Fast's face.

Tissidimit turned to Erik and the others. "It was I who told you that Two Elks Fighting and the woman who brought light were with child. It was I who told you that the spirit from Jumping Deer's lost son entered this child. Now it is right for the sister to take her sister's daughter. She must complete this circle of life."

Raven Woman cackled. She approached Runs Fast and glowered until Runs Fast pulled back. She approached Cusowat. "It is as Tissidimit says. I shall bring this child up to be a medicine woman for the people. No evil spirit resides within. Runs Fast is confused." A strange grin spread across her etched face as she eyed the man and cackled.

Erik released a slow breath. Shaking, he slowly released his hands that tightly clenched Hatchet's reins.

"I do not say that Raven Woman and Tissidimit are wrong," Runs Fast said, "but the trickster in little white boy does this. Little white boy has a spirit that confuses us." He spat. "I say we should allow Tendoy to decide this when he returns."

Erik realized that Runs Fast sought to buy himself more time to turn others against Erik and his child. The people could forgive Runs Fast and defer the decision to Chief Tendoy. Erik tensed. Glad Spirit's life had not yet been preserved.

"Hear this," Cusowat said. "I decide this for my people, not Tendoy. I accept Glad Spirit as my daughter and daughter to my wife, Jumping Deer. It is right that Two Elks Fighting brings her to us. As Raven Woman says, she will become a woman the people shall turn to."

Cusowat addressed Runs Fast. "Perhaps a trickster has entered you, Runs Fast. You should go to Tendoy. Take your family. Come back to us when the snow returns and Tendoy returns."

Runs Fast glowered. "No. It is for each man to decide how to live. I will accept Glad Spirit because you decide this." He pointed toward

Erik. "But *he* I will not accept. He is here because you allow it, and so I allow it. Hear this. I will destroy little white boy where I find him but not here at Sacred River." He shook his fist at Erik.

Crooked Leg and then Black Buffalo, their eyes hard, stepped to Runs Fast's side and folded their arms.

Cusowat said, "I agree that is your decision to make, Runs Fast."

Erik said nothing. He took a last look to where his daughter was nursing at Jumping Deer's breast. Jumping Deer resembled Bright Shell so strongly that looking at her brought a pain and numbing darkness within his chest. Three men had just sworn to take his life should they happen across him.

Erik rode north from the Sacred River band and, late day, skirted Salmon City. Two days later, he reached his cabin and Bright Shell's body. It remained undisturbed as he had left her, wrapped in robes on the cabin roof. He considered burning the cabin and Bright Shell's body with it.

"No, it is not like the Tukudeka to do such a thing," he whispered. Although she was of the Sacred River band, Erik chose to follow Sheepeater customs.

He found an outcrop above the hot springs. There he placed Bright Shell's body dressed in her finest gown, the one she had worn on their wedding day: the white elk skin adorned with elk teeth. He placed her favorite cooking kettles with her, as well as the mirror, her beads, and the fox robe she had never finished. He pulled an elk robe over her and tied it.

He prayed, asking the Great Mystery to receive her. "Take home this woman who gave her life to Two Elks Fighting. The woman whose smile lit my life. Let her walk the sky trails untroubled by the spirits who wish to lead her astray. Take care of Glad Spirit and her mother's spirit, which now resides with her."

Erik whispered to Bright Shell, "I will speak of you as the woman who brought the people light, as Tissidimit addressed you. That is how the Sacred River band will remember you." Blackness pinched inwardly. "My Bright Shell, my light, how can I live without you?"

Erik returned to the cabin. He pulled together the belongings he needed in order to survive and to hunt, including his sheep horn bow and his knife. All other things he piled inside his cabin. He pulled burning embers from the fire and scattered them about. The fire ignited, crawled across his belongings, caught in the roof timbers, and blazed into a living, screeching demon. He hoped it would erase the memories but knew it would not.

Erik backed away as the heat increased and the flames blazed higher.

He mounted Hatchet and, leading Leaf, headed down trail. Passing the hot springs, he turned and watched the black smoke snaking its way into the blue August sky. He gazed toward the outcrop. The wind fluttered the feathers he had hung above Bright Shell's wrapped body.

It was a holy place now. Good spirits would live there and keep Bright Shell company. Her child would grow, but unlike white people, Glad Spirit would never wish to come here. He had been right to give her to the people, and he was happy that Jumping Deer would be her mother. It was as Raven Woman had said. She would become a great shaman for the people. He and Bright Shell would no longer have a say.

Nearing the valley floor, Erik pulled up on Hatchet and looked over his shoulder for the last time. A thin line of smoke snaked upward into the sky. He was too numb to think and knew enough not to do so. His instinct to survive had taught him such over the years. He returned his attention to the muted tracks leading downward. He had no plan other than to follow them.

"To hell and back if necessary," Erik muttered.

Who were the attackers? Every sense told him they were the men who had been watching from Madam Holloway's porch. Bannack was the only place he had taken Bright Shell. Two men dressed in dark clothing. One was tall. But the men could have been anyone, not the two he had seen watching.

They had a week on him, but it mattered little. Erik touched his medicine pouch. Gray Owl, with Erik's first vision, had tried to tell him he would be tried. *How could the old man have known?* His finger traced the mountain lion tooth inside the pouch. A scalding bite shivered across his scalp. *The pinnacle in the burning-rocks land. That vision! Could it be? But the night cat said it was not my fight.* His entire body prickled. *What if it was?*

Like his helper spirit, the night cat, he would pursue—not quickly but relentlessly. When he caught them and, like the night cat, sprang from the darkness, they would never know of him until his knife had slit their throats.

Erik stopped when within half a mile of Bannack. He had eaten little. He dismounted and turned his ponies loose to graze but left them packed so he could more quickly resume his journey. He chewed some dried meat while he searched the surrounding country. The tracks of the men he pursued had traveled unconcerned, unrushed, and unaware that he followed. That was good. He would catch them.

Their act had been senseless. Had Bright Shell not fought back, she might still have lived. Erik shook as he became overwhelmed by the memories. She had cut one of the men on his face. Where? Was it a deep cut? One man had lost two fingers earlier in his life. Erik had no other description, only vague memories of the two men who had watched them. He knew they rode shod horses. One's right rear hoof left a distinctive mark.

He had found her covered in blood. The knife had been tangled in the robes. A cold realization washed over Erik. *She cut our baby free. Why? Did she not think I would return in time? Did she know she was dying? Did she intend to give our daughter her first milk, to give her a chance?* In doing so, had she made her own death a certainty?

Erik fought the memories. "Enough," he whispered. He released his arms from about himself and stilled his shaking. "We have a long journey ahead of us, Hatchet." The journey would end only when he caught up to the two men. Beyond that, there was nothing.

CHAPTER 31

Numbing darkness enfolded Erik, yet he had little difficulty in following the men's trail. At first, the men had retreated toward the Big Hole River, where their tracks turned north. John Owen's fort was north, and although it was in Flathead Indian country, it passed through the western edge of Blackfeet lands. The Blackfeet likely would not have tolerated their traveling through. *They might be heading toward Helena, another gold camp,* Erik thought.

Erik followed, trying to keep his head clear, pushing himself, occasionally switching to Leaf and giving Hatchet time to rest. After several days, the trail swung east, but instead of continuing toward Helena, it abruptly swung south.

"They intended to throw us, boy," Erik murmured. "They're heading back to Bannack, where there's grub and company. I wonder if they know who's on their trail."

Erik wished their trail had not swung toward Bannack. He had no stomach for encountering people he knew. He trusted Samstrung and Virgil, but others might tip off the two men he pursued. Not everyone would respect his choice to marry a Shoshone woman.

Besides, he felt it would be better to catch them outside Bannack. He wanted to catch them somewhere where they could not run, where their dying screams would be heard only by the wind. He wanted them to suffer agonizing deaths and to know he was the one who took their lives and would leave their bodies to be torn apart by scavengers and forgotten. A vision of the two men suffocating on their blood arose. The cold, twisting feeling that the image brought unsettled Erik.

Erik reached a dense stand of conifers within sight of Bannack and picketed his horses. At dusk, he made his way into the town.

He checked the saloons, looking for a man missing two fingers and another with a fresh cut on his face. He moved among the familiar buildings, avoiding contact, keeping in the shadows, and watching. Eventually, the two would visit one of the saloons. Despite his inner turmoil, it mattered little when. Time was his ally. He recognized some people but kept his distance. None fit the description of the two killers.

The corral was empty except for a single ailing mule. That meant Virgil and Lemuel were on the trail somewhere. When Pete Samstrung came from his mercantile, Erik wrestled with himself about talking to the man. His hurt and sense of failure troubled him until he turned away and stepped from sight back across the street. This path had been chosen for him, not for others. He would not burden Samstrung. After Erik took the men's breaths, he wanted nothing to lead back to Samstrung or his friends.

He watched men until all were familiar, and whenever he saw new arrivals in Bannack, he studied them until he was certain they were not the men he sought. He realized the men might have split up, so he individually reexamined each man. He began second-guessing himself but again convinced himself they had to be in Bannack somewhere. Had they seen him and holed up? If so, he would outwait them; it was only time.

Erik withdrew from the town and returned to watching the trails and checking tracks, looking for the distinctive mark from the one horse. He found it and quickly realized it was a mark entering Bannack and not leaving the town. It was too recent to have been made when he had first arrived. Was it possible the men had slipped past him, gone elsewhere, and then returned?

Erik brushed clear the trail that led north. They would eventually have to leave the town. This time, he would find their tracks and follow, but if they weren't staying in Bannack, what were they doing?

He stood up from where he had been erasing the tracks. "Virginia City!" He gazed east. "To blazes!" He had assumed the scum had come from Bannack. They could have just as easily come from Virginia City and traveled through Bannack.

A day later, as difficult a decision as it was, Erik led Leaf to Samstrung's corral. Erik could more easily care for one horse. Leaf would slow him down. The pack train had returned, but none of the mules alerted with Erik's presence. They remembered him. He turned his pony loose among the pack animals.

"You've been good to me, boy. If you're still here when I get back, I'll come get you. Come on, Hatchet," Erik murmured. "It's just you and me now. We're heading east."

He did not search for tracks. None would exist along the well-traveled road.

The next day, Erik entered Virginia City. He found it similar to Bannack. About the same number of saloons, brothels, mercantiles, and hotels lined the streets. There were a blacksmith and two livery stables. As it was the capital of Montana Territory, there seemed more of a sense of settlement. Perhaps it would last when the gold ran out.

Erik was less concerned about being noticed here than in Bannack. He would be scrutinized, just as any newcomer would be, but here he had no one to apologize to.

Erik visited the saloons and hotels and observed the brothels. He watched the streets and businesses. He found no sign of the two men.

He again considered asking. A man missing two fingers would be noticed.

"But if someone knows of them and, when I get done with them, they get noticed missing, I'd for sure have someone come looking for me. Nej, Hatchet. Not yet."

Erik searched in widening circles around Virginia City. This day, the lingering odor of decay and old cooking fires wafted to him, and shortly, he came upon a broad trampled ground covered in squalor—discarded hide remnants, broken poles, firepits, animal bones, and dung. Several crows mocked him and took to wing. The rotting odor persisted. A torn coyote carcass was partially the source of the stench. This was where Tendoy and the people with him had camped.

They had now gone, and it occurred to Erik where. Tendoy had left Virginia City and gone to the Three Forks of the Missouri to join with the Crow to hunt bison. "I guess I'm not destined to ever meet the man," Erik muttered. "But then meeting him now would not be under the best of circumstances."

He gazed about the barren earth devoid of grass and brush and trampled and fouled. Erik would not have kept a dog there.

A flurry of leaves scudded across the ground in front of him, and Hatchet faltered. The seasons had changed.

"Somehow, I'm wrong about those scum, Hatchet. They rode north at least once. Maybe they have business with the Indians—maybe even with Tendoy. These men come to Virginia City or go to Bannack for supplies. Maybe that's all. Otherwise, they're brush men." He stifled a laugh. "A bit like me."

Erik sensed he was correct. Instead of continuing up Alder Gulch, he veered northeast up Granite Creek. It lacked the heavy digging that marked Alder Gulch, indicating there had been less gold in its drainage. That meant less reason for men to use this route, and for those who did, it meant less chance of being noticed. Erik followed with an eerie certainty that the men were somewhere ahead of him.

Erik would pursue until he found and caught them. Only then would he decide how to kill them. Like any hunted animal, the men would yield clues for a fitting death.

He topped the low mountains and descended eastward into the Madison River drainage and turned north downstream. The valley was broad, marked by scattered cottonwoods and willows and choked with meandering streams and marshes. He kept to the higher ground.

He wasn't the only traveler to keep to the higher ground. He found tracks from shod horses, and unexpectedly, he found himself staring at the scuff mark. Erik drew a sharp breath.

He picked up the tracks and followed to where they merged with a game trail that dropped down into heavy grass and marshes. Bison trails cut through the area, as did deer and elk trails, and turned to mud. He spotted wolves slinking up from the river. It was no longer possible to follow the tracks, but they appeared to be heading north toward the Three Forks area.

By late afternoon, low, scudding clouds swept in over the western mountains, and a spattering of rain enveloped Erik.

"To blazes, Hatchet," Erik muttered. "Even if I did find a dry track, we won't be tracking much longer if this keeps up."

A penetrating, persistent, cold drizzle enveloped him, and he pulled his coat over his shoulders to stop some of the rain from running down his back.

He thought about stopping. A fire and a good cup of coffee would have been welcome. But he was close. The tracks had to have been made within the last couple of days. The men could not have been far ahead, and if they holed up for the rain, he could close on them while they were stopped.

Erik rode into the evening until the dim light had faded. He shivered from the cold. He had given up on spotting any further tracks.

"Guess this is all we can do, Hatchet." An ache numbed his chest as Erik swung down and picketed Hatchet. He climbed a small rise to the north and scanned the countryside, trying to catch sight of a campfire, hopeful but knowing how unlikely it would be.

I know I didn't miss them, Erik told himself. *They're close. Probably down under the trees, out of the rain. Also to keep out of sight of Indians.* He smiled inwardly.

Erik slept under some cottonwoods. Although barren of leaves, their thick, intertwined limbs gave some protection from the rain.

At early light the following morning, Erik gulped a few pieces of dried elk and some water and resumed following the river. Streams braided the area. He found himself pulling back to drier ground out of the wet grass and mud. Spindly cottonwoods lined the river, their branches lacing the gray sky. Swarms of flies and mosquitoes erupted from under Hatchet's hooves.

He reached where the Gallatin, Madison, and Jefferson rivers flowed through a lush, broad plain. Tissidimit had shared that this entire country had once been Shoshone hunting grounds before they were driven west across the divide by the Crow and Blackfeet.

The three rivers meandered, splitting into numerous channels that made it difficult to determine one from the other. In the rain and heavy grass, Erik knew he would never find the men's tracks in the near vicinity of the rivers, but he also knew they had to cross somewhere or turn up or down one of the rivers.

This was the Three Forks area, where the three rivers joined to form the Missouri River. Erik guessed the men would continue down the Missouri. He crossed to the west side, where he could reach drier ground, and found a large game trail. Below him, spanning more than seventy-five yards, the Missouri rolled deep and swift.

In a few miles, the river dropped between barren bluffs that climbed above the river. Rock voodoos and twisted pines crowned their summits. The dusty trail led high above the river, through stunted grass and prickly pear. Erik had not seen any shod tracks for some time, but pony tracks from Indian hunters abounded. When the pony tracks swung west and up through the cutbanks toward the pine-studded hills, Erik followed.

He angled west and crossed a series of low, windswept ridges before dropping into another river that meandered back toward the south. He followed until the river joined the Jefferson. Since reaching the Three Forks area, Erik had traveled a large circle, and he came out onto the Jefferson several miles west and upstream from where he had been a week ago.

Erik was not prepared for what he found. Signs of a bison hunt stretched for more than a mile along the river. The decaying odor of bones and carcasses enveloped him as he passed through old campsites with abandoned tepees and discarded belongings. Erik recognized Crow sign and then Shoshone sign. This had been the planned hunt, and from the signs, it had been successful. That meant that after two seasons away, Chief Tendoy should be on his return to the Lemhi Valley with hides and meat and would join Cusowat for the winter. Erik had come close to crossing paths with him.

It would not have mattered had he done so. He would have avoided Tendoy.

"Only when I've taken the breath of those men," Erik whispered. "Until then, this is my path."

He caught himself staring at the scuff mark, at first unable to comprehend what he was seeing. It was there and fresh. Erik's blood pounded. "Well, Hatchet, looks like they've been here as well."

He circled the area. Although it was scarred with pony tracks and bison hoofprints, he eventually found more shod tracks and the scuff mark.

Likely, the men had brought horses, some liquor, or possibly firearms and had illegally been trading with the Indians. It was little wonder Erik had not found them. They were practiced at keeping out of sight.

Erik gazed west toward Idaho Territory. "They aren't heading to Helena or down the Missouri, Hatchet. And it might be we aren't the only ones following them." Low forested mountains graced the western horizon. If Erik had guessed the men right, they were now avoiding the law in Montana Territory and seeking new opportunities elsewhere. They were heading west.

"I say we just go west, Hatchet. When we get to the goldfields, we're apt to run into them. With winter coming, if we sit here much longer, we won't be going anywhere."

Erik followed the Jefferson a short distance until it drained from the south. He eyed the line of timbered mountains to the west, which were now spotted with snow after the last cold rain.

"I tell you, Hatchet, they'll keep west into the Big Hole and then follow it until they decide to cross into Idaho Territory. I wager they'll cross twenty or thirty miles north of where I took Samstrung's mules across. If so, that'll put them into the Clearwater country, north of the Salmon River, near as I know."

Erik headed up a small stream draining from the west and topped a low divide. He dropped into a narrow stream-laced valley. The rapidly flowing creek wound its way generally toward the west. Game trails indicated the deer and elk cut between the drainages along the same route.

Erik wound his way along the narrow drainage until evening. As was customary, he picketed Hatchet near the creek, built a small fire for his meal, and then laid out his bedroll a few yards distant.

He thought of the men who eluded him and then of Bright Shell until exhaustion turned to sleep.

MUSKRAT

CHAPTER 32

Erik clawed from a deep sleep; the morning light shone pale. A sharp whinny brought him fully awake, and icy stabs raced up his neck. Hatchet's second whinny was cut short. *Mountain lion!* Erik scrambled up and grabbed his knife.

Hatchet pounded his direction, snorting. A voice pierced the early light: "Hiya, hiya."

Not a lion but an Indian had Hatchet! Except Hatchet thundered in his direction, snapping limbs and brush.

The horse burst into view with a small form desperately clinging to his back.

As Hatchet passed, Erik grabbed at a leg and jerked. The person cried out and fell, and Erik was surprised the thief had not the skills to hang on. The form crumpled and moaned.

Erik flashed his knife toward the form. The thief was not much more than a boy, he realized, as the youth struggled to back away, hurt from the fall.

Frightened eyes met Erik's but quickly calmed. The boy prepared for certain death at the hands of a white man.

"You take my horse!" Erik exclaimed in Shoshone.

"Are you a brother?" The boy gasped, his eyes wide.

"You are Shoshone." Erik lowered his knife. "I do not kill one of the people. How is it you come to take my horse? Where are the others?" He braced for the other raiders.

The boy grimaced in pain. "I thought you were Blackfeet." He gestured an ugly word and fell to his side, heaving, revealing the mangled form of his leg. Skinny and nearly naked, dressed only in a loincloth and tattered leggings, the boy had been hurt but not only from his fall, which explained why Erik had unseated him so easily.

"I take horse to go back to Sacred River," the boy choked out. His breath rasped as his face pinched.

"Be calm," Erik said. For the boy to show pain, it must have been extreme. "I can see you are hurt. By what name do they call you?"

The youth signed and said, "Muskrat of Tendoy's people." Muskrat's eyes searched Erik's face. "You know of Tendoy?"

Erik nodded. "I have been with Cusowat."

The youth appeared bewildered. "How is that? You are a white man." Pain again streaked his face.

"I am of the Tukudeka and know of the Sacred River band. But you are injured. Do not talk. Let me help."

Erik pulled back the ripped legging. Grisly blood and torn flesh greeted him. Blood ran from a reopened wound. "Lie still," he directed.

Muskrat trembled, his eyes searching and his breathing ragged.

Erik ripped a piece from his blanket and pressed it onto the wound.

Muskrat's hands jerked up as his eyes rolled. He went limp, passing out.

"A blessing," Erik whispered. The cloth blossomed red.

Muskrat must have been thrown and possibly trampled by his horse, Erik thought. He must have seen where Erik had stopped for the night and seen his chance to get Hatchet. The pain the youth had endured to crawl even a few hundred yards to try to take Erik's horse had sapped his strength.

The blanket Erik held bled through. He added another piece, holding it tightly, and although he felt the bone slip, he had no choice but to keep holding.

The boy was lucky to be alive. He had a knife but had likely been unable to feed himself. His eyes were sunken, and his skin was taught over protruding bones. He burned with fever. Erik guessed he had already eaten his moccasins.

At length, Erik released his grip. The bleeding had stopped.

Erik threw wood onto last evening's embers and coaxed a new fire. Carefully, he began a more thorough exam of Muskrat's injuries. An angry mass of purple and red surrounded cuts on his thigh. His lower leg and ankle were swollen. He feared the boy had somehow broken his ankle as well as his leg. He also found angry bruising on his chest and side. Dried blood matted his hair.

Muskrat's chest rose and fell haltingly. Erik wondered if this was what the Sheepeaters called the sleep that proceeded death—the same as when his mother had died.

"Not this one," Erik prayed. "I cannot let this one walk the sky trails. True, I will not find the two men this season if I abandon the trail now, but do not take this one's spirit, Great Mystery."

Erik propped Muskrat up with some brush behind him to keep his head up. He bathed the cut on his upper leg. It did not appear as bad as it had at first, but his skin and a portion of his flesh were shredded, possibly from being dragged across a snag. The cut on Muskrat's head had swollen closed. Muskrat had likely been knocked unconscious and been unable to call for help. For sure, he had not been alone. It made no sense that the other hunters had not found him, unless there had been other reasons.

He splinted Muskrat's lower leg with four short sticks and wrapped it tightly with a torn blanket and rope. The bone had not torn through that Erik could discern, but if Muskrat tried walking on it, which Erik guessed he had, he could easily do more damage. Any open cut could lead to blood poisoning.

Erik built the fire for some warmth. The sky brightened, but thick clouds had rolled in. Cold wind hissed from beneath them. This storm would not bring rain. It would bring snow.

Erik left Muskrat bundled in his blankets and scouted the nearby surroundings for shelter. He could drag Muskrat on a travois if necessary, but to where? They were in the bottom of a narrow valley. A wide creek cut along its length. Another intersected it a short distance to the west. Clumps of cottonwoods and willows spread along its length, and grassy benches opened to the north below a ragged, snow-dusted peak.

"I best bring a shelter to him," Erik whispered, deciding against trying to move Muskrat. "At least for as long as he still breathes."

Erik began cutting poles for a small lean-to. He did not anticipate being there long. The feeling of death hovered near. The thought of sending another on a journey to the sky trails tore at him. At least he could shelter and watch over Muskrat until the time came.

Snow was falling by the time Erik had finished piling brush and fir boughs on the lean-to and closing most of the entrance. Inside, he fixed a bed of boughs and spread a hide over them.

He hoisted Muskrat's frail form and carried him into the shelter. The youth's fever had subsided, perhaps because of the snow.

Muskrat stirred. His eyes grew wide, and he tried to scramble up.

"Be calm." Joy washed over Erik. "I am pleased you are awake. You do not yet walk the sky trails," he said, knowing that was what Muskrat might believe now that the world had become eerily white.

Muskrat found the splint on his leg and grabbed at it.

"No. You must not move your leg," Erik said. "The bone inside is broken."

Muskrat stared, panting.

"Here. Drink this." Erik gave Muskrat some water, and the boy gulped it down. He handed him some dried meat, and Muskrat devoured it. "Easy," he said. "A little at a time so you do not get sick."

Muskrat wiped a thin forearm across his lips and stared at Erik. "I do not know you. You say you are of the Tukudeka, yet you know of my people."

"I am known as Two Elks Fighting among the Tukudeka. That is the name by which your people also call me."

Muskrat gulped more water and heaved his shoulders, shaking.

"I will take you to Sacred River." Erik attempted to give him hope. "My horse can take us."

Muskrat's eyes flickered. Likely, the boy knew he was near death. He would wonder how it might benefit Erik to return many days to take him to his people. In certain times, it was acceptable to leave the lame and dying behind, and Muskrat surely expected that.

"I am a friend. I will not leave you," Erik said, guessing the boy's thoughts. "I will take you to your healer. I know Raven Woman."

Muskrat's eyes widened in recognition. He signed, "Thank you," and then he whispered, "I am of the Broken Tree band. Shadow Woman is healer. I go to her."

"You should rest," Erik said, pleased that Muskrat seemed hopeful. "When you are well, we will travel. Here. I have white man medicine to help. Drink this."

In truth, Erik had nothing except some sugar he had added to the hot water. Muskrat drank it, draining the cup.

"You should sleep. It is a long journey to Sacred River."

The boy lay back and soon fell into a fitful sleep.

"Thank you, Lord," Erik whispered. He pulled his blanket over Muskrat and tugged his coat more tightly about himself while he fed the small fire. It cast some heat into the shelter. Snowflakes hissed into the flames.

By morning, more than a foot of snow had fallen—the first heavy snow of the season. Thick flakes filled the muted sky. There were no shadows but only faint streaks of gray in the otherwise white. Erik worried briefly about Hatchet but knew the horse would find shelter under the cottonwoods along the stream.

At length, Muskrat woke, somewhat more alert.

Erik gave him more food and water. He was pleased with how the boy ate and drank. He allowed himself to believe the boy might live.

"I must go to Shadow Woman," Muskrat said. He pulled at the splint.

"No," Erik said sharply. "There is poison in your bone. You must not move your leg."

Muskrat frowned.

"I put the sticks on your leg so no more bad medicine can get in. When we get to Shadow Woman, she can take the bad medicine out of your bone but only if we keep on the sticks."

"How do you know these things?" Muskrat demanded with eyes wide.

"Porcupine Woman of the Tukudeka knows these things. She is a healer. She showed me many things because I am also a healer."

Muskrat's eyes followed Erik's, searching to see if he spoke the truth. Muskrat turned away, apparently accepting Erik's explanation. It was largely true. Erik had learned much from Porcupine Woman.

"How did it come that you are injured?" Erik asked.

"My uncles and I hunt," Muskrat said haltingly. "We follow some elk. Some *Duungagithe' gwidape,* Blackfeet dung, surprise us and want our horses. We try to fight. I run with my horse and fall down a rocky place and wake near here. My uncles do not find me." A shadow crossed his face. "Perhaps their hair is now on a Blackfeet lance, and they walk the sky trails."

"When was this?"

Muskrat spread his fingers twice.

Erik clenched his teeth. It was little wonder Muskrat was nearly starved. The boy had been crawling around for nearly three weeks, likely finding a few berries and nothing else. Muskrat was correct to believe the others with him had been killed. Otherwise, they would have found him.

Muskrat touched his lips and spread his hands. "I am thankful Two Elks Fighting has come to me. I was wrong to take Two Elks Fighting's horse."

Erik smiled. It was the closest Muskrat would come to apologizing.

"The Blackfeet are also my enemy," Erik said. He gave more meat to Muskrat. "Eat. When you are strong, we will travel."

Muskrat again slept. The light faded. Still, the snow fell.

By daylight, two feet of snow covered the camp.

Muskrat stared out. "We do not go to Shadow Woman," he said without emotion, but he could not hide a quick flicker of distress.

Erik nodded. "My horse is good, but he cannot go over the mountains in this snow. You must not travel either, or poison goes into your leg."

Muskrat's eyes searched Erik's.

"Be calm. We are safe here," Erik said. "I can hunt. When you are strong, we will travel. I know a way to where we can cross the mountains to reach your people."

But Erik guessed that by the time Muskrat's injuries had sufficiently healed, it would be December. By then, the only route would be to travel several weeks to the southeast, where he could cross at a lower elevation before returning to the Lemhi Valley. The near passes would otherwise be hopelessly buried under many feet of snow until May or early June. But why would there be any rush? Muskrat could live apart from his people just as Erik could. The challenge would be in keeping him from insisting on traveling too soon.

Erik glanced out at the relentless snow. This would not have been his choice for a winter camp. With the deepening snow, the game would soon leave the immediate area and seek the canyons, but this storm would pass, and he would have some time to hunt. He could also trap. Anything that crawled, flew, or swam was food. He had cut cottonwood and willow before to get his horses through a winter. That he could do as well. There were worse places to be stranded.

CHAPTER 33

Muskrat slowly improved, but for a few days, Erik did not dare remove the bandages or splint. He wanted to bathe the injury and take a closer look. Fearing the worst, he heated some water and pulled the padding away from Muskrat's leg.

At first, he could not see from all the dried blood. He washed the area. Muskrat's brow furrowed. The cuts remained purple red but, to Erik's relief, seemed to be confined around the torn skin and flesh. He dried the area and rebound it. Erik could only guess about the break, whether the bones remained together or not.

"You put it back?" Muskrat protested.

"A bad spirit is inside. Shadow Woman will take it out when we get to Sacred River."

"It does not feel like there is a bad spirit."

"If you stand on it, for sure there will be," Erik said sternly. "It heals, but there is still poison."

Muskrat gave him an uncertain look.

Erik produced a crutch he had cut. "You can use this for now when you must make water, but keep still otherwise. I will go and get a big-ears deer. Before we travel, you must have clothes, and we must have meat." Erik had already cut up one blanket, and Muskrat did not have a shirt. His loincloth and tattered leggings offered little protection.

Erik rode Hatchet north away from the camp and toward an open, aspen-fringed slope, hopeful the deer had not already left for the lower country. He studied the peak that broke above the slope. Wind scoured its west face and sent a plume of bright white into the blue sky. Mountain sheep would likely browse the windswept areas, he knew. Perhaps he'd try to get a bighorn and make another bow. Winter was a good season for repairing and making new weapons, and Muskrat needed more than just a knife.

Topping a rise, Erik began descending into a small ravine. He found a small band of mule deer bedded down under the aspens. They rose on spindly legs to watch him, and their mule-like ears swiveled in his direction. He killed two. He might not have another opportunity. He dressed them but took some of the organs for later. The deer would be a start to providing meat, hide, and sinew but not enough for more than a few weeks.

He said a thanksgiving for them.

When Erik brought the deer into camp, Muskrat could not hide his amazement. "Two big ears." He hobbled out to look.

Erik told him to sit. "I will have you help shortly."

One animal he hung from a tree for later. He built a small firepit outside the lean-to. Across it, he laced some narrow poles, on which he hung the lean meat. He cleared a place next to the fire and placed some spruce boughs. He threw down an armload of dry wood.

"There. You can tend the coals and dry this meat." He helped Muskrat out onto the boughs.

Muskrat scowled but took up feeding a small fire from which he raked coals under the drying meat.

Erik put the deerskin in the creek and built himself a fleshing beam like those he used for cleaning his pelts. He cut an aspen and buried it at an angle near the lean-to and rounded off its butt. He also built a frame on which he could stretch the hide.

The following morning, Erik brought the skin up from the creek and began the fleshing process. He buried the tip of his knife in a block of wood to keep from cutting himself. He then positioned the hide over the fleshing beam and drew the blade against the skin to remove both the hair and membrane and any remaining flesh and pieces of fat. The fat he retained for rendering. Muskrat watched with a bemused look on his face. Erik guessed the reason.

As he had done for his pelts, Erik stretched the doeskin onto the frame and resumed scraping, picking all possible bits of fat and membrane from both sides of the hide. When finished, he placed the stretched hide opposite the meat racks near the fire to dry.

He checked the drying meat. In the cold weather, the drying would likely take several days.

"This is women's work," Muskrat said at last.

Erik had guessed his thoughts. "Do you see any women here?"

Muskrat shot him a look.

"When you hunted with your uncles, did you not carry their moccasins and tend their ponies? Did you not gather wood and build their fire? Are you a woman?"

Muskrat opened his mouth and then closed it. His eyes flashed. "No."

Erik laughed. "You did those things so the hunters could hunt, yes?"

Muskrat sat silently. Erik knew his thoughts. Erik had endured ridicule with the Sheepeaters when he'd gathered plants, tanned the hides, or carried wood to the fire. Eventually, the other boys had accepted his behavior but only because they'd decided it was what white men did.

"You took the burden from the men so they could make meat. It is not women's work to share the burden from another, whatever the task may be."

Muskrat smiled and tossed a bit of wood onto the area where he made the coals. "You are a white man. I am *Ne`we*. Shoshone."

"Yes," Erik said. "And let me ask you this, Muskrat: How is it that a man shows a woman he wishes to marry?"

Muskrat shot him another look but could not suppress a smile.

"Does he not go to the stream with her and carry water back to the camp? He does women's work to show her that she is first. Or are you too young to know these things?"

Muskrat sputtered and gestured, rapidly flicking his fingers. "I am ten and three this winter. I know these things."

"It is because the woman honors the man that she keeps his lodge, and it is because the man honors the woman that he hunts and provides for her," Erik said.

Muskrat shook his head. "You make my head hurt, Two Elks Fighting."

"We both do what is necessary so that we can soon return to your people."

The following day, while Muskrat continued to tend the coals, Erik took the doe's head, split it open, and removed the brain. He pounded it into a paste mixed with warm water and then rubbed it into both sides of the stretched hide. He allowed the paste to dry and then repeated the process. When he had worked both sides twice, he again set the stretched skin aside to dry.

Erik left the camp and walked into the surrounding woods and gathered the remaining rosehips and kinnikinnick berries he could find on the sparse shrubs where they were yet exposed under the trees or in windswept areas. Those were about the only berries that remained after the first snows. Along with some spruce-needle tea, the rosehips and kinnikinnick might stave away scurvy.

Erik began butchering the second deer and put Muskrat to drying its meat as well. He could not attend the second hide immediately and so buried it for later.

He attended to Muskrat's leg again and washed it. It appeared better. Muskrat again protested when he wrapped and splinted it.

"It is because it is wrapped that there is no poison," Erik said.

The meat of the first doe had finally dried. Erik and Muskrat powdered it by hammering it between stones Erik had brought from the nearby stream. Erik no longer got any looks from Muskrat, who apparently had overcome his women's-work prejudice.

They added the powdered meat into hot liquid fat Erik had rendered from the hide scrapings. They mixed in some dried rosehips and allowed the mixture to cool into pemmican cakes. Erik could survive a week on a pound of pemmican if necessary. He had done so before.

The first hide had dried. He took it to the fleshing beam and began jerking it across the beam, running it back and forth across the log.

"You can do this, Muskrat. Sit and work it across like I was doing."

He helped the boy get situated. Muskrat had probably seen it done before in somewhat a similar fashion. He worked it hard, running it back and forth, eventually breaking it into soft leather.

Erik dug another small pit and set up a small cone of poles, over which he stretched the softened hide. He lined the pit with coals and added some punk wood, creating a billowing smoke. The remainder of the day, he had Muskrat smoke the hide, take it off after a few hours, and then do the other side. The process made the new leather almost waterproof.

Erik began tanning the second hide. He did not remove the hair from this one but prepared only one side. This hide would serve as a second blanket.

The following morning, Erik took the finished doeskin, cut a slit approximately in its center, draped it over Muskrat's head, and cut holes for his arms. He trimmed it to length, took the trimmed portions, and turned them into two tubes. He punched holes, and using twine from his possibles bag, he sewed the tubes on for sleeves.

When he handed the shirt to Muskrat, he said, "Your mother can make her son another when he returns."

Muskrat's eyes sparkled. He threw aside the blanket and immediately slipped into his new shirt. "You do good work. I have watched, and I should now like to make some moccasins."

"Is that not women's work?" Erik teased.

Muskrat cast a wry smile. He took the leather, pulled it over his foot, cut it, and stitched on a top. He did a second one, finishing late the following evening. It had taken the entire doeskin to make the shirt and moccasins.

"But we will let Mother put beads on them," Muskrat said.

Erik laughed to himself. Muskrat had to hold out at some point, but the boy's sentiment mattered little. Erik had no beads.

New leggings were the last thing Muskrat needed, at least where the old legging had been ripped apart on his injured leg. That would take a third deer, which Erik found and killed after a lengthy hunt.

While he was tanning the third hide, another storm came and went. Erik was surprised Muskrat did not remind him of leaving to return to the Lemhi. Possibly he recognized they could no longer cross the passes toward the west, and Muskrat did not know about traveling south to where they could.

This day, Muskrat was restless and said, "If it was not too far, I would go to bathe."

"And you would have to chop the ice," Erik said.

Erik guessed that Muskrat was feeling ripe. It was little wonder after his being sequestered in the shelter and sleeping in animal skins with his leggings and loincloth grimy with sweat and dried blood. *Like I'm feeling*, Erik thought.

"Perhaps we will," Erik said. "You should soak your leg to pull out the poison." That was how Erik explained it to Muskrat to allow him to wash the wound.

Erik pulled out his skinning knife and waved to Muskrat. "Come help." He began jabbing his knife into the frozen soil, breaking it up. He and Muskrat broke and scooped out the earth until they had a narrow depression about two feet deep, two feet wide, and three feet long. Erik lined it with his oiled ground cloth and began filling the depression with water.

"I see you bring the water to me," Muskrat said, bemused.

"And like your mother makes her stew hot, we shall heat the water." Erik pulled some stones from the fire and rolled them into the water, where they hissed and sputtered, sending up steam.

Shortly, the water was warm. He pulled the stones out to reheat them.

"You sit and put your leg in the water," Erik said, gesturing.

After Muskrat settled near the edge, Erik untied the splint and removed the blanket shreds. The wound had healed, although the area was still blue black and dimpled with scar tissue. The bone had held.

Muskrat soaked his leg for a while.

"You wanted to bathe. You can bathe here," Erik said. "Give me your clothes."

Muskrat gave Erik a look but eventually yielded his leggings and loincloth and slid deeper into the water. He brought his legs up a little, sitting. "It is like the stinky water place," Muskrat said.

"But not stinky," Erik said, laughing. Muskrat referred to hot springs' usual rotten-egg odor. "And it will be even less stinky after we both wash and I get these clean." He took Muskrat's leggings and loincloth and boiled them a piece at a time in his coffeepot. He wrung them out and draped them on sticks near the fire.

Muskrat rubbed himself and looked around as if he were done.

"Your hair as well," Erik said. "If you were in the river, you would."

Muskrat leaned forward and splashed water over himself. He gasped, sitting back up.

"Good. Now get out; I must fix your bandage. There is still poison in your bone."

While Muskrat sat bundled in a blanket, Erik wrapped his leg. Muskrat seemed to accept his fate now and didn't give Erik any trouble as Erik refixed the splint.

Erik added more water and reheated it for his own bath. It was a tight squeeze into the small depression, but he managed to wash away some of his old sweat and dirt.

I've got to do this more often, Erik mused. He missed the hot springs. Then thoughts of Bright Shell flooded in. He squeezed his eyes, trying to force away the images of her and the times they had bathed together.

I can do nothing about those men at the present, Erik told himself. He glanced toward Muskrat. *And somehow, I have to get him back to his people.*

He realized how pleased he was that Muskrat had survived, his wounds had healed, he had not gotten blood poisoning, and his bone should now be mending. All that was good.

CHAPTER 34

Snow enveloped the valley, and the peaks to the north shone white. Storms regularly came in from the northwest and swept down the narrow valley, burying the lean-to. Erik had been fortunate to build it where he had. They were protected from the wind.

In places, the wind scoured the snow away, exposing the hillsides. Hatchet grazed those areas or foraged on the cottonwoods and willows in the draw.

In other areas, the wind piled the snow deep and heaped it in strips along the leeward side of the rocks and trees. The drifts kept Erik from traveling any distance.

This evening, they sat near the fire and shared a snowshoe rabbit Erik had snared.

"You should tell a story," Muskrat said. "During the cold seasons, Yellow Horse would call us to his lodge and tell us of things."

Erik smiled. It had been the same with the Sheepeaters.

"But do white men do the same?" Muskrat asked, frowning, seeming to reconsider his comment.

"Yes, but I fear you would not understand stories of trolls and fairies and Midsummer's Eve," Erik said.

Muskrat raised his eyes. "No, I do not know these things. I would listen."

"I think it would be better to listen to a story of the Tukudeka, the people you call brush dwellers."

"I would listen even to brush dwellers," Muskrat said.

Erik figured he'd had enough of sitting around and doing little since they had finished preparing the last deer, or he might not have listened. "Then I shall share a story that Gray Owl, the one we turned to, told us when I was the same number of winters as you. It is how the Tukudeka got the sheep horn bow."

Muskrat's eyes gleamed. He pulled his blanket more snugly about his shoulders and tossed some dry twigs onto the smoldering cooking fire, where they soon brightly blazed. It was customary that a young person should do so for the person who told the story.

"In the beginning, First Creator made all animals, and to each animal, he gave different gifts. He gave Beaver big teeth so Beaver could make his lodges, he gave Bird feathers so she could fly and warm her nest, and he gave Deer strong antlers and long legs to protect him from Coyote."

"Yes, this is much like the people's stories," Muskrat said, smiling. "He gave Salmon paddles to move through water."

"And he gave Rabbit long ears so he would listen and hear when Coyote or Wolf was near." Erik eyed Muskrat.

Muskrat glanced down and then back at Erik. He understood. All children should listen when a wise one told a story.

"He gave Sheep thick wool to stay warm, pads on his feet to climb rocky areas, and big horns to push away enemies," Erik said. "He gave Bear great claws and Wolf sharp teeth. Each animal received gifts, and each animal used his gifts to take care of his family.

"And then First Creator made Man, but he did not give Man any gifts. Man did not receive sharp teeth. Man did not receive feathers. He did not get claws. He did not get fur. He could only dig in the dirt and eat roots and leaves. Man's family starved and went naked."

Muskrat raised sparkling eyes and smiled. Although he was on the verge of manhood, tonight Muskrat reminded Erik of a child. Whether or not he believed the story did not matter.

"First Creator asked each of the animals to give Man a gift because he did not wish for Man to starve and go naked. The animals told First Creator that if they did this then Man would hunt and eat them all.

"'No,' First Creator said, 'I will tell Man he will not receive these gifts if he eats all the animals. He must only eat those he needs.'

"So the animals gave Man gifts. Beaver gave Man sticks to make into arrows and spears. Bird gave Man feathers to fly his arrows. Deer gave Man antlers to shape stones for his spears and arrows. All animals but Sheep gave Man gifts."

Muskrat watched Erik intently, now caught up with the story as a young child might have been.

"The animals asked Sheep why he did not give Man a gift.

"Sheep said, 'I only have horns I can give Man, but my horns are too hard for Man. He cannot use them.'

"So the animals said it was permitted for Sheep not to give Man a gift, but some were afraid that First Creator would know this and would allow Man to eat them all.

"But it was not Man who ate them all." Erik eyed Muskrat, and the boy drew back. "It was Bear!"

Muskrat smiled.

"In those days, Humpback Bear liked to eat Sheep, so that was what he did. No one could kill Bear, so Bear ate all the sheep he wanted, and Sheep became worried. There were soon only old sheep and no young sheep.

"'It is because you did not give Man a gift,' the others told Sheep.

"'But what can I give him? My horns are too hard. He cannot use them. Oh, we will soon all be eaten by Bear!' Sheep cried.

"'It is because you do not give him a gift,' the animals said. 'Give him your horns.'

"And so Sheep gave Man his horns.

"And Man said, 'Sheep is right. I cannot kill Bear with Sheep's horns. I can only make bowls and spoons with them.'

"But Raven knew what to do. He took Sheep's horns and threw them into the stinky water that bubbles hot. 'Come back tomorrow, Man; you will have an idea what to do,' Raven said.

"So Man came back in the morning and found that the bubbling water made Sheep's horn soft, and he made a bow, for that was all he could think of to do. And when the horn became dry, the bow was very good.

"Now Man could kill all the animals. He could make weapons and lodges and clothes. He could eat Deer and Fish and Buffalo. And he could kill Bear.

"When First Creator saw this, he was pleased. And he told the animals not to be afraid, because Man promised to kill only what he needed for his family. And as long as Man did this, the animals and Man would be happy. And that is how Man got the sheep horn bow."

Erik spread his hands, sending flickering shadows racing. The story had brought back bittersweet memories.

Muskrat's eyes shone in the dancing firelight. "That is a good story, uncle," he said. "It is the same for the people." He stirred the fire. "But the Lemhi do not make the sheep horn bow. We get them from the Tukudeka, your people. It is a good gift."

Later, Erik lay in his robes, listening to Muskrat's peaceful breathing. *His world is not mine,* Erik thought. *And it is not the animals to be feared. It is man to be feared. Only man brings evil into the world.* He thought of the two men somewhere toward the west. He was now impatient.

CHAPTER 35

This day, Erik took Hatchet and pushed north through the deep snow, toward the wind-scoured peak. He paused near some stunted pines where the wind had cleared the ground and exposed some of the short bleached grasses. He studied the open slopes that ran above him into rocky outcrops barren except for some stunted shrubs and a few twisted firs.

A band of bighorn sheep grazed above him. They seemingly did not take notice, but Erik knew otherwise. He picketed Hatchet and climbed upward to a cleft. He strung his bow and began a careful hunt back in the direction of the band, which would now be slightly below him.

Erik came upon the animals where they had bedded down among the boulders. Two rams with massive horns pulled at grass tufts off to a side and a few yards above the ewes. Those rams he did not want. He searched the other animals until he found a younger ram with good but less massive horns.

The young bighorn stood broadside to Erik. His horns curved around the sides of his head better than halfway. They would make a fine bow, Erik thought. The meat would be welcome as well.

Seeing the place where his arrow would pierce the animal, Erik said a prayer and asked the Great Mystery to guide it true. It buried itself deep behind the animal's shoulder, piercing the ram's heart. The ram went to his knees and then folded forward into the reddening snow. The animal's head rolled with his eyes staring sightlessly in Erik's direction.

Erik whispered, "Thank you, great curved horn, for giving me your spirit. May your life be one with mine and provide me with a fine bow by which I can feed myself."

The smaller rams and the ewes that grazed nearby had startled when the animal fell and now watched as if they wondered why their companion did not rise. They moved off, stepping up the hillside as if moving from the smell of death.

Erik reached the dead ram, spilled its blood, and began dressing the animal. He took the liver and heart. The entrails he left for coyotes or magpies. He made a pack of the meat and hide, and tying on the ram's head, he hoisted it onto his back and, struggling, descended the mountain to find Hatchet.

Upon seeing the bighorn, Muskrat said, "You bring a curved horn. Will you make a bow?"

Erik smiled. "I have told the story of the sheep horn bow, but I have not shared the secret of the sheep horn bow. I know Muskrat is not of the Tukudeka, but the Great Mystery sees that Muskrat and Two Elks Fighting share a camp, so I will share the secret of the horn bow if Muskrat wishes to help."

Muskrat struck his fists together, excitedly nodding. "Yes, I would learn the secret of the sheep horn bow and help you, uncle."

Erik immediately began working the sheep's head, stripping away the hide and flesh. Erik had watched Whistling Elk build the bow that he presently owned. He had given it to Erik after his vision-seeking, when he became known as Two Elks Fighting, but Erik had never built one of his own.

"We first need to heat the sheep head in hot water and slip the horn sheath off the bone," Erik explained. "We can use our bathing place but with more stones."

Muskrat nodded and scrambled to put stones into the fire.

"We do this for two nights," Erik said. "Much like when we dried the meat. I prepare the meat. You keep the water hot with fresh stones."

When the water was near boiling, Erik submersed the skull. While it soaked, he skinned the sheep and butchered the meat. Some he smoke-dried, and some he roasted fresh.

Muskrat kept the water near boiling, tending it for two days, at which point Erik pulled the head out. He showed Muskrat how to cut some remaining tissue from under the horn and then twisted the two sheaths from the bone. Using his hatchet and knife, Erik began the laborious task of splitting the horns. He used the back halves only. The front halves might later be fashioned into ladles or shallow bowls.

Erik ran his fingers along the back halves of the horns, feeling for cracks. "It is good, Muskrat," he said. "There are no breaks. These horns shall make a strong bow." He set the split halves aside. "Remember these things. First, we talk always to the spirit of the curved horn that has given us his horns. The curved horn must know that his life was not taken without use."

"Yes," Muskrat replied. "We do this as well for all animals we hunt, like your story—the big-ears deer, the white rabbit, and even the redfish." He gestured for each animal.

"Listen, and the curved horn may talk to you. Look. Feel. He will share some of his spirit with you. And when we have completed this bow, its spirit will remain within its horns that become this bow. Treat the animal with honor, and the bow you make from him will lend his strength to the hunter."

"Even if the hunter uses the bow to take another curved horn?" asked Muskrat.

"The curved horn knows you take its life with respect and only as necessary, as the Great Mystery says. If the curved horn knows this, it will allow you to take others. It knows you will honor its brothers as well. That is why you talk with it while you fashion this bow."

Erik returned the back halves of the split horns to the bath and added more hot rocks to begin another heating process.

On the second day, when the horns had sufficiently softened, Erik strapped each to a flat, heavy piece of wood. When fully dry, each horn held its new flattened shape.

While the horns cured, Erik hunted the rocky outcrops along the creek for a rough stone different from the stones they had used for making the pemmican and heating the water. He recognized and collected some sandstone, the stone the Swedes used to smooth wood.

He began sanding each horn and worked on each over the next several days. Erik explained his work as he carefully shaped each piece until it was worked into a shape about an inch and a half wide that tapered to a blunted point about fifteen inches long—a limb.

Erik instructed Muskrat in sanding as well but only the rough shaping.

When both halves were finished, he began the final shaping. In turn, he tied each horn to the fleshing beam, where he continued working, sanding, and shaping. Frequently, he stopped to check his work. There were no shortcuts. He sanded for a short while and then untied the horn limb and checked it against the second limb. Both had to be equal in thickness for their entire length. Taking care now meant less time when balancing the bow.

He finally reached the point when the two limbs were equal and ready to be attached. He sanded each end until they fit snuggly and overlapped by about three inches. Then, using a small metal bowl from his cook kit, he started some water boiling. He cut hide shavings into it and began boiling them down. Periodically, he skimmed the water off, until he had a thick glue in the bottom of the bowl, something Muskrat was also familiar with. It was the same hide glue the Shoshone used for fletching arrows and making their sinew-reinforced wood bows.

Erik also softened and shredded some sinew into long strips.

He warmed the two limbs, and with Muskrat helping, he painted glue onto both halves of the joint and joined them. Erik pulled some of the sinew through the glue and whiplashed it around both limbs, joining the two halves tightly together. He next spread glue the length of the outside of the bow and layered strips of sinew along its entire length. He bound sinew around the bow at the midpoints of each limb, at the tips of the bow, and again around the center grip.

"Here. We now let the bow rest," Erik said. "Tomorrow we balance the pull of the bow so the arrow it shoots flies straight."

After setting the bow aside, Erik immediately began work on the bowstring. He twisted sinew into longer and longer fibers until the fibers were of sufficient length. He then twisted three of the resulting cords together, having Muskrat hold one end while he twisted. He fastened loops on both ends. One loop was static; the other he could adjust to tighten or loosen the string.

He cut a small notch in each wingtip so it would accept the string and then strung the bow. He pulled and checked the bend of each limb as he drew the string back.

"See? The upper limb comes back too fast," Erik said. He allowed Muskrat to pull the bow as well.

He sanded the lower limb some more. He didn't work fast or overwork the limb. Accidentally overworking the limb would have meant reworking the upper limb. Too much back-and-forth would weaken the bow.

"Now, Muskrat, we shall see." Erik stood with his new bow and stepped away from the lean-to. Muskrat hobbled after. To Erik's dismay, he no longer used the crutch, but Erik held his tongue.

Erik restrung the bow and gently pulled and released the string. He slightly shortened the string and then restrung it, getting more tension. He nocked an arrow and, at half draw, released it. It felt good. Twice more, he fired arrows.

"This is it, Muskrat," Erik said. He pulled back to full draw and released the arrow. It whistled into the dirt bank he had cleared of snow. "You shall try." Erik handed the bow to Muskrat.

The youth nocked and released an arrow. It thunked into the dirt. "You make a fine bow, uncle," he said, grinning. "Tomorrow we should go to the people."

It was the demand Erik had expected and dreaded. He shook his head. "Sickness still lives in your leg, Muskrat, and there is snow on the pass; we must wait awhile."

"But this I do not feel." Distress filled Muskrat's eyes. "You said there was a way."

CHAPTER 36

The seasons had turned. Erik figured it was late February or early March. The sun shone longer and gave him hope that the snow would begin receding from the passes, but this was also the time when the heaviest snows came.

Erik and Muskrat tanned the sheepskin and made a new loincloth for Muskrat. Sheepskin made a better cloth for that use than did the doeskin. Muskrat was no longer as skinny. He had regained much of his strength and some weight. He no longer used the crutch but hobbled around on his leg quite ably. Erik gave up trying to keep him off it. His story about poison had lost its effect. Muskrat wanted to get to Shadow Woman so she would fix his leg so he could run again and not wobble. Erik's chest tightened. The boy would never again run and would always have a limp.

Muskrat practiced with the bow. They worked on arrows. He enticed Erik to tell another story.

"We should go now," Muskrat said when Erik finished the story. "Surely this is the snow-eater moon."

Erik could see why Muskrat thought so. The sun shone in a blue sky. The last heavy snow had begun retreating. "Do you hear the longnecks honking, Muskrat? It is not the snow-eater moon. This is the time for the fools' snow."

Muskrat shook his head. "It is snow-eater moon. Soon it will be greening-grass moon. We should go."

Erik woke to the sound of hoofbeats. He turned over in time to see Muskrat atop Hatchet, moving quickly through the thinning snow.

He scrambled up. "Fool boy." He dressed. Muskrat had taken the new bow, of course. "To blazes. Think of that," Erik muttered. "I save his life, make him clothes, and make a bow"—Erik had not decided to give it to him—"and the kid runs off. On my horse!"

He grabbed some dried meat and set out, following Hatchet's tracks. "Hope he doesn't break his leg again—or this time, his neck."

Erik followed for half an hour before he caught sight of Hatchet coming back in his direction without a rider.

The horse came up to him, and he caught the animal's head. "So where'd you dump him, boy?"

Erik swung up onto Hatchet and retraced Muskrat's steps. He spotted Muskrat trying to hide in the timber and then run, hobbling badly. Erik shouted for him to stop. "You will make the poison come into your leg!"

Muskrat stopped trying to run and crumpled, gasping.

Erik slid off Hatchet and went to him. Pain streaked Muskrat's face.

Erik bent over the boy. "Was I not right, Muskrat? Did the poison not come back?" He felt Muskrat's leg. It already swelled rapidly. Thankfully, he did not feel a dislocated bone. Maybe it had held. He could not say the same for the small bones in his foot or ankle.

"I am sorry, uncle," Muskrat gasped.

"I told you I would take you to your people, Muskrat. It is not yet time, but soon."

As if to prove Erik's point, a sudden gust of shivering wind hit, singing across the snow, kicking it up. Shadows raced across the sky. A massive cloud billowed above and bore down on them.

Muskrat's eyes widened.

"Come on, Muskrat. We've got to get." He hoisted the boy onto Hatchet.

Muskrat grimaced and held Hatchet's mane.

Erik swung up behind him and clucked to the horse. "We've got to get out of here, Hatchet."

The wind hit again. Huge, wet, icy pellets bore down, stinging, and soaked them in moments.

In another hundred yards, the world went white. The wind howled like a screaming demon. Erik bent over Muskrat and prayed Hatchet could find the way back. This was the kind of blizzard that came in the spring—the storm he had feared.

They almost walked through the camp before Erik saw the outline of the shelter. He carried Muskrat into the lean-to and then turned Hatchet loose.

"Go find some trees, boy." He patted the animal. This was a strength-sapping, wet snow that could quickly kill.

Erik slipped into the shelter. Muskrat sat with pain yet streaking his face, shivering. Erik shivered as well. The wet snow had penetrated to his skin. He was soaked. Muskrat was not as soaked, mostly because Erik had had his back to the brunt of the snow, and Muskrat had ridden somewhat protected in front of him.

The light was dim, but Erik pulled away Muskrat's leggings and examined his leg more closely. It had turned angry blue black and was badly swollen.

"See? The poison is back, Muskrat." Erik found the old splint and padding. "And so this goes back on." He strapped the pieces back onto Muskrat's leg.

"I am sorry, uncle," Muskrat said.

By morning, two feet of new snow covered the camp, but as quickly as it had come, the storm had raced away. Patches of blue bled through. Erik grabbed a deer hide and headed out to find Hatchet. The horse was near the creek, under some timber. Erik rubbed the animal down and brushed off the snow that caked him. Hatchet shook himself, sending a shower of ice at Erik.

"Thanks, fellow," Erik murmured. He kept rubbing. "Glad to see you made it and that you were smart enough to get into these trees and get out of it." He patted the horse. "Thanks for not killing Muskrat. I can't blame him for wanting to get out of here. But now he just made it likely that we won't be going for some time."

Erik returned to the lean-to.

Muskrat sat outside near the fire with his splinted leg sticking out. He heated water. "I shall make some stew," he said. Apparently, he was trying to make amends.

Erik didn't chastise Muskrat. It was in the boy's blood to want to return to his people. Likely, he ached with the need to let them know he did not walk the sky trails. He had finally given in. Had he returned on a horse with a sheep horn bow, no matter the way he had come by it, he would have been received with great honor. *Until I showed up*, Erik thought. Then he might have been turned away from the Lemhi. But that was not how a young man thought—he thought not about what the repercussions might be but about what the honors might be.

A few days later, the wet snow had begun to melt. Erik caught up Hatchet and told Muskrat to behave himself. "Work on your arrows."

"Where does uncle go?" he asked.

"We need meat," Erik said. "It is a long cold season yet, and now we must stay here awhile longer."

Muskrat glanced away.

Erik returned the next day with another bighorn ram. Muskrat's eyes flew wide.

"Because we must remain awhile longer, Muskrat should make a bow."

Muskrat grinned.

Weeks later, the bow was finished. Muskrat practiced with it, sending arrows into the now barren dirt bank.

"It is good, uncle," Muskrat said, beaming.

"It is a man's bow," Erik said. "Perhaps Muskrat goes on a vision-seeking this season. I will tell Yellow Horse that a certain boy needs a man's name."

Muskrat's eyes widened. He stood taller.

Snow still clung deeply to the passes, but it was time.

CHAPTER 37

Muskrat killed a mule deer just outside their lean-to. Erik was with him when he did and praised him for his skill. They dressed the deer, packed some of the meat, and roasted some to eat. They struck camp, strapped on their bedrolls and gear, and headed west. Erik walked, while Muskrat rode. He would not walk the entire distance, but the less Muskrat was on his leg, the better it would be.

Erik and Muskrat talked little. They had survived the winter, but it was yet a long distance to the Sacred River. There could easily be a Blackfeet or Crow hunting party out.

Erik followed the valley where they had camped down into the headwaters of the Silver Bow River. Ducks and geese swarmed the countryside. He swung south and topped the low divide that again dropped him into the Big Hole River drainage, but instead of continuing to the Jefferson toward the south, he turned west up the Big Hole. He followed it through low mountains south toward its headwaters. He watched the high divide to the west and checked the passes for snow. This early, he doubted anyone had crossed.

Even if the snow had gone, Erik had no stomach for crossing into Idaho Territory over Big Hole Pass or continuing down the North Fork of the Salmon River to reach Salmon City, not with Muskrat in his company. He momentarily thought about retrieving Leaf, but that part of his life was finished. He took Muskrat south to the Lemhi only out of his promise to see the boy returned safely. He had not fulfilled his promise to avenge Bright Shell, and Runs Fast and others had sworn to destroy him unless he did. He decided he would not visit Cusowat or the others but simply would leave Muskrat outside the camp, and Muskrat could walk the distance home.

The weather was clear this day. He let Muskrat walk for a short distance. The boy was not in pain as near as Erik could discern, but the bones had not healed well. He walked with a bad limp, slightly dragging his left foot. Muskrat still might have hoped Shadow Woman could suck out the poison, but Erik doubted it. Likely, he accepted that he would be lame for the remainder of his life. But something also told Erik that Muskrat knew he needed only a good horse to be equal to any man, and Erik believed he would soon have one.

Erik took notice of the yet snow-blanketed pass where he had crossed with Samstrung's pack train on the way to the Dutchmen's strike. Farther south, he made out the narrow valley where his cabin had been. He pulled his eyes away. Even if he'd had the stomach to try that pass, it was also cloaked white.

He intended to try to cross where he would still be north of the Sacred River band's winter camp but south of Salmon City. He did not care for the east side of the divide, where now he was more likely to encounter others, white as well as Indian. He did not care to explain why he traveled with a Shoshone youth.

He turned west toward the divide.

Days later, they had crossed the divide and approached the Lemhi's camp. Muskrat had been having increasing trouble walking and rode double behind Erik.

When Erik caught sight of the encampment, he stopped in near disbelief. Instead of the dozen tepees he was accustomed to seeing, there were at least sixty lodges spread across the ground along the river. Tendoy and his band had indeed returned to the Lemhi River last winter. Erik wished to meet the chief he had heard so much about, but he would not. He told Muskrat to dismount. The youth protested.

"You said you would tell Yellow Horse it is time for my man's name."

An ache welled in Erik's throat. He tried to explain, but it was too late. A band of three horsemen, quickly joined by another three, trotted in their direction.

Erik immediately recognized Runs Fast, Crooked Leg, and Black Buffalo. He did not recognize the other three horsemen.

"I see Yellow Horse!" Muskrat exclaimed in joy. "He comes with Hunts Elk and Buffalo Tail. They do not walk the sky trails! Aiyee! Let us go to them."

"I cannot," Erik said.

Muskrat slid to the ground. He stared at Erik, frowning.

"Go to Yellow Horse," Erik said. "Tell him I bring you home. Tell him to bring Cusowat of the Sacred River band and Strong Wolf. Tell them I wish to see my daughter. Go quickly."

Muskrat's eyes widened. "You have a daughter with the people?" He shook his head. "Why do you not speak of her before?"

"I married Strong Wolf's daughter. We had a child. The reason I am where I find you is because I seek the men who took my wife's breath. She who brought the people light now walks the sky trails."

Distress filled Muskrat's eyes. "You turned away from seeking those men when you found me?"

Erik nodded. "I gave you my word I would bring you home, but I also gave my word I would not return here until I had taken their breath. That is why I cannot go with you to the village."

Muskrat shook his head, becoming agitated. The boy understood but found it difficult to accept.

"You can do this for me, Muskrat," Erik said. "My daughter is known as Glad Spirit. She is with Jumping Deer, wife of Cusowat and daughter of Strong Wolf. Watch over her for me as you can."

Muskrat visibly shook. "I can do this, uncle, but I do not understand." He held his bow tightly, seeking Erik's eyes.

Erik stared ahead until the riders had closed about him. He read the hate in Runs Fast's eyes and the scowls on Crooked Leg's and Black Buffalo's faces. The other three Lemhis, whom Muskrat knew, he could not read, but none seemed particularly joyed to see him or Muskrat. Erik wondered what other misfortune had befallen the Sacred River band and for what he would soon take the blame.

Muskrat glanced from Erik to Runs Fast, apparently recognizing the threat. "But for my life, you could have avenged the woman who brought light. You have sacrificed your honor for me! Aiyee."

"Perhaps, Muskrat," Erik said. He kept his eyes on Runs Fast, who fingered a rifle and brought it up to bear on him. "But I do not enter the village. Do as I have asked, Muskrat."

Muskrat limped toward Yellow Horse.

"Stand there," the man said loudly. "You have brought dishonor."

The boy froze.

"But for you who disobeyed, Buffalo Tail would not bear this scar."

A man pulled off his buckskin shirt. A jagged, white-marbled line crossed his shoulder.

Buffalo Tail spoke. "We should all walk the sky trails but that Yellow Horse leads us to where the Blackfeet cannot follow."

Muskrat stood with his head down. It appeared that neither Erik nor Muskrat was welcome.

Erik spoke. "I bring Muskrat back from the spirit world. He comes back to you so that he can prove himself." It was true that Muskrat had repeatedly expressed his desire to return to the people. Only now did Erik realize why.

"Ha, he is but a foolish boy who disobeyed," Yellow Horse spat. "He put us at risk. Good horses were lost. He brought dishonor to his father. It would have been better had he been left to feed the wolves."

Erik tried to steady himself. They were not overjoyed to see Muskrat's return. The youth stood unmoving and braced in shame. Apparently, he had not been invited on the hunt. It was common for a youngster to secretly accompany a raiding or hunting party. In some ways, it was expected; however, it was also not uncommon for a youth to bring disaster because of his inexperience.

Erik challenged Yellow Horse. "You say he brings dishonor. I see Muskrat as a fine hunter. He builds a fine bow and provides meat for us. He brings meat to the people."

Erik saw the men's eyes move to Muskrat's sheep horn bow. Of course, Erik had provided meat and helped Muskrat build the bow, but that was not what was important. That Muskrat had done his part as well was what mattered.

"But he loses his horse," Yellow Horse said. The man's eyes had softened.

Erik breathed more easily. This was but a test and means of telling Muskrat his place. It was a way of reinforcing that he must always obey and follow when directed to do so. Inside, these men were overjoyed to see Muskrat.

"Ah, but for being injured when leading the enemy from you, he would be bringing you *my* horse," Erik said. "I can tell you this of Muskrat: he has not yet done his vision-seeking, but he is already much a man. I know he leads the Blackfeet away from his uncles. He falls, and his spirit has nearly gone from his body, yet he steals my horse to return to his people. He fights me until he can no longer fight. He shows much bravery. Instead of challenging him for a child's mistake, the people should sing a song for him."

All had quieted.

"I tell all who will listen: Muskrat should seek his vision this season. He already carries a man's bow. He should carry a man's name."

For the first time, Muskrat raised his head and glanced toward Erik.

Runs Fast spat. "This man does not know this. He is little white boy. He is not of the people."

Yellow Horse and the others turned toward Runs Fast.

Erik said, "I am Two Elks Fighting of the Tukudeka. I know your ways, and I speak the truth of Muskrat."

Yellow Horse addressed Muskrat. "Are Two Elks Fighting's words true?"

Muskrat nodded. "But as you can see, Two Elks Fighting helps me as well. He gives me life. And this bow I hold is because he taught me the secrets of the curved horn. I have come back because it is right." He stepped toward Buffalo Tail and held out the bow. "I gift this to you, uncle. You pulled the enemy away so that I could lead them from you."

Buffalo Tail stiffened and held up his hand. "No, Muskrat. We both did what warriors must do. You must keep your bow. You will need your bow for when we go to hunt buffalo."

Trilling arose. The news of Muskrat's return had spread. Others from the village approached.

"You do not return with scalps, little white boy," Runs Fast snarled. "You dishonor yourself and Strong Wolf's daughter. You lie to Strong Wolf."

"It is true I do not return with scalps," Erik said. "This is why I do not come into the village, though I wish to see my daughter, and I wish to see my brothers. I honor my word. Yes, I will leave."

"We shall follow, and perhaps you will never return."

Yellow Horse shot a look toward Runs Fast. "It is each man's decision to do what he wishes, but I see that Two Elks Fighting has returned one who was lost. I see that he does not take a life but that he returns a life."

"Bah," Runs Fast spat. "He has no scalps. He should leave now."

Erik saw that Muskrat was now caught up in the arms and trilling of the others, perhaps his family. Erik held fast, still facing Runs Fast, Crooked Leg, and Black Buffalo. He hoped that Muskrat had relayed his message and that Jumping Deer would bring forth his daughter so he might catch a glimpse.

"I ask that Cusowat brings my daughter," Erik said again.

Runs Fast straightened. "You have no daughter," he said, and he spat.

A crawling cold bit into Erik. It couldn't be. He felt a weakness in his stomach.

"You must leave. You are no longer of the people. She is of the people."

She is of the people. Erik trembled as the cold vanished. She was alive, but Runs Fast intended to prevent him from seeing her. Erik now reasoned that he remained living only because he had brought back Muskrat.

"I tell you I will go, Runs Fast, but I wish to speak with Cusowat and to see my daughter. You will not see me again until I have avenged the woman who brought the people light."

Runs Fast spat again. "Bah, you say this before, little white boy. And as we can see, you lie. You bring only evil." He cocked his rifle. "As Yellow Horse says, I can choose."

Crooked Leg scowled. "I say we let Two Elks Fighting return to the shadow lands, for that is surely where he dwells. There is no need to kill him. The shadows will kill him."

Erik saw Cusowat approaching, and close beyond him were his wives, one being Jumping Deer. On her hip, she carried Glad Spirit, who was now eight months old. Erik swept his eyes to the small face. A stabbing numbness raced through him. Even as young as the baby was, he immediately saw Bright Shell gazing back. In anguish, Erik tore away to focus on Cusowat.

"I am glad to see my brother," Cusowat said. "Runs Fast does not speak for the people. It is good that Two Elks Fighting brings back Muskrat. I would welcome Two Elks Fighting to my lodge. Tendoy hunts. It is I who speaks for the people when he is away, not Runs Fast or Yellow Horse."

Erik swallowed. "Thank you, my brother, but you know I cannot. I have not taken the breath of the *wo'api-taa*, the maggot worms, and this is my promise. But I can see Jumping Deer with Glad Spirit, and this is good. It makes my heart glad. I will go now until I fulfill my word."

Erik straightened and looked out toward all who had gathered. "And for those who can hear my words, I renew my promise. And this I wish to present to Strong Wolf as a sign of that promise." He pulled the new sheep horn bow he had made and tossed it to Cusowat.

Cusowat examined it. He nodded. "Yes, I shall give this to Strong Wolf."

Before he could let his heart overwhelm him, Erik turned Hatchet and headed north. The soft trilling caught his ears before he was out of sight of the camp. Was it for a person now lost to the people, or was it a thanksgiving to Two Elks Fighting?

ELK CITY

CHAPTER 38

Erik debated his direction. He avoided Salmon City and headed up the North Fork of the Salmon River, uncertain if he should return to the Big Hole and start from there or just head into the nearest camp on the Clearwater River and hope to get lucky.

A few miles up the North Fork, he reached a somewhat dilapidated waystation. Smoke curled from its stone-and-mud chimney. A few chickens scratched around a low-slung outbuilding. A shoddy corral contained several horses and mules. A bit of a garden had recently been tilled. Nothing green yet showed. Something cooking smelled good.

Inside the log structure were a few crude shelves containing some mining gear and some food stocks mixed with odors of leather and whatever was cooking. A potbelly stove stood in the corner, with a coffeepot pushed to the back. Erik took note of a few rifles leaning in a rack and a couple of pistols hanging on pegs. A short, stocky man with a black mustache and a tattered gray shirt came from behind a curtain that partitioned the large room.

"Welcome, mister. I'm the proprietor, Hiram Eggert." He raised expectant eyes.

"Erik Larson." Erik nodded a greeting. "I thought if you had a meal, I'd have a plate." He glanced around. "And maybe a few supplies."

"Emma!" Eggert shouted. "Got a traveler, if ya can fix some vittles."

Muttering arose from behind the curtain amid clanging pots. "Be just a minute," a woman's voice sang back. Likely, the couple lived on the other side of the kitchen.

"If yer plannin' on going into the Big Hole—or the Bitterroot, for that matter—there's still snow, but you should get across. A couple a earlier travelers have been through."

"I'm thinking of heading west across the Clearwater drainage to some of the gold camps," Erik said.

Eggert squinted. "Cross it?" He ran a hand through dark hair. "You better have more'n a few supplies. Yer gonna be bucking snow up to yer ears unless yer not in a rush and can give it a week or two."

Erik sat heavily at the only table. "I have no stomach for sitting any longer," he said. "I'd go if it was the dead of winter."

"Coffee?" Eggert pulled the pot off the stove, poured a cup, and set it down in front of Erik. A strong, overdone coffee odor enveloped him.

"Thanks." Erik took a sip and quickly decided he might be leaving most of it. He did not need to spend what little money he had on a meal, but he figured it might get him some information. He had nothing to lose by talking to this man.

Shortly, a busty woman with a blue apron covering her calico dress delivered a plate of venison, beans, and corn bread. "Be four bits," she said with a dour face. The mixed tangy smells reminded Erik it had been a long while since he'd had a store-bought meal.

Erik dug out a half-dollar. "Thank you, ma'am."

Emma Eggert wiped her hands across her apron before taking the coin and pocketing it. She stood aside, appearing to want to be in on the news. The way they both behaved, Erik was surprised they didn't set plates for themselves and join him. Maybe they hadn't had many travelers to talk to.

"By chance, you see two men come by here, Mr. Eggert? It would have been last fall, about the time of the first heavy snow. They'd be heading south toward Salmon City. One man is short two fingers. The other has a scar across his face."

Eggert was silent for a moment. "Yer just checking whether they come this way but thinking they headed into the Clearwater country, ain't ya? You ain't interested in the gold camps."

"I'd be obliged." Erik avoided anything more.

Eggert shook his head. "No one comes to mind, but not many stop here since Salmon City's not much more'n a day south. Depends on how short a grub they are after comin' over the pass, whether they stop or not." He snickered.

Erik could not be sure the men had not come this way, but Eggert's answer helped solidify the feeling he had that they had gone to the Clearwater country. He took a bite of his meal. Unfortunately, the tangy odor was not validated by the taste, but he was hungry. The corn bread was the most palatable.

"You been looking all winter?" Eggert asked.

"I have a bit. I've got my reasons. They stole from me," Erik said, trying to preempt the *why* question.

"You ever been in the Clearwater country?" Eggert asked.

"I've been west on the Salmon some but never north to the Clearwater."

"Let me show you something then, Mr. Larson." Eggert unrolled a map. "I hope ya don't mind."

The map reminded Erik of the one Pete Samstrung and Virgil Williams had pored over when they were trying to locate the Dutchmen's strike. He should have paid more attention.

"More people than not get turned around up there. A lot go in that don't come out."

Erik did not think he would be one of them, but he was open to Eggert's perspective.

"There's three main rivers. About like the tines of a pitchfork. Way up here is the North Fork. The first gold was found at the west end of it." He moved his finger down the lines representing the river to a place marked *Pierce*. "Then there's the Middle Fork. It forms up where the Lochsa and Selway come together. No gold. Only timber." He traced his fingers from a spot marked *Lolo Pass* down to where two rivers converged. "And here's the South Fork, where yer headin'. Some good gold along it. From about this point west." He put his finger on Elk City and then Newsome. He swept his fingers across the map. "After the Clearwater picks up the South Fork, it flows north and then west to where it joins the Snake at Lewiston."

"I have been to Lewiston," Erik said. "Went up there from a place north of Boise City."

"So then you know where Mount Idaho is. Well, the country directly east of Mount Idaho is all Clearwater country." He ran the palm of his hand from Mount Idaho to Montana Territory.

Seeing the rivers laid out on the map sobered Erik. The two men could have been anywhere.

"When you reach the divide up the North Fork, go west nearly straight across the upper reaches of the Bitterroot to get into the Selway, and then go across part of the Selway to the South Fork. If you can get across. The timber is thicker'n porcupine quills, and snow'll be horse-belly high in places. When ya come outta all that, you'll be at Elk City. There's a good road west of there but none before ya get there." Eggert traced his fingers across from the divide to the west. "About a four-day hike if yer lucky but likely six or seven this time of year. The Nez Percé made a trail through, if you can find it. It mostly follows the ridgelines between the Salmon and the northern drainages."

"Thank you kindly," Erik said. "For what do I owe this?"

Eggert rolled up the map. "Seen you when you come in, and seen something was eating bad at ya."

Erik finished what he could of the meal, left the coffee, and then rounded up a few supplies that would get him across the country, which apparently was a timber jungle, from the way Eggert had described it, and one yet deep in snow.

He paid for the supplies. "Mighty obliged, Mr. Eggert. And you, Mrs. Eggert. Thanks for the meal." He nodded at her. She returned a slight smile, making Erik wonder if he were the first to thank her for a meal. Then, considering his meal, he figured he might have been.

"Good luck. I hope you can settle what's eatin' at ya, Mr. Larson," Eggert said as Erik stepped out the door.

CHAPTER 39

Erik had no difficulty in following the trail up the North Fork to the divide, but there the trail forked in several directions. The main trail seemed to veer toward the east, and a second branch continued north.

"The upper Bitterroot valley. Sure looks pretty, Hatchet. Wish that was the way they were heading, but only John Owen's fort's up there, and I doubt they'd be welcome."

Erik gazed west, looking for the third trail. He was met by an undulating blanket of snow and dark conifers. That was the direction he intended to travel. He scouted for some sign of a trail but found nothing.

"It has to follow the ridgeline," Erik muttered. He picked the broadest section and headed west.

Eventually, the conifers and snow thinned, and muddy parks opened. He was relieved when he finally found old travois marks.

For several miles, Erik followed the ridgeline, occasionally finding the marks but generally just heading west, until the ridgeline swung south and abruptly became a line of jagged peaks. South of the peaks was the Salmon River drainage. He avoided the peaks, dropped north of them, and crossed through several tributaries that made up the upper Bitterroot drainage. Erik quickly understood what Eggert had meant about getting turned around. This was a country of twisting whitewater streams and dense timber that appeared nearly identical in all directions.

Erik camped off the ridge near a lily pond in a small meadow. The ridgeline he had followed was barren of water, except for the snowfields, but it was not difficult to move down into the head of one of the many streams that drained the ridge. These mountains were unlike the divide that bordered the Montana and Idaho territories.

Although they lay unbroken in all directions, they tended to top out at a similar elevation. No great peaks blocked travel across the drainages, yet these mountains were deceptively rugged, and nothing was flat.

A day later, Erik reached the top of another ridgeline, where he again picked up travois tracks. He had crossed the upper Bitterroot drainage and now overlooked the Selway drainage. It was worse—nothing but thick timber and blowdowns clogging narrow ravines and whitewater streams met his view.

Despite his desire to remain on top, Erik was frequently forced to drop down to skirt the snowfields. When he did, thick timber blocked and slowed his progress until he could get around it and relocate the trail. The trail, when he could follow it, repeatedly twisted north and then south and only begrudgingly edged toward the west. A straight line did not exist. It was little wonder that it took five or more days to cross something that should have been crossed in three days.

Erik paused high above a turbulent stream with his way again blocked by snow.

"Hatchet, I admit those Nez Percé were smart. You'd be more than tempted to drop down into one of these streams. If you did, you'd never get out, and they don't much track west. No, sir, we wouldn't have stood a chance without this trail. Maybe if you want to stay in the bottom and prospect for gold, but if you're interested in crossing this country, you'd better stay up here, even in the snow."

Late afternoon, Erik crossed a low rise and descended into a small river valley. He smelled woodsmoke and soon encountered some Chinese working a small prospect, the first people he had seen in days. He had finally entered gold country. Automatically, he began checking hoofprints for the scuff mark.

The miners were friendly enough, but as he expected, they regarded him carefully. They had likely seen Indians, and with his buckskins, he somewhat resembled one. Erik closely inspected the workings to discern if the two men were there. He asked about nearby camps, recalling those Eggert had mentioned and indicated on the map, particularly Elk City and Newsome.

The Chinese he spoke with seemed not to understand him, but he kept asking until he met one who spoke some English.

"Oh Oh Ganday!" he exclaimed, grinning. "Ovah mountain." He pointed northwest.

Erik's blood rushed. Oh Oh Ganday was not one of the camps Eggert had mentioned.

He headed up a stream in the general direction the Chinese had pointed. Numerous signs of small placers quickly appeared. Remnants of old campsites, a few tattered tents, and a few log buildings were strewn through the timber. It appeared the easy gold was gone, and the earlier miners had gone with it.

He crossed the summit and descended into a gentle, timber-choked valley where smoke curled from several hidden buildings. Presently, he encountered a rapidly flowing creek that drained toward the north. A few log structures marked where a small town once had flourished but now was mostly abandoned. Dozens of Chinese milled about. He recognized their distinctive shops—a butcher, a mercantile, and a couple of saloons. One building had an old sign: Orogrande Saloon. Erik saw no whites.

The Chinese nodded at him and grinned broadly. He nodded in return.

The name Orogrande gave him pause. There had been a strike on Loon Creek named Oro Grande. Samstrung had considered heading there to outfit it, but Craig Weston, one of his competitors, had done so. Erik had been interested in locating the new camp because its location description matched one of the Sheepeaters' winter camps. This Orogrande was in the Clearwater drainage. There was no connection other than the name, and this Orogrande had passed its heyday.

Erik moved on, heading north down the rapidly flowing river. They called it Crooked River—a name well suited. Much of it had been placer mined, and the places that had not been had at least a dozen Chinese manning sluice boxes, wheeling dirt to them, and shoveling it in. Their singsong voices filtered down to him as he rode past. He spotted several of the rock huts where they lived. Windrows of neatly stacked and washed cobbles snaked up the draws and lined the creeks.

Maybe the rich gold had been dug, but apparently, there was sufficient remaining to satisfy the Chinese. None seemed idle. Work might taper off later in the season, but presently, there was plenty of water from the snowmelt, and they were taking advantage of it.

Where Crooked River joined the Clearwater, Erik turned upstream. According to what he remembered from the map, he was a few miles downstream from Elk City. The ground was equally dug, and he encountered more Chinese camps.

"Best we find a camp spot ourselves, Hatchet," Erik muttered. He turned up a draw that seemed to be less occupied and less dug. A trickle of water emerged from it. *That could be the reason. Not enough water to run a sluice.*

A mile up, he found a suitable site. Snowbanks rested against a low hill. Erik set water on to boil, and Hatchet grazed on the new grass. Erik watched the sun bleed from the sky as it painted the tips of the rocks across the valley an eerie pink and orange.

"Funny," Erik said. "I went more than a week without seeing a soul. Now I'm in the thick of others, even though they are Chinese. I think I rather prefer last week."

CHAPTER 40

In the morning, clouds flooded in, and rain threatened. Erik traced back to the Clearwater. South of Elk City, he noticed Nez Percé ponies grazing on a hillside a short distance from several tepees. The town of Elk City was on the Nez Percé Trail and several Nez Percé families had set up their camp nearby for trading with the townspeople.

Woodsmoke permeated the air as he caught sight of log buildings stretched along a muddy street. Several Chinese dressed in their customary loose-fitting blue cotton pants, tunics, and conical hats filled the street. It appeared this end of Elk City was where they had their shops and businesses. Despite several buildings in disrepair or vacant, these buildings were brightly lettered in Chinese red, including one that sported the Chinese flag. Their owners grinned and bowed as he passed. Erik nodded toward them, wondering what a proper greeting entailed. They clasped their hands inside their large sleeves, grinned, and bowed again with their black queues swinging as they bobbed their heads.

About the time he began wondering if Elk City was like Orogrande and populated only by Chinese, he noticed a US flag atop a building at the far end of the street. Several horses and some men were nearby. He passed a two-story structure with a sign above a wide door: "Elk City Hotel. Boarders welcome." Wickermsham mercantile was where the horses stood with the US flag. Directly across from it was the Buffalo Gulch Saloon. Another building had a sign—L. P. Brown and Company—but appeared boarded up. Possibly there were a few other open businesses he did not notice. Erik bet there were fewer than fifty whites and likely four times as many Chinese. He stopped near the boardinghouse.

Three men spilled out onto the street from the saloon, engaged in a loud argument. They paused long enough to carefully scrutinize Erik before resuming their argument. Two other men nearby had also taken notice of Erik. He nodded a greeting.

"Guess not many newcomers come into town," Erik muttered as he swung off Hatchet.

The odor of something delicious baking wafted out into the street from the boardinghouse. His stomach grumbled. Erik hesitated. Mrs. Eggert's fare had smelled appetizing as well.

He entered the boardinghouse and found the proprietor, Mrs. Abigail Hanson, to whom he introduced himself.

"The only woman in the district," she said with crinkly pale eyes. She wiped work-worn hands on a green apron that covered a brown print dress. She was slender like a beanpole, with salt-and-pepper hair tied in a bun. "Welcome to Elk City, Mr. Larson." She closely scrutinized Erik. He guessed why: his hair needed a trim, and he wore buckskins. Probably she could smell his woods-and-smoke odor.

Erik glanced around. A torn lace curtain blew back from the entry of a dining area off to one side. The wooden tables and chairs appeared marred and worn.

Mrs. Hanson must have guessed his thoughts. "It is what you see." She straightened her apron. "Indeed, I believe Mr. Hanson and I will be leaving this season unless, by God's grace, the War Eagle pays out. Otherwise, this is not a fitting place anymore. Only a few miners too stubborn to go looking for new prospects, and they ain't much good for paying their bills. And to beat all, the Chinese are settlin' in."

"But you do have a room?" Erik asked.

"Course I do. Supper and a bed is a dollar, and if you want, I can round you up a hot bath for another dollar."

"That's what I'm in mind for," Erik replied. He mentally counted his remaining money.

"I'll see if Sam Chung can lend me a hand," Mrs. Hanson said. "I've finished with breakfast, unless you need something. I might have some biscuits and ham remaining. I can rustle up a plate for four bits. Supper is at six o'clock sharp."

Despite his watering mouth, Erik declined. "I had breakfast." It explained the lingering odor. "Is there someone who can tend my mount? I didn't notice a livery stable."

"Sam Chung can take your horse as well," Mrs. Hanson replied. "The Chinese have a place. Used to be where Alonzo Brown kept his mules."

Erik caught the sound of muted thunder rolling down from the timbered ridge beyond. For a moment, he thought it might have been dynamite, but a glance at the clouds streaming in told him otherwise. At least he had made it to town in advance of the rain. From the look of the black cloud bellies, anyone on the trail would soon be drenched.

"Well, Mr. Larson, looks like you're in good time." Mrs. Hanson had also noticed. "You can carry your packs inside. Your room is at the far end. Sam Chung will be here to get your horse."

"How much for the care of my horse?"

"Another dollar."

"Three dollars?" Erik sputtered. A man didn't make that much in a week.

"Take it or leave it. You'll be wet in a minute no matter which way you decide." Mrs. Hanson eyed him and glanced at the building thunderheads.

Erik didn't move. He could just as easily stay the night in the timber, but thoughts of some greens and beefsteak tugged at him almost as much as the hot bath did. It had been better than a year since the Potters' in Bannack. Oddly, he recalled coming into Bannack in a similar thunderstorm.

"Well, look at it this way, Mr. Larson: we ain't making much these days. Mr. Hanson's *Lewiston Tribune* costs him a dollar a paper, and these here hairpins cost me twenty-five cents a dozen."

"Three dollars it is then," Erik said. He turned back to the street, intending to get his gear.

"I don't mean any disrespect," Mrs. Hanson said, "but I can't afford no more credit." She squinted at Erik.

"Uh, no, ma'am." Erik showed a half eagle "I'd like to pay tomorrow, if that is fitting. Might even stay for another meal."

Mrs. Hanson glanced toward the saloon. "A lot can happen before tomorrow." Her lips tightened as she held out her hand.

Reluctantly, Erik dropped the half eagle into Mrs. Hanson's outstretched palm. "I reckon you're right, though I'm intending to keep that at a minimum." An uneasy feeling washed over him. As poor as things appeared in Elk City, he didn't care for the word to get out that Mrs. Hanson had a paying customer—one who paid with gold coin. Others might not realize it was nearly the last of his money.

A brilliant flash and earsplitting explosion jolted Erik. He pulled his packs off Hatchet as he felt the first raindrops. He was relieved to see a Chinese man come running up.

"I am Sam Chung," the man said. "I take horse now." He grinned and bowed.

"Thank you." Erik found himself inexplicably bowing. Sam Chung again returned the bow and led Hatchet away.

To where? Erik wondered. The next shimmering flash and crash of thunder and sudden pelting rain made him dismiss the thought, and he carried his belongings into the boardinghouse. Mrs. Hanson led the way to the far room.

"When would you care for your bath, Mr. Larson?"

"Soon as practical, ma'am. Just let me stow my gear."

Mrs. Hanson opened the door to his room and lit the kerosene lamp near a single bed. "I'll fetch you in about an hour," she said, giving Erik another going-over. "The facilities are out back. You can use the back door." She nodded in the direction of the outhouse, which was now shrouded in a curtain of rain.

Erik shut the door, sighed, and flopped down onto the bed. He hadn't seen a real bed for more than a year. He surveyed the tiny room. It had a single window prominently situated toward the outhouse. He pulled the lacy curtain across it. The kerosene lamp flickered light across flower-patterned wallpaper that peeled in numerous places. A portrait of George Washington hung near a dresser. There was also a washbasin, a bedchamber, the customary chair, and a small table.

From its musty smell, Erik doubted anyone had used the room in quite some time.

"Probably even the ghosts have moved out," he murmured. Then, curiously, he wondered where they would have gone if they had moved out. This entire town was just about to become given up to ghosts— well, the ghosts and the Chinese.

Cautiously, he checked the bedding. It seemed clean enough and free of bugs. *One night,* he mused. He regretted not moving on and now missed his half eagle. He had no idea when he would see another town, however. He had just crossed a huge swath of territory inhabited by no one. He hoped Mrs. Hanson wouldn't forget she owed him two dollars. Maybe the bath would be worth it.

The sky had continued to darken, and rain hammered the boardinghouse, vibrating a loose board somewhere. Fortunately, the back room where the bath was positioned was dry and warm. The bath *was* worth it. Sam Chung came in twice to check on things. Erik wasn't about to move until directed to do so. He took the hint that he had overstayed his dollar when Sam Chung returned with a stack of towels.

"Soon suppah," he said.

Erik pulled himself up, thinking it could not have been that late, but it had been a polite reminder. Maybe there was something to be gained by civilization. Tomorrow night, he would be under the trees again, probably in another thunderstorm or possibly snow.

Erik dried himself and dressed. He put on his dark brown shirt and beige trousers he had worn while working for Pete Samstrung. He threw on his short frock coat. This was as civilized as he would ever appear, and now that he was out of the mountains, these clothes would be more passable than his buckskins.

When he stepped from his room, Mrs. Hanson eyed him and nodded her approval, smiling. "Glad to see some civilization under all that Indian garb. Now, don't be late for supper. Mr. Hanson will be here, as will a couple of boarders. They eat like horses."

"Thank you, ma'am." Her demeanor had brightened in response to his appearance. He stepped outside. The rain had slackened in the slate-gray sky but was not finished. Another streak of lightning flashed over the trees, quickly followed by a low, booming, drawn-out rumble.

CHAPTER 41

Erik crossed the street to Buffalo Gulch Saloon. A half dozen miners wreathed in cigar and pipe smoke were drinking and playing cards. An unattended honky-tonk piano sat in one corner. Stairs led to rooms above. Erik doubted there had been much recent use for them, especially since Mrs. Hanson claimed to be the last woman in Elk City. A barkeeper stood behind a grandiose bar. Erik couldn't help but wonder from what gold camp it had been transported and how. Elk City was at the end of a hardly passable trail. Lewiston had to have been well over a hundred miles west, and that was by crow flight.

The bartender, a slender man with straight black hair, greeted him. "What's it be, stranger?" He sported a large handlebar mustache now graying. "Name's Ben Humphries." He squinted through washed brown eyes. "Don't get newcomers much."

Erik introduced himself. He caught a look from Humphries.

"Swede, huh?" His eyes roved over Erik.

"I came from Sweden when I was a youngster," Erik acknowledged.

Six sets of eyes turned to take him in. This was different, Erik mused. For a year, he had been with the Shoshone. He was back in the white world. He was thankful he had dug out a shirt and had stowed his buckskins.

"A whiskey." Erik set four bits on the counter, hoping it was enough. After a dollar for room and board, another for a bath, and a third for his horse, he wondered.

Humphries eyed the half-dollar, poured a drink, and tossed the coin underneath.

The barkeeper would ask nothing else unless Erik offered. Most barkeeps respected a man's privacy.

Lightning flashed, flickering light through the window, followed by the crack of thunder. The men at their tables hardly glanced out.

Erik found a table and sat. He swirled the amber liquid and watched it smoke the sides of the glass and bleed into droplets. The swallow burned, rolling down his throat, biting. He drank little, occasionally with the Swedes, but he admitted to himself it was good to do so on occasion, especially after a winter in the woods. He tapped his glass on the table and tried to catch the conversations around him. He needn't worry. The men he chased weren't there and wouldn't be. What had he expected? That he would cross over a hundred miles of empty wilderness and find them at the first saloon he happened upon?

Near as Erik could tell, the talk was about mining, hopes that the War Eagle would come into production, the cost of freight, the Chinese taking over, and what to do about the Chinese flag.

"Let 'em keep it. If the War Eagle don't come in, I say we're all finished. The town might as well belong to the Chinese."

A man with red hair and broad shoulders stepped to Erik's table. "Mind if I join you, Mr. Larson?" The man was well dressed in a coat, high-collared shirt, and string tie. "I heard you introduce yourself to Ben. I'm Austin Chase. I own this place." His watery gray eyes shone. Chase had a bottle of whiskey in hand and a glass.

Erik nodded at the chair. "Guess you can." He grinned. "You just said it's your place." For some reason, Erik figured Chase was the owner.

"From where do you hail?" Chase asked, settling himself.

Muted thunder filtered through the bar, dampening the other men's conversations.

"Just passing through," Erik said.

"I was afraid you'd say that. I was hoping you'd be looking at mining properties. You're dressed right, if I can be so forward. Figuring on you being someone out buying."

Erik wondered at the comment. At twenty-one, he'd never thought he might be taken as a businessman or investor. He laughed. "No, sir, just on my way through. Nowhere to go. Maybe to Lewiston."

The swing doors burst open, and three men, talking loudly, jostled in, followed by a blast of wind and rain.

"A bottle here!" the youngest of the three men, not much older than Erik, shouted. He peered at the barkeep with pale eyes from a pockmarked face. He was shabbily dressed and wore a heavy coat, as all three of the men did.

The other two men pushed back chairs at a corner table and sat. The tallest wore a battered wide-brim black hat with scraggly black hair protruding from beneath that matched a tangled bear. His eyes glittered behind a hawk nose and briefly settled on Erik before he turned back to his partner.

The third man was short in stature and probably in his early thirties. His eyes appeared an unhealthy yellow. He had a stubble beard and a scar across his cheek.

Erik's chest tightened, and then he relaxed. *No, plenty of men have scars.*

"Some more newcomers, Mr. Chase?" Erik nodded their direction.

"They been in and out a few times." Chase clenched his jaw. He appeared a bit perturbed by their presence.

Things went quiet as Ben Humphries delivered a bottle with three glasses to the men's table.

Erik caught the sharp-nosed guy eying him again as the sandy-haired kid poured the drinks. They weren't miners or packers. Their clothes and appearance said they had been riding. Erik hoped these weren't the boarders Mrs. Hanson expected.

The three raised their drinks, muttered to one another, and downed them. It appeared they congratulated the kid for something.

Uneasy, Erik returned his attention to Austin Chase. The man seemed a bit haggard, as if every time he found hope, it was dashed.

"So what's to keep a man here?" Erik asked. "If I was to say I was looking for work, I mean."

Chase raised his eyes. "Nothing if the War Eagle doesn't come through."

"I'm guessing that's a hardrock mine?"

"Mr. Shelton's back East, looking for capital. Those you see here are his men, just working on empty air." Chase nodded at the men playing cards.

"Can't do that for long," Erik said. "Gotta come up for grub sooner or later."

Chase almost laughed. "Which is drawing nigh." He tipped his bottle in Erik's direction. "May I?"

Erik nodded. He didn't need another drink, but he didn't want to turn down Chase's offer.

Chase recharged their drinks and downed a swig, and Erik fingered his. "You really want work?"

Erik shrugged. "Besides the War Eagle, anything else?"

Chase shook his head. "Chinese have pretty much moved in. They operate all the old placers. Folks said they were exhausted and not worth a buck a day, but the Chinese seem to be doing well enough." He swirled his glass. "Of course, you can't tell with those people. They stick pretty much to themselves at their end of the town—which is now most of it." He laughed and then waved his arm about. "Except for this, Mrs. Hanson's boardinghouse, and Wickermsham and his mercantile. Wickermsham's partner, Jim Witt, is making out all right because he owns all the ditches and leases them out to the Chinese. I own the rest of the town, which now amounts to mostly empty buildings that the Chinese don't want.

"At first, we did good, selling to the Chinese, but after that, those making the sales moved on. A friend of mine, Alonzo Brown, did good business until the Chinese brought in their own pack train. Alonzo packed goods in and out of Mount Idaho for his brother. They had a well-stocked store until last November, when Alonzo finally pulled out."

"I saw that it's boarded up."

Chase nodded. "It and most everything else."

"What about the rest of the country? I came through Orogrande. It appears that's all Chinese now," Erik said.

"Newsome is about fifteen miles northwest of here. It's still running some good placer. There are probably a couple dozen souls there, but the Chinese are moving in there as well," Chase said. "I mean, if that's what you're looking for." He set his jaw. "But I'm not taking you for a miner."

Erik recognized it as another invitation to explain his intentions. "Nej, not a miner. I used to do some packing for Samstrung and Harpster out of Bannack and Salmon City. I've seen when lode mines open up that someone needs a packer."

Chase eyed him. "Samstrung and Harpster. I know them. They're well?"

"Still chasing new strikes. We took a train to a place they're calling Dutchmen's Flat. I thought there might be opportunities up here."

Chase appeared skeptical. "So you're not just passing through to Lewiston?"

"I am unless I find something of interest," Erik said.

"Besides the War Eagle, there are several hardrock prospects in the area, but none have proved up. You're right; if they did, that would change things."

Erik took a swallow of whiskey to be cordial. He appreciated his senses, and more than once, being alert had saved his life. In fact, every time, being alert had saved his life.

"So if there's no work here, why are those three hanging around?" Erik nodded toward the newcomers. "You indicated the others are working for the War Eagle."

Chase leaned over the table. "They're hanging around for no good. Quinton Dudgin is the short one. Ramey Smith is the tall one. The kid is new. I haven't met him yet."

Erik nodded.

"Rumor is, the Chinese are sending out a shipment of placer. It wouldn't be the first time that road agents have come to town, biding their time, waiting to jump a pack train."

"And why wouldn't I be doing the same?" Erik asked. He allowed himself a smile.

"Except for your fancy shirt, you act like an Indian, because you sometimes use hand talk, and I don't think it's your line of work. Second, one man isn't enough to stop a Chinese mule train. Despite the laws, the Chinese have firearms and can usually get some whites to help with the packing. Now, that would be where you would come in. I could see you being the kind to get hired on as a guard. On the other hand, Dudgin and Smith and that kid strike me as ones who'd be doing the jumping."

"Anyone going to tell the Chinese?"

"I already have," Chase replied. "I'm deputized by Sheriff Sinclair over in Warrens to handle things in these parts if necessary. Unfortunately, some of the War Eagle miners might join Dudgin and Smith if given a chance. Not much love for the Chinese hereabouts. Miners can't tolerate American gold dug up by noncitizens and then shipped out of the country, particularly when they don't have jobs."

Erik nodded. "Seems to make sense, but the Chinese worked to get the gold, didn't they?"

Chase leaned back. "I see it the same as you do, Mr. Larson. The Chinese dug it. They earned it." He threw down the remainder of his drink. "I hope it doesn't come to that. I wish I could offer you a job. I own half the town, but I don't see much future."

"Maybe the War Eagle will come in," Erik said. "Thanks for the company. I'm figuring Mrs. Hanson is about to serve supper."

"Yes, that's one good thing we still got around here. Mrs. Hanson serves up some wicked-good grub. Her husband has the placer grounds up Buffalo Gulch. Those always were some of the best grounds. I think they've always done better with the boardinghouse, though."

Erik stood up and turned for the door, thinking about the coming meal, his mouth watering.

CHAPTER 42

Pushing his chair back to leave the Buffalo Gulch Saloon, Erik glanced again toward the newcomers. The tall man with the black beard and hawk nose, Smith, was pouring drinks. His hand, missing his two small fingers, gripped the bottle.

A blinding red enveloped Erik. He pulled his knife and leaped toward the man. "It was you!"

He slashed downward, catching Smith's arm, knocking the bottle spinning, ripping through his sleeve, and spraying blood. Smith staggered back, sending his chair clattering across the floor and knocking the table askew. The bottle smashed onto the floor. Swearing, Smith frantically grabbed for his gun belt, missed it, and lurched back.

Dudgin scrambled up and away. The kid sat in a daze, unmoving.

Erik slashed again at Smith. He was a head taller than Erik, but from Erik's force, he slammed into the wall.

"Easy!" Austin Chase yelled. He grabbed at Erik, spinning him away.

"She was my wife!" Erik shouted. The miners jumped from their chairs to join the fray.

Dudgin pulled his pistol. Erik lunged and slashed again at Smith but felt himself being tackled and pulled back. An explosion ripped near Erik's ear and peppered him with stinging particles. Glass and wood splintered.

A War Eagle miner headed toward Dudgin. Another grabbed the kid. Chase corralled Erik's arms. Erik struggled, spinning against the man, and tumbled with him, but they separated as they impacted the floor.

Dudgin, his yellowish eyes glaring and breath stinking, stood over Erik, leveled his pistol, and cocked the hammer. "You're a dead man."

An explosion rocked the saloon, and dust and wood fragments rained down. "Not in my place. The next one, and you're the dead man, Dudgin." Ben Humphries held a smoking shotgun.

Dudgin held up his pistol, let it dangle, and stepped back, grinning. Erik tore to his feet and slashed again. Chase grabbed his arm and wrenched his knife away, sending it clattering across the floor.

"What's the cause of this?" Chase spat.

Something inside Erik had shattered. Images of Bright Shell floated before him. "Those two men— My wife," he choked out.

"What's he talking about?" Chase asked, turning toward Smith.

"Hell if I know. Never met him in our lives. Don't know his wife," Smith spat.

"We ain't been with no man's wife, least any we knowed about," Dudgin said. "Ain't no law against that." He guffawed, and the scar across his face rippled raw.

Erik cursed in Swedish and struggled to get at Dudgin.

"Arrest him, Deputy," Smith said. "I'm pressing charges for assault." He examined his arm. Blood soaked his sleeve and dripped onto the table.

Chase's arms locked more tightly about Erik. "Easy, Mr. Larson." He pulled Erik back from the table. "I've got no choice but to lock you up. We'll sort this out." He shot a look at the three men. "Better go have Mrs. Hanson look at your arm, Mr. Smith."

Two of the War Eagle miners helped Chase escort Erik outside. The cold rain hit Erik and brought him partially back to his senses, and he quit struggling.

At the jail, Chase swung the door open. "Haven't had much of use lately. It's lucky I even know where the keys are."

Erik slipped inside the cell and sat. He hoped it wouldn't have much additional use. He had no intention of staying for long.

Chase eyed him. "What the hell, Mr. Larson? You acted crazy."

Erik smoldered but tried to keep his head. All this time, he had been following the two, searching near hopelessly. Now it was almost as if he would not accept that he had found them. Dudgin and Smith were their names. Seeing three men and not two had thrown him off.

Chase paced about the room, peered outside briefly, and then lit a kerosene lamp. He reached into a drawer and set a loaded pistol on a small table before pulling up a chair and sitting. He eyed Erik. "Don't know how long I'd better keep watch on you, but I figure I'd better for a bit. That Smith is likely to take the law into his own hands. You'd already be dead if he'd've gotten to his pistol." He glared at Erik. "He'd've been in his rights."

Erik didn't respond.

"In case you are wondering, those two men you decided to tangle with aren't too keen on arguing. I didn't tell you this when you asked about them. Word is they killed a man in addition to jumping a Chinese pack train. We couldn't prove it. I was watching them, working on it."

Erik remained silent.

"So don't talk!" Chase slammed his fist against the table. "I sure had better things to do than wet-nurse someone tonight." He began rummaging through some papers, found a ledger, and began making notes.

Footsteps clomped across the boardwalk, and Ben Humphries entered.

"I'm pretty sure they've lit out," Humphries said. "They were mighty hot. By the way, the kid's name is Clay Bender. You wanted to know that." He nodded in Erik's direction. "You figure out what set him off?"

"Only that he claims Dudgin and Smith had something to do with his wife. He won't talk. I'll see what Smith intends if he comes back."

"He ain't gonna be back unless it's to shoot our prisoner. I'm betting they're the ones that held up the pack train and were looking to do it again." He glanced in Erik's direction. "He might have inadvertently stopped them for a bit."

"I'm figuring the same," Chase said.

Erik had heard, but his head was not in it.

Chase closed the ledger. "Might be you should get us some chow from Mrs. Hanson in a bit," he said. "It's going to be a long night."

Numbly, Erik recalled that he had paid for supper. It was the least of his worries. He considered what had caused him to lash out as he had—with only a knife. Where had the uncontrolled rage come from? He hadn't buried things in the least.

Humphries approached Erik. "So was your wife an Indian?"

Erik stared ahead.

"That's it, Larson, is it not? Dudgin let drop something about him and his friend having some fun with an Indian squaw up in Montana Territory. He told me, 'No harm in that. That's what they want.'"

Blood pounded in Erik's head. The lies they told among themselves perpetuated stories such as this.

"They've been visiting the Nez Percé camped nearby as well. But then so have others. Trading, they say." Humphries shook his head.

Erik sprang up, striking the bars. "Did Dudgin explain the cut on his face? Did anyone ask? That's not something a woman would do if she was getting what she wanted!"

"So that's what happened? That was your woman?" Chase came to the cell.

Humphries's eyebrows narrowed. "They said they did no harm."

The blackness began suffocating Erik.

Chase's lips tightened. "Tell me what you know, Mr. Larson."

Erik began trembling. The feelings he'd had when he saw Smith's missing fingers boiled up. Heat coursed through him.

"You're Swedish, right?" Chase said. "Might be you don't know the trouble you're in around these parts of the country. People have been hung for less. You'd better hope Smith doesn't come back."

Erik turned toward the wall, unable to focus.

"Hell," Chase said. "Can't help you if that's your way."

Things Erik had seen flooded back. His being was drawn into the blackness with the wolf-bears. Chase and Humphries were still talking, but he no longer heard voices, only a dull noise coming from a black pit that seemed to stretch forever.

Mrs. Hanson's voice brought him back. Fragrant cooking filled the room, but Erik's stomach turned. Mrs. Hanson confronted him, scowling. "Do not think you will get a refund. And here I thought you were respectable." She glowered, shaking her head. "You're just like all those Indians that come around here, getting drunk and fighting."

An abrupt calm overcame Erik. He spoke emptily, addressing no one. "Those two men did the unspeakable to my wife."

Chase and Humphries approached Erik's cell.

"After it was done, she cut our daughter from her belly. I tried, but I could not save my wife." Erik heard his words but felt nothing. "I placed her body on the rocks near our cabin."

Mrs. Hanson clutched at her throat. "Oh, my dear boy! Your child too?" She stumbled.

Chase eased her into a chair.

"It was by God's grace that I saved my daughter."

"Oh dear Lord," Mrs. Hanson whispered. "Where? Where is she—your daughter?"

"With the Lemhi." Erik leaned against the metal slats, shaking. "I have dishonored Strong Wolf. I have given my word to take those men's breath. They are no longer men."

"I am so, so very sorry," Mrs. Hanson whispered. She staggered up and touched Erik's hand. "I shall pray for you." Angrily, she turned toward Chase. "You let him out of there."

Chase shook his head. "That is my sentiment, Mrs. Hanson, but not something I can do—not until Dudgin and Smith and the kid are gone. I can't be responsible for more people getting killed—most likely him." He jerked his thumb toward Erik. "He isn't thinking right."

Mrs. Hanson continued gasping, shaking. "Let him go. It is not right. Not right."

Ben Humphries took Mrs. Hanson's arm and gently led her from the jail. She continued protesting.

Chase approached Erik. His voice eased. "I reckon you should try to get some sleep, Mr. Larson. Based on what you say, no one's going to be pressing charges. I can't tell you what to do, but you won't get a second chance if you go at them like you did tonight." He paused, eyed him, and shook his head. "I thought you Indians were more savvy than that."

Erik pulled his fingers from the iron slats and glared at Chase.

"I don't know your story, Mr. Larson. I don't need to know it. Somewhere you picked up being Indian. Just remember, you're in a white man's world at the present. You have a daughter to go back to."

"I'm Swedish. I spent time with the Sheepeaters. That is all. I do have a daughter to go back to. And I have my honor to restore."

In the early morning, Austin Chase woke Erik, unlocked the cell, and handed him back his knife. "As I guessed, no hide or hair of them. Of course, you know they're probably down trail, waiting for you."

"I'm hoping on that," Erik said. He sheathed his knife.

Ben Humphries came inside. "Your outfit's outside, Mr. Larson. Sam Chung brought it by and got your gear from your room. Mrs. Hanson said you should come by for some breakfast."

Erik shook his head. "I don't imagine that's a good idea."

"She figured you'd say that. She's wishing you well and said for you to come back when you've shaken your demons. She says this is yours."

Erik received two silver dollars, a bit surprised. "Tell her I'm obliged." He swung onto Hatchet. "I don't know what overcame me yesterday, Mr. Chase. Sometimes we Indians are visited by bad spirits. I spect that's what happened." He grinned slightly. "Doubt I'm going to have the same ones visiting next time."

"I won't presume," Chase said. "I can't condone it. I also know you'll never get any help from the law about your Indian woman. I don't agree, but I can't do a damn thing about it. I only wish I could loan you a rifle, but you understand why I can't."

Erik managed a smile. "I get along fine with my bow." He glanced toward the trail. "It would be good, though, if I had an idea of their mounts. It'd only be so I can avoid being shot, you understand, being's all I *do* have is a bow."

Chase glanced at Humphries. "I can't rightly say. Can you, Ben?"

Humphries gave Chase a slight smile. "Now, I'm not entirely sure, but I believe Dudgin is riding a gray. If I recollect right, Smith has himself a big black, and I think Bender rides a bay."

"Much obliged," Erik said. "I'll be sure to keep my distance."

Erik headed east, downriver. He'd catch Dudgin and Smith. He'd spare the kid if he could, but the wo'api-taa would soon no longer exist.

CHAPTER 43

Erik recognized the hoofprint with the scuff—slight but noticeable. He sucked in his breath. He had never been blinded by hate as he had been when he recognized Smith. Months of searching could have done it. Things he'd thought he had controlled had overwhelmed him. "Never again, Hatchet," he whispered. "They do not know that I ride behind them this soon. Smith figures I'm locked up for a while."

Erik considered what the men intended. He had a feeling Dudgin gave the orders. Smith was the man who pulled the trigger, and Bender was a wet-behind-the-ears recruit needed to give them the numbers to jump a pack train. A former packer, Alonzo Brown, had been packing into Elk City a year past and was now gone. Maybe Dudgin saw this as an opportunity to take on a Chinese pack train, something few people would be concerned about. The Chinese still needed supplies, and they still needed to pack out their gold.

Possibly the men would not travel far, believing Erik was in jail, and would simply allow things to cool down. They also might remain nearby at Newsome and wait for the Chinese shipment. After all, Erik reasoned, they would consider him just a kid with a knife and no threat to their plans.

Newsome lay northwest across the mountains, also along the Nez Percé Trail. Alternately, it could be reached by following the Clearwater River and then turning up Newsome Creek. Erik guessed if the men were heading for Newsome, they would follow the Clearwater, as it would be easier to keep watch on their backtrail.

"Then I'll take the Nez Percé Trail, come in from around the back, and be waiting for them, Hatchet."

Erik headed along the trail, but when he topped the first false summit, he left the trail and headed up the ridge. The main trail was to the south and below him. Past the highest point, he swung north and then dropped down the next drainage into Newsome Creek, well upstream of the town. He immediately encountered scattered mining operations and retreated into the timber. He surveyed Newsome from a distance and checked for the men or their horses.

Newsome was much like Elk City but with half the buildings, and unlike in Elk City, most of the inhabitants appeared white. The Chinese appeared to have set up establishments downstream of Newsome. The larger of two saloons seemed to sport rooms above it, and Erik noticed two ladies standing out on the balcony. A couple of mercantiles, a livery stable and blacksmith, and a boardinghouse completed the town.

After watching at length, he entered the town. No one seemed to take undue notice of him other than as someone new in town, a further indication the trio had not been there. Inquiring at one of the mercantiles, Erik tried to determine when the next pack train would be coming in but got only curious looks. As was true for Elk City, the only mule trains serving the town regularly were Chinese. The other packers had come and gone and weren't expected again for several weeks. Then Erik asked if anyone had seen the three riders, but that brought only suspicion.

He left Newsome by way of the Nez Percé Trail, again heading northwest. He abruptly stopped after a few miles when he failed to spot the distinctive scuff.

"Blazes," Erik muttered. "They're down on the Clearwater." He shook his head and chided himself. Trying to outguess the men in this enormous country was almost senseless. The knowledge of how close he had been in Elk City gnawed at him. Yet he had also been close to getting killed. He touched his medicine pouch.

Erik turned back and headed down Newsome Creek toward the river. "At least we know we're behind them, Hatchet," he said. "Unless they've holed up back in the direction of Elk City, intending to circle back for the Chinese pack train."

Erik reached the Clearwater, turned downstream, and inspected the damp sections for tracks. He found nothing in the first mile and convinced himself the men had holed up. He started to turn back, when he spotted it: a slight scuff mark. The horse's left hoof. He guessed it was Smith's horse, the black. At least that was what he pictured—Dudgin leading, Smith either at his side or behind him, and the kid following farthest behind like a stray dog.

He clucked to Hatchet. The men were down trail in front of him. He had a vague notion of a plan but knew not to settle on anything. Whistling Elk had taught him that just as the hunter adapted to the prey, the prey adapted to the hunter, including turning things about on the hunter.

Erik's chest tightened. He had lost time with his visit to Newsome. He urged Hatchet on, moving quickly and fighting a feeling of desperation.

Presently, the men were heading west. When the river swung north, they could continue toward Mount Idaho and Lewiston or possibly cross into the Salmon River country and look for other opportunities there. It no longer appeared they might circle about and return to Elk City.

Late that day, Erik reached one of the stage-and-freight stops. He saw a sign: Clearwater Station. A lengthy sluice was set in a fast-rushing stream emptying from the thickly timbered hillside. A crew of five men worked it.

Inside a low-slung log building, he found the proprietor, Mr. George Reed. He was a balding, short man. Erik asked about any pack trains coming through or mail stages.

"You got a letter to post?" Reed asked.

Erik shook his head. "I'm hoping to catch up to my party. Three men, riding a bay, a gray, and a black."

Reed gave him a skeptical look. "From Elk City, by chance?"

Erik became uneasy but chanced it. "I went up to Newsome. I think they continued downriver."

"You only carry a bow?" Reed eyed him more thoroughly.

Erik guessed he knew the answer, or he would not have asked. "I lost my rifle."

"Funny thing. There were three men through. One had his arm bandaged. Said something about a crazy white Injun lover. Might that be you?"

Erik rubbed his brow. "Probably." He nodded. "Best be on my way if I plan to catch up by supper."

"No concern of mine, mister. They were too interested in my sluice for my liking." Reed eyed him. "You won't catch them by supper, however."

"I'm obliged," Erik replied. Reed's comment meant they were better than a day ahead of him. He was thankful Reed had assessed him more favorably than the three men he followed. His thoughts darkened. "Come on, Hatchet."

He encouraged Hatchet into a quick trot and pressed him for the remainder of the day.

This morning, high clouds blocked the sun. A penetrating, cold breeze accompanied by a misty rain pestered Erik, but it was good. The men might hunker down and not travel, giving Erik a chance to close the distance.

Midday, he came around one corner from where the trail snaked along the river in a long curve. Three riders were ahead. Blood rushed to Erik's temples. He watched from the edge, where he was partly concealed in the trees that bordered the trail, until he was certain it was them. Bender, not Dudgin, rode in the front on his bay. Dudgin and Smith rode together, Dudgin on the gray and Smith on the black. The black slightly swung its left hoof—the reason for the occasional scuff.

Erik glanced about. This was not good terrain. The heavily timbered walls climbed steeply along both sides of the narrow, turbulent river. Downstream, the timber had been gouged out where slides had taken out the trees and piled them into the river. The canyon was too narrow for him to overtake the men without being seen.

Erik wanted to get downstream of them and prepare a night ambush.

No, not at night, Erik decided. He wanted to catch them near evening when they passed within his bow range. He needed only two good arrows. Bender was of no concern, and he'd likely run, believing it to be an Indian attack.

The men rounded the river's far curve and passed from sight. Erik eased back onto the trail and followed at a hidden distance. He watched the ridge above him. If he could get to the top, he could cross and eventually drop down in front of the men. The river trail would follow a longer, more tortuous route around every entering tributary and descending ridgeline.

The rain increased. Erik grew more hopeful that the men would soon stop.

He glanced upward again, wondering if it were possible. Thick timber reached down from the ridge.

"Only one way to find out, Hatchet." Erik turned off the trail and headed up a small draw.

For a short distance, he moved easily among the timber, but then the trees crowded in and became a maze of spindly cedars and firs with slender trunks spreading in all directions. The timber became so thick that he could see no landmarks but only the trees' spidery black branches reaching upward, draped with lichen and witch's beard.

Erik urged Hatchet up and around the deadfalls and over the slickened trunks. One direction looked the same as another. Only the steep slope kept him oriented—that and knowing the river and trail lay downhill.

The route proved painfully slow, and Erik nearly turned back. This country could easily reduce a man to futile cursing and lashing out. It was the timbers' nature to clog the hillsides, splay skeleton logs downhill, and form barricades to anything that wished to pass. It was man's nature to fight the barricades and clutching limbs. As Whistling Elk had taught, it was an animal's nature not to fight the country. "Become like the deer," Whistling Elk had said. "She does not go straight. She picks her way around. Remember, sometimes you must go backward to go forward."

Erik settled and gave Hatchet his head. The horse, like the deer, picked his way in the direction Erik encouraged.

Finally, they reached the summit that bordered high above the river. A game trail followed the apron of timber and made traveling a little better until it opened onto a sheer drop where the land and trees had been torn away and plunged into the river. Below, he caught sight of the trail. The men were much farther downstream. He had not caught them.

A mountain rose back and above Erik, but he had guessed correctly. He could now cut north and intersect the river well downstream of the men.

He tested the air, breathing deeply, knowing he would be able to discern woodsmoke from a campsite if the men had stopped. Although the rain tended to beat down the smoke, its faint, distinctive smell sharply contrasted with the scent of rain and wet conifers.

251

Woodsmoke, horses, or talking. Any one of those would give the men away long before they knew of his presence.

The shadows thickened until the gray shapes of timber were nearly indiscernible. It had become too dangerous to continue. Erik could not afford to have Hatchet walk into a broken limb or go lame by stepping wrong over a log.

He followed a trickling creek into a small grass-carpeted clearing. Its brightness surprised him and made Erik realize how dark and muted the timber had become. He tethered Hatchet and spread his bedroll with its oilcloth under a thick spruce, where the ground was relatively dry. He figured the men he followed had already holed up. If he had not already passed them, tomorrow he would. He could then pick his place and end the blackness that had plagued him these past months.

CHAPTER 44

The morning broke bright and clear. The steam from the rain rolled from the timber, and the heat gathered into a dense, almost suffocating blanket. Erik had been working his way northwest for several hours. The timber thinned and opened into grassy, barren slopes. He dropped down, crossed a shallow stream, and then began climbing an open ridge, at last swinging back in the direction of the trail. He was a good two miles back and above it, much farther away than he had intended. Above him, the land ascended into thick timber. Below were the gray and purple shadows of the Clearwater canyon. He continued across an open slope in the direction of the river, now confident he was well downstream of the men.

An open expanse abruptly unfolded before him. It was as if a giant hand had raked away the earth down to the river, scooping out a giant bowl that funneled into a rocky black gap. The rock was a basalt flow, much like the fractured rock along the Goodale Cutoff.

"To blazes," Erik muttered. The basalt formed a series of steep, rocky ledges covered in grasses and thick brush. Midway across, a silvery ribbon of water fell from the rim and tumbled across the ledges before it disappeared into a narrow cut above the Clearwater.

Erik had not been prepared for this change in the country. Turning back and dropping below the cut would mean the men would likely move ahead of him again. Climbing above and around would mean losing at least another day, and the canyon would not keep them confined much longer. They would soon reach intersecting trails, where they might change their route.

The day had been stifling, and sweat ran from his neck. Erik might as well have been sitting in a sweat lodge. Some flies took advantage of his pause and buzzed about his eyes, trying to catch the moisture on his eyelids or inside his nose. He swatted at them.

A fragrance, perhaps kicked up by the heat rising uphill, caught his senses, something like strong mint. Memories of the Swedes and their valley washed over Erik. He tightened his grip on Hatchet's reins. Katrine had her life. His had been taken from him. A bitter taste flooded his mouth, and he spat.

"We're going across, Hatchet. The wo'api-taa are about to breathe their last."

The first bench extended to the opposite side, where it became masked by rock breakdown and scraggly conifers. It lay about fifty feet below Erik. Toward the center, the rim towered much higher where the stream spilled in a dizzying falls. The stream was a concern. After collecting below the rim, it appeared to cut through a rift in the rock, which, he knew, could be impassable.

A rush of wind pricked Erik's scalp and cooled the droplets of sweat. He had pushed hard this day. He could not now afford to let fatigue dull his senses. In a few short hours, he would intersect the trail in front of his prey. *If not tonight, tomorrow night*, he thought. He'd been on their trail for ten months. It was June. Another day would not matter. Often, the hunter's best weapon was time.

He would wait until they had camped and then jump them. He wanted the wo'api-taa to know it was him. He wanted to see their eyes when he confronted them—to see their fear and hear them plead for mercy before he slit their throats or pulled their intestines from their bowels and strung them out to cook in the sun.

Erik glanced at the sky. "Great Mystery, I know these two are no longer men. They deserve to no longer breathe. Am I wrong in wanting this?"

He gazed at the far edge of the bowl.

"Come on, Hatchet," Erik whispered. "We can't cross it if we don't try." He turned Hatchet into a grassy draw that cut through the tortured blocks of basalt toward the first bench.

Hatchet hopped downward, sending rock and gravel skittering and sliding. Erik rose in the stirrups to keep his balance as the horse scrambled down and out onto the bench. "Good boy." Erik patted his horse. He gazed back toward the rim. He wouldn't be going back up.

Erik headed across, feeling like an ant trapped in a kettle as the rim towered above. The bench was open, covered by scant grasses and some ragged buckbrush. A faint game trail, likely made by mule deer coming down to reach water, had been scuffed into the rock and thin soil.

Erik reached where the stream crashed from high above. Spray broke into a white mist, and the late sun cast a rainbow against the gleaming black rocks, but the beauty was short-lived. The stream cut across the bench through a sheer cleft ten to twenty feet deep. The game trail wound down through a breakdown of basalt blocks, but nothing came up the opposite side, at least not that Erik could see.

He came to the foot of the falls a few yards above where the stream entered the cleft. Water thundered into a cooling spray off breakdown near the cliff face. Erik dismounted and stepped out onto the slick blocks. "Come on, boy," he encouraged. "We've been through worse." He led Hatchet into the rushing water. It tore at him as it funneled into the narrow chute below. Hatchet obediently followed, and soon they stepped out onto the opposite side.

"Good boy." Erik patted Hatchet's muzzle. He was thankful Hatchet had been an Indian pony. Most horses would have shied at the water crashing down from above. Horses usually tried to run from danger and often didn't last long in the mountains. When spooked, they would just as likely go over a cliff as not.

Erik scouted for a way off the bench. The few breakdowns he found abruptly ended in sheer drops.

"Patience," Erik muttered. "There has to be a way down for us somewhere, Hatchet."

He reached the distant side and edged around the corner, fearing what he might see. The basalt ledges continued into the distance until masked by timber.

"Good," Erik said. "Where there's trees, there's a way down."

Erik reached the edge. Below him, the basalt had broken into huge blocks. He caught a quick flash. A mountain lion leaped across a cleft and stopped and crouched on a slab, gazing back at him.

"My friend," Erik whispered. He touched his medicine pouch and found the tooth. "What are you trying to tell me?"

He studied the breakdown. One cut appeared broader than the others, and for the visible distance, it appeared he could get down.

He clucked to Hatchet to head downward. A dozen shapes erupted around him. *Grouse!* They exploded in all directions with their wings pounding the air, and a whirring blur surrounded him. Hatchet jumped and turned, trying to get uphill. Erik grabbed to balance himself but found only empty air. He hit hard. Pain engulfed him before a blinding light erupted and snuffed into blackness.

CHAPTER 45

Numbing pain brought Erik to his senses. Stars sprinkled the night sky. He fought to remember what had happened and recalled running into the grouse and being thrown. He tried to sit up, and a flash of angry, numbing red engulfed him. His head pounded. He touched it and brought away his fingers, wet with blood. More blood soaked his buckskins and stained the ground where he had lain. He could not feel his lower right leg and discovered that a rock lay atop it, pinning it against the sharp edge of another.

Erik lay back, woozy with pain. He wondered where Hatchet was, if his horse had tumbled with him, and if his horse was even alive. He could make out shapes beside him only where they blocked the stars. Nothing appeared to be a horse carcass, at least from what he could see.

He clenched his teeth and tried again to sit up. He leaned onto his left side and grabbed the chunk of basalt that pinned his leg. He pulled. It slid across his leg and sent new stabs of pain through him as it grated across his flesh. Desperately, he twisted the jagged rock off his leg. He was loose.

Grimacing, he shoved his leg outward but felt only dead weight. He flexed it. His bloody thigh blazed with fire where the rock had slid across it. He didn't dare try to stand but pulled himself backward upslope a few feet before he slid back down.

Even if he could see, he doubted he could climb out, up or down. His throat cracked dry, and he couldn't swallow.

He stared up at the quietly blazing stars indifferent to his plight. His heart beat strangely fast, and a wave of dizziness engulfed him.

He picked out a solitary star. "Was I wrong, Great Mystery?" he whispered. He considered Dudgin and Smith again. Memories of Bright Shell replaced them. Her face floated above him until darkness again engulfed him.

He woke. Bright Shell had left him, and images of Dudgin and Smith refocused. He fought the bile that rose and then calmed himself.

"What does it matter if they live or die?" he whispered. His voice cracked. "If they are no longer human beings, what does it matter if they know it is I who killed them? It does not."

He let out a wheezing breath. "I need your help, night cat. Perhaps you tried to warn me, and I was not listening. And perhaps you now feast on Hatchet." He knew the mountain lion would care little how it found its meal.

Some feeling began returning to his leg, and along with it came a tingling, stabbing pain.

Erik swallowed, and his swollen tongue stuck. It was a long distance back to the falls, but he needed water. He heaved himself a few feet up the side of the ravine and then a few more feet. Hatchet's nicker startled him. The horse shook his head, rattling his bridle, and blew his nostrils above Erik's face.

"Thank God you're okay, boy," Erik gasped. He grabbed the animal's leg and pulled himself up. His head pounded fiercely. He found his canteen and, shaking, swallowed the cool, life-giving liquid and then slumped back to the earth, dizzy and unable to focus. The pounding, reverberating throbbing inside his head was nearly unbearable. His hands twisted on his canteen. He lifted it again and gulped the remaining water.

Erik continued sitting, unsure if he could do much in the darkness but desperate to try. Gingerly, he felt along his leg and felt where his leg had been cut. He pulled his knife, cut a thin strip from his buckskins, and tied it over his injury. The bleeding had stopped. His leg was not broken, he did not think, but his head—dizzying lights erupted.

He lay back and sucked in the cool night air. He shuddered. The strange lights again blossomed, and pain enfolded him. He found a twig and bit on it. Agonizingly, he searched the sky for a hint of approaching dawn.

At length, almost imperceptibly, a pale light began to streak the sky, and the timber and rocks emerged as faint silhouettes. The western sky yet blazed with stubborn stars.

Morning light bathed the ravine where Erik lay. Hatchet had not wandered far but busily pulled at the thin grass that grew from the otherwise ragged rock.

"Here, boy!" Erik called. He rubbed his hands as if he held some feed. Hatchet shook his head and came down to him.

"Steady," Erik whispered. He grabbed Hatchet and hoisted himself, wobbling, to his feet. He knew it would be nearly impossible to swing his bad leg over the animal. He bit his lip, reached to offside of the saddle, and pulled himself up, trying to roll his leg across Hatchet's back. Pain numbed his senses, and he dropped back. He rested, took a breath, and tried again. This time, he succeeded. He tried to hold himself upright, but the world swam before him. A pounding, throbbing numbness flashed through his head.

"Go find water, Hatchet," Erik whispered. He turned the animal's head downhill toward the river and got him moving. Erik could only pray the ravine cut through the basalt and did not end on another cliff.

Each step jarred Erik's senses, but mostly, he was unaware of things. The sun's heat beat down. He sensed brilliant light but no form. He closed his eyes.

Katrine stood in his way. "You should not have left us, Erik," she said. "But I know you had to. I know what your name means now, Two Elks Fighting. You don't belong anymore. Not to us or the Sheepeaters. You don't belong to anyone."

He saw Björn take his sister into his arms and enter their cabin.

He forced his eyes open. Blurred shapes and numbing pain seized him.

Hatchet moved downward and into the timber's cooling shade. The slope lessened, and Hatchet surged onto more level ground. They neared the river. Its rushing sound and wet scent filled Erik's head. Hatchet lowered his head, and Erik slipped from the animal's back, unaware he was falling.

CHINESE PLACER CAMP

CHAPTER 46

Light slowly bled into Erik's senses. At first, he thought he was in the Lundgrens' old cabin, the family whose cabin he had lived in for a time in the Swede's valley. The walls were stone, however, and the light seeped in through a rude open doorway and not through windows. Singsong voices filtered in from outside, as did unusual aromas, including garlic and ginger. The tangy odors might have awakened him.

A shadowy form rose from beside Erik. A Chinese man had been sitting nearby.

Erik tried to sit up. His weakness and the numbing pain in his head surprised him. The man chattered excitedly, called out in Cantonese, and ducked outside. Erik caught sight of two other Chinese through the small door. One came inside.

"Hehwoh," he said, and he bowed. "I am Hong Sing."

Erik propped himself up a little, staring. He wondered how long he had been out. His head and leg were bandaged. He lay on a thin pallet inside a stone hut. Its roof was of wooden poles. A tiny stand held a washbasin and oil lamp. Some boots stood near the door. It appeared other mats were rolled up against a wall.

"I'm Two Elks Fighting," Erik said, unaware he used the Sheepeater language. His head pounded.

Hong Sing appeared confused but smiled. "Indyun?"

"Nej." Erik recognized Hong Sing's confusion. "I'm Erik Larson," he said.

Hong Sing shook his head. "Ehwik Lahson."

"Call me Erik." It didn't seem Hong Sing would be able to pronounce his name easily.

Other Chinese came to the door, and Hong Sing introduced them: Chen Yuen, Pon Kan, and Pon Heing. Erik was a bit thankful they did not enter. There was little room for himself and Hong Sing as it was.

"Ehwik." Hong Sing gestured and addressed the others. "Ehwik."

They smiled and chatted, all seemingly pleased he was awake.

"Thank you, Hong Sing, for taking me in," Erik mumbled. "Tell everyone thank you." Bright flashes crashed through Erik's head, and he slumped back. Apparently, these men had found him.

Hong Sing spoke briefly in Cantonese and turned back to Erik. "Are you hungry? We have rice and sahmon. Big sahmon are in rivah now."

Erik nodded. It explained the fragrant odors from the fire outside. What Swede wouldn't have wanted salmon? But pounding numbed his vision, and he wanted to sleep. "Ja, I'll try to eat."

Hong Sing spoke to Pon Kan, the man who had been at Erik's side when he awakened. Pon Kan quickly left and returned with a bowl of rice mixed with bits of rich salmon and steeped in the spicy smell of garlic.

Erik managed a few bites, scooping the food to his mouth with his fingers. He wondered where Hatchet was. Without his horse, he never would have reached the river. The Chinese never would have found him. He shivered and lay back as the world again faded.

When Erik again woke, his head pounded more fiercely. He tried to focus. Except for the tiny oil lamp and a sliver of light around the door, the hut was dark. Hong Sing was present and greeted him. Pon Kan threw back the covering on the door and brought in a crock with warm water.

He settled next to Erik and removed the bandages from his leg. From his knee down, his skin appeared angry purple and black, bruised and torn from the rock. Above his knee was a second wound from when Erik had pulled the rock free. His leg reminded him of Muskrat's leg. From a small crock, Pon Kan scooped out what appeared to be stringy dark green moss. He washed the area around the wounds, covered them with the moss, and bound the cloth over them. Erik felt an odd numbness on his lower leg where it had been pinched. Not all the feeling had yet returned.

Pon Kan unwound the bandages on Erik's head, dipped the cloths in warm water, and wrung them out. He dabbed at Erik's cut on the back of his head. The small movement caused a burst of shimmering light. Erik drew in a short breath. He fought away thoughts of his father's death. He had died of a head injury.

Finished and with new bandages affixed, Pon Kan instructed Erik in Cantonese while Hong Sing interpreted: "You sleep. Do not move."

Erik gave him no argument and settled back.

Over the days, Erik grew accustomed to Pon Kan caring for him, changing his bandages, and bringing him rice or broth. Afterward, Hong Sing often visited. The other Chinese remained outside, where they ate their meals and visited with one another. Infrequently, they glanced in on Erik. All were seemingly happy to see him improving.

The Chinese worked a placer. Hong Sing explained they were there like most of his countrymen. "This is land of the golden mountain. We are sojourners. When we get gold, we go home."

Fleetingly, Erik wondered if there was room for an additional miner. Mining gold could be how he would acquire a rifle. His bow had its limits, which had been made all too clear. With a rifle, he could already have killed Dudgin and Smith from a safe distance without their ever having been aware.

The first few days, Erik's pounding head awakened him. The headache came and went, sometimes with the flashing lights. Often, he felt confused. Some days were better, and this day, he woke without the dull drumming. Even so, Pon Kan insisted he rest. It humbled him when he realized that since his arrival, the others had given up their hut to him and slept outside.

Hong Sing said, "You come to us nearly dead. Look like Indyun. You are saying things as if you come from the shadows. Pon Kan sees you are hurt and so helps you. Chen Yuen thinks you come to us for a reason."

"I am grateful," Erik replied. *What reason?* The Sheepeaters believed he was sent to them as a gift from the Great Mystery, and similarly, the Sacred River band believed he had come to teach them farming. Was it a good reason the Chinese sensed? Others, such as Runs Fast, had made it clear that he also brought misfortune.

This day, when Pon Kan and Hong Sing came into the hut, Erik's head had calmed. Pon Kan cleaned the wounds on Erik's leg. It yet felt numb, especially around his foot, but Erik saw no red streaking and no blood poisoning. Pon Kan noticed as well and seemed pleased. He removed the bandage from Erik's head. It felt slightly numb where Pon Kan touched, but that was all. A wave of gratitude washed over Erik when Pon Kan left the bandages off.

"Hong Sing, please tell Pon Kan that I am indebted to him for his care." Erik reached out and took Pon Kan's hand. "I owe you my life. Thank you. Whatever I can do for you, I will do."

Pon Kan gently pulled away. It surely was strange to have someone take his hand as Erik had done. Chinese did not shake hands, nor did they embrace as white men did.

Pon Kan bowed and rapidly spoke, nodding at Erik.

Hong Sing interpreted: "We are all men of this earth. You owe me nothing. You would do the same."

Erik frowned, wondering.

Hong Sing gestured toward the door. "Come. It is time to go out."

Erik stood, stooping because of the low ceiling and uncertain of trying his leg, expecting to feel pain. Instead, his lower leg and foot tingled. The sensation felt like insects running up and down, and it was difficult to sense when he put weight on his foot. He hopped onto his good foot.

Pon Kan offered him a forked stick. Erik leaned on it and hobbled out the door. The sun blazed brightly, and the summer heat touched his skin. He surveyed the tall cedars and firs that reached into a brilliant blue sky. The Clearwater River rushed past and slipped behind deep green conifers and muted gray rock outcrops that jutted from the river.

After his having been confined to the small rock hut for so long, nothing appeared more beautiful. Erik lifted his eyes. "Great Mystery, thank you for my life." But his thoughts immediately turned to the men he followed, and his stomach tightened.

The others who were working the placer greeted him and smiled and bowed. Erik walked in their direction, trying his leg, trying to overcome its numb, tingling sensation. He tripped and caught himself, and a flash of pain raced upward from his foot. It was difficult to judge his leg. Possibly the nerves had been damaged where the rock had lain on it for so long. Nerves could not repair themselves, and a bit of despair rushed through Erik. He fought it off.

Erik caught sight of Hatchet grazing on an open knoll beyond the camp. As if he sensed Erik's presence, the horse raised his head and shook it. Erik warmed. Like Muskrat, he might need a horse to be complete, but that was insignificant. He was alive.

CHAPTER 47

Erik took his place with the Chinese and helped them work the placer to the extent he was able. He took his meals when they did. They usually ate rice with a relish or sometimes rice with some trout or salmon but rarely any other meat other than rabbits the Chinese snared.

Erik fixed a shelter a distance up the hill, under the trees, away from the stone hut. He told Hong Sing he preferred the limbs of the conifers to rock walls. "I like the stars for my roof." In truth, he wished for the Chinese to have their sleeping quarters back.

"And when it rains?" Hong Sing asked.

"I have an oilcloth for when it gets bad."

"Maybe we build another hut," Hong Sing said, smiling.

After their morning meal, the men returned to the sluice, although Pon Heing frequently tended their small garden for a time before rejoining them. He had diverted a small tributary to bring water across a simple terrace they had cut. Among the vegetables he grew were garlic, onions, and cabbage.

The Chinese ate again near noon and rested afterward before again returning to the sluice, where they worked until the light faded, which, at that time of year, was nearly fifteen hours. They finished with an evening meal.

Outside the huts, the Chinese kept a fire on which they cooked and kept a constant kettle of water. After their evening meal, Erik retired to his shelter, but the Chinese sat about the fire with their long-stemmed pipes and talked, sometimes well into the night. The flames danced and snapped, sending occasional showers of sparks skyward. The breeze wafted the woodsmoke and pipe smoke to Erik's shelter.

Mostly, they lived outdoors. They used the stone hut for sleeping or to get out of severe weather. At night, the four Chinese rolled out their mats and slept beside each other with their tunics hung on pegs and their boots aligned nearby. Occasionally, Erik saw the glow from the oil lamp they lit inside the hut but often only on nights when it rained.

There was another custom Erik learned to appreciate. Contrary to stories he had heard, on frequent evenings, Chen Yuen and Pon Kan tended a larger fire and heated a large kettle of water. They poured the heated water into a smaller pot not much larger than an oversized pail, and each man took turns washing. They scooped the water and vigorously swabbed themselves with cloths, sometimes jumping about. It amused Erik. This was not just once a week, as he was accustomed to.

Erik had not elaborated on his shelter much more than necessary. He had stacked brush on the roof to keep out the rain and shored up the sides a bit, somewhat like the shelter he had built for Muskrat, but little else.

He took advantage of quiet time to work on his bow and arrows, which the Chinese admired. They had no weapons other than knives and, if it became necessary, large cleavers and axes.

The evening was also the time when Erik checked on Hatchet. He would ride him for a bit and then afterward brush him down and talk to him. Each time he worked with Hatchet, he wondered about the men he pursued. He considered leaving, but finding the men now would have been like finding a certain leaf on a forest floor.

Other travelers came through. If they were white, the Chinese were pleasant enough, but they stayed to themselves while they passed by. If the travelers were Chinese, Hong Sing invited them to stop for a meal. Once, a lone traveling Chinese man stopped and introduced himself as Ah Wong. Although Erik found it difficult to judge the Chinese men's age, Ah Wong seemed younger than Erik was. Possibly he was eighteen or nineteen. Ah Wong's arrival became unsettling for Erik because it reminded him that he should be moving on. He could get about now, except for when spasms of fiery pain shot through his leg. Then he sat, unable to walk, until it subsided. His leg also remained numb, and he had to concentrate on his steps. He wondered if the feeling would ever return. Sometimes, after he vigorously rubbed it, it seemed improved.

Ah Wong remained with them for a night and then a second night. When he began helping with the mining, the men began building a second hut. Like the other Chinese, he sought protection and comradeship as well as the gold.

This day, Erik glanced up to see a Chinese pack train coming down the trail. The Chinese immediately broke from their work and noisily gathered around the packer.

"Lee Pow," Hong Sing said, introducing him.

"I'm Erik," Erik replied, and he found himself bowing to the man. Lee Pow was shorter in stature than the others, had darker and livelier eyes, and moved about more quickly.

"He comes from Mount Idaho but goes to Lewiston to get Chinese goods," Hong Sing said.

Mount Idaho was a day's difficult ride to the northwest and more than two and a half thousand feet above the Clearwater River. Lewiston was nearly a hundred miles farther. Lee Pow packed his goods into the numerous small Chinese placer camps and frequently allowed the Chinese to accompany him on his return trip to Lewiston with their gold.

Pon Kan helped as Lee Pow unloaded the packs and spread the many items out for inspection. The supplies consisted largely of crocks of preserved vegetables, tea, rice, and spices. This load also contained a pair of mining boots, a shovel, an oilcloth, and some rope. Erik guessed there was some opium along with plenty of tobacco for their long-stemmed pipes.

Lee Pow knew considerable English and wanted to talk. Erik shared only that he was a trapper, but he inquired about Lee Pow's possibly having seen Dudgin, Smith, and Bender.

"Not them," Lee Pow said, shaking his head. "We have bandit— Kan See. You watch for him. Vehlie bad man." He grinned broadly and nodded vigorously.

They talked for a long while, and Erik accepted a small gift of tea from Lee Pow.

"For when you are trapping," Lee Pow said. "Maybe bring me some furs?"

Erik laughed. "If we catch up somewhere next spring."

"Come back here. I come through sometime. Ahlees bring supply to Hong Sing."

Lee Pow and the others repacked the mules, and the man continued in the direction of Elk City.

Erik wondered why Hong Sing did not send someone out for supplies, as Mount Idaho was a long day's ride and an apparent staging area.

"We are not safe," Hong Sing explained. "Our camp is not safe. Too few of us."

It was the same reason that smaller placer camps depended on Pete Samstrung and Chet Harpster.

This morning, as he had become accustomed to doing, Erik made his way toward the creek, where the Chinese were already busily shoveling dirt into their sluice, chattering to one another—something Erik had come to expect. Never had he seen more industrious men; they were always talking and grinning, as if they took great joy in their work or passed a joke among themselves.

He stopped once to let a spasm of pain pass through his leg before he reached the side of the sluice. They greeted him.

Sometimes Erik washed the cobbles in the water entering the sluice. When he had asked the sense in washing off the rocks, Chen Yuen had grabbed a muddy cobble and washed it in a gold pan. Erik had seen the dozen or so specks of bright yellow that clung to it and understood.

This day, Erik watched for errant stones that washed through the sluice and disrupted the water's flow. Whenever one did, it caused turbulence that lessened the sluice's effectiveness in trapping the gold—not that he ever saw much of it. Rarely did Erik spot a piece larger than a grass seed. Most of the gold was flour gold: specks that could be removed only by amalgamating with mercury. Chen Yuen had lined the first several cleats with the silvery metal to capture the bits as the silt containing the gold flowed through the box. Later, he collected the mercury and retorted it, driving off the mercury and capturing the gold.

A chunk of white quartz clattered through the box a short distance and stopped. The water bubbled up around it. As he had done with a thousand other stones, Erik snatched it up and flung it toward the pile of washed cobbles. The instant he released the stone, he knew. His breath caught. The stone winked unmistakably with spots of bright yellow from where it rested on the pile. He grabbed it and held it up. Masses of gold shot through a piece of stark white quartz, and Erik whooped.

The five Chinese immediately surrounded him. He held out the rock. For a long moment, only the gurgle of water in the sluice could be heard. Everyone then burst into joyous cheering and began passing the rock around, jabbering. Nearly as quickly, they dashed for the hole in the hillside from which the last shovelful of earth had come. In short moments, they turned over two more chunks of white quartz equally speckled with gold.

Erik stood aside, watching the excited Chinese tear at the bank as more rocks emerged. They had found a glory hole where several pieces of rich float had caught up in the alluvium.

During the ensuing days, the Chinese found a few more gold-rich quartz chunks before their streak dimmed. It seemed to make no difference. They worked with the same exuberance and diligence, as if the cobbles were multiplying instead of dwindling. Erik wondered to where the gold ore disappeared. He guessed that Hong Sing kept it separate. It would need to be hauled to a mill to be crushed to release the gold.

This evening, while Erik worked on an arrow, he watched the stars appear. A meteor streaked across the sky. It reminded him of a time with Bright Shell and how she'd insisted a meteor was a falling spirit. He wondered if it were possible. He imagined Bright Shell coming to visit, and he warmed to the vision. Then Dudgin and Smith flashed back to his mind, and his stomach turned. He thought of the mountain lion that had leaped out onto the basalt block when he was injured. It had been sent, but for what reason? It had been to warn him not about the grouse but about something else.

Erik had tried to bury his memories, but at age sixteen, Erik, and his brother friend, Badger, had killed two men. They had done so to save their own lives, yet it had deeply bothered Erik. Gray Owl had explained that the men had done evil and were no longer worthy of being human beings. They were wo'api-taa, maggot worms, and no longer deserved life. Since Bright Shell's death, Erik had lived for revenge. But the meaning of Gray Owl's words was now becoming clear. To seek revenge meant acknowledging Dudgin and Smith as human beings and gave credence to their lives. They deserved death but a nameless and faceless death.

"How is that possible, Gray Owl? To think of them gives them existence. You would wish me not to give them existence. How is that possible?" Erik spoke loudly to the night sky.

He replaced Dudgin's and Smith's names with a single thought: squirming white maggots—two maggots that awaited squashing between his fingers. He calmed. It was not his to do. It was in the hands of the Great Mystery to do.

He lay back on his elk skin, inexplicably at peace—something he had not experienced for a year. It had been a while since his head had throbbed with the flashing lights, and he walked with fewer episodes of pain, although his leg was yet numb. Maybe he was becoming used to it like a person with a wooden leg.

"It's time," he whispered. "I've been here long enough." Come morning, he would say goodbye and ride out—not to seek the maggots, for that was no longer his to do, but to where? He would trust the Great Mystery.

CHAPTER 48

Loud Chinese voices woke Erik—voices he did not recognize. He reached for his knife and bow and started to scramble to his feet, but his leg didn't work, and he slipped. A flash of pain raced up his leg. Struggling up, he hobbled down the hill toward the Chinese stone huts. Moonlight glinted off moving figures. It flashed silver from raised knives and cleavers. His friends were among a throng of bodies, fighting, shouting. A blade slashed down, and Pon Kan fell, writhing and holding his neck. Glistening black flowed across his naked chest. He struggled onto his knees and tried to rise with one hand raised protectively as the clever fell again, knocking his head crazily to the side. Sparkling black sprayed his shoulders, and he collapsed in a heap.

An unearthly howling filled the night air. Maybe another of his friends had been cut by the dark assailants.

Pain shot up through Erik's leg as he fought to run. He slipped and stumbled again. From where he had fallen, he watched, unable to reach his friends, who were now fighting for their lives.

A figure clutching bags ran into the night, down trail. Two men joined him with their blades flashing and then winking into darkness, followed by others.

Erik reached the huts. Two figures lay slumped.

He reached Ah Wong, the newest member of the group. He was cut across his arm, but otherwise, he was seemingly unharmed. The youngster knew no English, but Erik saw in his eyes and understood what had happened.

Erik examined Pon Kan but did so unnecessarily; the man who had been considered the doctor and likely had saved Erik's life lay dead in a pool of glistening blood from slash marks to his neck. His head had nearly been severed.

Erik returned to Ah Wong and helped wrap his arm to stop the bleeding. He gazed in the direction the others had run in chase of the assailants. He turned his attention back to Ah Wong, built up the fire, and put the kettle of water on.

At length, Hong Sing and Pon Heing emerged from the shadows, half carrying Chen Yuen. Breathing hard, they released him to the ground. Chen Yuen clutched a badly bleeding arm. Another gash crossed his back, slightly below his neck.

Pon Heing slumped to his knees over his brother's body, swaying, keening with grief.

"They take gold," Hong Sing said, his breath coming hard. "We follow but cannot beat them. Chen Yuen hurt."

"I'm sorry," Erik said. "I should have helped."

Hong Sing shook his head. "You too far away. You came anyway."

Hong Sing pulled the kettle of water from the fire and began washing Chen Yuen's cuts. His arm gushed blood. Erik pulled apart a long piece of cloth and wrapped it around his arm above the cut. He twisted it until the bleeding ebbed. In the firelight, he could see the depth of the cut. The artery had been cut. Chen Yuen's eyes were frantic.

"Where are Pon Kan's medical things?"

Hong Sing spoke rapidly to Pon Heing, who straightened and retrieved his brother's implements.

Erik reached for them, but Hong Sing raised his hand and said, "I do this."

Fumbling through the items, Hong Sing found a needle and silk cord. They moved Chen Yuen closer to the fire and brought out one of the oil lamps. Pon Heing managed to get a liquid down Chen Yuen's throat. Ah Wong held the lamp while Hong Sing reached his needle inside the open cut and began to sew the artery. Erik wondered at the man's abilities.

Erik stood up; his leg was now on fire. There was nothing there for him. He hobbled back uphill and saddled Hatchet.

"Come on, boy," he whispered. "We've got places to go tonight."

He glanced skyward and wondered how long it would be until daylight. Stars slightly dimmed by the bright moonlight blazed in a wavering blanket overhead. He located the Great Dipper and, by its position, judged it to be well past midnight. Even at this latitude, he had several hours of darkness.

"Nothing I can do about it," he whispered. He turned Hatchet downstream and rode quickly after the three Chinese. The moon, a silver orb above him, cast his moving shadow onto the faint trace in front of him. He would have no trouble finding the men. They would not expect a man coming behind them on horseback.

But Erik did not intend to overtake them from behind. Instead, he judged their location and pulled Hatchet off the trail.

"Come on, boy; we've played this game before. It's just timber and not much at that. You and I can find our way."

Fortunately, the canyon walls had pulled well back from the Clearwater along this section, and unlike with the area upstream, Erik had room to move away from the river and upslope above the trail.

Erik topped the ridge and momentarily paused. The trees and rocky outcrops shimmered softly in the moonlight. It was as if a silvery blanket had been laid over the land. Where the light could not penetrate, shadows etched the draws and the river gorge. He found it eerily strange how the night's beauty deceptively hid the recent evil: Pon Kan lying hacked and dead. Chen Yuen would probably soon be dead as well. Erik fought the crawling feeling in his belly.

"We have to drop back down there, Hatchet," he whispered. "Back into those shadows to do what I intend."

He had considered getting far enough downstream and waiting for daylight, but it wouldn't work, he realized, not in this country, not with just his bow. He needed surprise. He studied the next shadow-drenched ravine.

"Come on, boy. Let's hope this one gets us close."

He crossed the ridge, slipped down into the shadows, and intersected the river trail. The moonlight was blocked by the canyon wall and tall timber. Erik turned downstream, seeking a patch of light.

After a mile, the trail arced back and broke into the moonlight. Erik rode out into its soft brilliance. He continued for a short distance until he found a slight rise that would give him the advantage he needed. He tethered Hatchet and returned to the spot he had selected. He pushed a half dozen metal-tipped arrows into the ground near his side and checked his knife.

He heard the men coming. They were moving swiftly, almost jogging. The weight of the gold ore had not slowed them. None watched their backtrail, and they moved steadily in his direction.

Erik waited. He would have little opportunity if he missed. *Forty paces. Thirty.* He strung his arrow, rose to a knee, and pulled back, locking his thumb against his cheek, aiming. The near man came into certain range.

He released. The arrow pierced the man's neck, and he stumbled and fell. Instantly, Erik nocked his second arrow. The man's companions stopped, frantic and confused. One tried to step from the trail, and Erik's second arrow buried itself in his chest. The man fell, writhing. The third man spotted Erik, screamed, and ran at him, flashing his knife.

Erik grabbed his own knife and jumped up and to the side. He slipped the blade into the man's belly as the man slashed downward. Erik jerked his knife upward into the man's lungs and then wrenched his knife free. The man gasped, gurgling; dropped to his knees; and then sprawled over onto his back, holding himself, staring at the blood welling from where Erik's knife had plunged into him.

"There is no honor in this killing," Erik murmured. He reached down, pulled the man's head back, and drew his knife across the man's neck. Moonlit blood erupted from the man's throat as Erik released the dying body back into the dirt.

Erik stood quivering with fire in his leg. He hobbled to the downed men. The first was dead. The second gasped with blood pouring from the wound. He would soon be dead. Erik cut his throat as well. The surprise in the man's eyes dimmed to a vacant stare.

"Forgive me, Great Mystery," Erik breathed. "Though these men lost their right to life, I am not pleased with what I've done."

Erik reached down and pulled his arrows from the two men. It would not be good for someone to find that an Indian had killed some Chinese.

He found the pouches with the gold dust but not the ore. That explained why they had been able to move so quickly. Erik was not concerned. It should not be difficult to locate a hundred pounds of ore come daylight.

A sudden wave of nausea hit Erik. He swayed. How had it come that he had done this? Had he layered onto these Chinese the hate he felt for Dudgin and Smith? He sucked in the night air in deep gulps and tried to clear his head.

"These were not men!" Erik shouted. "Gray Owl would agree. These men forfeited their lives when they killed Pon Kan." But Erik no longer believed his echoing words.

CHAPTER 49

Erik swayed on his feet, numb with what he had done, and stared at each body. He thought about burying the men and then rejected the idea. It mattered little. Their spirits were no longer there. He limped back to where he had tied Hatchet, with the pain again stabbing through his leg. Trying to run had made it worse. He dragged his leg over his horse's back and turned up trail.

Sunlight, like a glowing coal on the eastern horizon, bled through low clouds and pierced the uppermost limbs of the timber on the ridge above. Silently, it crept downward along the needles of the conifers and drenched the limbs in golden splendor. Erik wondered again how such beauty could dwell in this evil place, how it could not care what he had done.

The Chinese believed he had been sent for a reason. Had this been the reason? And for what good? Hadn't he now brought evil to his Chinese friends, or wouldn't he soon?

He reached the stone huts. Hong Sing, Pon Heing, and Ah Wong, with his bandaged arm, came toward him. Erik did not see Chen Yuen and feared the man had died.

Erik grimaced as he swung to the ground. "The others are dead," he said.

The men glanced among themselves, all having understood his words.

Hong Sing nodded.

Erik handed the three pouches of gold dust to Hong Sing, who received them and bowed. "We are indebted," Hong Sing said.

"They did not have the ore," Erik said. "If they took it, it is probably along the trail. I did not see it."

"They took. Tomorrow we will look," Hong Sing said.

"How is Chen Yuen?" Erik had dreaded asking.

"He rests."

Erik felt a surge of relief. He did not ask if the man would keep his arm. Likely, he would not.

The Chinese picked up their shovels and picks. Pon Kan's body lay to the side but was now dressed. It was then Erik noticed a second body—one of the assailants. The men headed up a slight knoll to the side of their sluice and dug two shallow graves.

They wrapped Pon Kan in a blanket and carried him to one of the graves. They then dragged the second man to the second hole.

Erik watched as they rolled the bodies into the graves, which were so shallow that when filled, the earth barely covered them. Seemingly satisfied, the Chinese headed back toward their camp.

"Now we have a meal," Hong Sing said.

"You buried one of the bandits next to Pon Kan," Erik said.

"Yes. He is Chinese. It makes no difference now."

"I left the other three down trail," Erik said.

"We go to bury them next. But we will not bring them here. Too far," Hong Sing replied.

"You didn't bury them very deep," Erik said. He could not help but wonder if an animal would dig them up. He recalled the settlers burying his boyhood friend Mark Stiles along the Goodale Cutoff. They had buried his body six feet under the wagon road and burned a fire on top of the spot to hide it from not only the animals but also the Indians.

Hong Sing turned to him. "It is so the worms will eat the flesh. The devil is in the flesh. The worms eat the flesh. Flesh gone. Man's spirit no longer troubled by the devil. Man's spirit is in his bones. We take the bones back to China."

"How?" Erik asked.

"Bone collector. In two years, maybe three, bone collector come to take bones back to China—even the evil ones who attack us," Hong Sing said. "We do not belong to the land of the golden mountain. We belong to China. We go home to China."

Erik nodded. "I understand." He wondered what would be proper for his own burial—a churchyard or atop some stone outcrop.

The following day, the Chinese accompanied Erik to where he had left the three bodies. They dug three shallow graves and buried the bandits a distance off the trail so they wouldn't be readily noticed.

Hong Sing cut a Chinese character into a tree near the trail. "To tell the bone collector where to look," he said.

Afterward, they searched for the missing ore. Erik was surprised they hadn't already spotted the bags along the trail. He had not paid close attention to how many cobbles the Chinese had found that held visible gold, but he believed they had at least fifty pieces. Hong Sing had told him they would take it to Orogrande, where they knew others who would mill it.

Erik had not considered the ore's possible value until now. He recalled Hank Hailey had assessed a similar piece—one Badger had found during his vision-seeking. Hailey had proclaimed it must have had nearly an ounce of gold—twenty dollars. The Chinese might have had more than fifty ounces. Erik was not adept at ciphering numbers, but he finally arrived at $1,000. Was it possible the bandits had cached $1,000 in gold somewhere along the trail?

Two days later, Erik and the Chinese gave up the hunt.

"Maybe to spite you, they threw it into the river," Erik said.

"No, we look there."

It was true. They not only had looked behind rocks, in crevices, behind logs, and under shrubs but also had walked the river to check for the bags. Erik thought the thieves could have dumped the bags out into the water, but the ore was distinctive white quartz and would have been easily seen. They turned up nothing. Somewhere between their camp and where Erik had killed the men, the gold ore had vanished.

Erik remained with the Chinese. It was as if he could not escape what had happened. Although it was unlikely, Erik wondered if it might happen again. How many other road agents, Chinese or white, might take the chance of robbing these men? Yet the Chinese worked as if nothing had happened and, more so, as if nothing was going to happen.

A few weeks passed. The South Fork of the Clearwater now ran shallow in the late-summer heat. The tributary the Chinese had been working dried up. They moved down to the river and began working the newly exposed gravel along the riverbanks with two rockers. One man dug gravel from their pit on the hillside and carried it in buckets slung on a pole over his shoulders to the rocker, where he sprinkled it into the grizzly on the head of the box. The second man dipped water from the river and, while gently rocking the box back and forth, washed the gravel. The water carried the bits of gravel across a set of shallow riffles in the bottom of the box, where specks of gold caught behind them.

Erik decided the process was never-ending and nearly fruitless. The men had recovered their best gold while the gulch near the stone huts carried water. Now it was dry, but they continued operating along the river, painstakingly washing bucket after bucket of gravel. The pittance of gold they accumulated each day could hardly have paid for a cup of tea. This was no way to make a living, Erik decided. Yet the Chinese remained patiently at work.

"Will you stay here this winter?" Erik asked.

Hong Sing shook his head. "We go to Elk City. Come back next spring. Maybe not if someone else here. Maybe find new place. Maybe go home to China." He grinned.

Erik shook his head. Despite all this, they remained optimistic.

This morning, Erik approached Hong Sing. His head had long ago ceased giving him trouble, and his leg was better. It had been some time since he had experienced any stabbing pain. Sometimes his leg was numb, but Erik could manage that, especially when on the back of Hatchet. His leg had been the worst when he'd tried to stop the bandits.

"I'm moving on," Erik said. He held Hatchet; the animal was fully packed.

Hong Sing studied him. "We eat first." He beckoned to the others. "They would ask that much of you."

Erik had wrestled with even telling Hong Sing. He had known he would be leaving, especially after he killed the Chinese men. Doing so had rekindled thoughts of Dudgin and Smith. Despite his best efforts to erase them from his thoughts, he could not. He wondered if their paths would cross again. If so, he knew what he must do, despite his new understanding of Gray Owl's words.

"Ja, a meal with you would be good," Erik said.

They gathered at the stone hut nearest the fire. Chen Yuen sat in the doorway with his arm bandaged. They exchanged greetings. Pon Heing served rice with a customary salmon-and-vegetable relish and tea. Erik could not help but wonder what Pon Heing felt at having lost his brother, especially in a foreign land.

The men lit their pipes. Each took a turn and addressed Erik. Hong Sing interpreted. They expressed their thanks. Erik was a man of honor who risked his life for people not his own. Hong Sing summarized by saying, "You showed us what a true man is."

Erik raised his eyes. Those were the words the Sheepeaters used to describe a young man who had completed his vision-seeking.

"Thank you. You have taught me much," Erik said. "You are the hardest-working people I've ever known. I hope you can each return to China someday if that is your wish, but you are welcome in America."

Erik read Hong Sing's eyes. They might have been welcome to some but certainly not to all, and America was not their home.

Hong Sing spoke. "We say you come to us for a reason. We know you seek three men. Before you come to us, these men come. Chen Yuen believes evil follows them. They stay one day with us and try to take gold, but we show them we have none. In two days, you come to us, and we know this is the reason you come. Chen Yuen knows you seek these men, but you are not the evil."

Erik recalled that Chen Yuen had been the one who said he had come for a reason. He wondered how Chen Yuen had sensed that. "Ja, they are evil men," he said. "Perhaps not the younger man with them, Bender, but he soon will be. The other two, I no longer speak their names. They are not worthy to be called men. But you should know them. The one missing two fingers is called Smith. The one with the scar across his face is called Dudgin." Erik glanced at Chen Yuen. "You are correct, Chen Yuen. They bring evil. They would bring death."

Hong Sing interpreted, but the Chinese understood.

"The men go to Mount Idaho," Hong Sing said. "From there, I do not know. Maybe Lewiston. Maybe Salmon River."

Erik's skin crawled at the reawakening thoughts. "Thank you, Hong Sing." He bowed. "However, you should know I no longer seek these men. If the Great Mystery brings them to me, I will kill them. If not, it is what the Great Mystery desires, not I."

Hong Sing again interpreted for the others, and they nodded. "We say that you must take this with you." Hong Sing offered Erik a small pouch. "It is your share of gold."

Erik took the pouch and hefted it. "I cannot. Pon Kan saved my leg. He gave me my life. This is his gold. It is now his brother's gold to take to their family in China." He handed the pouch to Pon Heing.

Pon Heing shook his head and pressed his hands into his thighs.

"You must take," Hong Sing said. "You save our gold. We can never go back to China without gold. Maybe someday we can go."

The Chinese stood. The discussion was finished. They briefly bowed, and Erik returned the custom. He swung back up onto Hatchet and turned down the Clearwater.

He might now head to Lewiston to purchase some supplies and a rifle. He had been incredibly lucky with the Chinese. His bow was good in most cases but would not be if he came upon Dudgin and Smith, who were heavily armed.

After Lewiston, he was uncertain. Another winter would soon be upon him. He might search for another area to trap.

CHAPTER 50

Erik thought of the pouch of gold dust inside his saddlebag. He figured it was several ounces, a considerable sum. The Chinese owed him nothing for what he had done. A strange sensation crept over him. This was blood money. He shook his head. No, he had killed the thieves because it had been the right thing, and now it was the right thing to move on.

Lewiston was a distance of three or four days if he took the Nez Percé Trail. He could get a decent meal and a bath. The Chinese rice and vegetables were decent fare, especially when he brought in wild game, but nothing tasted as fine as a beefsteak with potatoes, rich gravy, and perhaps some onions. He and the Chinese had heated water and taken bucket baths, but he wanted a real bath, a sit-back-in-the-tub-with-soap kind of bath. But the rifle had to come first. Luxuries would come afterward if he had enough dust.

He could not help but wonder about the lost ore. Perhaps the thieves had hung it in a tree? He searched for a final time but to no avail.

He approached the burial site, and the putrid smell of decaying flesh wafted to him. Hatchet shied.

"Nuts, Hatchet, just what I feared. Something's dug them up."

He picketed his nervous horse and walked up off the trail to where the graves were. The graves had been opened. The three partially naked bodies lay a few yards away, covered in flies and maggots. A pair of crows hopped about, tearing at the bodies. Upon seeing him, they bobbed their heads with their ebony eyes glinting and, croaking, flapped away.

"Guess that's one way to get the flesh and the devil off the bones," Erik muttered.

He buried his nose and mouth in the crook of his arm and wondered why the bodies had been pulled a distance from the holes. He could not imagine any animal digging them up and dragging them off. They did not appear to be much eaten either.

The sickening odor began overwhelming Erik. He gasped, choking, but forced himself not to leave. It was because of him the men were dead.

He pulled the bodies back into the holes and threw some rocks and brush onto them. He pushed over a few dead snags and dragged them over the top. Probably it would make little difference, but he had no intention of returning to Hong Sing's camp to inform them.

He stripped off his buckskins and waded into the river, where he washed them. He wrung them out and redressed. It would be better for his buckskins to dry while he wore them, he thought, as they would not stiffen as much.

Hatchet still shied when he returned to the horse.

"Sorry, boy. I know you don't like dead things." He stepped back. "Come to think on it, I don't much like dead things either, unless it's roasted venison or beefsteak."

He broke a conifer branch and rubbed it across his wet buckskins. He then rubbed his hands in the grass.

Hatchet finally accepted him, and he rode a distance in the sun until his buckskins had dried. He stripped off his shirt and rolled it and then let the wind and sun further cleanse his skin.

At length, Erik smelled woodsmoke and spotted a camp a few yards off the trail. He figured he was near the junction to Mount Idaho. Two unkempt men stood in the trail with their rifles loosely pointed in his direction.

Erik raised his hands. "I'm friendly. Just passing through."

The men studied him, until finally, one of them guffawed and lowered his rifle. "Just looks like an Injun." He waved at Erik. "Come on. You damn near got yourself shot."

The other man, with a hawk nose, continued sizing Erik up, particularly his bow. "You see what those red heathens did to those poor bastards up the trail? We found them dug up by wolves or somethin'. Ain't that right, Gerard?"

"That's right, Ned." Gerard ran a finger under his nose and continued eyeing Erik.

"I saw them and tried to rebury them," Erik said. He pulled his buckskin shirt back on. "You must have found them a while back. They're stinking bad. I had to go for a swim." He dismounted and loosely wound Hatchet's reins over a sapling.

Maybe that satisfied Gerard a bit, because he glanced back at his partner and seemed less suspicious.

"It was a few days ago we found 'em. They was kilt by Injuns. Did you notice?" Ned stepped over to a smoldering campfire and pulled off a coffeepot. "Care for some coffee?"

Erik wanted to continue up trail, but he didn't refuse the coffee. The men didn't give their surnames, and Erik didn't give his. Both men sported scraggly whiskers and matted hair. Their soiled and ragged clothes reeked. Why did Erik get the impression Ned was using the coffee as an excuse to engage him? It made his skin crawl.

Erik took the proffered tin cup, swallowed a bit of burned acid, and immediately began looking for a place to dump it. The entire camp smelled. Bits of hide and animal remains were scattered about, but the men weren't trappers. This was the wrong country for trapping. It was too hot and dry.

"We were gonna head up to Mount Idaho and report what we found," Ned said. "Must have been Nez Percé renegades. Injuns don't much like the Chinamen."

"You said they were dug up by wolves," Erik said. "Indians wouldn't have buried them."

Ned straightened and worked his jaw. "You doubtin' me, boy?" he spat. His eyes narrowed. "It was Injuns."

"Could be that other Chinese buried them," Erik said. "They don't bury them deep, you know. On account of the bone collectors."

"On account of bone collectors?" Ned raised an eyebrow, and his mouth half turned into a grin.

"Chinese bone collectors come around every two or three years and send the bones back to China," Erik explained.

Gerard interrupted. "They was done in by Injuns just the same. I seen three arrah holes, and they all had their throats slit. I sure as hell know what arrahs do to a body. Saw that when I was packin' the Bozeman."

Erik didn't reply. He knew the truth.

"At first, we thought the poor bastards were waylaid by some road agents and then got buried to hide the bodies," Ned said. "Wouldn't be the first time some Chinamen got robbed. Them road agents are thick around these parts."

"When we found them, they was gettin' eaten by varmints," Gerard said. "We thought we'd just rebury them and tell the sheriff, but we didn't have a shovel."

"So that's what you intend?" Erik asked. "Head on up to Mount Idaho and let the sheriff know?"

"Figurin' so. We were hopin' we'd get some more company, though," Ned said. "Nez Percé hang around Mount Idaho. If there's renegades about, I don't fancy ridin' up that canyon and gettin' massacred. Be a perfect place." He squinted at Erik. "You goin' that way?"

Erik swirled his coffee, still looking for a chance to dump it. "That's not my intent. I'm coming from Elk City. Maybe going on to Lewiston. What about you?" The questions were like dancing with a porcupine—not quite getting to the point.

"We just back and forth in this country, lookin' for a bit of gold to wash and maybe doin' some packin' when someone needs a hand," Gerard said. "Livin' it easy."

Erik's skin prickled. *Gold without a shovel? These two might be road agents themselves.* The fact that they had happened on the bodies was curious. Hong Sing had intentionally buried them back up off the trail.

Erik stopped his hand, remembering the look in Gerard's eyes. *Ned and Gerard dug them up, not some animals. Leastwise wolves.* Wolves preferred killing their own prey. A sudden chill raced down Erik's neck, raising his hair. He had stumbled into a camp of scavengers. Ned and Gerard had dragged out the bodies and robbed them of anything they might have still had on them.

They might well report the bodies and the arrow holes. Both had noticed his bow. They could easily blame him for the deaths and likely would. It would deflect attention from any of their other deeds. A clammy feeling crawled across Erik's neck. They would not suspect he carried some gold, but it wouldn't stop them from taking his bow and horse and leaving his body in the river.

Erik decided the visit was over. He emptied his coffee cup into the grass, tossed it to Ned, and caught up Hatchet.

"It wasn't Indians that killed those Chinese you dug up," Erik said. He touched his bow, and both men's eyes widened.

Ned started up, scrambling for where his rifle rested against a tree.

"You won't need it, Ned," Erik said. "Other Chinese buried those poor bastards because it was those bastards that robbed them. They were settling the score. You'll find two more graves upriver at a Chinese placer. Ask for Hong Sing; he'll confirm what I've told you. It was not Indians."

Erik spurred Hatchet into a trot and headed north. The scum would not question Hong Sing. They likely weren't on friendly grounds with anyone along the river. He regretted telling the truth, but it would have been impossible to quell any rumors, and he did not want to see a war erupt because of something he had done. But now he had a new worry. The US government was obligated to answer to the Chinese government for any Chinese citizens killed by Americans. Sooner or later, word would reach the sheriff, especially if Ned and Gerard could figure out something in it for themselves.

"Well, Hatchet, I fixed our hides good, didn't I?" Erik muttered. "We've disappeared before, but I sure could have used that rifle and grub. Winter's going to be mighty long without a few supplies."

CHAPTER 51

The following morning, Erik was surprised to find a waystation at the crossroads of the Clearwater River and the Nez Percé Trail. He had not expected to find a place where he could pick up a few staples and had resigned himself to heading back into the high country without. Erik hoped to purchase a rifle but learned the station manager, John Clindinning, offered only a few knives and axes.

"Rifle's too much of a temptation for a drunk renegade," Clindinning said. He closely scrutinized Erik with a wry grin. Erik guessed he had noticed his bow in addition to his buckskins.

Erik gathered up some cornmeal, salt, sugar, coffee, and beans. Clindinning raised bushy gray eyebrows that matched his wispy graying hair and bushy beard. He smiled as he started jotting the items down.

"Could have done yourself better at Mount Idaho," Clindinning said. "But I thank thee."

Clindinning seemed even more pleased when Erik handed him the pouch of gold dust. Erik nervously watched as a goodly amount of his dust was weighed and then swept into a small canister.

Clindinning's gray eyes pinched. "Didn't take you for a prospector." He handed Erik's pouch back.

"I came by it legally," Erik said. "Trapping and packing."

"No offense," Clindinning replied. "I get plenty of durn men through here who have acquired it illegal-like, but then those kind are likely to just help themselves to what I got anyhow. That's one of the problems of being out here by your lonesome on a busy trail."

Clindinning offered Erik a cup of coffee, and Erik quickly accepted, figuring that it had to be better than Ned's and that where he was headed, he'd run out before spring.

Clindinning's arm shook a little as he poured, betraying his years. He was a tall man dressed in a dark brown waistcoat over a white cotton shirt that buttoned at the throat.

"William Jackson first settled here," Clindinning said. "Got here in '61 and built himself a durn toll bridge. Folks call it Jackson's Bridge. Some call this place Bridgeport on account of it. I've only been here a short time." He refilled his own cup and nodded toward Erik.

Erik took a swallow. This coffee was much more palatable than the last cup he'd had.

"The Nez Percé reservation is a stone's throw northwest of here. They come across here regular-like on their annual trek to hunt buffalo in the Big Hole. As far as I know, Jackson never had a lick of trouble with them, nor have I. I follow the rules. I don't sell them firearms or liquor, and not having any makes it easier to avoid the temptation." Clindinning nodded stiffly. "Though some folks around do sell them weapons, it's just inviting trouble. I have enough trouble with white scalawags." He frowned. "Never any trouble with the Chinamen either. They have their own pack trains and come through here regular-like as well.

"So what are your thoughts, Mr. Larson, if I can ask? You going back doin' some trappin'?" He eyed Erik's supplies.

"I planned on it. This country isn't fit, though." Erik said it as an invitation for Clindinning's perspective.

"Nope. Not around here. Go upriver on the Middle Fork for the best. It forks into two rivers, the north being the Lochsa and the south being the Selway. Lochsa has always had good fur but durn little else. It has a trail along it into Montana Territory." He squinted at Erik. "Ever hear of the Corps of Discovery? They come over Lolo Pass down the Lochsa. Durn near starved. Nothing but timber up there. No elk. No deer. Maybe a few salmon at the right time of the year. Otherwise, only squirrels. They ended up eating most of their horses before they got here. Nez Percé saved their hides.

"Probably won't see another soul up there either. Durn few gold camps. Now, farther north on the North Fork, that's a different country. Some of the best goldurn gold ever found. The first strike was at Pierce. Still a goodly amount around there, but up the Middle Fork, nary a thing." Clindinning raised his bushy eyebrows. "Never can figure gold. It's down on the South Fork and up on the North

Fork, nary a bit in between. Maybe could be, but so durn much timber you couldn't see it unless it crawled out of the ground and bit you."

"Any trouble with the Indians upriver?" Erik asked.

Clindinning guffawed. "Not with the Nez Percé. Maybe some Blackfeet coming raiding from Montana Territory but not the Nez Percé.

"At least there hasn't been. Maybe now. Two men were by a few days back, saying some Chinamen got killed by Indians. Said some animals had dug up the bodies. It could be, but I'm doubting it. Sometimes the Chinamen and Indians don't get along, but I never heard of the Nez Percé killing any."

"Ned and Gerard," Erik said. "I ran into them. But just so you're straight on things, those men were robbing graves. They're the ones who dug up the bodies, not some animals."

Clindinning raised his eyes. "Surprises me not. Durn scavengers is what they are. Always coming by here with something doing. If I smell them coming, I just bar the door."

"Exactly how I figured them," Erik said, recalling the unforgettable stench that had hovered about their camp.

"Claimed the Chinamen had arrow holes in them, though," Clindinning said. He raised his eyes. "Don't suppose someone wanted to make it look like Indians?"

Erik had hoped not to share more information than necessary, but he now decided word would catch up to Clindinning soon enough. "I spent some time with some Chinese on the South Fork. Some of their countrymen robbed them, hacking them up. Those who survived took the law into their own hands." Erik swallowed the remainder of his coffee and handed the cup to Clindinning. "It was not Indians who killed those Chinese."

Clindinning worked his jaw with his whiskers bobbing a bit. He started to say something and stopped. He eyed Erik for a long moment. "You sure you don't need some more ground coffee or sugar or something?" He weighed out another pound of coffee and some dried apples and packaged them up for Erik. "See you again? Maybe next spring?"

"I'm obliged," Erik said.

Leaving Jackson's Bridge, Erik continued north along the main river trail. The slopes receded from the river and climbed in brown folds like giant stairs into the basalt cliffs that now lined both sides of the canyon. An occasional conifer spotted their crowns. The early autumn sun had bleached the short grasses nearly white. Cottonwoods with heat-crinkled leaves grew scattered in the hot, dusty draws. Scraggly bitterbrush, sagebrush, and spindly sunflowers stretched over the dry hillsides.

"Hotter than blazes down here, Hatchet. Hard to believe winter's coming."

Erik reached the confluence of the South Fork with the Middle Fork of the Clearwater. He headed east up the Middle Fork; it was nearly three times the size of the South Fork. The trail he followed quickly ascended from dry sagebrush to areas with chokecherry, mountain ash, and sumac. Conifers began reaching down in thick aprons from the ridges.

Erik glanced upriver toward the timber-cloaked peaks. "A day and we'll be up there, Hatchet. Be a lot cooler."

The sun bled orange the following morning, peeking through a brown haze and accompanied by the acrid smell of woodsmoke.

"Fire upstream, Hatchet," Erik muttered. "Doubt it will be trouble. Plenty of country. We just go where the fire isn't."

The river split with one of the tributaries coming in from the north and the second joining from the south. Erik forded the river and headed north. According to Clindinning, this was the Lochsa. The fire seemed to be toward the south, along the Selway.

He was now in dense timber. Cedar, fir, and spruce towered a hundred feet into the sky, making it difficult for Erik to believe he had been in a barren, heat-scoured canyon a few days past. Sunlight fought to reach the forest floor. In the scattered openings, mountain maple, birch, and alder were ablaze with fall foliage.

"Clindinning was sure right about the timber, Hatchet."

This was great fur country but nearly a desert for big game, such as deer or elk.

Erik followed the Lochsa for several miles until he reached a small tributary that tumbled down through a narrow valley. It reminded him of the valleys he had wintered in at other times. He turned up it. He sought a base camp where the timber was more open and there was sufficient graze for Hatchet.

Even after he reached the higher country, it took Erik several more days of scouting the drainages to determine where the fur animals were before he decided on his winter camp.

He found where a turbulent creek raced through a narrow valley and wound its way through a series of small, willow-spotted meadows. Mountain maple and alder merged into heavily timbered ridges.

A recent burn had cleared several hillsides of timber. The trees' charred skeletons jutted stark and twisted from thickets of orange and russet huckleberry bushes and beargrass clumps. Thick, waist-high grass carpeted the open areas along the creek.

"Good feed for you, Hatchet," Erik said, "and likely some deer."

As if to prove the point, two mule deer broke for cover into the timber.

He scouted the country above the stream, searching for sign of fur animals, and was rewarded with good sign. That meant there were also predators, such as fox, coyote, and possibly lynx.

"Well, Hatchet, this will be home for the next few months. This time, we won't have to build a cabin in a snowstorm, and I might even be able to store up some hay for you." Erik gazed toward the west, aware that the air had cooled. A curtain of dark clouds he had not noticed earlier towered above him, threatening rain.

He glanced south to where the fire plume rose in the still air. "Maybe the rain'll put that out."

CHAPTER 52

Water dripped from the icicles, catching the early spring light and reflecting sparkling diamonds onto the earthen floor. Erik stood gazing south. Absently, he pushed a moccasined toe through the mud. The seasons had turned. Shortly, it would be time to head down out of the high country. A few hides yet cured on their stretchers.

His cabin had held up. It had given him a place to sleep, prepare his meals, and work on his pelts. The snow had been considerably deeper in this valley than in the other places where he had trapped. Hatchet had not had as much grass, except that which Erik cut and the grass exposed under the brush and along the edges of the creek. He did well enough with the sumac, willow, and aspen. On a few occasions, Erik trailed him down the valley to where there were some exposed grassy slopes near the river.

Erik had come to this valley somewhat in haste, concerned that trouble might be looking for him because of the dead Chinese. Likely, no one would any longer be concerned. Clindinning had tacitly agreed that it was business between the Chinese and not whites. If anything, the sheriff might ask a question or two.

Erik had made no decisions regarding the new season, despite a long, lonesome winter. Should he return to the Sacred River band? He could not as long as Dudgin and Smith breathed life. And would he ever? His time with the Chinese had revealed that he could not seek revenge—to do so acknowledged Dudgin and Smith as human. They were not human. If their paths ever crossed, Erik would take their lives. They would know death at his hand, but it would be detached, unemotional, and nameless.

An icicle broke from the roof and fell, splintering into shards of sparkling crystal. Erik kicked a piece and watched it skitter across the muddy earth. He stepped from the door into the bright sunshine. The winter had been long, with too many memories and too many ghosts.

"Great Mystery, these mountains give me too much time to think. In truth, I am but a leaf tossed about in the wind. What am I to your great plan?"

Erik decided he would take his furs to Lewiston and attempt to acquire a rifle. The Great Mystery would lead his path after that.

He packed his furs onto Hatchet, and leading the horse, he snowshoed his way back out of the high country to the Lochsa. It was high with meltwater and pounded white. Lingering snowbanks made it nearly impossible to traverse the river, and in places, he found himself slogging through flooded areas, trying to keep to the trail. No horses had been through.

His progress improved when he reached the confluence of the Lochsa with the Selway, where they joined to become the Middle Fork. He noted a few horse tracks had turned up the Selway. Down the Middle Fork, the canyon broadened, and the snow receded, but the trail became mud and matted grass. The mountains above and behind glistened white in deep snow.

He continued until he found good grass. The Sheepeaters called this season the new sheep moon. He camped early and allowed Hatchet to leisurely feed. He was in no hurry to get to Lewiston, and Hatchet needed to recover from the winter.

Erik built a travois for his furs, and in a few days, he resumed his travel to the confluence of the Middle Fork with the South Fork of the Clearwater and turned north. The river ran swiftly, with high water from the melting mountain snow. He had dropped more than two thousand feet in elevation. A warm, summerlike breeze buffeted him and brought the scent of fresh grasses and sagebrush. Shrubs had unfurled their leaves. It was difficult to believe a week ago he had been deep in snow and kicking icicles across his cabin floor.

He met a few parties of prospectors and, shortly beyond them, two pack trains. The second pack train was Chinese. This early in the season, many of the gold camps were still snowbound, but supplies often were deposited at the snowline, and men would pack them the remaining distance on snowshoes. Each time he came across travelers, they asked similar questions: "Where are you coming from? How deep is the snow?"

At the confluence with the North Fork of the Clearwater River, Erik continued west down the Clearwater. He rounded a corner and unexpectedly met two riders. His scalp immediately prickled. They could have been Ned's and Gerard's twins—they were unkempt, with ratty clothes and scraggly beards.

The trail curved into a small draw and out, but Erik would have been cut from sight for only a brief minute or two. How had he not seen them? A chill raced over Erik. They had been off the trail in the rocks above, watching, and had dropped onto the trail when they spotted him.

The men studied him, especially his bow. One of them spat into the mud. They had rifles. Thoughts of the dead Chinese leaped to mind. Erik figured they were judging their chance or the value in jumping him. A bow offered no defense against two rifles. His load of furs held value but not to them. His horse held value. Erik rose in his saddle, making a show of his knife. If they judged him to be a mountain man, they would likely figure he knew how to use his knife, despite his youthful appearance.

One of them fingered his rifle. A shiver crawled down Erik's neck. He knew it would take nothing for the man to put a bullet into him and for them to pilfer his body for anything of value and then roll it into the river. Hatchet would be theirs. They'd unload the pelts and find his gold a bonus. He fought an uneasy impulse to glance at the river below.

"If you men are heading upriver far, you'll be running into deep snow above the Selway and Lochsa. I'm coming out of there."

Neither acknowledged him. Erik stiffened. He had one chance: he could run at one and try to unseat him and grab for his rifle. A bead of sweat gathered and slid down his neck as he tried to read the men's intentions.

Movement on the trail beyond the men caught his attention. Another pack train was coming into view. Quick relief washed over Erik, and he clucked to Hatchet, continuing down trail and heading past the men.

They nodded. "We ain't heading that far," one of the men said as Erik passed. The man spat again, wiping a sleeve across his beard, his eyes following Erik.

Erik moved off the trail to let the pack train through but then continued toward a low ridge. He pulled his bow and a couple of arrows and strung it. He continued moving up the ridge, dragging his travois. If necessary, he would cut it free and run. He stood no chance against rifles, but at least one of the men would get an arrow. The trail behind and below him remained empty. He let out a slow breath.

It did not matter. He knew the men could easily circle back and follow the travois tracks. Erik reached the ridge and turned to watch. He was becoming tired of traveling alone, at least along trails on which he could be jumped. In timber, he had the advantage, but here on these open trails, he was easy prey.

The men did not reappear. Likely, they had found a spot from which to watch for another straggler. Erik continued along the ridge and then down, keeping off the trail for another couple of hours before stopping for the night. Lewiston was yet half a day away.

"Used to be a man could live in this country on his own, Hatchet," Erik mused. "Now if you even look like you have a dollar, you're likely to be jumped."

CHAPTER 53

About midday the next, Erik rode into Lewiston. He passed the Bitterroot Saloon, where he and his bow had been pitted against the six-shooter. He glanced across at the Clearwater Hotel, where four and a half years ago, he had spent a few nights and taken his meals when he turned eighteen. He'd come to Lewiston to look for a wife and raise a family. He hadn't met the right woman, and now that he understood more the ways of the world, he knew he never would have met the right woman in a bustling outlaw supply and shipping town—not one who was not already married.

There were fewer tents but more and taller buildings than he remembered. People, horses, and wagons filled the streets. Lewiston had sprung up in 1861 on the Nez Percé reservation to supply the gold camps springing up along the Clearwater River. The reservation soon had been reduced to a tenth of the size, so Lewiston and the gold strikes were outside the new boundaries. The Nez Percé retained their hunting and fishing rights on the old lands, but they could no longer occupy the former reservation. Of course, many did, particularly young Chief Joseph and Chief White Bird.

Erik entered the Bitterroot Saloon and asked where he might be able to trade his pelts. One man sized up Erik and his buckskins and mentioned that Andrew Spaulding down the street was known for trading furs. "He deals with Celestials and Indians. He ought to deal with your kind."

Meaning he deals with mountain men, Erik presumed. He nodded his thanks and made his way down the street until he found Spaulding's Mercantile.

Andrew Spaulding was a lanky, weathered older man, and he and Erik struck up a good conversation. Spaulding was familiar with the country above the Lochsa, where Erik had spent the winter trapping. He recalled the old days when Indians had brought in bison and elk hides. He was most pleased with Erik's lynx. It would fetch good money.

After considerable bartering with the furs and still falling short of being able to buy all he intended, including an old Spencer rifle, Erik pulled out the Chinese placer gold.

Spaulding's eyes widened. "Maybe you should consider some civilized attire. I have some new canvas pants with reinforced pockets." He set his hands on a pile. "Or a shirt." He indicated some shirts piled on a shelf. A white shirt hung nearby, displayed on a peg.

"My kind thanks," Erik said, "but let's settle on this for now. Take the difference out of my dust, and if you can change it out for some coin, I'll be back for some additional supplies for your trouble."

Spaulding eyed the gold dust. "I can do that. Maybe twelve dollars an ounce?"

"I trust your judgment," Erik said.

Spaulding weighed the gold. "Three ounces point two. How about thirty-eight dollars, less what you owe me?"

"How about you give me ten for now? I'll take the balance on other goods when I pull out."

"My pleasure." Spaulding seemed a little giddy while handing Erik two half eagles.

Erik left his goods behind, except for the Spencer and some ammo and a few things he could use back in the hotel. He found the livery stable and asked the owner to give Hatchet some extra feed. He paid a dollar in advance. He then returned to the Clearwater Hotel.

It did not appear crowded. A stout middle-aged lady with graying hair and deep creases, especially about her pale blue eyes, met him.

Her initial smile turned to a frown as she sized up Erik. "Nej, we have no room." Her eyes turned to flint, and she turned away, muttering.

Erik's smile spread across his face. "Är du säker på att du inte har utrymme?" (Are you certain you have no room?)

The woman abruptly turned, her eyes sparkling. "Svenska?"

"Ja, Svenska." Erik nodded, grinning. "I'm Erik Larson. I came to America when I was a young lad." He noticed some of the decorations inside the boardinghouse. White candles stood in a traditional red three-bulb holder, and a carved rose-mailed red horse sat on a ledge above the fireplace.

"Dear Lord, I'm Mrs. Simon Steele," she rattled in Swedish, staring, dumbfounded. "You are from the old country, ja. Well, I just have a good bed, I do. That Mr. Varner—he is not back. I will just fix up his room, and you shall have it, Mr. Larson."

Erik grinned. "It is a pleasure meeting you, Mrs. Steele. I promise I'll be more presentable shortly if you can direct me to where I can also get a bath."

Mrs. Steele peered intently at Erik before fluffing her skirt and wringing her hands. "Ja, sure we have a bath."

Erik laughed.

"What be so funny?" Mrs. Steele demanded.

"You remind me of Mrs. Olafson. She's from Sweden as well." He picked up his belongings. "I have a shirt she sewed for me. You will see."

"Ja, well, that is good," Mrs. Steele stammered. "You call me Ma Steele. Everyone does. And yes, you can get a bath, Mr. Larson. It will be four bits. Your bed and meal is a dollar."

"That suits me just fine," Erik replied. He reached for his pouch.

"How long do you plan for?" Ma Steele eyed the pouch. "I take five dollars for the week, plus four bits for the bath." Erik fingered the pouch, and she quickly sweetened the offer. "It be five dollars, and some evening, you and I share some stories of the old country," she said.

Erik pulled out a half eagle. "I intend a couple of nights," he said. "Keep the five dollars. If anything remains when I do head out, I'll settle with you then, if that would suit you."

"Ja, ja." Ma Steele's eyes lit. "It sure was better around here in the early days, when everyone was going to the gold country. Now, not so busy." She eyed him more closely. "We get some of that dirt off of you; maybe then I can see some Swede."

Erik smiled. "I have a story about the Olafsons that I can share at supper if you wish."

Ma Steele showed Erik his room, the dining room, the facilities outside, and the room where he could take a bath. "I will heat some water now if you wish," she said.

"That would be kind. Show me your woodyard so I can bring in a load."

"Might not be more than a load that's been split," she answered.

Out in the back, Erik discovered Ma Steele had been correct. Only a few pieces of wood lay scattered about, but a pile of lengths of log awaited splitting. Erik gathered up the last of the pieces, carried them inside, and then returned to the yard and began splitting more wood. When Ma Steele came into view, she said, "You have already paid, Mr. Larson."

Erik swung the blade, splitting a block. "It is my pleasure. We shall have more time to talk about the old country if I do this." Truthfully, Erik remembered little of Sweden. What he knew he had learned from the other Swedes while in Minnesota before they headed west, but as he swung the ax, he warmly recalled the customs—the stories of fairies and trolls, the songs, the special food, and the celebrations, especially Midsummer's Eve. Those were good memories.

He sank the ax into another block of wood and sent the pieces spinning and clattering to the ground.

As it turned out, Erik was the only one for a bath. As near as he could guess, there were three or four regular boarders. Ma Steele had made an exception for him. Bath night was usually Saturday.

Afterward, he returned to his room, slipped on his beige canvas pants, and then pulled on the shirt Margret Olafson had made for him. It was a traditional open-collar white shirt with narrow blue stripes and was made from the cloth he had purchased in Lewiston. He fastened his suspenders and slipped into his short dark brown frock coat. He examined a frayed sleeve. He wondered if he might have enough money remaining at Spaulding's Mercantile for a new one. He pulled on his boots. "I guess I'm back in civilization," he mused.

When he emerged for supper, Ma Steele looked him over and gave him a pleasant nod. Two other men were already present. Erik was surprised when a young girl brought him a plate of food—Ma Steele's daughter, Elise. Erik guessed she was maybe nine or ten. She reminded Erik of the Swedish youngsters in the valley, except she had curly brown hair that reminded him of Mrs. Lundgren's daughter, Emma. Elise joined Erik with a plate of food for herself.

"Now, do not you be bothering Mr. Larson," Ma Steele told her. "I am sorry, Mr. Larson. I told her you were from Sweden and that you might have a story."

"My pleasure," Erik said. He told Elise she reminded him of Emma, a friend of his sister, Katrine.

Elise wanted to know why he wasn't with his family and having supper with his sister.

"I sometimes wonder that as well," Erik said.

He asked Elise if she had heard stories about Jeppe the elf. She had not, so Erik began a story about how Jeppe journeyed west on the wagons. He had hardly finished, when Ma Steele shooed Elise to bed.

Erik and Ma Steele shared some coffee. He could not remember any as good, until he remembered the Olafsons'. The evening brought back memories of the Swedish settlers. Ma Steele professed her longing for the Swedish people. She had come from Sweden a dozen years ago. Elise had been born in America. Erik found himself wondering if he had given life with the Swedes a fair effort.

They talked long into the night.

It was not right, Erik finally decided, for he and Ma Steele to talk together alone, and he excused himself.

Back in his room, he decided he could get used to civilized living, but he would need a job. What kind of job could he do? He had experience in packing. Lewiston was the hub from which the pack trains and freight wagons headed out toward the gold camps. Although many of the early placer camps were now dying, others were still thriving, and some lode claims were coming in. The hardrock mines would need tenfold the freight that the placer operations needed. He began to warm to the idea and decided he would check around come morning.

Erik hardly slept. The bed was too soft; some boarders were having a party; and he worried someone might try to break in and take his rifle or remaining gold, having seen him freely spending it. Finally, he got up, dressed, and walked out to watch the sunrise.

CHAPTER 54

After breakfast, Erik tracked down some of the merchants and learned that with few exceptions, they shipped their goods by wagon and not mule train. None needed assistance. He could remain available in case they came up shorthanded, but the wagons and pack trains were already on their way with the first goods for the season.

Erik recalled Lee Pow, the Chinese packer who had come through when he was with Hong Sing. Lee Pow packed his goods solely by mule train.

He found the Chinese section of Lewiston. It consisted of several dozen buildings and numerous tents scattered along the Snake River near where the Clearwater joined. Several Chinese boats and rafts were moored at the docks. Goods from China arrived in Portland and were shipped 350 miles, first up the Columbia and then up the Snake. Other goods were brought overland from Sacramento to Portland and then shipped up the Columbia. Either direction, freight had to be unloaded and portaged around Celilo Falls and then reloaded onto smaller boats for transport upriver another 250 miles to Lewiston. River transport was largely possible because the confluence of the Clearwater and Snake rivers was less than eight hundred feet in elevation.

Erik's efforts to find Lee Pow brought quizzical looks and little help, until he stumbled onto Man Wah, an elderly Chinese man who supplied Lee Pow. Man Wah became excited when Erik inquired if he knew Hong Sing.

Man Wah grinned broadly and exclaimed, "You are the one! Vehlie good to meet you, Mistah Ehwik. You are friend of Hong Sing and Chen Yuen. I know them."

301

Two other Chinese men seemed to take interest in their meeting and edged in their direction. Man Wah noticed as well and immediately said, "You come have tea inside, Mistah Ehwik."

Erik closely followed Man Wah through the crowded mercantile, between shelves of crockery and mining gear. He noted gold pans, rubber boots, picks, and shovels were piled in heaps in one area, and crocks of rice, relish, and roots were piled in another. Fragrant spices, including ginger, anise, and cloves, permeated the air. Brightly colored scarves floated on the breeze, along with colorful rice paper and paper lanterns. Erik guessed they were to remind the Chinese of their homeland.

Near the back of the store, at a small table, Man Wah indicated a wicker chair for Erik to sit and took a chair across from him. A younger man materialized and quickly poured a steaming cup of fragrant tea with a sweetish spice. Man Wah gestured to the younger man and nodded toward the two men Erik had noticed outside. They had come inside.

Man Wah's eyes followed the men, and he set a cleaver on the table. The men noticed and paused.

Man Wah smiled. "You be okay with me and Man Ling, but you are not safe in this place."

"Lewiston?"

Man Wah nodded. "You kill the bandits."

"I had a debt to pay," Erik said. His skin prickled. "Pon Kan healed me. They killed him."

"Yes," Man Wah said. "We are happy you kill bandits. The white Indyan with bow. But you kill Kan See men."

"Kan See's men?"

"The bandits work for Kan See. He is powerful man. He does not harm me because I am my own man. He harm others. Maybe he harms Lee Pow, who trades with me."

"And if he knows I'm here?" Erik asked. He nodded in the direction of Man Ling, who had the two men cornered and escorted them toward the entrance. "Am I in danger?"

"Maybe. Chinese do not like for white man to interfere. Chinese take care of Chinese." Man Wah shook his head. "You keep watch. You have a rifle. That is good."

Erik sampled some of the spicy tea. A knot grew in his chest. Had he again brought evil to others who knew him? "Thank you, Man

Wah," he said. "I shall watch. I had hoped to run one of your pack trains, but I can see it might not be good for you."

"No. It would be good," Man Wah said. "You have rifle. Kan See men leave you alone." He smiled. "You come back when Lee Pow is back. Maybe go with him."

Erik briefly considered the idea, but Man Wah had also just warned him to become scarce. He felt it might not be prudent to hang around Lewiston for a couple of weeks for Lee Pow to return. Much could happen. "Thank you. I will consider checking back," he said. He stood, bowed, and left the store.

Outside, the two men continued watching him. Maybe because Man Ling stood nearby, they made no effort to follow. Of course, if the Chinese wanted him dead, he would not know until his throat had been slit.

A dozen mules filled the street in front of another mercantile. Chinese busily packed the animals with large wicker baskets that held chickens and piglets. The Chinese would take them into the gold camps, where they would be raised and slaughtered. They favored pork over beef.

Erik briefly considered inquiring whether they needed assistance, but after his conversation with Man Wah, he decided otherwise.

"I guess I didn't need to do any packing," Erik muttered.

He did not like it. He had hoped to stay for a few days and enjoy Ma Steele's cooking and hospitality, but he now knew he would be moving on, especially because of a man named Kan See. Well, he had gotten what he came for: a bath and a rifle.

CHAPTER 55

Erik had an hour before supper. He found an empty table in the Bitterroot Saloon and began nursing a whiskey. He watched other men come and go through the cigar haze and listened to the honky-tonk piano. Mule deer and elk antlers graced the walls, along with a fox pelt. There was also a Nez Percé bow and quiver of arrows. He thought of Gray Owl. Although the men he had killed were Chinese, would Gray Owl have agreed with his killing them? Would he have considered them not men for their having killed Pon Kan? Was Erik now hunted by Kan See?

Erik reflected on the time he had prepared for his boyhood vision-seeking. Gray Owl had shared his own boyhood vision. A snake had come down from the sun and repeatedly attacked an owl. The owl had fought it and, in the end, grabbed up the snake and flown it to the sun. Gray Owl had received his name from that vision and had been the one to lead the people. Some seasons had been good; others had ended in suffering.

The whiskey in Erik's hand vibrated. Had the burning-rocks vision been a second vision? The one his spirit helper had said was not his? The wolf-bear creatures had repeatedly attacked the night cat. Gray Owl had told Erik he believed Two Elks Fighting would become the one to whom the people turned. Twice, evil had risen against him, and it would rise against him again.

No. That is spirit talk, Erik told himself. He took a swallow of whiskey and felt the burn. *Where have these thoughts come from? I'm no longer of the people's world.*

Erik glanced around. These men were oblivious to the spirit world. For a time, he had been unaware of it as well. Now he could not shake his burning-rocks vision of the wolf-bear beasts that had risen against the night cat, his spirit helper. "That's what it's telling me. It's time to go back to the people," he whispered. He drained his glass.

Three men in boisterous conversation at a nearby table caught Erik's attention. The oldest man wore a coat with a fancy waistcoat. The other two were not much of a step up from the scum Erik had recently met on the trail. Both were raggedly dressed and dust-covered. The older man seemingly barely tolerated the younger two, as if he had an obligation to be there but desired to be elsewhere. The conversation centered on something about cattle.

The dance hall lady addressed him twice before Erik realized she was talking to him. Generally, because of his dress, ladies didn't talk to him, but presently, he wore civilized clothing. Then he figured his unruly hair might yet bespeak his long winter in the brush, and she would still recognize his nature. He glanced up.

"Uh, pardon me, ma'am."

"Name's Dolly." She smiled, and Erik noticed the rouge applied liberally to her cheeks and her smeared red lipstick. "I said if you're interested in anything you see here, you just let me know."

Dolly wore a rather frilly dress, and heavy perfume followed her movements. Erik noticed her low-cut front and flushed as he pulled his eyes away, although he found no sin in harboring the fleeting thoughts that accompanied his gaze.

"Thank you, ma'am." He pulled back. "Just biding some time."

"Over here, Dolly," the older man called from across the room, beckoning her with a raised empty glass.

Dolly touched Erik's arm. "You just let me know, honey." She gave him a sidelong look and pursed her lips before whisking away toward the men with the perfume's fragrance racing to keep pace with her.

Erik couldn't cage his eyes as Dolly made her way to the men's table. The three men seemed to know her, especially the older man. He was a large man with graying hair at his temples and confident eyes. He made familiar motions toward Dolly. She pretended him her attention, smiling and laughing and entering a conversation that Erik could not make out, while she poured new drinks.

Erik burned with recognition of her earlier actions within his presence. It was an open-letter invitation—and she had presented it neatly to him, even in the midst of the other men. Her eyes glanced back in his direction, and he quickly looked away. They settled on the new drink she had placed unnoticed in front of him. He could not help but wonder what Dolly saw in him. Why him? There were others besides the three men she now entertained. He glanced around as if to prove to himself his point. A least a dozen men were spread out in the noisy saloon, smoking their cigars with their whiskeys in front of them, some playing cards. Why not one of the others?

Erik nodded in return to Dolly and took a swallow of the new drink, thankful she had momentarily pulled his darkening thoughts from the spirit world. The whiskey warmed him. Her smile was genuine.

Despite his misgivings, a warm shiver washed over Erik. It had been a while since he had been in the company of a woman. But when he thought about it, his thoughts snapped back to Bright Shell, and a sudden darkness seeped in. His stomach tightened. His hand shook, and he pushed the drink away. He returned to studying the three men, making certain they were not Dudgin, Smith, and Bender. There seemed some similarity. His mind clouded in turmoil. Could it be that the one with lighter hair had a scar? He watched the other man to see if he was short any fingers. Cold, clammy sweat collected on the back of Erik's neck. The wolf-bear vision crept back. Was evil rising?

A lanky, unkempt youth stumbled into the room, clearly intoxicated. "Whar ya at, Unter, ya snake?" The young man glanced about before he stumbled toward the table where the three men sat. He headed directly for the older man.

Something seemed familiar about the youth. Erik tried to make it out. The kid was dressed shabbily in a torn vest over a dingy high-buttoned shirt, and his clothes were caked in grime.

"You owe me!" the kid shouted, slurring his words. He tossed his head to get his scraggly dark hair out of his eyes. His slender hand nervously twisted on a pistol.

Erik's chest tightened. He was about to see the kid get killed.

The two men on either side of Unter slid back.

Unter eyed the kid. "Don't be a fool," he said. He remained steady. "You were paid."

Drake Minton! Erik scrambled to his feet, knocking his chair away.

"Not what I was owed. I want my share," Drake spat, his fingers pushing at the pistol.

"Drake!" Erik shouted. He started toward him.

The youth jerked around, his brown eyes wide. As he did, Unter slammed back from the table and leaped toward him. His fist flashed, and he caught Drake square with a hard right. He slammed his left into the boy's gut and then struck again with his right. Drake crumpled to the floor as his wind gushed out, and his pistol slid from his hand and across the floor.

"Bastard whelp," Unter cursed. He let fly with a boot, catching Drake on his side. "No one calls me a cheat."

Erik slammed into Unter, pushing the man off Drake. "Leave the kid be. I'll take care of him."

Unter pulled his pistol and aimed it at Erik. "This ain't your fight, mister. No one calls me a cheat, and no stranger jumps me." The hammer cocked.

Drake writhed on the floor. Blood bubbled from his mouth and nose. Dolly reached him and pushed him down, saying something Erik could not make out. Erik stared at the cocked pistol aimed at his chest.

Erik raised his hands and stepped back. He recalled the time he had jumped Dudgin and Smith. He sucked in a breath. "You're right. Sorry, mister. This is not my fight. I know the kid—that's all."

Unter lowered his pistol. "You know him?" He waved the pistol at Drake.

Drake tried to get up. "Le' me be." He weakly swung his arms, trying to get away from Dolly. "He owes me." He grabbed at his pistol on the floor.

Erik kicked it away. "You're drunk, Drake. Leave it." He grabbed the boy under his arms and pulled him away. "I'll try to square things, mister." Erik said it as a mild apology to Unter.

"Look, stranger, he's no account to me. We're finished. He cost me plenty." Unter holstered his pistol. "Get him out of my sight."

Blood wet Drake's grimy shirt. "I need my share," he mumbled.

Somehow, Erik managed to get Drake from the saloon and into the street, where he slumped in the dirt.

"I gotta go back in there," Drake protested. "He owes me."

Erik shook him. "Tomorrow, Drake. You aren't fit for taking on anyone today." Of course, Erik had no idea what the situation was.

Drake's watery eyes settled on Erik and then opened wide. "M-Mister Larson," he stammered. "What you doin' here?" He groaned, holding his side. "That snake busted my ribs."

"Later, Drake. Let me get you off the street." Erik got an arm around Drake and pulled him up.

Dolly watched from the door with a hurt expression. Others stopped briefly but then continued walking past. A drunk man in the street was common outside a saloon.

Drake's breath and clothes reeked. Erik guessed he had been working on building up his courage to confront Unter for some time before he came in.

Erik led Drake, stumbling, toward the Clearwater Hotel. Drake got sick and fell to his knees, coughing and spitting his stomach's contents into the dirt. He wiped his mouth with a grime-caked sleeve.

When he was finished, Erik hoisted him up again and half carried and half dragged him up the steps into the Clearwater. Ma Steele met them.

"Herregud."

"I'm sorry, ma'am," Erik said. "He's taken a beating. I'd be obliged if you can help me clean him up a bit."

Ma Steele wrinkled her nose. "Lord's sake, Mr. Larson, I appreciate what you did for me yesterday, but this? Take him out!" she exclaimed.

"He about got himself shot," Erik said. "I know him. He's traveled a hard road."

Ma Steele leaned in for a closer look. "Why, it is young Mr. Minton." She frowned. "I have not seen him in weeks." She stared at Erik. "It was that Mr. Unter, was it not? I wish Drake had shot him, I do." She got an arm around Drake, and the youth immediately groaned.

"Careful. Unter kicked him in his ribs."

Gingerly, they propped Drake up and helped him toward the room where the baths were.

"Well now, Mr. Larson, I do not really mean it. About Drake killing Unter. I do not. He is a bad one for sure. A sorry excuse of a man. I believe Drake had his fill. The only reason he stayed with the man before was he had nothing else."

Between them, they got the water poured. Drake seemed to be coming around a bit, and Ma Steele washed around his nose and examined his eye.

"Lucky you are that you did not lose your eye," she muttered.

Drake groaned. "It's my blamed side that hurts the most."

Ma Steele helped him out of his shirt and immediately tossed the rag into the corner. She gently prodded Drake's purple-and-red-bruised side, and Drake winced. "You may have broken ribs. For sure you need a doctor." She eased him to his feet.

"Can't pay for a doctor," Drake said. "Get me a bandage to wrap my ribs. I'll be okay."

Ma Steele appeared dubious, but Drake was correct: a doctor could have done little for him other than give him some laudanum for the pain.

"Do you think you can get in the tub all right?" she asked Drake. To Erik, she said, "I shall wash his clothes."

Drake stumbled, reaching with his good arm for his boot.

"You should help him, Mr. Larson. Throw the rest of his clothes outside the door." She turned to Drake. "Lord's sake, lad, do be careful."

Erik assisted Drake into the water. If he recalled rightly, Drake was now sixteen. He appeared younger. He hadn't filled out much. Erik expected he hadn't been favored with abundant meals. He wondered about his father but did not ask.

"Don't go to sleep in there. You'll slide in and drown." Erik handed Drake a brush and a bar of lye soap.

Drake mumbled something and propped himself up.

"Holler when you want a bucket of water for your hair." Erik often had rinsed his father's hair on Saturday nights before they left Minnesota.

Drake nodded, and Erik poured the water. Drake yelped. He tried lathering himself but struggled with having the use of only his left hand.

Erik helped him rinse. When finished, Drake was practically passed out again.

"Come on. You'd best get out." Erik held out a towel.

Drake didn't seem to recognize anything as Erik helped him from the washroom to his room. He was asleep before Erik had gotten out of the room. He hoped Drake had finished getting sick.

Erik found Ma Steele in the curtained area next to the bath where she heated the water and washed clothes. She was busily stuffing Drake's clothes into a pot of scalding water. He realized this was not the first time a similar scene had played out at her boardinghouse.

Why had it not occurred earlier to Erik that Ma Steele had no assistance? Where was her husband, Elise's father?

She nodded at him and frowned. "It will take more than one washing for sure," she muttered. "Better off he be burning them and buying some new ones. For sure he has no money."

"I admit those were my thoughts," Erik said.

She eyed Erik. "I do not know what that lad got into or where he has been. For sure he has not been out of these clothes for months."

"So he just showed up today?"

"Maybe he be around, but I have not seen him." Ma Steele added some soap to the boiling water. "He was here for some time after his papa died. Stayed in the room you're in. Poor lad. He said they were looking for his mama. Never did find her as far as I ever knew."

Erik stiffened. Had Drake's father died, *or* had he been killed? Ma Steele did not know that the two of them had been looking to kill his mama—in truth, Drake's stepmother. Had Drake's stepmother's new husband killed Drake's father? *Randolph*. That was his father's name. Wilhelmina was the stepmother.

"For sure he was working for that Mr. Unter, running cattle south of town here. Driving them to some of the gold camps. I do not know why he was gone for so long this last time."

Erik could guess. He could have been trailing cattle to Umatilla or south into Boise Basin—anywhere. From hearing Unter's comment, Erik guessed Drake had cost him money. He had probably lost some cattle. Unter might have withheld the price, which would have explained why Drake didn't feel he was getting what he was owed.

Ma Steele looked up. "How come it is that you know Drake?"

"I met him and his father four summers ago on the Goodale Cutoff. They were returning east with his younger half brother and sister. Twins. About five years old, if I reckon right. They were taking them someplace in Kansas—to an aunt, I believe."

Ma Steele frowned. "And then they came back here to look for their mama? There is a story for sure."

"I don't rightly know." Erik felt no need to share everything, especially if Drake hadn't explained. "You said they were looking for his mama. What'd Drake tell you?"

Ma Steele tightened her lips. "Only that they never found her, and then his papa died from consumption. Terrible death. He spent his last days here. That is how I met Drake. He was here a good deal. Helped me out, he did. Poor lad."

Erik breathed a little easier. They had not caught up to Wilhelmina. "Well, I thank you for doing this, ma'am."

"I would not do this, mind you—I run a respectable place—except it be for Drake." She was silent for a moment. "It is not over, Mr. Larson. Tomorrow or maybe the day next, Drake will be back at that Mr. Unter." She clasped her arms about herself and squeezed her eyes. "Drake has made up his mind. For sure, once someone makes up his mind to do something that foolhardy, he is not to be talked out of it." She shuddered. "My Simon—" She raised her eyes and shivered. "Herregud."

"I'm sorry," Erik said. He had guessed something similar might have happened.

Ma Steele nodded. "I have a daughter to raise, and I will. I have a few menfolk who watch out for me. Maybe one of them will settle down."

"You have done enough. I'll have a go at Drake after he sleeps it off. Let me know what I owe you for all this."

Ma Steele fished out Drake's shirt and began rubbing it across a washboard. "I would not ask a thing, but I must care for a daughter." She shook her head.

Erik straightened. "I spect Drake will be out for a bit. I figure on going over and introducing myself properly to Mr. Unter and to that dance hall girl, Dolly. She seemed to have an interest."

"Dolly?" Ma Steele stopped washing. "Those two were thick when Drake first got here, they were. He was just a lad, he was. You can imagine with her being a dance hall girl, he had the wrong notions." She smiled. "Young people." She shook her head. "They have to learn for themselves." She resumed scrubbing the shirt.

"There might be a connection between Dolly and Mr. Unter, which could be helpful," Erik said.

"Of course," Ma Steele said. She began wringing out Drake's shirt. She eyed him. "Now, do not go getting yourself into a fix, Mr. Larson. Supper is still at six. Maybe you could get Drake down here. I am sure he is famished. You saw him. Nothing but skin and bones, he is." She shook her head again.

CHAPTER 56

Erik did not intend to engage more than cursorily with Mr. Unter. He was more concerned about whether the man considered Drake to be in debt to him.

Dolly met him inside the saloon door and immediately asked about Drake.

"He's sleeping it off," Erik said. "Ma Steele patched him up. He'll be fine except for a cut lip and some bruised ribs."

Dolly hung her head. "I watched it storming up. Mr. Unter—he's that sort of man," she said. Her eyes glistened. "You probably saved Drake's life." She fumbled with a lace near her throat.

"How do I find Mr. Unter?" Erik asked. He had looked around and not seen the man.

"He might be down at his mercantile. He'll be back here later. You might as well know he's the reason I'm here. He owns this place as well."

Erik considered the information. Ma Steele had been correct. If there was still something between Drake and Dolly and between Unter and Drake, the kid would end up dead. "Does Drake owe Mr. Unter anything that you know of?"

Dolly tightened her lips. "Mr. Unter has a way of making everyone owe him something. It's more like he owns him. Don't ask me to explain."

"Like he owns you?"

Dolly's eyes shot up. "No!" She glanced about. Her lips quivered and drew into a line.

"I apologize," Erik said quickly. "I had no business—"

"No, likely as not," Dolly said. "It's my choice. It's my life now." She smiled and pulled a chair back from a table. "Do you wish to wait? I'll get you a drink. I owe you that at least for what you've done for Drake."

Erik touched the chair but did not sit. "No, thank you, ma'am. I still haven't paid for the one you left me the last time." He caught her eyes and smiled.

Dolly blushed. "You looked so dog-drowned lost I just had to. Don't think anything about it, please."

Erik felt a little disappointed, considering his previous thoughts. "Well, just the same, Dolly, thanks." He glanced at her, trying to read something more, wondering if there had been anything at all. He realized he was good at misreading women and slid the chair back. "I best be off. I'd still like to catch supper at Ma Steele's, and I'd better check on Drake."

"At least tell me how you know Drake," Dolly said. She sat, indicating she would not let it be.

"Ja." Erik had no choice. He pulled the chair out and sat. "I met him on the trail a few years ago." He continued the story and briefly explained, but as he had done with Ma Steele, he left out the reason Drake and his father had been looking for Wilhelmina.

Erik learned Dolly also knew that Drake and his father had been looking for his mother but not their intentions. Drake had never indicated that Wilhelmina was his stepmother.

"We were close," she said. "I was his first love." She laughed gently. "He wanted to marry me, but of course, when he found out more about who I worked for, he backed off. It like as not broke his heart. But that was nigh on a year ago." Her hand trembled where it rested on the table, and for a long moment, she appeared lost.

For the first time, Erik took a closer look. It surprised him to realize Dolly appeared not much more than a girl herself.

He touched Dolly's hand. "Thank you for your time, ma'am, and thank you for helping Drake. I'll share with him that you inquired and wished him well. I'm guessing come morning, he'll be just fine."

Erik stood and left Dolly sitting and staring. He no longer needed to meet with Mr. Unter.

Erik joined the other boarders at the long table where Ma Steele served the meals. Elise joined him again. Erik could not help but wonder about the child's future in this setting. Drake still slept.

Erik complimented Ma Steele on the supper and then borrowed some spare blankets. He spent the night in the corner of his room while Drake occupied the bed. He told himself he slept better on something hard in any respect. He remained uneasy. Drake had plenty of reason to wake and leave in the middle of the night. Erik intended to stop him if he tried.

In the morning, Erik had no difficulty in getting Drake to breakfast. Ma Steele kept bringing the biscuits and ham and eggs until both were stuffed. Drake remained silent while eating.

"I don't need an explanation, Drake," Erik finally said. "You are finished with Mr. Unter. I know about your father and about Dolly. I'm sorry you lost your father."

Drake quit eating. He frowned. "You're wrong, Mr. Larson. I hain't done with that snake Unter."

"You are, Drake. I said you were. If I hadn't waded in when I did, you'd be planted under."

Drake stared, working his jaw. "I hain't a kid anymore," he spat. "I can settle my own blamed affairs."

Erik nodded, recalling a similar conversation along the Goodale Cutoff. "I reckon you can, but I'm asking you to put things aside awhile." He paused. He had not decided until that moment: he was not going back to the Sheepeaters. "I'm asking you to ride with me, Drake. Afterward, if you still have a mind for settling with Mr. Unter, I won't stop you."

Drake pushed at a piece of ham; his eyes were now glued to the plate. Erik sensed that something had begun breaking apart within him.

"I spect I do owe you, Mr. Larson. You helped me and my pa before. I'd be obliged to ride with ya. I hain't like that snake Unter. I pay my debts."

"You owe me nothing, Drake. It's your choice," Erik said. "One thing you do owe me, though. You and I are going to go visit the barber."

Ma Steele had been listening. "If you be riding with Mr. Larson, you shall need a few things." She brought out some clothing she had bundled up—a shirt, some pants, and a coat. "My Simon doesn't need these."

Drake's eyes widened.

"You just go change now so I can toss those rags you been wearing."

314

Drake mumbled a thank-you and presently came back neatly dressed. Both the shirt and pants were a bit loose, but the suspenders held them.

Before noon, Erik and Drake left Lewiston behind. Erik allowed Drake to say a short goodbye to Dolly after checking first to make certain Unter wasn't present. Erik was pleased with some things. Drake had a good horse, a red-and-white-spotted gelding he called Paint. The horse reminded Erik somewhat of Leaf, but he was a bigger, more powerful animal. Drake also had his father's pistol and rifle.

GROFF FERRY

CHAPTER 57

Erik had not planned on it. It just seemed the right thing to do, and now Drake rode with him. Before Drake had come into the saloon, Erik had convinced himself to return to the Twisted River band. His thoughts of the vision and Gray Owl had convinced him it was time. The night cat had told him he would know when it was time. Like two of the wolf-bear creatures that had risen against the night cat, Dudgin and Smith had risen against him. Kan See might have sent men after him. Had evil now risen a third time? He had reason to keep Drake from Unter while things settled, if ever they did. Possibly he and Drake could pick up a packing job or help at one of the ranches—if he could keep the kid alive until he got the chance. Erik would have time enough afterward to return to the people.

Erik chose to skirt the Nez Percé reservation for a few miles, and then he cut across Camas Prairie toward Mount Idaho. A good wagon road marked the route. He and Drake encountered several freight wagons as well as frequent riders, but Erik made it a point to keep their distance.

At length, the tall-grass prairie gave way to shorter grasses and drier country. A ribbon of dark pines marked the eastern horizon. Mount Idaho was perched on the eastern edge of Camas Prairie. Beyond it lay the Clearwater canyon, where Erik had recently traveled.

A large log hotel and tavern sat at the end of the road in Mount Idaho. Two other log buildings sprawled nearby—a livery stable with a blacksmith and a saloon. Another six dwellings were scattered about, some in the thick timber on a nearby hillside—the town's namesake. As with Elk City, a few Nez Percé families camped nearby. Mount Idaho was the mustering point for much of the freight that continued by wagon or pack train to Elk City and the other gold camps.

Erik entered the tavern and ordered a meal for himself and Drake. He inquired about meeting Loyal Brown. Erik remembered that his brother, Alonzo, had packed for Loyal and kept a store in Elk City.

Loyal Brown came out to greet him, clearly curious about who had asked for him. He was dressed in a black coat, waistcoat, and bow tie—business attire. He appeared to be in his forties.

They shook hands. Erik invited him to sit with them, explaining he had an idea.

Brown laughed and stroked his dark beard. "I usually don't get folks through here that aren't gold struck and only interested in prospecting. What idea fancies you that might interest me?"

"I've been through Elk City and have experience packing. I've also spent time with the Chinese. I could help you start some commerce with them." Erik got to the point.

"It is rather ironic what you propose, Mr. Larson. I recently closed up at Elk City. The whites have largely moved on, and the Chinese are running their own stores and pack trains." Brown spread his hands. "I believe I have all the business I need right here. Mount Idaho is quite the crossroads. It has been since gold was discovered at Florence Basin back in '61. I bought this place in '62 from Moses Milner, California Joe himself, after he cut a trail into Florence. He tapped his fingers. "Freighters can also drop into the Salmon River drainage and make a stop at Slate Creek. I thank you, but I do believe I've enough business here."

As if Erik had not heard a word, he continued. "As for experience, I worked for a man by the name of Pete Samstrung out of Bannack. I mostly served as an outrider, keeping watch for road agents and as an interpreter with the Indians."

Brown raised his eyes. "Yes, road agents have always been a problem. We had a dickens of a time with them when we first started packing out of here. My brother and I were both held up on occasion. Fortunately, those times seem past." He hesitated. "Except things might be getting heated up again. A Chinese placer got hit down on the South Fork last summer. Some Chinese got killed."

Erik drew a careful breath.

"We think it was Chinese. They have different tongs, and they frequently go at one another. Someone tried to make it look like Indians," Brown said. "We don't need something like that to boil over and get the Indians riled."

"It was. Those were the Chinese I spent the season with. Some Chinese bandits jumped them, and some got killed."

Brown scrutinized Erik more closely, and Erik figured he wondered what his role had been in the killings.

"The Chinese like to settle their own differences," Erik said quickly. "I believe that is all the concern we should give."

Brown nodded. "You are correct."

"Lee Pow is their packer. You likely know him because he comes through here. He can verify what I say," Erik said.

Drake's eyes flicked between Loyal Brown and Erik. Brown cocked his head in Drake's direction.

"Young Mr. Minton wasn't with me at the time. I met him in Lewiston," Erik said. "We both need work. I thought if you were still wanting to pack goods to Elk City, we might be able to open the store again, especially on account of my ties with the Chinese."

Brown ran his hand through his hair and raised his eyes. "I took you to be a newcomer to this country," he said evenly. "You know Lee Pow and some of the other Chinese. You clearly know your way around, Mr. Larson." He drummed his fingers on the table. "If I thought there would be enough business, I'd take a go at it again. You saw the Chinese who are there, however. I doubt they will want me to pack for them, especially now they are packing their own goods. Only if the lode mines open up. Then you should avail yourself if you hear news of such."

Brown stood and excused himself. At least the man had listened.

Erik set his jaw. He believed Brown might have considered hiring him until he admitted his connection to the Chinese killings.

Drake eyed Erik. "You never said ya were on the river last year with the Chinamen." He pushed his fork at some beans. "Mr. Brown said someone made it look like Injuns." His eyes narrowed. "What happened?"

"I had to make some things right for the Chinese I was with. That's all."

"Sort of like what my pa and me were trying to do, right? And ya gave me hell for it."

Erik put his fork down. "I didn't want you to make a mistake that you'd be living with for the rest of your life, Drake."

"Oh, but you can just go and take revenge. That's what ya did, didn't ya?"

"I've already made mistakes, Drake. At the time, I was not thinking past stopping some men who had just murdered one of my friends." Erik watched Drake as he wrestled with himself. He pushed his plate away.

"We found her, you know. Pa nearly got shot. Ma begged for his life, so he didn't, but it was sickening. He just gave up after that. Then he got sick and died. That was near when we first got to Lewiston, almost two years ago."

Pain flooded Drake's eyes. "I told Ma where the twins were. She said she was glad but didn't want to see them. Can you believe it?" His eyes blazed. "Then she had the blamed gall to ask me if I wanted to come with her. Pa said I could. That's when I was done. I didn't care what happened anymore—to either of them. I stayed in Lewiston with my pa until he died. I met Ma Steele and Dolly. Mr. Unter gave me a job. We got stopped by road agents once, and I handled myself okay so he kept me on, but then he started cheatin' me. I couldn't get another job, so I stayed with him. I had my fill of it the last time. I was on trail for two months and lost some cattle while crossin' a river. He didn't say a blamed thing about his takin' it out of my pay, but he did. I worked for two months for nothin'. I had to call him out. He owed me."

Erik had nothing he could say. He realized he might have done the same thing. He pushed his hands across the table and drew in a breath. They had come to a crossroads. There was a real possibility Kan See would send men, and now Drake was in the crosshairs of that as well.

"Look, I thought I could find us some work and that you and I could maybe run a pack train. It doesn't appear anyone needs us. I've appreciated your company, Drake, but I'm not sure much lies ahead for either of us." He paused. "I'm going to head south into the Salmon River country. If you still want to ride along, you can. There's no promise of anything there, though."

Drake shrugged. "I know you got me out of Lewiston because ya knew I'd go back and have another go at that snake, and I woulda. He still owes me, but now it doesn't seem to matter. I'll go where you're goin', Mr. Larson, even if ya got Chinamen comin' after ya."

"I do not believe they will," Erik said, and then he smiled. "But thanks, Drake. I admit I like talking to someone other than my horse."

CHAPTER 58

The following day, Erik pushed on with Drake. About midday, the broad expanse of the Salmon River canyon opened before them. Like a giant, wrinkled robe, the grassy fingers of early summer ridges cascaded downward into purple shadows. A few green-black conifers scattered themselves along the rim, and clumps of cottonwoods speckled bright green in new foliage filled the draws. Buckbrush and prickly pear spotted the ridgeline where they rode. This was typically dry country, but the spring rains and snowmelt had greened up the short grasses and sprinkled wildflowers about.

As was his habit, Erik kept from the trails and followed a narrow ridge. He preferred to see what lay hidden along the trails, and being on the ridge gave him a better view. Below them, a few elderberry shrubs and thickets of blackberry lined the narrow draws. They traversed the steep, rock-strewn slopes by following a faint game trail that wound itself down into a deep ravine and then back out onto a barren slope.

Erik traversed back, steadily dropping in elevation, working his way across the open slopes. It was steeper than expected, and he worried Hatchet or Paint might take a wrong step and roll. Thus far, Drake's horse had held its own.

At length, some livestock appeared as dark specks on a distant barren slope. They neared Slate Creek, a freight and ranch outpost. Erik thought maybe he would try again to find some ranching work.

Erik caught the flash of light from dancing water amid the scattered trees and steep bluffs.

"There's the Salmon, Drake. The River of No Return."

"Why they call it that?"

"Legend has it those who travel down it don't make it back upriver. I don't know if the Indians called it that, but for a fact, they cautioned against going down it."

"First I've seen it like this. My pa and I crossed at its headwaters when we came back from Kansas. There it wasn't much bigger'n a creek."

They were nearly down. Erik spotted some mountain maples in a small reentrant and angled toward the spindly trees. Mountain maples were a sure sign of flowing water.

Erik found the trickling stream, and they let their horses rest. The sun beat hot, reflected from the surrounding hills. Even early in the season, as it was, the temperature would climb into the eighties.

They continued upriver, now following the main trail; the Salmon River lay to their right. Erik marveled that where the Lemhi entered the Salmon, the Salmon was about a hundred feet wide. Here it was between four hundred and five hundred feet across. Its green waters flowed rapidly, deep and swollen.

An uprooted tree bobbed past. Drake shuddered. "Hell with River of No Return and goin' down it. Ya hain't even gonna cross it. I for sure hain't," he said.

"You can cross on a ferry here and there, as I understand," Erik said. "Now it's full of meltwater."

Erik turned up a rapidly flowing stream he took to be Slate Creek. Several clapboard buildings stood in the distance along a bench above the river.

Drake hesitated before following. Erik guessed Drake had expected to head into the town.

"Seems to be a fair-sized spread up this way," Erik said. "I spotted cattle."

Shortly, they reached the ranch buildings and a low-slung house with yellow prairie roses near the front door. A set of steer horns tacked to a log had a lariat wrapped around them. Behind the house lay a fenced garden with lush new growth and a dozen or more hens.

Mrs. Stromback, a bosomy, slightly plump lady with blonde hair and teal-green eyes, met them. Erik recognized the Swedish name, but she spoke with no accent, so he did not ask. She indicated they might find Mr. Stromback farther up toward a spring, checking on cattle.

"He and his two hands," Mrs. Stromback said. "I'm not thinking he needs any new hands, however." She gave them close scrutiny. "He had one a few weeks back."

Erik took it to mean that Mr. Stromback had recently turned a man loose. He decided it was unlikely they'd need Drake's or his services. Then he caught sight of a golden-haired young woman maybe a year or two older than Drake peering from the other room. From appearances, she was related. Drake noticed her as well. Maybe it *would* be worth visiting Mr. Stromback. *What are the chances?* Erik thought.

They were escorted from the door by a boy of maybe eight. "Josef," he said, introducing himself. Out in the yard, a boisterous dog wiggled with excitement. "Roundup," he said.

"Is that your sister?" Drake croaked.

"Nah, that's Cousin Bonnie. Our hand Rex is crazy about her. She doesn't like him, but she's got another fellow she likes. He's up at Warren's Camp, mining gold. He'll be back, I'm pretty sure."

Disappointment etched Drake's face. Erik bit his tongue to keep from laughing.

Josef pointed in the direction where they might find his father. "A cow path takes off past that fencepost and goes up the hill yonder to the timber. That's where they're at."

As they headed in the direction Josef had indicated, Drake said, "You know, I do believe that I could get used to settlin' down on a ranch."

"You heard the boy, Drake," Erik said. "She's spoken for."

"But she hain't met me yet," Drake quipped.

Erik laughed to himself. It was unlikely, but what else were they doing?

In a mile, they found the spring and scattered cattle.

Three men, including one who was likely Erik's age, appeared to be fencing off an area of the spring with split rails. He straightened when he caught sight of them. A second man somewhat stooped, with graying hair, moved toward his rifle.

"I come in peace," Erik said, and he laughed. Then, on a chance, he greeted them in Swedish.

The third man, at best thirty, jerked up, grinned broadly, and shouted, "Svenska? Hallo, hallo." He quickly strode toward Erik.

"Ja," Erik said. A strange feeling overtook him. Something about the man seemed familiar—his appearance. He was tall and had broad shoulders, blond hair, and vivid blue eyes. Crow's-feet etched the corners of his eyes.

The man stopped in front of Erik, studying him. "Name's Jon Stromback. I come across from Minnesota with a wagon train of Swedes."

"Mr. Stromback?" A chill raced over Erik. The name had been familiar, and now Erik remembered. He could hardly speak. "I'm Erik. Erik Larson." He slid from Hatchet, hitting the ground solidly.

"Dear holy God, Erik. It *is* you. You survived."

They clutched each other and laughed.

"Ja, I did. So did my sister, Katrine, and the Olafsons. Most everyone survived, though some turned back after reaching the valley."

The others had drawn about, open-mouthed. Erik learned the older man was Art, and the younger was Rex. He introduced Drake, who stood watching, bewildered, with his mouth held in a crazy grin.

Stromback fairly danced. "Then you know I got your sister and the others to Fort Boise." He laughed and paused. "All these years, I never knew. We thought you dead for sure. You were just a lad."

"Ja, I was twelve. I always thought you were so much older. You're not—maybe six or so years."

"I'm twenty-eight. Still, that was ten years ago. We've both changed," Stromback said. "Herregud, Erik, how are you?"

"My parents didn't make it."

Stromback sobered. "I'm sorry." He waved toward Art and Rex. "Finish up here, boys. I'm heading back with Mr. Larson and Drake. It shall be time for chow when you get in."

They rode back off the ridge, talking.

When they reached the ranch house, more proper introductions were made. Erik and Drake sat with Jon Stromback. Bonnie was in and out occasionally, as was Josef with two younger girls. Mrs. Stromback had shooed them away, but Josef insisted on listening in.

Erik told Jon Stromback about the valley and the Swedes who were still there, or at least had been there when he left, including the Adolphsons, the family Stromback had been hired to assist. Informally, Stromback had adopted his younger sister, Katrine, along with the Olafsons, the family who had promised to care for Katrine after the wagons split up.

"When we got to what's now Boise City," Stromback said, "I knew it was too late in the season to turn north with them, and I didn't favor spending a winter in that country. Mr. Adolphson arrived, so I figured my job was done. Gold was being discovered up in this country, and I was young and wanting my chance at making a strike. When I reached Mount Idaho, I learned the goldfields were snowbound and that I wasn't going anywhere.

"Like others, I figured I could winter on the river, and I planned on heading into the goldfields in the spring. As the Good Lord had it, I met some of Chief Whitebird's people when I reached here. I learned there was rarely snow in this part of the canyon and got to thinking that I might be able to raise some beef. It would be a better bet than chasing gold, especially because others had told me the entire country had already been claimed up."

Stromback offered his cup toward Bonnie and nodded toward Erik and Drake. Drake quickly gulped his remaining coffee and shoved his cup toward Bonnie for a refill as well, grinning even more crazily.

Erik caught a slight frown from Stromback.

"I had the money from helping Adolphson and made an offer to buy the land. Then it was part of the Nez Percé reservation. They agreed to sell after I threw in my rifle and promised them a horse from time to time." He laughed. "I've lived with them without trouble since." He nodded at Erik. "What about you?"

Erik briefly told him about life with the Sheepeaters, his stay with the Swedes, and his jobs of packing and trapping. "I thought I might consider working on a ranch for a bit if the chance got thrown my way."

Stromback glanced at Drake.

"He's about like me," Erik said. "He lost his parents. He could use some work."

"Sorry to hear that, lad." Stromback slowly shook his head and nodded in the direction of Bonnie. "Bonnie's already got interest from my hand Rex as well as a miner back up in Warren's, where he and his father have a strike." He nodded at Drake. "His name is Samuel Chambers, in the event you two ever cross paths. He worked for me a few weeks past, and he's a right good hand. To be honest, I tried to talk him into staying. He indicated he fancied doing so but had his claim to work. I'm expecting him back."

Drake's face fell. Erik knew his feelings since he had shared a similar fortune.

"I could keep you both on for a few days if you just wanted some chow and a place to stay."

Josef immediately cheered. He made it clear he wanted to know why Erik acted like an Indian.

Erik briefly considered it, but other thoughts had arisen. It would not do to remain long, especially if Drake got any hopes up about Bonnie.

After a supper of beef with gravy and potatoes and a dessert of apple pie, the men shared more of their stories. Mrs. Stromback and, on occasion, Bonnie kept them in coffee. Stromback smoked his pipe. Erik and Drake declined. Erik did not speak of Bright Shell or the Lemhi Shoshone. He did not intend to mention anything about Dudgin and Smith, until it occurred to him that their type could try to take advantage of the Strombacks.

"Besides Drake and myself, I reckon you frequently encounter drifters seeking work."

"I do," Stromback said. "And you might guess the main reason I keep my eye on them."

"By chance, have three riders come through? Two men in their late thirties and the third maybe twenty. The shorter, older man has a scar on his cheek. His name's Dudgin. The taller man has black hair and is missing two fingers on his right hand and goes by Smith. The other is a kid named Bender."

Stromback drew on his pipe. "Can't say those three match up to any lately. I'd likely notice one with missing fingers."

"He wears gloves."

Stromback shook his head. "Why do you ask?"

Drake straightened.

Carefully, Erik measured his words. "Two of them dry-gulched me. Not Drake. He wasn't with me at the time. They took something of mine. Your niece reminded me."

Stromback studied on it a moment longer. Erik guessed from the man's look that he had deciphered his message.

At length, Stromback spoke. "I am truly sorry. I will keep a close watch."

Erik accepted the offer to use the bunkhouse with Art and Rex, despite a bit of misgiving about Rex. Both hands had turned in by the time they joined them. Rex cussed them out when they lit a kerosene lamp. Art was more amiable. Erik would have enjoyed talking more with Art, but it was late.

Early morning, they managed to rise in time for breakfast. Erik insisted on lending a hand with chores to pay for the hospitality and grub. They rode up the creek with Jon Stromback to check on some of the drift fence and found a few areas that needed some repair. Erik and Drake remained on the mountain to fix it.

The moment Stromback turned back, Drake challenged Erik. "So ya gonna tell me about those men? Or is it like the Chinamen, Erik? How many men you chasin', or is it men that are huntin' you?"

"I'm sorry, Drake," Erik said. "I don't think they're a danger or going to be of any account. I chased them for a while. I'm done unless I happen on them. I wanted Mr. Stromback to be aware in the event they showed up."

"What'd they do to ya? You said something about Mr. Stromback's niece remindin' ya. You have a woman? They do something'?"

Erik swallowed. The blackness began flooding back. "Look, Drake, now's not the time, okay? Someday, when the time's right and you need to know, I'll share it with you. Now's not right."

Drake studied Erik for a long moment. Perhaps he could see how Erik was being torn apart. "All right, I reckon I'll trust ya. Just no more, okay?"

"Not unless I take you to meet my Indian brother." Erik tried to smile.

Drake frowned and shook his head.

They both returned to cutting poles and fixing the fence.

At dinner the next day, they said their farewells. It was expected not to overstay a welcome.

Erik said he'd pass on the news of where Stromback had ended up. "You never know; someone might get up this way."

"Ja, I'm going to have to do better than that," Stromback said. "I told your sister I'd visit someday. I was never certain where they ended up and have just recently heard of some Swedes in what some are calling Long Valley. The Payette River runs through it."

"That's them. It's a great valley for raising cattle, but the winters are tough," Erik said.

"Which is why I'm here," Stromback said, laughing. "It might be possible to trail some cattle into a valley like that and back out here for the winter. I've thought about Salmon Meadows, which is fine range as well. It's between here and Long Valley. The Nez Percé might take exception to us being in Salmon Meadows, however. It's not on the reservation any longer, but they still have hunting rights. The problem is getting a herd of cattle across the Salmon River in the spring."

Erik raised his eyes. "What about us getting across?"

"This time of year, you'd never make it, except John Groff put in a ferry a few years ago. Late in the season, you could swim it."

Erik saw Drake stiffen. Drake did not like crossing rivers, likely because of the cattle he had lost.

"I'll let Katrine know you'll be visiting," Erik said.

"Ja, maybe in a year, when Josef's a bit older. Let Katrine know we'll be coming."

Erik grinned. "I will. Make it around Midsummer's Eve. They do it up grand."

"I shall do so," Stromback said.

CHAPTER 59

Erik and Drake turned south, heading upriver. By noon, they reached Groff's ferry, which was located just south of the confluence of the Little Salmon with the main Salmon. The river appeared to be a moving, rising, falling mass of living, racing water. It seethed through the limbs of uprooted conifers that had caught up against the bank.

The ferryboat bobbed on the opposite side. Erik fired his rifle. "Like Mr. Stromback said, this sure would have been the end of the trail, Drake, had they not put that in."

Drake sat uneasily. "We gotta go that way?"

"If you want to reach the Swedes."

A large man came from the cabin across from them. He waved and shouted, pointed at the river, and shook his head. His words were lost.

"Doesn't look good, Drake," Erik said. "He's not coming across. I reckon the water's too high."

"There's nowhere else to cross?" Drake asked.

"Nej. According to Stromback, the next ferry upriver is Shearer's ferry. Trails there don't go the direction we want to go. Not for several hundred miles."

"I can't believe that in this whole blamed country, this is the only spot where ya can cross to go south. What about the Injuns? They can find a trail anywhere."

"Not them either." Erik gestured at the steep slopes that rose from the canyon floor. "The Snake's probably not ten miles on the other side of that mountain. I suppose we could go back up to Lewiston and down the west side of the Snake. We'd be able to cross near Fort Boise and then reach the Swedes coming up from there, another hundred miles or so."

Drake stared. "Unbelievable."

"Otherwise, we wait here a bit." Erik considered the truth. This was the only spot. The Little Salmon River drained a narrow canyon from the south that ended in cliffs at the Salmon River. There was no trail on the opposite side. A few Chinese had a placer in one area that they had passed a short distance downriver, but it appeared they had a raft for crossing back and forth. Upriver, the Salmon swung west but emptied from an even more rugged gorge.

Drake allowed a slow smile. "Maybe we should go back to Mr. Stromback's ranch. Do some more fence or somethin'. I could fancy that."

Erik laughed. "I'm sure you'd like that." He shook his head. "Nope. We camp. Might be we get some cooler weather and the runoff locks up in ice again." He pointed toward a notch upriver to where some ragged peaks glistened white.

Erik waved his arm in a slow arc. The man waved back. "He knows we're here. I'm sure Mr. Groff's seen it before. Early travelers. We just stay put until he can come and get us."

They took the horses to where there was some greening grass and prepared a campsite in an area marked by previous travelers. Erik took his bow and scouted for rabbits. When he returned to their camp with two, Drake shook his head.

"You should teach me that with your bow," Drake said. "Like ya did throwin' sticks at the grouse. I've done that a couple a times now."

Erik nodded. "There are easier ways to get rabbits, like the snares I showed you before, but only if you're going to be camped for a length of time. I'd be pleased to give you a try with my bow, however."

Erik found a suitable dirt bank where an arrow tip wouldn't be ruined and set up a bundle of grass for a target. He showed Drake how to string the bow. He explained how to sight along the arrow and anchor it against his cheek for more accuracy. "It's necessary to use a fixed spot so your aim is the same each time. Some men will sight along the arrow, judging the pull and the position of the arrow. Others just know where to hold it because they have used it so often. I have found if I anchor it against my cheek, its flight is more predictable."

Erik demonstrated and loosed an arrow into the grass tuft.

Drake struggled and put his first arrows anywhere but near the target. Erik remained patient. He recalled his own first efforts and how his arrows had kicked up dust many feet from their intended target. His Sheepeater brothers had mocked him. Only Badger had had the patience for his clumsy efforts, and that patience had come only after Erik saved Badger from drowning. *In this river,* Erik realized, *but well over a hundred miles to the east.*

"When I was with the Sheepeaters, we boys shot arrows for hours on end. First thing in the morning, we'd race each other out to where we practiced. We shot all day until our arms were too sore or we got too hungry. That was our fun, but it was also our training. You'll get it."

Drake continued shooting. Erik stood aside and made only minor suggestions. Finally, Drake hit the target several times.

"Enough," Erik said.

"Good," Drake said. He examined his wrist. Blood seeped from it where the bowstring had repeatedly struck.

"Come on. I have some salve we can put on that. Not much you can do except keep at it. You'll get to where you won't snap your arm as much."

"Yeah, but I like it. How do I get a bow?"

"Maybe someday I'll help you get one of those as well."

Drake glanced at Erik. "I already got an arrah. It's the one you gave me. I've kept it."

Erik's throat tightened. "I'm glad you did. I always wondered how you made out. I'm glad you're riding with me."

Erik salved Drake's arm. They dressed and roasted the two rabbits over some willow coals and then made some coffee. A cool wind from the snow-blanketed mountains upriver buffeted them. Dancing firelight illuminated the window of the cabin across the waters and leaked through the logs.

At first light, they were surprised to see John Groff bringing the ferryboat across. They were equally surprised to see that the river had dropped by nearly four feet.

"By this afternoon, it will be as high or higher than when we arrived yesterday," Erik said.

"The territory has set my rate at a dollar for each horse and rider," Groff said as he greeted them.

Erik retrieved two silver dollars from his pouch and counted his blessings that he had not used all his money in Lewiston or Mount

Idaho. Erik and Hatchet loaded onto the boat for the first trip. Groff didn't trust two horses and riders with high water.

Initially, Erik believed the man had little inclination for conversation, but he learned otherwise when, as they pushed into the current, Erik asked about the country where they were headed.

"Be a lot of high water, and you might not have a trail in a few places, particularly in Salmon Meadows, but you should get through."

"I hear it's good graze for cattle. Has anyone tried to take up a ranch?"

"Nope. The snow's what gets you. If you summer grazed, you could take them out through Indian Valley and then into Boise Basin, but it's too long a trail. It's shorter and easier to come this direction and take 'em up to Warren's Camp, except for crossing the river. But I wouldn't mind. I'd get two bits a head." Groff chuckled.

"What about through that valley where some Swedes have got some farms?"

Groff smiled. "Same problem. Getting the cattle to market." He eyed Erik. "You a Swede? I heerd of some Swedes tryin' to settle there. I'm guessing they got snowed out. Is that where you're heading?"

"I am, and I hear a few Swedes are still scattered about." Erik grinned. "They settled there partly because the snow and country reminded them of Sweden."

"They can have the snow. From Prussia, I am."

The boat bounced and heaved in the swift current. Erik soothed Hatchet, whose ears swiveled and hooves stamped, as they crossed.

"So no one's settling Salmon Meadows?" Erik had begun wondering about graze midway between the Swedes and Slate Creek.

"Nope. There's been a few packers put up cabins for caching supplies and such. You'll pass one along your route over Goose Creek. It makes a good stopping point. John Welch built it."

"John Welch? Packer John?" Erik shook his head. "The man who got killed by road agents over near Lemhi Valley?"

Groff's eyes shot up. "He did? I never heerd that. You knew him?"

"I heard of him. I did some packing in that country." Erik told the story.

"Hell of a thing," Groff said.

They reached the south bank of the Salmon River, and Erik led Hatchet off, happy to return to solid land. He watched as the boat returned for Drake and then made its way back, straining against the heaving river. Drake appeared a bit pale and extremely relieved when he led Paint off the boat.

Groff offered them a meal for an additional dollar, but Erik declined and told him they wanted to get upstream as far as possible. Erik wondered if Drake had any money. With too many crossings, they'd be swimming, high water or not.

"Any surprises where we're heading?" Erik asked as they headed out.

"You might encounter some Nez Percé at Salmon Meadows. They shouldn't bother you, but they favor horses more than anything. Yours or their Indian brethren's—it makes no difference," Groff said.

Erik thanked him, musing that the horse he now rode once had belonged to a Nez Percé.

For the first few miles, the steep canyon walls remained covered in scant grass and no trees. Elderberry and blackberry thickets lined the draws. Mountain maple, willow, and cottonwood choked the west- and north-facing ravines. As they slowly gained elevation, heavy timber appeared on the rim against the skyline and gradually began reaching down toward the river. An occasional ponderosa now grew along the banks.

The canyon floor broadened where another river came in from the west. A few miles farther, it appeared a ranch was being laid out. Three men were working on a log building situated on a grass-carpeted bench above the river. They hollered a greeting to the men but pushed on.

Shortly, black basalt pillows jutted outward from the bluffs and squeezed the river into narrow chutes. The water exploded into bouncing whitewater below the chutes. The trail that closely followed the river became submerged in foaming water. Twice, Erik had to climb up and around by following faint game trails that wound far up the steep walls and down again to the canyon floor. He would have chosen to cross to the other side, but the torrent prevented it.

Toward late day, the horses were becoming tested from working around deadfalls and the washed-out trail. A loud booming crescendoed above the river noise. Whitewater flashed through the trees up trail.

"Ya better hope this trail goes around that," Drake said.

Snow-white water thundered down a series of falls. The highest was close to twenty feet. Fortunately, the trail swerved and threaded its way upward past the falls.

In another mile, the canyon opened onto a rich, grassy meadow spotted with clumps of willow—Salmon Meadows. The river, now about twenty yards wide except in places where it flooded farther into the meadows, meandered from the south, deep and silent. Scattered ponderosa pine drew back from the meadows and covered the low hills. Heavily timbered mountains rose beyond and caught the glow of the setting sun.

Erik's chest tightened. This country resembled the Swedes' valley.

"Good place for the night, do you reckon?" Erik asked. He had considered trying to reach John Welch's cabin, but it was half a day distant, and they had been considerably slowed by the swollen river. "I wanted to get out of that canyon. Didn't know if we ever would."

"I can't believe this country," Drake said as he drew up beside Erik. "Never seen blamed grass so tall or thick. Water everywhere. Be good ranchin' land for sure."

"Salmon Meadows is one of the spots Mr. Stromback talked about. It's like where we're heading. Though after late October, it'll be buried under several feet of snow."

Erik led Drake off the trail and upward onto a drier, timber-covered hillside before finding a camp spot.

"We can watch the trail and avoid some of the mosquitoes," Erik said. He slapped at one. "Let's get us a fire going and some smudge. It might help."

Soon they had a fire crackling and threw on some green limbs for smoke.

"I wouldn't do this if I was concerned about Indians," Erik said. "No sign of them or any travelers on the trail. We could be the first."

"Mr. Groff said he'd only crossed a couple of others other than Mr. Pollock," Drake said. "That was his place being built back on the bench."

"That would make a good winter ranch for cattle out of this country," Erik said. "Ever think of raising cattle?"

"To be honest, I was thinkin' about it, but I'm not for having to cross that blamed river. You'd have to so's you could take them into the gold camps, unless there's some camps this side."

"Ja, that's the problem as I see it. It might be that where we're heading, the Swedes have a foothold and can winter where they're at. You'd take cattle out in the fall and bring them back in the spring."

"Ya still gotta figure the river," Drake said.

Erik watched the fading sun. Ducks and geese spotted the open waters. A doe and her new spotted fawn crept out and down to the river.

"Beautiful country nevertheless," Erik said.

Drake agreed.

PAYETTE LAKE

CHAPTER 60

The following morning, mist shrouded the valley and river. It wrapped its way through the low areas and crept up into the trees where Erik and Drake had spent the night. Some geese passed above them, honking, swinging downstream and then, in a wide arc, circling back. The wind whistled through their pinions as they flew close above.

"They're trying to find a hole they can settle through," Erik said. Other geese, buried in the fog, honked in reply, seemingly giving directions. "It'll burn off," he added.

He fixed some breakfast. They loaded their gear and headed back down toward the trail. Erik's heart quickened. *We should reach the valley today.* It was a couple of months short of four years since he had last seen his sister.

The fog began lifting, rolling up into the timber and fading into a warm blue sky. Erik was again struck by the country—high grass meadows with thick green willows that bordered the river. Deep eddies with trout. Ducks and geese scattered everywhere. Red-winged blackbirds clacking, balancing on last season's cattails. A band of elk moved through the timber at the valley's apron. Erik took a second look to make certain they were not Indians.

Soon he turned east along Goose Creek. Near a low, pine-shrouded ridge near the creek, he found Welch's cabin. It was in disrepair but obviously a camping spot for travelers.

"I see someone's been here," Drake said.

"Ja, Mr. Groff told me about it. It's John Welch's cabin. For me, it's like seeing a ghost."

Drake eyed Erik.

"I heard about him when I was packing out of Leesburg. He had a store there. He was one of the first packers to take goods into the Boise Basin and then went on to Leesburg. He brought goods out of Walla Walla and built this place to cache his goods for the winter. The following season, he headed out and across where we're headed and where the Swedes are and on through to Boise Basin. He built some other cabins along the route and intended to continue bringing in goods, until he got killed."

Drake shifted uneasily in his saddle and arched his eyes.

"He got jumped by road agents south of Salmon City when he was taking out gold, intending to go back for more goods." Erik finished the story, including the part about Sheriff Ramey.

Drake eyed the cabin. "Now I can see why ya talk about ghosts."

"I share this with you, Drake, not to make you untrusting of others but as a lesson to take to heart."

Drake shot Erik a look. "I got robbed, too, ya remember. It was a different way, but it was the same end. I lost two months of wages."

"You didn't get killed."

Drake didn't reply but glanced again at the cabin. Erik led down the trail that now angled up the low ridge.

The swiftly flowing creek wound between tall ponderosa pine, Douglas fir, and occasional tamarack. Many soared more than a hundred feet, as straight as arrows, into the blue sky. The timber reminded Erik of the trees along the Lochsa and Clearwater, but the slopes here lacked the dense undergrowth. The trees' lowermost branches were upward of twenty feet above the ground. Their red-bark trunks and lowest limbs were spotted with bright green lichen. There was little need for a trail through the open country.

They ascended a narrow, steep granite-walled canyon. Somber speckled gray-and-white boulders stacked like a castle's ruins reached upward from the edges of a tumbling creek.

At length, they topped out and overlooked the adjacent valley. A line of jagged mountains still spotted with lingering snow rose to the east. Big Payette Lake lay below them but was masked by timber. Erik headed downward, cutting through the timber, until near the shore, where the lake suddenly opened like a blue jewel spreading outward to meet the far mountains reflected in its still waters.

"Beautiful," Drake mumbled. "Never seen anything like this."

A rocky bank jutted into the azure water, and Erik stopped to let the horses water. Huge trout lazily swam out away from the shore, seemingly not bothered by the horses sucking up the crystal water. The trouts' shadows were cast against the pristine bottom until they disappeared into the velvet depths.

Erik turned south along the shore for a short distance and then headed southeast across the broadening valley. Stands of timber and aspen groves spotted the grassy hills—hills that were now familiar. The valley shimmered in the late-spring sun.

"We're at the north end of the valley," Erik said. "Guess according to Jon Stromback, they're calling it Long Valley. Good name for it. It's about forty miles long."

"Grass like this the whole way?" Drake asked.

"Ja, and up some side valleys as well." Erik gestured around them and pointed east. "Anton Wikstrom's place is a few miles that direction, about where the valley meets the ridgeline. His place has a hot springs. There's at least a dozen hot springs in the valley."

They had reached a small rise. Erik sat Hatchet for a moment and pointed east. "You see that line of mountains? Beyond them, you'd drop onto the South Fork of the Salmon. It drains north. The Payette River, which drains this valley, runs south. Think about it. We've just come up out of the Little Salmon River, which drains north. Two miles in that direction, you'd be back in the Salmon River drainage. That's all that separates the two drainages. It's one reason this valley is overlooked. You can't find it." He laughed. "The last winter I was with the Sheepeaters, I was northeast of here, near the mouth of the South Fork. The Sheepeaters call it Sandy Water River. If I'd known where this valley was, I could have found my sister a lot sooner."

"Crazy country," Drake murmured. "I like it. Plenty of game. For sure ya can raise livestock. I think better than Salmon Meadows. Is there any gold?"

"Some gold at a few places on the edges of the valley and along the river. There's Copeland's diggins and Pearsol's diggins down the valley on the east side. Or there was, last I was here. Otherwise, I never heard of enough gold for someone to make much more than grub. The salmon and trout are better."

Late afternoon, they reached the Wikstroms' farm. A young boy of about seven and a beautiful young woman came into the yard.

Erik shouted and waved. "That must be you, Jon, and you, Linnea." He slid from his saddle.

It took Drake a few moments to collect his wits before he dismounted.

Freda emerged with her blonde braids bouncing, and she, Linnea, and Jon swarmed over Erik. "Erik, you've come home!"

Drake stood awkwardly aside until Erik made introductions. When Erik introduced Drake, he watched Drake's and Linnea's eyes meet, catch, and then brighten as they exchanged smiles. Linnea was seventeen. So were Mia and Emma, Erik realized—if they were still in the valley. He wondered what Drake's reaction would be when he met them.

Linnea snuck a long look at Drake and then ran to fetch her father and brother from the field.

When Anton Wikstrom and thirteen-year-old Laurens arrived, there was a new uproar of greetings, hugs, and handshakes.

Like before, when Erik had first found his sister and the settlers, Anton set Laurens out on one of the horses to spread the news.

"You'll wish to see your sister right away, I do believe," Anton said. "She and Björn did not waste any time, you shall see. Ja, they have two wee ones—a toddler boy and a baby girl."

Joy and pain raced through Erik. He felt joy at the news that he was an uncle. He already had known he was, based on a revelation from his spirit helper at about the time the boy would have been born, but to hear that it was fact caused a strange sensation. Pain was brought by memories of Bright Shell. He wondered about his daughter, Glad Spirit, and whether she yet lived.

"Are they still at the old Lundgren place? Katrine and Björn? The Lundgrens came back about the time I was leaving. And another family. Are they all still here?"

"Nej. Björn moved to where you spent the winter trapping at that hot springs south of us. The O'Donnells did not stay. They lived there a bit and decided to move somewhere to the north on the Salmon. I think the snow got them."

Erik understood. The valley's deep snow ended a lot of dreams.

"Sometimes drifters come through and stay for lengths. Some are trying to find work, and most of them are trying to entice Adolphson's Ingrid to elope and go with them or things worse," Anton said, shaking his head. "Adolphson encounters too many travelers where he's at."

"He's doing a good trade, I wager, being on the main trail like he is," Erik said.

"It costs him and his family," Anton said. "They don't use the hot springs as much because all the drifters use it and snoop around, but I'll tell you about that another time. We sure hope you are back."

The Wikstroms' place had stayed much the same, with the addition of two rooms and a barn. Jon had been three when Erik left. Now seven, he was a tall lad, and Erik could see some of his mother's likeness. He had Freda's rosy complexion and a mask of freckles. The other children—Anna, Björn, Linnea, and Laurens—were Emma and Anton's children. Emma had died at Fort Boise.

Now seeing Laurens ride off, Erik swore he was watching Björn. He had the same grin and high-arching eyebrows that always gave Björn a look of surprise. Erik felt he could have taken an interest in Linnea if she hadn't been five years younger than he was. She was strikingly beautiful and had a fine figure. She was so much like his sister, Katrine, it seemed eerie, but then all the Swedes were quite fair, and nearly all had the same vivid blue eyes. Freda, Anton's new wife, was German and had coarser and darker yellow hair that was still braided as he remembered. Maybe she was a bit more rounded. Anton had aged, and his hair had gray mixed with his darker blond. Creases around his eyes had deepened. His hands were worn. Life in the sun and wind, raising crops and stock, had taken its toll.

"I have no mind to leave in any hurry," Erik said. "I brought Drake, partly thinking that with summer on, maybe someone might take on a hand."

Anton gave Drake a closer look. "I need a farmhand, Erik. Laurens works hard, but he's just not got a man's strength. But I shall need to see. I cannot have someone up and leaving on me." He nodded slightly in Linnea's direction.

"You can never say," Erik said, smiling. "Is everyone well?"

Anton's lips tightened. "Anna and Lars lost their first baby. God has blessed them with two more. Little fellow had complications from birth. Just died one night. And another tragedy: right after you left, Pelle lost part of his leg. Fell from his horse and got dragged into some trees. Snapped his leg. I cut it off." His eyes pinched. "Came close to losing the lad, we did."

Erik shivered. Pelle was Mia's age and her childhood friend. They were all the same age, Erik realized, or within a few months of each other—Pelle, Mia, Linnea, and Emma. All were just a few months older than Drake.

"Adolphson sure didn't need that," Anton said, "but Pelle gets around. Might not ever be on his own, but he mostly minds the waystation. Anna and Lars are doing well otherwise."

Anton gestured for Erik to sit. There were a few well-crafted chairs under the log house's overhang. Freda brought out some cold, sweetened mint tea.

"It sure seems Adolphson got dealt more than his fair share," Anton said. "He's still the one that keeps us together, Erik. It was always his dream. We've done well all in all, and he sees good things from his dream. We all do. Raising our families. Seeing grandchildren. Seeing the land tamed and providing for us. You being here would make it more of a blessing." He gave a hopeful look toward Erik as he drank some tea.

Erik avoided an answer. "I should go and see my sister. You'll understand."

Anton slapped Erik's shoulder. "That I do, lad, but give Laurens another hour, and I'll bet Katrine and a good number of the others will be here. You can bet they're packing their wagons with fixin's as we speak. Adolphson has perfected his *brännvin* whiskey. It's early for Midsummer's Eve, but we are celebrating."

Erik grinned at Drake. "You'd better plan on staying here for the night. The hot springs is just up the trail. We can get the trail dust off." He nodded in the direction of the springs.

Drake grabbed his head. "All those women comin' with us?" He cast his eyes toward Linnea.

Erik wasn't sure how to respond but laughed.

Shortly, wagons and people on horseback arrived, including children and a few dogs. Erik was taken aback and experienced a complete loss of words as people from throughout the valley arrived. First came Lars and Anna and their two children, Karin and Jens. They were but a mile down the creek. Then Sven and Margret Olafson arrived with Mia and Torsten, who was now almost nine. Torsten held back a bit at first, not believing it was Erik. Immediately, he wanted to know about the Indians. Erik told him there would be time later. Mia and Erik hugged. Mia was Katrine's adoptive sister. She was a strapping, beautiful young woman quite like Linnea, only with a bit more heft.

The valley's patriarch, Nils Adolphson, and his wife, Astrid, arrived with their oldest daughter, Ingrid. Nils was the one who had sent word back east to Minnesota about the valley and convinced them to settle here. Ingrid caught Erik's attention, and he drew in a sharp breath. He tried to remember her age—maybe nineteen. She was tall, an image of her mother when she was younger, and not at all unattractive. Ingrid smiled lightly. Pelle had remained at the waystation in the event travelers happened by.

Next were Magnus and Louise Lundgren and their three children, Emma who was Mia's age, Oscar who was born when Torsten was, and Elizabeth who was five.

Last to arrive were his sister, Katrine, and his brother-in-law, Björn, and their two youngsters: Carl, a toddler of nearly two, and Ruth, who was not quite a year old.

Erik embraced his sister. As he reflected on their first reunion six years ago, similar feelings overwhelmed him. Erik lifted Carl to his shoulders. The boy immediately reminded him of Torsten at Carl's age. Then he nearly dropped the child. His own daughter, Glad Spirit, was Carl's age. Shaking, he put the boy down.

Erik wondered if he would ever tell anyone about her—if he would ever tell Carl that he had a part-Shoshone cousin his age. He bit his lip. No, that was another life.

He embraced Björn, thankful that Katrine had him. Björn had always impressed Erik with his hard work and also his steadfast support of his father. Björn and his father had built this place, planted and tended the crops, and raised some stock.

It was a long and joyous night. True to Anton's proclamation, Nils produced some of the finest brännvin yet. Erik never had been much into drink, but tonight he was obligated to answer all the shared toasts. Tomorrow he would likely be going nowhere, and for once, it mattered little.

Erik made a good effort to catch up with everyone. They were especially excited to hear the news about Jon Stromback and his family and that the Strombacks planned to join them next summer during Midsummer's Eve. Erik refrained from repeating too much about himself. There would be time for that, and much of it, he would never share. Nils reminded everyone of Sunday meeting and said to bring a special dish for this weekend's gathering. They had much for which to give thanks.

The four young women—Ingrid, Emma, Mia, and Linnea—cornered Erik. They demanded to know about Drake. Where did he come from? Was he a farmer, or was he prospecting for gold? Why did he talk funny? Erik fended off the questions by summarizing how they'd met and saying he was good with cattle. If they had other questions, they could ask him themselves. He got pointed looks from each of them.

His approach seemed to work. He later observed Drake engaged in animated discussion with each of the young women at various times.

The night deepened. Families began returning home. Katrine and Björn piled their young children into the wagon and turned down the road. It amused Erik to see Björn driving a farmer's wagon with his sister next to him, with Carl's small blond head bobbing from the box behind and Ruth's small form sitting between her parents. One of the dogs, which Erik had not matched with a family, sat with Carl.

Erik had wondered about pushing on to Katrine and Björn's place to spend the night with them, but he then thought better of it. He and Drake found sleeping quarters in Anton's barn.

"I can't figure ya, Erik," Drake murmured. "Why'd you ever leave all this?"

CHAPTER 61

In the early light, after a hearty breakfast, Erik and Drake bade farewell to Anton and Freda. Erik intended a longer visit with Katrine and Björn, and afterward, he wanted to check over the old Lundgren place. After the Lundgrens had returned, they had decided to build a new home on new acreage upriver, perhaps because of the memories associated with their original place. They had lost their oldest son, Harald, when he fell through the ice. He was buried near the old cabin, which now stood abandoned.

Drake begrudgingly followed. Erik guessed he would have preferred to visit longer in the near vicinity of Linnea.

"If you wish to stay here for a bit, Midsummer's Eve is in a few days," Erik said. "You'll learn about a few Swedish traditions, which I believe you will appreciate."

"Are you seriously asking me that question?" Drake shot Erik a look. "If I wish to stay a bit?"

"I have only your welfare in mind," Erik replied, smiling.

"What is that supposed to mean?"

Erik did not answer; instead, he headed south. A preemptive hint might be appropriate with Drake, he thought, and if necessary, he would explain later.

Erik cut across the familiar ridge to the south and dropped down and past the Olafsons' new place. Erik and the others had built a real house after a fire had burned the homestead cabin. He continued past and directly over the next ridge and dropped into a small basin. This was the valley where Erik had wintered and trapped. It was now Katrine and Björn's place.

A cabin constructed with the familiar Swedish square-notched logs stood on the level. A good-sized garden grew adjacent to it, surrounded by a sturdy fence. Beyond were some small outbuildings—likely storage buildings for hay and a stock shed. Björn had a couple of milk cows and, from the pungent odor, at least one pig.

The longish-haired yellow dog came bounding out to greet them. Close behind were Katrine and Björn. Katrine carried Ruth, while Carl peeked from the doorway.

Erik felt warmed by the sight.

They had a second cup of coffee and spent much of the morning talking. Drake was lost on a good deal of it and took outside with Carl and the dog for a bit.

Erik toured the homestead with Björn, giving him a few pointers, but he quickly realized Björn had a much better grasp of things than he did, though perhaps not on horses. Björn had a team for plowing, but they were not particularly fit for riding.

Erik declined to stay the night, knowing his sister lacked the room inside. He was certain he would spend the night on occasion, but likely, he would stay in the stock shed unless he was not in Drake's company.

Erik and Drake reached the turnoff to the old Lundgren homestead and turned up the overgrown road.

"I spent a winter trapping over where Björn and Katrine now have their place. They stayed in this cabin until they got theirs built. If there aren't too many pack rats, you and I could use it if you wish."

Drake cocked his head. "It beats stayin' in stock sheds, but I'll wager the grub won't be as good."

"Not if you're cooking," Erik said.

Not much had changed. The two beds needed new ropes since rodents had chewed them in places. They would need a good rain to determine the condition of the roof. The remaining structure seemed sound.

After clearing out pack rat nests, they succeeded in getting a good cook fire in the stove and prepared some supper. Afterward, they settled back with cups of coffee.

This had been a good cabin, Erik decided. He wondered if he might take a hand at farming again. Before, he'd had a garden of sorts. He admitted to himself that Ingrid had turned into a fine woman. He was but three years older. Before, she had been but fifteen, and at the time, he had not been drawn to her.

Drake studied Erik, twisting his hands on his coffee cup. "I know what you're thinkin'," he said at length. "What's the answer? You gonna take up farmin' again?"

Erik shot him a look. "I'm not pushing any decision," he said evenly. "I had intended to farm before, and it didn't work. But I have family here. I don't know. It's something I can't rightly explain."

Drake nodded. "I can explain it. Too much Injun in ya, makin' it hard for ya to decide."

Erik glared at Drake. What gave him the right to read his thoughts? Recently, he had been doing it way too often.

"Well," Drake said, "you told me to keep my eyes open more than my mouth. I've been noticin'."

Erik slapped his cup down. "And so have I. And I'm thinking you'd better learn a bit about some Swedish customs and Swedish women before you find yourself staring down someone's shotgun barrel."

"What?" Drake straightened and swung around on his chair. "Is it that obvious?"

"Ja, it is. A Swedish woman is going to be right nice to any man, Drake, but be careful to see anything past that. Some of our customs would lead you to believe more is going on when it isn't." But Erik knew it might be, particularly with Linnea.

Drake's eyes sparked. "I think I can see okay."

"You'll especially think that during the Midsummer's Eve celebration. It's a time when things get a little carried away and a little loose, with some kissing and maybe a trip to a hot springs, but even that you can't read too much into. Remember, every man in this valley is going to be watching you."

Drake hesitated and swallowed. "Maybe ya better brush me up on things. I admit I hain't been much around women. Leastwise not the marryin' kind recently."

"Perhaps you and I will go for a ride tomorrow." Erik wanted to kick himself. Who was he to advise on women? He had chosen Indian women. Pain darkened his thoughts.

"Why not now?"

"I think more clearly from some mountaintop, and I might say something I'll regret."

Over the next few days, Erik and Drake settled into the old Lundgren cabin and made the rounds, visiting and offering some work. He took

Drake with the intent of finding him some full-time work and, of course, because Drake insisted on visiting with the women.

Lars and Anna were well. They accepted the loss of their first child by knowing it was not unusual, particularly in this wilderness. Margret and Freda had helped her deliver.

They had made good progress on their farm. They had torn apart the Andreasson cabin and built a completely new one. The sawpit had remained in steady use, but that was soon to change. They were installing a water-driven saw this season a short distance above the Wikstroms' hot springs.

Anna told Erik that her father and Björn were trying to run a few more cattle. Anton had successfully taken some to Boise Valley and sold them for good money. The difficulty was in carrying stock, even a single milk cow and a single horse, over the winter. They farmed enough oats and had a barn and stock sheds, but it was a struggle. She admitted that her father found it even more difficult without Björn at home, but Laurens was a good hand, and Björn visited weekly.

This day, Erik visited the Adolphsons. Only Pelle was present. Nils and Astrid and Ingrid were up at the Wikstroms'. Nils had turned their homestead into more of a waystation than a producing farm. They still grew vegetables and raised beef for travelers and the mining camps. They had a stock of goods, and they boarded travelers in a large boardinghouse they had built. The boarders used the hot springs to bathe.

Pelle managed on his one leg. He had become accustomed to remaining at the waystation, especially when his parents were gone.

"Too dangerous to leave it," Pelle explained. "We have some whiskey for serving travelers, but that's not what a lot of them want. They want my sister." Pelle grinned. "Pa's thinking about building another house but like the Olafsons' house farther up the creek, so we're not so near the trail. Still, that won't stop them. I mean, Ingrid helps serve meals and does wash. Every man around knows she's here."

Pelle caught Erik's eyes. "Of course, they also know about Emma and Mia and Linnea. Mia and Linnea don't have as much to worry about because travelers don't go their direction, but they go near enough to the Lundgrens' place, so I keep my eyes on Emma as well.

"Most of the time, travelers are fine, but you can tell when some snakes come slithering in. I usually hang out of sight with my shotgun. With one leg, I can't do much plowing, but I can sure use a shotgun." Pelle smiled. "It's mostly those who set up at one of the cabins or camp awhile along the trail who are the worst. They like to hang around the hot springs in case Ingrid or Emma goes down there. We watch that right close." He laughed.

"Have you had to use it?" Erik asked. "The shotgun, I mean."

"No, but I've come mighty close. Twice, I came out with it. One guy had a knife. He knocked the shotgun out of my hands, and it went off." Pelle laughed again. "You can still pick shot out of the logs over there." He pointed to the wall, where a picture hung in an odd position. "Pa was here and put an end to him. I mean, he sent him packing. He might have been one of the scum who visited us a few nights later and set some of our haystacks on fire. That's what we worry about the most."

"How about the Chinese?"

"They're a bit queer but never any trouble. They have their own food and won't sleep in our boardinghouse. They just want a place to gather for a while. Sometimes they buy vegetables. Usually, they want to sell us vegetables. We've even bought some." Pelle chuckled. "Indians are different. They don't buy a thing. It's like they expect us to give them stuff or trade us some ratty old hides we don't need. We usually do. Pa always reminds me they were the ones whose trails we followed to get here. Sometimes they come here to go fishing at the lake farther north. It's crazy when the salmon are running. The whole river turns red from their spawning colors."

Erik wondered if Pelle was content. He didn't figure Pelle would marry. How could a man manage a farm on one leg? As Pelle had admitted, he couldn't much handle a plow. Erik felt it was good for him to be around when travelers came through.

"You pay pretty close attention to travelers. Have you seen three men—two older men, one missing two fingers who's about your pa's height and has dark hair and the other with a scar across his cheek, and a younger man about twenty who travels with them? He's got a rough face."

Pelle shook his head. "You're right that I see a lot of travelers. I'd've noticed one missing two fingers. Why?"

"I crossed paths with them. They'd likely take what they want, including your sister."

Pelle's eyes narrowed. "Which is why I have this." He pulled the shotgun to his lap.

CHAPTER 62

Erik leaned on his hoe and watched Drake hacking at weeds. The sun beat warm. He tried to read the young man's mind. Did this sort of work suit him? Or like Erik, did he prefer being among horses and cattle?

"What did you think about Jon Stromback's ranch?" Erik asked.

Drake gave him a wondering look.

"I mean, it seems he does fine for himself in wintering packers' stock and raising beef cattle for trailing into the gold camps."

"Yes, however, I distinctly recall that his niece has been spoken for," Drake said. "I thank you, but I'm stayin' put for a bit. Besides, I'm likin' what I'm seein' around here."

Erik laughed. "You have to be able to make a living."

Drake hacked at some more weeds and eyed Erik. "Well, if you wonder which I prefer—cultivatin' crops or ranchin' cattle—I prefer work where I'm on the move, which would mean ranchin' cattle and raisin' a few horses. But I hain't got my blamed head in the clouds either. I know ya got to feed yourself, and that means growin' some crops as well."

Erik had been stopped short. Drake knew the truth. "I was thinking—you and I both saw the country in Salmon Meadows as great summer range. This is great range as well. The problem is getting any number of cattle through six months of deep snow. Stromback said he would trail cattle to Salmon Meadows, except for ferrying the river. In the fall, it's low enough in places you could swim a herd, but spring and summer, you'd have to ferry, and that would be costly."

Drake leaned on his hoe. "Depends on how much you can get for a head of cattle at the gold camps."

"Ten dollars. Maybe more. That's better than taking them to Boise City for sure."

Drake returned to chopping. "I'd say that would be plenty. What ya considerin'? Raisin' cattle here and wintering them at Slate Creek? Working with Mr. Stromback?"

"It might be something to ponder," Erik said. "There also might be closer winter pasture where you don't have to ford the rivers. I hear areas along the Weiser River and the Council Valley have less snow. Where we came up Goose Creek is where you would turn southwest to get there."

"Yes, and everyone says it's Nez Percé country."

"Not if you honor their hunting rights and maybe trade them a beef or two. I think it could be done."

"Until they get stirred up," Drake said. "I get the feelin' a lot of them don't consider they gave up this land just 'cause some of their blamed cousins did."

Erik considered the truth of Drake's comment. Stromback had worked something out, but that had been before the reservation was reduced in size. Still, he had done it. Maybe other settlers could as well.

Erik returned to chopping weeds. The potato plants looked good. They would soon be under attack by worms. That was what chickens were for. Maybe he'd better acquire a few from Olafson, he thought; Olafson had a bunch. Besides, he would welcome having his own supply of eggs.

Erik turned to head back to the cabin to get out of the sun, wondering what he was doing in a garden again. Was it for him, or was it for Drake? Maybe Drake could put up with it, but he wasn't sure he could.

A horse and rider approached—a rather small rider.

Torsten? Erik marveled as the eight-year-old marched Whitey, one of Sven Olafson's horses, up to the cabin.

"Hallo, Uncle Erik." Torsten brought the animal to a stop. "Kin you help me down?"

"Sure, Torsten." Erik reached up and swung the boy down. He was certain Torsten was away from his house without anyone's knowledge.

The boy stood grinning. "I did it. I got Whitey over by a big stump, and I got on her, and I came all this way by myself. Whatcha think?"

Drake had joined Erik.

"Well, I'd say that's pretty good. Does your pa know?" Erik asked.

"You won't tell him, will you?" Torsten's eyes fell. "I'll go home pretty soon. I just wanted to visit."

"I'm pleased you did. You can help in the garden for a bit, and then we'll all ride back."

Torsten's eyes widened. "I don't like to garden. I want to ride horses with you."

Drake laughed. "We were just talking about that, your uncle and me."

Erik said, "Well, I've been meaning to say hello to your folks and Mia. Maybe now's a good time. You can lead the way back. How's that?"

"Sure."

"Mr. Minton and I need to saddle up."

"I know," Torsten said. "I can't lift my saddle, so I don't use one."

"Soon enough, lad." Erik chuckled.

As Drake and Erik saddled their horses, Erik said, "I'm sure you wouldn't mind visiting the Olafsons with me for a bit?"

Drake glanced at Torsten. "Is your sister home?"

"She and Ma were in the garden. I was supposed to be."

Erik frowned. He realized Torsten was heading for a bit of trouble, although the boy did not seem to realize it. Torsten seemed to be that way. He got a notion to do something and just did it, which was partially the reason he had been taken by some Shoshones four years ago, and Erik had had to go fetch him back. It had cost him a good rifle, but that had been a small price compared to a life.

"You ready?" Erik asked Torsten. He knew Torsten needed a stump or a boost. He wanted to see how the boy handled it.

Torsten frantically searched Erik's eyes and glanced up at Whitey.

"Don't worry about telling folks what you need, Torsten. There is nothing wrong with asking for help." He reached down, made his hands into a stirrup, and raised the boy as he stepped up and over Whitey's back.

Torsten beamed. "Thanks, Uncle Erik."

The horse was a good choice for Torsten. She was an old gray-speckled white mare that did not mind children climbing on her. She also knew the way home, whether her young rider was in control or not.

"Okay, Torsten, lead us out."

Erik watched as the boy raked his bare feet against Whitey's flanks. "Git up, Whitey," Torsten urged. He turned the animal's head and kicked again. "Come on."

The horse begrudgingly turned, probably well aware of where it needed to be going, and led out down the trail toward the Olafsons'.

Erik and Drake rode behind.

When Torsten reached his home, he seemed as proud as ever, yet oblivious to his misdeed. "Ma, I'm home. Uncle Erik and Uncle Drake are here."

Margret and Mia came running out. Their frantic expressions quickly faded.

Margret helped the boy down about the time Sven rounded the corner on his horse. His worry gave way to anger and displeasure, and he jumped down and approached his son, towering over him. "Into the house, Torsten," he snapped.

Torsten's face crumpled.

"Do you not think he is a good rider, Sven?" Erik asked.

Torsten quickly looked back, hoping for some reprieve.

His father glared. "In!" he thundered. "You shall not be out here when you're disobedient."

Erik and Drake swung down. Of course, the matter was between Torsten and his father.

"It is what gets someone killed in this country, it is," Sven snapped.

"I reckon so," Erik said. "Which is why I brought him home. I will say he was mighty proud of himself for climbing onto Whitey and taking her somewhere. Might be good for him to be riding by himself at his age."

Sven glowered. "He knows the rules."

Margret interrupted. "Erik, would you and Drake like some coffee?"

"Something cold would be better, ma'am," Drake said, "if I may."

"I can get you some mint tea," Mia said.

Drake grinned more broadly, and the look he gave Mia was not lost on Erik.

Erik relaxed a little, feeling the affair with Torsten had been defused. He resolved that he would talk with the boy at some point to help him realize his error. As the Sheepeaters often stressed, a boy was more likely to listen to reason from an uncle than from a father. Erik was near enough to being an uncle, and it warmed him that Torsten referred to him as such.

"I've been meaning to come and visit," Erik said. "I've had a thing or two on my mind. First, as always, to again thank you for Katrine. You and Mrs. Olafson took care of her when I could not. I will always be grateful."

"Ja," Sven said. "You owe me nothing, Erik. You brought Torsten back." He frowned. "Twice now."

"It was easier this time," Erik said, grinning. "One thing I've been thinking: it just might be better for Torsten as well. He's not a farmer, Sven."

Sven stiffened. "If he keeps running off, he won't grow up enough to know if he's one or not."

"He favors the stock. He always has—except those chickens—if I recall correctly. You've seen that. Have you given thought to running more cattle on your place? Give him a couple of years. I think he'd be good at handling them."

Sven sat glowering, but then his eyes eased.

"You aren't only a farmer, Sven. You built this place." Erik waved his hands. "You've built all the rocking chairs, cabinets, and furniture in this entire valley. You still building skis?"

"Ja," he said as Margret put a cup of coffee into his hand. "Tack. Thank you." Sven touched her hand. "I still build everything."

"Torsten will do farming as well," Erik said. "I don't know what the best balance would be. I visited with Jon Stromback, and he's doing right well for himself. They have a vegetable garden and an orchard, but they raise mostly cattle. The winters up here keep you from doing that unless you can take cattle to lower elevation and out of the snow.

"I've been thinking that soon Laurens, Torsten, and Oscar will all be of an age that they could trail out a few head in the fall and bring new ones back in the spring. You could fatten and sell a few every fall. Stromback can trail them into the gold camps. Maybe Torsten would get to that point as well."

"Ja," Sven said. "Wikstrom. He's been thinking on that. He took some to Boise and did well." He abruptly turned to Mia. "Go get your brother, Mia."

"Oh, Sven, Torsten is too young to understand this," Margret said.

"He showed me today he's not too young. If he starts getting the idea, it might give him some direction to his growing-up years."

Shortly, the boy was seated with Erik and Sven. Drake excused himself, which Erik had known he would do. He kept company with Mia, which Erik also had known he would do. Margret remained busy in the kitchen, near enough that she could keep her eyes on Drake.

CHAPTER 63

The sun shone brightly on Midsummer's Eve day—the summer solstice. Erik found it difficult to believe that after this day, the daylight hours would again shorten.

Last evening, he and Drake had ridden down to the Adolphsons' hot springs and cleaned up the best they could. Erik preferred Wikstroms' hot springs, where they could almost swim, but the Wikstroms were a distance farther. Björn's hot springs were as well, and from what Erik remembered, Björn had not built a suitable place to bathe.

Erik shook Drake out of his bed. The youth glared and then swung his feet onto the plank floor.

"Chores to do, Drake. Get them done early. On Midsummer's Eve, it's a requirement. Tomorrow you won't likely be fit for doing much of anything. This is your big day to see if you like being a Swede or not."

"It hain't hardly light out," Drake complained. He stood and stretched his lanky frame, pulled on his pants, tucked in his shirt, and slipped on his suspenders.

Erik eyed his ill-fitting attire. His clothes had belonged to Mr. Steele, a larger man, and were now growing shabby as well. Erik's clothes were not much better. He realized with what they wore, they would be showing up like orphans at Midsummer's Eve, unless he could do something about it.

Both worked through the chores—they took care of the horses, the cow, and her calf, which Erik had convinced Nils to let him raise, and fed the hog.

Erik charged Drake with preparing some firewood and took Hatchet up the creek to visit Margret Olafson. Mia and Torsten were already putting on their finest clothes for the day's happenings.

Torsten quickly challenged Erik to wrestle, but Erik bowed out. "Got to get some things for Uncle Drake," he told the boy.

At nearly seventeen, Drake was near enough to a full build that he could fit one of Sven's shirts. Erik had provided Margret with cloth in the past, and he figured she was likely to have an extra shirt to lend.

"I do declare," she said, giving Erik a closer look, "that shirt of yours is practically in tatters as well."

"But this is the one you made for me."

"And that is nigh on five years ago, it is." She examined his sleeve, which was thin and showing through.

In the end, Erik did not refuse the loan of two shirts—one gray and one light blue.

Heading back, Erik hoped he wasn't making a mistake. He and Drake had been in the valley for almost three weeks. They both still appeared as if they had just come out of hibernation. Drake had a spattering of scraggly black whiskers and unruly hair that covered his neck. Erik's hair and fuzzy light-colored beard were little better.

Back at the cabin, Erik demanded, "Now, get that shirt off; we gotta get you looking presentable. Those women won't be getting any nearer than a rod to you unless we can get you fixed up some."

Drake's eyes bulged when the razor appeared in Erik's hand. Erik had never given anyone a razor cut other than himself, let alone a shave.

"Now, I wouldn't be moving around too much while I'm attempting this." He threw a towel around Drake's shoulders, lathered him up, and poised the razor. "Hold still."

Drake didn't budge. Erik scraped down from his earlobe toward his chin and then quickly checked for blood. He took a couple more scrapes, thankful he had gotten the hang of it.

He shortened Drake's hair around his ears and the back of his neck. Erik didn't think he looked all that bad. Only one small nick drew blood, and that was on the back of Drake's neck. It would do.

Drake washed himself off. "Ya know you're next, right?"

Erik shook his head. "I can manage myself."

"So coulda I."

"What?"

"It wouldn't have been the first time, ya know. Just no reason to get all fancied up before."

"And now with all those women, there is," Erik said, finishing for him.

Erik *was* next. Afterward, Erik tossed Sven's gray shirt to Drake. He put on the blue one. They snapped their suspenders into place.

"If you had a nicer hat and a vest, you'd look full Swede. Guess what you got will have to do."

"Where's *your* hat?" Drake eyed Erik.

"Never wear one. You know that."

Erik and Drake headed out and met the Olafsons at the turnoff. Björn's wagon with Katrine and their children approached from downriver. They waved.

Erik's last Midsummer's Eve celebration four years ago had been the only proper one he had experienced other than when he was a young boy in Sweden. During that last Midsummer's Eve, Björn had made his wish to marry Katrine known. Erik had sat with them near the bonfire. At that time, it had been as if his spirit helper visited to remind him of another unfulfilled promise. The feeling of the night cat's presence had partially caused Erik to move on. Oddly, his promise to return to the Sheepeaters remained unfulfilled.

It was a grand sight at the Wikstroms', and it stirred Erik's blood. The Midsummer's Eve pole, decorated with evergreens, flowers, and ribbons, had already been raised. The women and girls were in their best dresses. The young girls had made flower wreaths for their hair. The men and boys were dressed sharply and slicked up as well. Erik glanced at Drake. He'd fit in.

Tea, coffee, and mint tea were served with some cakes. Men caught up on their farming. Women caught up on babies and children. Erik had little to offer, but the men all gave Drake a thorough inquisition.

Magnus Lundgren grabbed his fiddle, and the dancing began around the pole. Lundgren limped around as he increasingly became caught up in his playing.

People sang familiar Swedish songs. The children, including Torsten, formed an inner dancing circle. Next were the single men, including Erik, Drake, and Laurens. They danced with the single ladies—Mia, Linnea, Emma, and Ingrid. Pelle stood nearby, hopping about, with his missing leg hardly slowing him down. The ladies made clear efforts to take turns with him, although Erik noticed Pelle favored Mia. Emma and Linnea vied to be Drake's partner. The married adults danced in a circle outside them.

When the first dance broke down, the circles changed.

Erik preferred to watch. More than once, Drake pestered him on how to do things. Erik admitted it had been a long while since he had done any Swedish dances, and he wasn't the best to be teaching Drake. That was not satisfactory to Drake. Erik recruited Lars. He breathed more easily when Lars happily gave some instructions.

After a few more dances and songs, someone escorted the children to the hot springs, and the adults gained a respite.

The women laid out the dinner: peas in thick cream, new onions, new potatoes, green nettles with salt and butter, smoked salmon, venison, beef, and a goose. Dessert was traditional wild strawberries sprinkled with sugar crystals and smothered in cream. All was exactly as Erik remembered.

Erik was a bit taken aback when Linnea cornered him. She pushed at the crown of flowers she wore and nervously slid her fingers down her dress.

"I should not be asking this, Erik, but I think Drake is sweet on me."

Erik suppressed a smile. "I would wager so."

"He's funny, and he makes me laugh. He works hard, but I don't know if he'd ever stay here. Papa needs me."

Erik knew Linnea's meaning. A farmer's work never ended, and to get ahead meant sacrifice. Life in this valley, in addition to the usual farmwork, meant surviving severe winters.

"He also makes me feel funny. I don't know. Is he an honorable man?"

Erik took a deep breath. He had not expected something like this from Linnea. He remembered her as a young teenager and not as a young woman. He thought of her as somewhat shy, though it was likely because she had been the younger sister to Anna. He was somewhat humbled that she trusted him enough to ask such questions.

"Drake believes in doing what's right. He's stood by me. I believe he leans to be a rancher. We've been talking about it. We think it's doable in this valley, just not carrying cattle year-round. The families here have proved living here year-round is doable. I think if he had a reason to stay here, he would. If I might be so bold, you might be his reason."

Linnea's blue eyes sparkled, and her cheeks glowed. It was as if Erik could see her heart nearly bursting.

She threw her arms about Erik and hugged him. "Oh, you make me so happy."

"You should talk to Anna about your funny feelings, though," Erik said. "I would dare say she has a better understanding of such matters."

"Oh, I will." Linnea fairly danced. "I'm so happy you're here. I'm so happy you brought Drake."

"Hallo, hallo!" Nils shouted for attention. He waved a bottle of brännvin. "Another Midsummer's Eve. We have been in this valley for nine years. Is it not something to behold? Look at our families. Look at our farms. Praise God."

He poured a small glass for each of the eight men, including Drake and Pelle. They all raised their glasses; squared their eyes; saluted one another; and shouted, "Skål!" before downing the strong liquid.

Anton began a drinking song. As was customary, the younger boys, led by Torsten and Oscar, joined in with the adults' singing and then began their own antics, hoping to induce someone into sharing a small sip of brännvin.

The women gathered in the shady places with the babies and swapped their own stories. Louise shared a drink with them, which they passed around but not as noticeably as the men. It was more acceptable, however, as Louise was English. Erik noticed Linnea talking somewhat animatedly with Anna and Mia. He believed it to be good.

Drake shadowed Erik. Erik tried to explain things the best he could, but the youth seemed too caught up in everything to care much for the details. Erik wondered if he had any idea just how deep Linnea's feelings for him were.

They lit the bonfire. The blaze reflected, dancing and flickering, from the creek that rushed by. As during the bonfire a few years ago, Erik kept Katrine and Björn company and watched the sparks ascend into the night sky.

Some persons slipped away to enjoy the hot springs. Erik noticed Drake and Linnea were missing. He hoped it would be well. After all, as Nils Adolphson had advised, "There should be nothing wrong with being a little foolhardy one night a year," but judging by what he now knew, Erik could not help but to worry a bit. "Blazes," he muttered. "They're not children."

Midnight passed. The night chilled. The Lundgrens and the Adolphsons departed for their homes. Sven loaded up his wagon and headed out with Torsten and Mia. Katrine and Anna, with their young children, stayed and crowded into Anton's home to spend the night along with Freda and her children.

Lars, Björn, Drake, and Erik found themselves in one of the stock sheds.

"We want you to know, Drake," Lars slurred, "you are welcome here."

"What do you say, Erik?" Björn asked. "Would Drake make a good Swede? We need one since you abandoned us." He laughed, also a bit tipsy from the brännvin.

"He has to learn what side's up on a plow and where the faucets are on a cow, but I reckon he might do," Erik said.

Drake eyed them but didn't comment. He hung his clothes on a peg and settled himself into his blankets.

"And what about that brännvin, Drake?" Björn asked. "Is it not better than any whiskey you've ever had?"

"I ain't disagreeing on that," Drake mumbled.

"Ja, my pa makes the best," Lars said. "Otherwise, what was the best of this day, Drake? I wager the hot springs."

"Especially with my sister," Björn hooted.

"Ja, we could see," Lars said, laughing.

Drake sputtered and reddened. "I can't help that. It's what happens around a pretty gal."

Lars and Björn laughed even louder. Erik bit his lip.

"How well we know. We've been there," Björn said.

"Ja, two children's worth," Lars said. "And it was you and Katrine who made that catch basin in your hot springs, after all. You thought no one could see."

"You are the one to talk, Lars," Björn sputtered. "You and Anna, all the way from Minnesota."

"Nej, we waited until it was proper," Lars said.

"So did we," Björn said, "though there were times."

Lars turned toward Drake. "And you, Drake? As one of the respectable Swedes of this valley, what are your thoughts?"

"We already saw what his thoughts were!" Björn said.

"No, seriously, Drake," Lars said. "We agree you'll fit."

Drake laced his fingers behind his head, staring upward, smiling. "Linnea is the best thing that's happened to me. I never thought about farming, though."

"I don't know, Lars," Björn said somberly. "What's my pa and Freda going to do if Linnea leaves? If Drake ain't a farmer and they go away?"

"Maybe you'll get another brother or sister," Lars said.

"Helvete! Such thoughts!" Björn threw something in Lars's direction. "Seriously, Drake."

"Keep them away from the hot springs," Drake said deadpan.

Björn shoved at Drake. "Enough."

Erik shook his head. "It does sound like those hot springs have a way of bringing on those younguns."

All three turned toward Erik, staring. Erik understood the reason. No one knew of his daughter, Glad Spirit.

Erik woke sometime in the early morning. It was cold, but that had not awakened him. Drake was stumbling about. Erik figured he had to relieve himself. Drake eventually found his way outside. Shortly, he returned, nearly tripping over Erik.

"Sorry," he mumbled.

Erik refrained from saying anything. Drake crawled back into his bedding and lay tossing about for a long while before he finally rolled over and settled. Erik smiled inwardly. With Linnea in his thoughts, as Erik knew she must have been, he doubted Drake would be leaving Long Valley, farmer or not.

CHAPTER 64

After Midsummer's Eve, it was no longer uncommon for Erik to see Torsten riding Whitey down the trail to visit. Often, Erik rode with him from there to visit Katrine and Björn or the Wikstroms. Frequently, Drake rode with them. Torsten was becoming a skilled rider. He could not completely saddle Whitey, but Sven helped him and then sent him on his way. Usually, the boy had a mission, which was sometimes to deliver a message and other times to deliver some bread or some other treat. Occasionally, Erik sent him back with a gift in return.

More important than his riding skills, Torsten learned to care for Whitey. He also helped Erik with Hatchet and Drake with Paint. He did the same with the horses of whomever he visited, Björn, the Wikstroms, or the Lundgrens. His life had become centered on horses, including helping Lars as a blacksmith's shop lad at the waystation.

He did every chore for tending the stock, including brushing, cleaning stalls, and pitching hay. Torsten also helped in the fields, of course, but it was clear his heart was now with the horses and cattle. Erik believed that on Torsten's ninth birthday, it was more as if Torsten had reached his eleventh.

Erik helped him set up a set of horns like those he had seen at the Strombacks', and soon the boy was practicing roping as well. But the horns weren't enough, and he was soon roping one of the calves. Drake joined in, giving good instruction to Torsten. Erik and Sven watched. It was not long until Torsten was able to gallop Whitey out from the corner of the yard and set a loop over the calf's head.

"Maybe he *will* be a rancher," Sven said one afternoon to Erik and Drake, who had ridden up with him. Torsten remained on Whitey's back and practiced roping for his father to see.

Erik welcomed the time visiting. Drake did as well, especially with Mia around, but other than some pleasantries, Erik no longer sensed anything between them. On the other hand, Drake seemed to find any reason to go with Erik to visit the Wikstroms.

"I'm thinking of helping Björn build a larger house," Sven said. "We might get a good go of it by winter."

"I know someone who would be happy to skid logs to the sawpit," Erik replied. He glanced to where Torsten had just settled a loop around the horns again.

Sven's eyes had settled on Erik, however, and also on Drake.

"Drake and I can get started cutting timber right away," Erik said.

"Ja," Sven said. "Some logs are seasoned and up at the sawpit. We'll put in a water saw soon."

Sven waved at Torsten, and the boy came and sat with the men. "I have another job for you, Son. You think you and Whitey can skid some logs?"

"You bet!" Torsten's eyes lit up. "Only you have to help me hitch them up and undo them."

Sven rumpled Torsten's hair. "Been a hot one today, has it not? I bet the creek after a bath would be mighty nice. Go fetch some towels, would you, Son? I haven't enjoyed a bath for some time. You two care?" He glanced at Erik and Drake and then nodded at the *badstuga*, the bathhouse, which doubled as the smokehouse.

The three men cut some willows, started a fire, and heated the stones. Torsten brought up a pail of water and the dipper. He turned to go.

"You should join us, Son."

Torsten's eyes widened. The boy must have been feeling some embarrassment but also some pride.

"We must talk a bit about herding cattle, do not you think? You think we should raise us a bull this season?"

"Y-yes, sir." Torsten's grin split his ears.

CHAPTER 65

At length, the old Lundgren cabin transformed into Erik and Drake's cabin. Even with a late start, the two managed to put in some potatoes, turnips, and onions, though not much else. They fixed the outbuildings and began bringing in hay to get the cow and calf through winter.

They joined in at the Adolphsons' during Sunday gatherings, as Erik had done in the past. Nils Adolphson always had some words to share and reminded everyone of their blessings in the valley. His positive outlook had convinced others to stay when, with the deep snows, it made more sense to try to homestead in the lower valleys or up on the Salmon River drainage, as the O'Donnells had apparently done.

As the season turned, Erik enjoyed his visits with Katrine, Björn, and his nephew and niece. He visited the Olafsons frequently, especially to ride with Torsten.

Erik had approached Ingrid, but nothing was there. It seemed to him she was content in remaining with her father and mother and helping Pelle in making the waystation her home. Maybe she had hopes of a good man traveling through who might decide to stay in the valley. Most travelers were prospectors still intent on striking their fortunes, and none had intentions of settling down. Others who came through were packers taking in or bringing out supplies and equipment and sometimes gold. A few camped along the river and contemplated homesteading, but they never lasted, and they frequently threatened trouble. More than a few wanted to avoid attention.

Erik accepted this turn of events. He and Drake could work a farm until Drake decided to move on or settle down. His interest in Linnea was known. Some openly hoped that in a year or two, they would marry. Anton Wikstrom had shared his thoughts, as had Nils Adolphson. Most doubted he would last the winter, however, and they doubted he had the heart to be a farmer.

This day, a late-autumn day with leaves yellowing, Drake left the cabin earlier than usual. Erik did not pay much attention to his comings and goings as long as their work was caught up. A farmer's work was never complete.

About noon, Erik decided to visit the Adolphsons. He meant to pick up some sugar and flour. In a few days, the men would load up crops and head toward Boise Valley for some trading and to restore dwindling supplies. Other than the crossing of the Payette River, which was still by a troublesome bridge, the trails had improved and had made it easier to take produce to Boise Valley and particularly to Boise Basin. A second and even third trip would be made as more of the crops came in, as close to the first killing frost as possible. Although, when the Swedes' wagons were gone, it was a risky time for unwanted attention from either Indian hunting parties or ne'er-do-wells who squatted along the river.

Erik reached the Adolphsons' waystation and noticed Drake's horse as well as one of Anton Wikstrom's. Briefly, he wondered why Anton was there. He half wondered if Drake and Anton were attempting a meeting on neutral ground regarding Linnea. It would have been proper for Drake to do so.

He found only Pelle inside the store.

"I thought Drake and Mr. Wikstrom were here, and where's Ingrid and your pa and ma?"

Pelle laughed. "Ingrid's at the house, and the reason you see one of Mr. Wikstrom's horses is because I am the only one here. My pa and ma are at the Wikstroms'."

"Then it's Linnea who is here with one of their horses," Erik said, laughing. "I bet she's not up at the house with Ingrid either."

"You are correct," Pelle said. "Drake and Linnea walked down to the hot springs. And in case you accuse me of things, no, I'm not covering. Everyone knows." He hobbled over to a stool and swung up onto it. "Want something to drink?"

"Everyone knows they're at the hot springs?" Erik questioned. He sat with Pelle.

"Well, not exactly. They know they're seeing each other."

"Better not be starting any cradles a-rocking until it's proper."

"It's all right." Pelle caught himself and laughed. "I don't mean *that's* all right. It's all right that Drake is seeing Linnea. It means Mia will quit paying him attention."

Erik laughed. "Ja, I thought she was sweet on you. I'm happy for you."

Pelle raised his eyes. "I'm just not certain how we can manage— me with a wooden leg. I think that's what Mia worries about—why she was giving Drake her attention."

"I didn't know she was." Of course, he had observed Drake with Mia, but lately, it did not seem Drake reciprocated much.

"Really?" Pelle rolled his eyes. "All of them were." He laughed. "It is good that he seems to have settled for Linnea."

"It seems Linnea is settling for him. Now it's up to Mr. Wikstrom, and if Drake isn't careful, he's going to get run out of the valley by a shotgun. Wikstrom's done that before."

"It was more like all the Wikstroms did it before—Anna, Björn, Laurens, *and* Mr. Wikstrom," Pelle said. "When that prospector laid claim to Freda and wanted to haul her away."

Erik laughed. "It's good I was not here."

"They are only soaking," Pelle said soberly. "Trust them."

Erik looked up and smiled. "The way I hear it, the kind of soaking that takes place around here tends to lead to younguns."

Pelle started laughing. "You're right, now you mention it. Lars and Anna *and* Björn and Katrine."

A gunshot exploded from the direction of the hot springs. Then came another.

Erik scrambled up. "They aren't soaking."

Erik slammed out the door with Pelle hobbling after him. He leaped onto Hatchet and put the animal at a full gallop down the river trail toward the springs, which were about a half-mile distant. Only then did he realize he had no weapons. In the valley, he rarely carried any.

Two riders bolted by in the distance, heading upriver.

Erik hesitated. He could catch them. Then what? Drake and Linnea might be in trouble. He spurred Hatchet downstream instead.

Drake was in the trail with blood wetting his scalp, leaning over Linnea. Drake had covered her with her dress. He had on only his pants. A pistol lay in the mud.

He held Linnea, rocking with her. "I'm sorry. I'm sorry."

His eyes found Erik's as Erik swung to the ground. Erik reached Linnea, fearing she was dead. Gashes of red crossed her neck and upper body. She bled. She breathed but was unconscious.

"Bastards spied on us and jumped us," Drake choked out.

"Are you okay?" Erik pushed back Drake's hair and examined his scalp. "Press this onto that cut." He tore some material from Linnea's dress. He gently examined Linnea. She began moving. "You think you can hold on for a bit? I'm sure Pelle's behind me. I'm going after those men." He grabbed the pistol and checked it. *Three rounds.* At least he had a pistol. "Is this their pistol?"

"Yeah. I managed to get it from one of them bastards."

The kid had guts. Erik hefted the pistol. It and his knife would have to do. His best chance to stop the men was now, and if any horse could overtake them, Hatchet could.

Erik said, "Hang on, Drake. Pelle's on his way."

He kicked Hatchet into a gallop and started up the trail. The men he chased might try to dry-gulch him but not with other settlers nearby who surely were responding to the gunfire by then.

The trail was well traveled. The men seemed to know where they were heading, and Erik guessed they had ridden it before and possibly stopped at the springs before to spy, as Drake had indicated. The men had two directions they could choose: in a few miles, they could turn west and head into the Little Salmon River drainage, or they could continue north to Payette Lake and follow along its west shore toward the gold camps. Erik bet on their going north. No one lived north of the Swedes. Then another possibility occurred to him: they could reach Salmon Meadows and swing south into the Weiser River country. It mattered not. He would follow.

Erik urged Hatchet on. He had few options. If he were lucky, he could shoot their horses and put the men on foot. That would buy him time. He would slit each of their throats by his schedule.

Gunshots exploded a short distance ahead. A bullet whistled high overhead. Instantly, Erik pulled Hatchet off the trail. He cocked the pistol and frantically tried to spot the shooter, who was seemingly a bit distant. Several more shots exploded nearby. Then there was silence. They had missed him, and Erik guessed they had turned back up trail, maybe hoping for a better ambush site.

"We're lucky, Hatchet. I didn't expect that. Glad they were overeager." Cautiously, Erik moved forward. "I can't press them, Hatchet. They'll try it again and maybe pick me off."

A horse lay in the trail. Pelle pushed at the writhing animal. The youth was pinned underneath. Pelle had not followed Erik to the hot springs but had spotted and gone after the two men.

Erik leaped down. "Easy, Pelle. Easy."

Wikstrom's horse wheezed, rolling. Erik hesitated only a second before he fired a bullet into the animal's brain. With any more thrashing, Pelle would have been crushed. He might already have been.

Pelle pulled free. "Thank God," he gasped. "There were two of them. Got the jump on me." His face pinched. "Are Linnea and Drake—how are they?"

"A mess, but they will survive. You?" Erik tried to examine Pelle.

"Sore." He coughed. "Herregud. That hurts wicked bad." He grabbed his side with pain flashing in his eyes.

"You may have some busted ribs," Erik said. "Take shallow breaths."

Pelle sat heaving on the ground. He looked at Wikstrom's horse. "Mr. Wikstrom's not going to be happy."

"He's not our worry right now."

Blood oozed from cuts on Pelle's arm and a gash on his head. Erik coached Pelle through moving his limbs. Pelle managed but grimaced as he stretched his arms.

"No limbs busted that I can tell," Erik said. "Maybe your ribs."

Pelle laughed and then caught himself. "Helvete, that hurt. Can't laugh. I was going to say it might have been good for once to be short part of a leg." He pointed. His wooden stump lay pinned under the horse's carcass.

"I think you're going to be okay, Pelle," Erik said. "You didn't bring your shotgun?"

"I had this." He shoved a pistol into Erik's hands. "Might be two rounds in it."

Erik checked and saw Pelle was right. He shook his head. *Two pistols. Four rounds.* Better odds than he'd had before. He took the ammunition and loaded the two rounds into the cylinder. "Think you can hold on? I can't stay with you if I'm going to catch them."

Pelle grabbed Erik tightly, gasping. "Ain't going to catch them now anyhow. Let them think you've turned back."

Erik hesitated, recognizing the youth's fear. "Maybe you're right."

Pelle gasped harder, his chest heaving. A bit of blood had formed at his lips. A cold numbness began enveloping Erik. Something inside Pelle might have busted open, and he was filling with blood.

Erik wrestled with himself, knowing the men were getting away, knowing his chance of catching them was slipping away, and wondering if it would become a protracted chase like seeking Dudgin and Smith. The image of two wolf-bear beasts overwhelmed him, and blackness began seeping in.

Pelle coughed. Blood bubbled up. His eyes blinked.

Dear God, not Pelle. Erik fought off the thought.

"Easy, Pelle. Easy. I'm right here. You're going to be okay. I know it." But Erik didn't know it.

Ingrid found them. She burst into tears. Her hands felt her brother and patted him. "Pelle, Pelle."

Pelle managed a smile and clutched her hand.

"Easy, Ingrid. He's going to be okay," Erik said. Somehow, he managed to hide his concern. "He may have something busted inside. Be careful in moving him. Drake and Linnea are back by the springs. They are cut up but otherwise seem good. You and Pelle will be fine. Help's going to be here." He stood. "I'm going after those bastards. I made the mistake one time before of not doing that. I'm not going to do it again."

Pelle's eyes followed Erik. Though pain streaked his face, he nodded.

"God be with you, Pelle. Hang in there." Erik reached down and touched Pelle's shoulder. "You've done your father proud. Mr. Wikstrom won't care about his horse. You did what you had to do."

Erik swung up onto Hatchet. He took a last look at Pelle, who lay bleeding and gasping on the ground, praying it would not be the last time he saw Pelle alive.

Ingrid remained bent over her brother's form as Erik rode upriver. They would soon have help. Gunshots did not remain unheeded. Only by pressing these men did he have a chance at stopping them. He had already lost precious time.

Erik followed quickly but cautiously. After a few miles, the men stopped running. Erik grew hopeful but knew even if he closed the distance to pistol range, it wasn't a good risk to try to shoot their horses. He had to be close enough to put a bullet in the animals' brains.

The men turned west. In a mile, they topped the low divide between Long Valley and the Salmon River drainage. They headed downward across an open park and picked up the Goose Creek trail.

"Good. They just narrowed their options, and now I know I'm not going to lose them. That's the most important thing," Erik whispered, patting Hatchet. He sensed the horse knew what was happening. They had been together similarly before. "Steady, boy." He stroked Hatchet's neck.

Twilight encroached. The two men emerged from the canyon and rode out into Salmon Meadows. The Little Salmon River gorge was a few miles north. Erik waited to see the direction they would travel. He figured they would continue into the gorge, but it was still possible they would head west into the hills, double back, and drop into the Weiser drainage. That would have been Erik's choice, and he knew this would be the place. Entering the gorge would make it difficult to turn back and difficult to climb out until it opened onto the main Salmon, where there was a single place to cross: Groff's ferry.

Erik considered slipping past the men while they were still in the meadows and waiting for them in the gorge, but he would have been only guessing on their direction. The men might have been thinking the same thing, which was why they had stopped.

"Patience," Erik whispered. "Let them decide our actions. I can't do a thing until I know where they're headed."

He had to follow well back to remain out of sight. Only a few willow clumps grew throughout the meadows. The men reached a small timber-covered knoll. Fortunately, a line of timber a half mile away offered a safe place for Erik. He could watch the direction the men took come morning.

He considered sneaking in under darkness and slitting their throats. As much as he hated to admit it, he needed to take the men alive and turn them over to the sheriff. Too many things could go wrong if he tried to kill them. He already had Kan See after him and possibly the sheriff. He couldn't risk endangering the Swedes.

"And how in blazes am I going to capture two armed men?" Erik whispered. "Sneak in there tonight and tie one of them up? Sure, the other one's just going to sit and watch." It was one thing to slip in and cut their throats; it was another to try to take them alive.

CHAPTER 66

In the faint morning light, Erik spotted the men moving. He prepared himself to follow. They continued north into the Little Salmon River canyon.

Erik was pleased. They had no choice now but to go down the canyon. He did not believe the two men would worry about a bunch of farmers on their trail. They might believe they had killed Pelle and would push harder to get through the gorge. Knowing their type, they likely were already running from the law. At this pace, they would reach Groff's ferry before evening and cross the main Salmon.

"Nothing I can do about it if they do, Hatchet. I might end up following them for a bit longer." With four rounds and nothing else but a knife, Erik could not afford a mistake. He still had only a vague idea of how to capture them. Somehow, he had to separate them from each other. Maybe he could get past them and get help from John Groff, but why would Groff believe him? If they turned down the main Salmon, he might be able to get help from Stromback, but he was days away. "Patience," Erik whispered. "Things will reveal."

Erik continued to hang back. Now, in the gorge, there were scant places free of brush and timber where he could see beyond a hundred yards down trail, and where he could see, the trail quickly turned behind a rock outcrop. It reminded him of the Lochsa and most of the Clearwater when he had been behind Dudgin and Smith and trying to get around them. Here the terrain was no different. He knew it would be impossible to go up and around the two men. Possibly, he could find a wide spot where a creek entered, but he would have to practically be on top of them to have enough time to skirt around. He recalled the barren slopes near Pollock's ranch, but there, he likely wouldn't be able to get ahead without being spotted. "Patience," Erik hissed to himself again, touching his medicine pouch.

Something cold washed over him, and the hairs on his neck prickled.

He pulled up on Hatchet and, from cover, scanned the section of trail ahead. He saw nothing and turned and checked his backtrail in the unlikelihood the men had tried to double back. Surprise was his best ally, but surprise worked for both sides, particularly if you thought something couldn't be done and somehow it got done. Having one man behind him and another in front of him would have put him in a death box. Thus far, the men had not attempted to hide their tracks, which suggested they knew he was following. All they had to do was stay ahead of him or wait for a good chance to kill him.

"What is it, night cat?" Erik did not like those thoughts.

He reached another open section. The trail followed the river and hugged some rocky outcrops before it climbed across a shrub-covered hillside and rounded the river bend. His skin prickled. He fingered his medicine pouch and peered intently ahead. "They know I'm here, Hatchet," Erik whispered. He studied the areas above the trail and any shrub that could have concealed a man. He had an unsettling feeling he was sitting in the iron sights of a rifle. He pulled Hatchet back.

A fleeting movement behind Erik caught his eye. Drumming hooves crescendoed. "Drake!"

The boy was riding hard.

Erik turned Hatchet and blocked the trail.

Drake immediately raised a wobbling rifle. Lather wet his horse's shoulders. "Erik!" He gasped, breathing hard. "Did ya catch the bastards?" He brought Paint to a stuttering stop.

"Just ahead, I think."

"I got to get 'em." Drake slammed his heels against Paint and tried to shoulder past.

Erik managed to grab Paint's reins. He nearly pulled Drake from his saddle.

"What the hell?" Drake spat.

"Listen to me," Erik hissed. "They've holed up. They're waiting to dry-gulch us."

Drake glared. "They're gonna get away."

"No. Time is our weapon, not theirs. There is no easy way out of this canyon. Remember? You and I rode it coming this direction. I'm not going to let either of us ride into a trap." Erik released the reins. "First, is anyone else coming? Are you running from Mr. Wikstrom?"

Drake rubbed his head where it was bandaged and grinned weakly. "I could be. I don't know."

"How are Linnea and Pelle?"

"Good as can be, I think. Pelle's alive. Linnea is crazy shook up but not hurt too bad. Soon as the Adolphsons showed up, I went and got my stuff and got on the trail. Oh, and I got ya your rifle and bow." He unstrapped Erik's rifle, handed it to him, and then pulled Erik's bow and quiver from out behind his cantle.

Erik received the weapons. He checked the load in his rifle. "Thank you. I feel much better now." Drake's foresight impressed him.

"Hell, if they're stopped ahead, here's what we do. We jump them so we can see where they're at. I stand decoy. While they're trying to keep me pinned down, you sneak in there with your bow and kill first one and then the other. They won't even hear you. That's why I brought it."

Erik tightened his jaw. "We can't kill them, Drake. I'm taking them in."

"What the hell? I hain't doin' that. I'm goin' after them." He tried to shoulder past Erik again.

Erik blocked the trail. "You're not, Drake. If anyone goes, it will be me. I told you: I've made some mistakes. I can't let you do the same. You owe me that much."

Drake glared. "You do not know, Erik—" He bit his lip but settled.

"It's been good riding with you, Drake, but now I'm saying how things will be. If not, one of us is likely going to get killed."

Drake's eyes briefly blazed before he nodded. "I'm listenin'."

"Good," Erik said. "Now, let's get on them. They've likely moved on. They can't afford to be stopping much to check on us, or they won't get across the Salmon before nightfall."

Erik resumed heading down trail with Drake following, safe beyond sight. He studied the landscape ahead, watching for birds, a flash reflecting from metal, or anything else that would indicate where the men were. This was not the right place or time. Erik touched his medicine pouch. "Where are you, night cat? These are the wolf-bears, are they not? Where are they?"

The whine of a bullet shrieked past Erik's shoulder, enveloped by a rifle's report. Then another round blazed past with a second rifle explosion. Erik grabbed his rifle. White smoke marked where the men were in the rocks. He fired a quick shot toward the smoke and spurred Hatchet forward. Closer to the rocks, they would not be able to get an angle on him. Behind him was wide open. He prayed Drake would figure things out and not advance.

Another whining bullet and rifle shot stopped short in a sickening thud. Erik turned to see Drake thrown back with his rifle spinning and his shoulder blossoming red. He hit the ground and crumpled. His horse spooked, ran a few yards, and stopped.

Erik fired at the rocks. He caught movement from a man dropping down. He quickly loaded another round and took a bead on where the man's head might reappear. He caught a flash and then nothing. Likely, they had him in their sights.

He wheeled Hatchet back and jumped down, landing next to Drake. Drake moaned and struggled to get up. Unable to do so, he pushed himself along in the dirt with his left shoulder dangling. Blood stained the ground.

Another round whined and kicked up dirt next to Erik's foot. The report reverberated through the canyon. It had come from lower in the timber.

Erik caught Drake by the shoulders and dragged him into a thicket near the trail. "Hang on, Drake."

Drake cried out, his eyes frantic and his left shoulder and arm limp and wet with blood.

Erik tore away Drake's shirt. A black hole seeping bright blood glared back from Drake's upper left shoulder. A fragment of white bone protruded, covered in oily red orange.

The youth shuddered, and his eyes rolled back. He was going into shock.

"Hang in there, Drake. It's going to be okay. The bullet went through." Erik grabbed both sides of Drake's shoulder. "This'll hurt, but I've got to stop the bleeding." He pressed.

Drake cried out and went limp.

"That's a blessing," Erik whispered. He continued holding. Slowly, he released his pressure and tore leaves from a young cottonwood. He stuffed the leaves into the hole and pressed again. While they held, he ripped pieces from Drake's shirt and packed the hole front and back.

He pressed the bandages against the wound. At length, the heavier bleeding stopped. Erik wrapped the remaining pieces of Drake's shirt tightly around the packing to keep it in place. He then cut strips from Drake's blanket and bound his arm to his chest.

Erik figured the men would not come back to finish their work; nevertheless, he kept his rifle close. He had to get Drake to some help. Tom Pollock might be working his place maybe twenty miles down the Little Salmon, he thought, and Groff could fetch help. But Erik quickly dismissed the possibilities. He wasn't going to ride into a death trap. The men would finish him off.

Behind him, at best a day and a half away, was the Wikstroms'.

"Help might come down the trail, Drake, but for now, I'm not counting on it." He began searching for poles for a travois. "I've done this before." Then, considering the time it would take to build a travois, Erik stopped. "And I've done this before as well," he muttered. He caught Drake's horse and tied his reins to Hatchet. "Come on, Drake." He hoisted the youth over his shoulder like a bag of wheat and got him astride Hatchet. Erik settled behind him and hooked his suspenders with a hand to keep him from falling off.

He turned Hatchet toward the Wikstroms' cabin, moving as quickly as possible and hoping the bleeding would not resume. He could manage only a couple of miles before his arms were too numb to hold any longer. He stopped.

"I have no choice." He regretted losing precious time, but he needed a travois.

Drake moaned and began moving, coming around.

Thank God. "Hang in there, Drake; we're heading home. Think you can hold yourself?"

"M-my blamed shoulder's on fire," he gasped in ragged breaths.

"We'll stop ahead. Now that you're awake, I want to make sure you aren't bleeding."

Drake shuddered. "I need water."

Erik wanted to push another mile, but he stopped at the next point where the trail drew near to the river. He slid off and eased Drake down. Drake tried to keep his feet, and Erik helped him walk a few steps before he crumpled into the grass. He watched as Drake gulped water from his canteen. Erik took some himself and refilled the canteen. He checked Drake's bandages. They were wet with blood, but the wound was not actively bleeding.

"Think you can hold on to your horse? We might make better time."

"I can try."

"Not good enough, Drake. Do it, or I need to build a travois. I can't hold on to you any longer."

"I'm sorry," Drake said. His face became strained. "It's my fault."

"You don't have to talk, Drake. It's still thirty miles to any help."

"If we hadn't a gone to the hot springs, nothing woulda happened."

"You were sweet on Linnea."

"It wasn't right. We were together. We both wanted it, Erik, but God saw to it that we didn't do it." Drake began shaking. "Those men musta been watching us. I'll never forget that bastard and what he said: 'Hey, Earl, kid's got himself worked up and don't know what to do with it.' He started pullin' down his pants, laughing like hell, sayin' he'd show me. It made me sick what he said.

"Earl had this crazy grin and held a pistol on me so his partner could have his way." Drake's eyes grew frantic. "Then the bastard grabbed Linnea, and she started kicking and screaming. I didn't care about the gun aimed at me. I went after the bastard—Gill, I heard Earl call him. Earl hauled me off a Gill and hit me—knocked me senseless a second."

Drake's eyes glistened. He swallowed. "Oh God, Erik, when I came around, Earl was getting on top of Linnea. I went crazy. I got my knife and went at him. Cut him good. Gill clubbed me again, and the pistol went off. I grabbed his arm and twisted it away. They grabbed Linnea and said if I didn't want to see her dead to drop the gun. They started down the trail with her and took shots at me. I shot back. Oh God, Erik, I coulda hit Linnea. I wasn't thinkin'. They dumped her. I guess that's when she passed out or something. I got her clothes when you came up."

Drake's shoulders heaved. "I'm so sorry, Erik. So sorry."

"Take it easy, Drake. No fault of yours for what they did."

"I hain't ever gonna forget their names or faces," Drake choked out. "And I know what I said—that I was listening—but I lied, Erik. I wasn't gonna let you take 'em alive."

Erik fought his own memories while hearing Drake talk of the near rape. A searing white heat burned through him. They wouldn't be alive when he finished with them either. They were not men. A vile taste rose in the back of Erik's throat. *Dudgin and Smith, and now Earl and Gill.*

He helped Drake onto Paint. "Hang on. I'll lead. Paint should follow. If you start falling, fall forward and to the right if you have a choice."

Drake said nothing. He gripped the saddle horn with his head bent. Erik led out, numb with what Drake had said.

He thought of his second vision. It was not as the night cat had said. The vision had been for him four seasons ago. The wolf-bear creatures had risen twice. The night cat had not thrown them back into darkness. How many times had the snake struck at the owl? How many times had Gray Owl been tested?

He pushed on, moving as quickly as possible, glancing back occasionally at Drake, who was slumped but somehow hanging on. Had he brought evil into Drake's life?

"You still with me, Drake?"

The youth stirred and partially raised his head. "So far."

They reached the Wikstroms' at about three in the morning, having traveled the last several miles in weak starlight. Laurens came to the door, and the house woke. Freda pulled Drake into their home. Linnea let out a cry and sob. Erik wondered how Anton would react.

The man said nothing about Drake. He addressed Laurens. "Go get Mrs. Adolphson." He turned to Erik. "I guess you found them."

"Two men," Erik said. "One goes by Earl, and the other goes by Gill. I got some distant catchings of them. Pelle got a good look." He thanked Freda for the coffee she handed to him. "You aren't going, Anton. Give me an hour to rest. I'm going alone. I'd be obliged for a packhorse and a few provisions."

Anton worked his jaw, appearing as if he wanted to argue and were wrestling with himself. "Ja. It is your way," he said at length. "What about him?" He jerked his head toward Drake, who was now lying in a makeshift bed in the living area with Linnea and Freda bent over him.

Erik hesitated. "He can have my cabin. Maybe he'll stick around if you Swedes will still have him."

They both glanced at Drake. Linnea held his good hand; her eyes were wet. Freda gave out orders for hot water and bandages.

LONG VALLEY

CHAPTER 67

Erik returned to his cabin and finished packing. He quickly made his rounds. He visited Pelle and was relieved to see he was on the mend.

"I probably busted all my ribs, Erik," he said, "but nothing bad inside near as anyone can tell."

They talked about the chase.

"I wish you well in catching them. Put them both under for me, will you? Neither one is worth the cost of Mr. Wikstrom's horse."

Katrine and Björn had received the news and met him at the Olafsons' with Carl and Ruth. Erik hugged his nephew and niece.

He clasped Torsten. "Maybe when you get those cattle going, I'll give you a hand. Now, you just help your ma and pa. Promise."

Torsten's eyes gleamed wet. "Y-you can ride trail."

Erik turned to his sister. "I said goodbye one time before, Katrine, telling you that there was no word for it in the Sheepeater language. It's for a reason. The people believe they will return and see each other—if not here, then in the sky. I'll return. I need to see these children of yours growing up."

Katrine wiped at her eyes. "I fear you will get yourself killed, Erik. You don't have to go after those men."

"It is not the men, Katrine. It is me. You should understand that now. The Sheepeaters believed I was a gift from the Great Mystery and brought good things. Others said I brought only evil. I know I have allowed evil to live, and it is given to me to end it. I do not know why."

Katrine shook her head with tears welling. "No one thinks you brought evil, Erik. No one."

"Perhaps it is not here where people still believe that." He held his sister tightly. He had never told her of Bright Shell. He had told

382

no one. He had come close to telling Drake to ease the younger man's guilt, but he never had. Bright Shell, White Eagle, Muskrat, and the others belonged to another world. His family and friends could not cross the boundary to that world. Each time he crossed it, he wondered if he could endure another journey. One time, he would not return. On which side would he be when that happened?

He asked Björn to watch Drake and Linnea. Björn laughed and said not to worry; Drake was a fine man.

Back at the Wikstroms', the packhorse, a chestnut named Willow, was ready, as were some provisions.

Linnea caught Erik in the yard. "Drake told me how you met. You helped him and his pa get back to Kansas. He told me you saved his life in Lewiston." She hugged and kissed Erik. "I owe you so much."

Erik was at a loss as to what to do. "I told you he was an honorable man." Gently, he separated from her.

"He means so much to me I can hardly bear it."

"I'm happy for both of you. Truly I am."

Erik made his way into the cabin. He was met by Freda and Anton. He said a quick goodbye and managed to leave Linnea with them. He wanted a moment with Drake.

"What's that all about?" Drake asked.

"They worry you might be like me and leave the valley, even with the place I've given you," Erik said. It was not entirely a lie, but Erik figured it would have embarrassed Drake to hear what Linnea had said.

Drake adjusted his bandage on his shoulder. "Mr. Wikstrom would never allow it, Erik. It's true what ya said about the shotgun, ya know."

Erik took a second before he caught Drake's slight smile.

"No, Erik. Linnea would never allow it. My family really were farmers. I'm not intendin' on farmin', but I figure some of us can run cattle. I'm stayin'. You have my word on that. Linnea and I wanna have a family."

"She's a wonderful woman, Drake. She'll be a fine mother. You'll be a fine father." Erik clasped Drake's hand. "I've got to be riding now. I just wanted to tell you thanks for riding with me. It was an honor."

Drake's eyes pinched. "You do not need to hunt those men, Erik. I may never forgive myself, but it brings no good end." He pulled himself up. "Once, you told me to be listenin' for when God talked to me—when my pa and I were huntin' for my stepma to kill her. I had the chance to kill her. I didn't do it. Maybe it was your words I remembered. Maybe it was God talkin' to me. I never believed it then. When those men tried to have their way with Linnea, nothing was going to stop me from killing them. But I did get stopped. By this." He lifted his bandaged arm. "I think it was God telling me I had what he intended for me here with Linnea and the others—if I wanted it." He steadied his eyes. "I do. Linnea and I love each other. I think Mr. Wikstrom's okay with us. At least so far." He grinned. "He's letting me stay here till I mend."

"I know you will have his blessing, Drake. He's a bit stubborn, but he sees much in you." Erik glanced toward Anton and the women. "You may be right about not killing those men, Drake, but I blame myself for what has happened as well. Things may be right for a time, but if those men are not brought to justice, someone else will be hurt. Evil begets evil."

Erik bit his lip. How could he tell Drake or anyone what he had felt when he discovered Bright Shell dying from the same unspeakable act? Now the feeling consumed him. The farewells had been a mask to his true emotions, which, until this moment, he had kept buried. For what reason he did not understand, but this path had been chosen for him. He would not be on the hunt for men; he would be hunting evil. Evil had to be cut down. Although he could never completely kill it—no man could—if unchecked, it would fester and grow. The vision from the burning-rocks land had revealed this. He had not understood. It simply was.

The men Erik sought were in the Salmon River drainage. He would never speak their names. He mentally renewed the details shared with him by those who'd gotten good looks at the men. The men had been sighted before at the springs. Linnea had recognized them. Both had scraggly dark hair and stubble beards. Both wore dark brown or black coats. Both rode bays. Possibly they had served in the Confederacy—if Drake had been correct in mimicking their southern drawl. They had tracking sense and could cope in the wilds. They had rifles and, for now, a single pistol. Erik had the other. One had a new cut on his neck and shoulder, and both lived on borrowed breath. The last was Erik's observation.

He tracked them steadily, having carefully studied and memorized their horses' prints.

There had been snow, and more would soon come. The trees had shed their leaves. Frost coated the landscape in the mornings, and ice formed on the edges of the streams. Erik desired to catch the men before winter, but as with the others he had pursued, it was in God's hands.

The second week, he found where another set of prints joined the two—a third man. Erik followed. The new prints showed a distinct drag on the right rear hoof.

A chill of recognition washed over Erik. He had not seen this track for more than a year, almost a year and a half. He was uncertain until he had followed the tracks for another day. When they remained together, he forced himself to accept the truth. Erik had deciphered Smith's horse before. Smith now rode with Earl and Gill, or more appropriately, Erik sensed, Earl and Gill rode with Smith. But where were Dudgin's and Bender's tracks?

With his blood racing, Erik urged Hatchet and Willow onward. He knew he was close. The more distinctive track made his job easier. He continued to watch for Dudgin's and Bender's tracks to join, but they never did. Likely, the men had split up. Most men did not ride for long together.

He found himself in snow again. Still, Erik pushed on. As he had done before, he avoided people. He watched the towns, waystations, and ferryboats. Then the tracks vanished, masked by other tracks and obliterated by worsening weather and increasing snow. Another winter was on him.

Erik found himself along the Clearwater, back near one of the warm springs. He built a brush lodge. He brought in feed for Hatchet and Willow. This would be a long winter. The furs he would trap would bring him enough come spring for necessary staples and ammunition. He also had a winter to work on arrows and his bow. He ran his fingers over his bow and recalled how his uncle, Whistling Elk, had presented it to him. Free Hawk, Erik's adoptive father, had presented White Eagle with his own sheep horn bow the same day. Did White Eagle still possess his?

This night, it was cold and some time past the turning of the year. The snow crunched. Erik's breath hung in clouds as he reached his brush cabin. He cleaned off his snowshoes. Hatchet and Willow stood in the shelter he had built for them and stamped at his return, nodding a greeting.

He caught the glow on the snow—wavering, fleeting colors. He gazed north, the direction from which he had come.

Softly at first and then more vibrantly, the sky began filling with thin, glowing veils. Pale tendrils of green materialized—luminescent, shimmering, and silent. The veils floated across the northern sky, reaching upward, expanding outward, and lighting the snowy mountain peaks. Now more brilliant, some were edged in rosy pink and lavender.

Erik shivered and became one with the spectacle.

"When I was known as Sky Eyes, this I observed," he whispered. "Then I was of the people. I came from the lodge while everyone slept, and I saw this. Everyone came out and danced in the snow. 'The snow spirits,' they told me. 'They dance. The Great Mystery has brought us this boy with eyes of sky. It is good.'

"And Katrine told me that when she saw the northern lights that night, she wondered about me. I wondered about her. In my heart, I knew I would find her, and I did.

"And tonight? What is it you are telling me? Is my sister reaching across this sky? Is there trouble, or are the snow spirits dancing with happiness? No, for Katrine, it is happiness. Perhaps another child?

"And is my true brother watching? Does he wonder what has become of his white brother? Am I to return to him?"

Erik turned from watching the sky and surveyed his lodge under the trees. He gazed back toward the stars and the white outline of mountain peaks softly glowing from the now nearly faded lights.

Evil had brought evil. It was meant that they had come together—Smith, Earl, and Gill—but what did it mean?

Since his burning-rocks vision, Erik had frequently tried to recall Gray Owl's vision and what he had said about it. The snake and the wolf-bears were similar. The owl had prevailed. The night cat must prevail. But Erik was Two Elks Fighting and not the night cat. How could the night cat prevail?

"I know this," Erik whispered. "When the seasons break, I will go to the people—not for my brother, though I will be glad to see him, but for Gray Owl. I know he must now be very old, Great Mystery, but not once have you shown me that he walks the sky trails. He will be waiting. He will have the answers to the burning-rocks vision. And I will know then how to stop the evil that has risen. Of this I am certain."

ACKNOWLEDGMENTS

Many people have inspired and encouraged me to write, and each has had a part in this book, as with my others. My brother Pat was a good source of firsthand information on the Idaho backcountry, hunting, and big game. Rob Morrow provided insight on the forests and forest management. My sister Linda Dorris helped in the research of old trails and in reading the manuscript. Her insight into character and story-line development greatly helped. Of course, I've continued to rely on my Chicago Swedish cousins, Jay and Ross Anderson, and my wife, Susan, for help with the Swedish customs. Sadly, my cousin Jay passed away during editing of this book.

Of special note, Jack Chamberlain was a great source regarding early farming techniques and life on the farm. Some of his experiences are indirectly captured within my characters. He did ride his horse to the one-room schoolhouse and met and married his wife, Doris, while they were yet teenagers. They remained happily married for more than seventy years until their recent passing.

I will always owe thanks to my three children, Scott, Tim, and Krystle, for tramping the hills with me and listening to my stories. Their lives have continued to provide me with anecdotal experiences for my books. Krystle has always taken a special role in keeping me on track. And I could do none of this if my wife, Susan, didn't keep the wolf at the door from having puppies.

As a boy, I grew up in McCall, Idaho, and wrote down the stories some of the pioneers of the region shared with me. They are long gone, but I wish to recognize a few: Sam and Jesse (Tim) Williams (pioneer gold miners), Carmel Parks, Ray Beseker, Sylvan Hart (Buckskin Bill), and Dave Spielman. My father, William Dorris, a game warden and bush pilot, took me hunting in this country and related his stories, especially about the Sheepeater Indians.

Published sources for information on the Chinese included Sister M. Alfreda Elsensohn's two-volume *Pioneer Days in Idaho County* and Dr. Liping Zhu's *A Chinaman's Chance*. I relied on several of Brigham D. Madsen's books on the Shoshone and Bannock people, including *The Lemhi: Sacajawea's People*, *The Bannock of Idaho*, and *The Northern Shoshoni*. I also used Thomas E. Mails's *The Mystic Warriors of the Plains* in depicting Plains Indian culture and beliefs, and I used Stephen Ambrose's *Undaunted Courage* regarding Lewis and Clark. Other sources included *Valley County Idaho: Prehistory to 1920*, edited by Shelton Woods; volume 1 of *Centennial History of Lemhi County, Idaho*, compiled by the Lemhi County History Committee; and several national forest histories, including *A History of the Nezperce National Forest* by Albert N. Cochrell, *A History of the Salmon National Forest* by Don I. Smith, and *The Clearwater Story* by Ralph S. Space. The latter sources give good descriptions of the gold camps, pioneer freighting, and historical figures of each region.

The cover illustration is from my oil painting titled *Northern Lights over Jughandle Mountain*, a prominent peak on the east side of Long Valley. McCall is near the forty-fifth parallel, and although the northern lights are infrequently seen in Long Valley, seeing them as a child is one of my fondest memories.

The pen-and-ink illustrations are also my work and are based on locations and subjects from this novel.

AUTHOR'S NOTES

Seeking Two Elks Fighting: Erik Larson: Sheepeater Indian Series continues Erik's story after he leaves his sister in High Valley (Long Valley). Erik intends to return to the Sheepeaters but finds himself torn away by intervening events.

I chose Long Valley as the setting for the Swedish families, although there were no permanent residents in this immediate area in 1863, at the beginning of this series. As soon as a gold strike was made, the packers and freighters began taking in supplies, and towns were established near the goldfields. Waystations along the trails sprang up, and the people who ran these businesses were the early residents of places such as Long Valley. Some offered supplies, meals and boarding, horse and mule exchanges, a blacksmith, and entertainment. They raised crops, generally a vegetable garden, to the extent possible. Some became towns, but most disappeared when the gold ran out.

In this light, I describe the people and activities during this period in Long Valley. I do not pinpoint where my fictional Swedes had their farms and waystation, so I can accurately depict these other historical activities and locations. For example, had the Swedes been in Long Valley, they might have met Packer John Welch and the prospectors and miners who ran several placers on the Payette River and the east side of the valley, particularly near what is now Gold Fork.

This same pattern of settlement was seen in the surrounding drainages, such as the Weiser River and Indian Valley to the west of Long Valley. Traditional farmers and ranchers began taking up permanent homesteads in the late 1870s. Finnish settlers arrived in Long Valley in the late 1880s. Farming, ranching, mining, and logging remained the primary industries in Long Valley up through 1977, when the McCall lumber mill was closed.

The region in which Erik's story takes place is today the largest uninhabited wilderness in the United States outside of Alaska. Erik's story spans four years, from when he leaves the Swedish settlers in August 1868 to when he returns to Long Valley in the summer of 1872. His circuitous route covers approximately 1,250 miles, excluding his travels to Lewiston and his many travels between towns and regions within his route. The area his route encompasses is approximately 28,000 square miles. A few scattered gold camps existed within this area in the 1870s, but otherwise, the towns and settlements were on the fringes.

The Native Americans also largely had their winter camps outside this region. They traveled through it, particularly the Nez Percé, to reach the western Montana bison herds. Otherwise, the predominant Native Americans in the region were the Lemhi Shoshone on the eastern edge and approximately 150 Sheepeater Indians along the Middle Fork of the Salmon River. These first people hunted in parts of this region, most notably the Little Salmon River, the Weiser River, and north along the Salmon River but generally not within the interior. As I have depicted, much of this country did not support big game animals, particularly along the upper Clearwater.

Today this area remains little changed, and the interior is considerably less inhabited than during the days of the gold miners. Portions of seven wilderness areas, including the Frank Church-River of No Return Wilderness, and eleven national forests, including the Salmon, Nez Percé, Payette, and Clearwater forests, cover this region.

I based the maps on USGS maps and historic maps of the region. I've indicated Erik's primary routes. The main trails I've indicated were the existing trails through the region in Erik's time, including the Nez Percé Trail, which cuts through on the north edge of the Salmon River drainage and the south edge of the Clearwater drainage. This was the only route east and west through this region and, ironically, was missed by Lewis and Clark, who went north over Lolo Pass.

I have tried to capture snapshots of the settlements in the region as they existed in this period—Elk City, Newsome, Orogrande, Leesburg, and Salmon City. Additionally, I included the active waystations, such as the North Fork, Jackson's Bridge, and Clearwater Station. I have based Alonzo's and Loyal Brown's history on the history of Mount Idaho and Elk City.

Most of the historic events involving the Lemhi Shoshone are based on my listed sources. I used a Shoshone leader, Tissidimit, to reveal a brief history to Erik, including Lewis and Clark's meeting with Cameahwait, who was Sacajawea's brother. Chief Tendoy's absence from Lemhi Valley is correct. A remnant band did remain in Lemhi Valley. Cusowat wanted to return to farming, as the Lemhi once had done with the Mormons. The bison hunt involved five thousand Nez Percé, Shoshone (including Tendoy's band), and Crow hunters but took place between the Missouri River and the Yellowstone River, where the men engaged a massive bison herd. Tendoy returned to Lemhi Valley in the winter of 1871. The fictional character Muskrat could not have been reunited with the Lemhi except at Lemhi Valley. Although established in 1868, Lemhi Reservation was finally acknowledged through an executive order in 1875. It remained a reservation until 1907, when the order was rescinded. The Lemhi who wished to do so moved to Fort Hall Reservation. Others remained in the Lemhi Valley on private land.

The Lemhi were a horse people and adopted much of the Plains Indian culture. The Sheepeaters began obtaining horses during this time, and some wintered with the Lemhi Shoshone. Some cultural and spiritual aspects are based more on the Plains Indian culture— for example, vision-seeking. Although practiced by the Shoshone, it was not as significant as I have portrayed.

What fascinated me regarding this region during the nineteenth century, in addition to the geography and wildlife, was the presence of three cultures: the Anglo whites, the Native Americans, and the Chinese. Conflict did arise among the cultures, but there was significant conflict within each culture as well. There also were compassion and unity within and among the three cultures. Most frequently, I found the latter to be the case within this region.

In the forthcoming book in this series, Erik will meet Samuel Chambers in the spring of 1873, when Samuel returns to the Salmon River country to marry Bonnie McCracken. The story will take place more in the central region, around Warren, and west to Slate Creek. Events will lead up to the Sheepeater War of 1879.

CPSIA information can be obtained
at www.ICGtesting.com
Printed in the USA
LVHW022241101121
702983LV00011B/886